Jail Bait

Marilyn Todd was born in Harrow, Middlesex, but now lives in West Sussex with her husband, one hare-brained dog and two cats. *Jail Bait* is the fifth novel in her series of Roman mysteries, following *I, Claudia*, *Virgin Territory*, *Man Eater* and *Wolf Whistle*.

Claudia's latest mystery, *Black Salamander*, is available in hardback from Macmillan.

Marilyn Todd

Jail Bait

PAN BOOKS

First published 1999 by Macmillan

This edition published 2000 by Pan Books
an imprint of Macmillan Publishers Ltd
25 Eccleston Place, London SW1W 9NF
Basingstoke and Oxford
Associated companies throughout the world
www.macmillan.co.uk

ISBN 0 330 37737 X

1 3 5 7 9 8 6 4 2

A CIP catalogue record for this book is available from
the British Library.

Phototypeset by Intype London Ltd
Printed and bound in Great Britain by
Mackays of Chatham plc, Chatham, Kent

This one's for Barbs, who understands that too much of a good thing is absolutely wonderful

I

No one could say for certain quite how it started. Some blamed that pot-bellied quarrymaster, home from Numidia. Others suggested it was the legacy of two Lebanese flautists passing through on their way to Iberia. Who could say? But like the first blue wisp of a heath fire, it passed virtually unnoticed, for the citizens of Rome had more pressing things on their minds.

The first two weeks of May had been treacherously hot, a vicious reminder of why so few festivals were scheduled in a month set aside not for rejoicing but for restraint. For purification rites rather than revelry. Some years the problem was cold, scorching the vines and wizening the buds; other years rain, inducing the blight and the mildew and worms in the cattle. In fact, so grim were May's auspices, marriages were rarely contracted and, as crops in the countryside shrivelled, cityfolk discovered that, virtually overnight, Rome was transformed from a glamorous metropolis into a stinking, fly-riddled furnace.

What use were great soaring arches, triumphal basilicas, if your children had no air to breathe? When the meat for your dinner turned rancid, fruit rotted and the poison from the quills of the wryneck bird could not hold back the rats? No longer confined to the slums, vermin scampered openly over the Forum and left droppings on tables and plates and on pillows. Sleep was impossible. And when people arose, crotchety and drained, their tunics would cling to their flesh regardless how often they bathed. Purple hollows formed under their eyes and even Old Man Tiber began showing his age. Dark brown and sluggish, his treacly current stank worse than the sewers, and although aqueducts fetched treasured water down from the hills, the channels were covered and this generated heat of its own.

Thus, as a million souls gulped tepid water and prayed to Jupiter for mercy's sake, for all our sakes, please send a change in the weather, so the little blue wisp gathered strength.

At first it was just the wife of a carpenter. A slight hoarseness. A fever. A few livid spots on her chest. Crushed by the heat and mistrustful of doctors, she dosed herself with fenugreek and took to her bed, smug at the money she'd saved.

Then two small boys, the sons of a wheelwright, succumbed and their mother had no such qualms about medics. They had expelled her husband's bladder stones, cured her sister's colic and eased her father's pain with henbane when he lay dying. But by the time the physician arrived at her home, four more cases had been reported on the Quirinal Hill.

And the little blue wisp that was Plague prepared to lay to waste its territory.

II

One hundred miles to the north the air was no less sultry, the heat every bit as oppressive, yet the plague was the least of Claudia's worries. She'd needed out, and she'd needed out fast, and this luxurious spa was as good a place as any to lie low for a while. Only—

'Hrrrrow!'

Inside her cage, Drusilla, Claudia's blue-eyed, cross-eyed dark Egyptian cat, took the opportunity to remind her mistress how uncomfortable it was inside this wooden crate and how long it had been since she'd had a proper mouse, adding that if Claudia had any decent feelings whatsoever, she'd stop buggering about and get the hell indoors.

'Stow it, you flea-riddled feline,' Claudia hissed back. 'I could have left you in Rome!' To contend with feral dogs scavenging the runnels, to be chased from the bakeshops, kicked aside by the hucksters, snarled at by beggars. 'You, my girl, should count your lucky stars. Just *look* where I've brought you!'

Stretching out before them, the placid waters of Lake Plasimene shimmered in the haze, its reed-lined shores a blur, the wooded hills which sheltered them the merest blue smudge. In place of the multitude of sweating humanity all snapping, bumping, joggling their way

3

through a maze of twisty lanes, day crickets rasped among the pines like blunted woodsaws and a spotted lizard scampered over the flagstones to disappear into a crack in the wall. Here, the air was redolent with bay trees and balm, and lavender and pinks filled the place of stale wine from smoky taverns and the sulphurous stench from the fullers' yards.

From the corner of Drusilla's wooden crate came a subdued 'Mrrr' at the pronounced absence of screaming children, the graunch of mill-wheels, the deep piles of mule shit.

'I know.' Claudia sighed aloud in sympathy. 'Hell, isn't it?'

She paused outside the gold-painted gates to tip the lackey who had carried her trunk. It was not too late to turn back . . .

Oh, come on, who are you kidding! Thanks to the epidemic, half the city's emptied out. There isn't one god-damned bed from the Alps to the Sorrentine peninsula which has not been laid claim to, be thankful you're booked in here! She shifted Drusilla's crate to her other hand and passed through the archway. Nailed to the gate was a schedule of events and Claudia scanned the list. Thanks to Pylades the Greek discovering a spring on this cliff-like promontory which projected several hundred yards into the lake, all manner of diversions appeared to be on offer, from mud wallows to massage, perfuming to pedicures, and let's not forget the spa waters themselves, but . . .

'What's on at the arena?' she enquired of the janitor.

'No arena.' He sniffed. 'Only the foundations dug out so far.'

Fair enough. 'The theatre?'

'Well, the walls is mostly up. I reckon first production should open, come autumn.'

Good grief, a girl could have popped her clogs from boredom long before then. 'Then,' Claudia lowered her voice, 'where will I find the dice games?'

'Dice?'

'Yes, yes, I know they're illegal.' That never stops them. 'Where can I join in?'

'Ah,' he said, scratching his beard, 'there's a choir performing tonight.'

'Hrrrrroww.' The sound might have come from Drusilla or her mistress.

With a depressing sense of foreboding, Claudia followed the travertine path towards the flight of red marble steps. Catering purely for the monied classes, Pylades had spared no expense in constructing this magnificent lakeside retreat, incorporating libraries and loggias, museums and great works of art . . . *and choirs!* Across the lake, a great crested grebe dived for molluscs and a black tern hovered over its reflection in the shimmering waters. Dammit, this exile into purgatory wouldn't be necessary if she'd been given half a chance to explain! To point out that she'd looked upon that money as a loan. That come the end of the month she'd intended to replace those wretched coins, perhaps even add a spot of interest, should a certain Syrian charioteer finish first again.

I mean, the cash had been in a depository, for heaven's sake. Who the hell checks their depository?

The answer, unfortunately, was one Sabbio Tullus, owner of said fortune. With the plague having no respect for status, age or gender, Tullus adjudged that now might be a prudent time to vacate the city and spend a few weeks overseeing his estate in Frascati and, fearing robbery in his absence, decided to take his silver along for the ride.

Claudia couldn't say who was the more surprised. Tullus, finding a gaping hole in the repository wall. Or Claudia, loading up her satchel.

The instant that key had rattled the lock, she was out through the gap like an elver, but there hadn't been time to reposition the loose block of stone. Tullus, goddammit, had seen her!

Typical that for all the resort's opulence and splendour, there wasn't a living soul to be seen. Not counting the gateman, the only other human on the planet appeared to be an immense Oriental, standing with his feet set solidly apart and his arms folded across his tight black leather vest, staring towards the misty blue hills which cradled Plasimene. Apart from a topknot on the poll, his head was shaved and glistening, and the only other outcrop of hair sprouted from his upper lip, which, like the topknot, hung disproportionately long. Pegging him as the sort of chap whose idea of releasing an animal into the wild meant kicking a cat off a cliff, Claudia reckoned he'd be just the sort Tullus would send to ask for his money back.

But then again, a dozen bruisers on her tail was better than the course he had actually taken.

As the searing heat beat down upon her back, Claudia groaned. The gods must be wetting themselves on Olympus at the mess she'd gotten into. I ask you, fancy calling out the *army*! Jupiter, Juno and Mars, what was the silly sod thinking of? Not that the military was concerned with the theft of a few silver denarii – no, no, that was a civil, as opposed to a criminal, misdemeanour. Rather,

Claudia believed, their ears pricked up because one of the caskets in that strongroom happened to belong to Tullus' nephew, who in turn was related by marriage to a second cousin of the Emperor's wife.

The connection was distant. But not so distant that it failed to qualify as potential treasonable theft!

The authorities could prove nothing, of course. A feeble little thing like me, officer? Surely a case of mistaken identity? I'll have you know, I'm a respectable young widow, and just look at this house, it boasts two storeys, a peristyle and an internal bath room, do I look like a common criminal? But the authorities weren't stupid. This theft concerned the Emperor and, like the tiger, they were prepared to stalk their prey, waiting for that one, fatal mistake.

Then the letter came. Luck? Or was the motive more sinister?

Mounting the red marble steps, Claudia glanced back towards the spa's bath complex, its limestone walls sparkling white in the sunshine with red valerian tumbling from urns set on pedestals. Relax. No one there. To the right of the path, nestling in a grove of immature walnut trees, sat the tiny, circular shrine dedicated to Carya, the nymph of the spring. There was nobody there, either, apart from a toothless old peasant woman rocking herself back and forth, and why should there be? Heaven knows, she'd taken a convoluted enough route to arrive here, had left enough false trails to confuse even the most zealous trufflehound.

In any case, why shouldn't an old friend of Claudia's husband cancel his furlough in order to deal with the crisis in the public water supply? And why, having done so, shouldn't he take pity on the pretty young widow and offer her the booking here instead? Paranoia is setting in once I suspect every stroke of luck which comes my way! There was nothing, she decided, nothing at all which could trouble her here, except maybe her jaws locking open from yawning too much.

'There you go, poppet!'

Slipping the latch to Drusilla's cage, Claudia marched towards the entrance, where two liveried Nubians heaved open the mighty oak doors and where, inside, Pylades himself was waiting to greet her.

'Welcome!' He stretched out both hands. 'Welcome, my dear, to Atlantis!'

III

Would you believe it! If someone had asked the resort's founder what he was expecting, Pylades would have demurred that, with her accommodation paid for by a man whose name was not Seferius, it was really none of his business, and largely this was true. He'd seen them come, he'd seen them go; some loud and blowsy, some blushing and timid, some actually believing their married benefactors loved them and intended to set up home one day. In this instance, however, when Claudia swept into the Great Hall like a whirlwind, ignoring the vast rolling seascapes which covered the walls and the honeycomb ceiling inset with ivory and mother-of-pearl but complaining instead of a lack of stimulating entertainment, Pylades resolved to break with tradition and make this young lady his business!

When the tornado finally paused for breath and became aware that the temperature in the Great Hall was several degrees cooler than outside, thanks to canvas awnings which shaded the clerestory windows and the cascade of iced water which rippled down a channel in its stepped marble floor, the Greek had already drunk in the rounded curves of her hips, the tilt of her luscious chin, the tumble of her wayward curls – now, there was a neck ripe for nuzzling! He imagined his tongue gliding down to that sumptuous cleavage, where ... Clasping his hands together, he held them in front of his body to conceal the change which was beginning to take place.

'You travel light, I see,' he said, referring to her single trunk. Always an encouraging sign.

'Alas,' she smiled, and he had cause to thank his prudent use of hand space, because her fluttering eyelashes induced a further quivering in his loins, 'since there was but the one place left on the ship which set me down along the coast, my servants and baggage were forced to follow by road.'

'Ah, the plague, the plague!' Pylades nodded wisely. 'Indeed, my dear, you're fortunate this reservation was made before the contagion broke out, we are turning even senators away for lack of space.'

Was it too soon to make his move? Like curving a shepherd's crook, you had to judge the temperature of the chestnut pole absolutely right. Too hot and it'll snap. Too cold, the wood won't bend. He considered the accommodation – a room with a wide double couch and a view directly overlooking the lake. Then he considered the sparsity of her luggage and ways she might reward the gift of a brand-new wardrobe complete with slippers, stoles and parasol. Maybe a pendant or two, if she performed that little trick he liked so very much ...

'Your man friend is not accompanying you?' he ventured.

'The term, Pylades, is *family* friend.'

Holy Mars, it excited him the way her eyes flashed. Hrrrmph. 'To the right, across the bridge over the watercourse, is the banqueting hall,' he explained, 'and beyond that the twin-storied sun porch. Straight ahead of you is our famous Athens Canal, with the domed loggia leading off to the right.'

As he continued to acquaint her with the layout of Atlantis, Pylades could only think of her eyes shining with gratitude at the magnificent embroideries, the shawls, the sandals he presented her with every time she spread herself across that wide double couch . . .

'You will, of course, need a man to guide you,' he told her, his gaze latching on to the points of her breasts. 'A red-blooded male, a real man, who can steer you to unimagined pleasures.'

'Can you point me one out?'

Beneath his clasped hands, something went limp and the arrival of a tall, middle-aged man striding across the hall could not have been better timed. With only a cursory smile at the guest, the newcomer peered at Pylades. 'Everything all right?' he enquired. 'Only you seem somewhat red in the face.'

The Greek smiled wanly back. 'Kamar,' he introduced weakly, 'our resident physician.'

'Who is either sorely overworked,' the Seferius woman said tartly, 'or else has nothing to do.'

'Pardon me?'

Pylades was glad it was Kamar who stepped in, his own wounds were smarting enough.

'There seems,' Claudia waved her arm to embrace the whole resort, 'a distinct shortage of patients for you, suggesting Atlantis is either deserted or they're all laid up sick in their beds.'

'No, no, I told you,' Pylades had a notion his voice had acquired a peculiarly plaintive quality, 'we're full up. It's just that your arrival coincides with siesta.' He turned to the Etruscan for support. 'Kamar, you see, swears by afternoon naps.'

'He would, wouldn't he? And should he make a mistake, he can cover that up, as well. With six feet of earth.'

Pylades felt his head spinning. He'd been mauled in public and in private. His resident physician had been savaged. Yet his only desire was to yank the tunic from her body and take her here and now, on the spot. 'Kamar,' he growled, 'could you spare a word in the office?' Anything to break free of this witch's spell! Clicking his fingers, he summoned a lackey to take the young lady's trunk and unpack but as he strode off, he heard his visitor tell the servant that he'd better feed Drusilla while he was about it.

'Would that be your maid, madam?'

'She has a preference for sardines and cooked chicken, unless –' over his shoulder, Pylades saw Claudia delve into her trunk and retrieve a crisp parchment fan '– you happen to have a mouse handy?'

As the feeling of faintness engulfed Pylades, he thought that at least now he had genuine grounds on which to consult his physician.

Quite what a Greek architect had been doing on a remote Etruscan promontory in the first place no one had bothered to ask, but his discovery of the spring combined with his perspicacity to develop the site had made Pylades a very rich man, you could tell from the gold clinging to his fingers and hanging round his neck. Even his fawn tunic, a masterstroke in understated elegance, had not escaped the soft breath of Midas. Claudia studied the retreating back of her host. Greek, of course, could mean anything – blond Adonises to strapping gladiator types, snooty Athenians to the proud Andros islanders – but unless she missed her guess, Pylades, with his swarthy skin and stocky frame, hailed from shepherd stock!

And as for that beanpole strutting at his side, either Kamar had no use for the likes of tonic waters, manicures and mudbaths or the remedies weren't working. With lips that turned perpetually inwards, he seemed as devoid of humour as he was of hair – in fact, he reminded Claudia of a tortoise with a particularly spiteful attack of the piles.

Still. At least, Kamar hadn't tried to make a pass at her – unlike that dirty-minded little toad, Pylades. Who the hell did he think he was dealing with? Some little bit of fluff playing second fiddle to a man who wants the best of both worlds while she has the worst of one?

'I am no man's mistress,' she informed the gurgling watercourse as she strode across the footbridge. Claudia Seferius is master of her own damned destiny, thank you.

She began to hum a jaunty marching song. It wasn't strictly true, of course, what she had told Pylades about her attendants following on. In situations such as this, a girl couldn't be too careful and it was best she brought no servants, not even her bodyguard, and even more advisable she left no forwarding address. When the heat over the Tullus incident died down, she'd slip home, but until then? Until then, no one knew where to find her. Unless one counts the sender of the letter . . .

Whilst for the slaves there was no such luxury as siesta (sweatroom furnaces still need stoking, mud heated, towels aired), the silence in the banqueting hall was unnerving, broken only by the crackle of frankincense resin which burned in the wall-mounted braziers and the slap of Claudia's soft leather sandals on the mosaic. With her eyes ranging over the gilded rafters and the statuary set in niches along the length of both walls, the voice made the hum catch in her throat.

'I don't advise the sun porch.' The voice belonged to a young man sprawled across one of the couches. 'It faces south and is far too hot this time of day. You'll be burned lobster red within minutes.'

'Will I really?'

'The name's Cal.' He leapt off the seat and, to Claudia's astonishment, performed a backward flip which ended in an elaborate bow. 'Short for Calvus, and since you're a new girl in school and this resort is vast, you'll need to be shown a few ropes.'

'Not by you.' He was young. Maybe twenty. Which made him a full five years younger than herself.

'I feel you—'

'You'll feel nothing,' she said, sweeping past. 'Better men than you have tried today.'

Man? Even as it formed on her tongue, the word jarred. The quality of his clothes and the rings on his fingers suggested he was the son of a senator, or possibly a legate or a judge or a general. His education would have taken place in Athens, he'd have attended university in Alexandria, no doubt he'd have a year's experience in a public department under his belt, say the Mint or the roads or temple rebuilding. In all likelihood, he'd have wed at sixteen and could well be the father of two with a third on the way!

'No,' he laughed, 'I was about to say, I feel you misjudge me! You think I'm too young to know what's what around here, but I have to warn you, there's nothing I don't know about Atlantis.'

Claudia studied the crinkling green eyes and spade-shaped jaw and thought, I'll bet there isn't! 'Like, for instance?'

'Like, for instance, your name is Claudia Seferius, you're a widow, you've recently arrived with your cat – the same cat, incidentally, which has already caused chaos in the kitchens, terror in the tackroom and absolute pandemonium in the parrot house.'

Claudia stiffened. How could he possibly know so much?

'Easy.' He grinned, suggesting he read minds as a means of acquiring his knowledge. 'While Pylades was greeting you in the hall, I nipped into his office to look up your registration!'

Simple as that? Well, why not . . .?

Cal, she noticed, had remained beside his couch as she headed towards the sun porch, therefore it came as something of a surprise to see a blur of blue linen flash by.

'Most people,' she pointed out, 'walk or even run to catch up.' She'd never met one before who cartwheeled through life!

Cal jumped upright to block her way. 'You don't listen,' he said, and his corn-coloured hair flopped back into place. 'It's too hot on the veranda this time of day, you'll make yourself sick. Walk with me, instead. Everyone enjoys a walk round the museum—'

Claudia pushed her face close to his. 'Do I look like you could shear me for wool?'

'I beg your pardon?'

'Or cut me into lamb chops?'

'I'm afraid you've still lost me,' Cal said.

'Neither,' she added, 'do I go "baaa", is that sinking in? Good. Because, now we've established I'm not a sheep, perhaps you'd allow me to do my exploring on my own.'

'Nonsense.' He slipped his arm into hers. She slipped it away. He slipped it back again. 'Everyone needs company and Atlantis,' he whispered, steering her towards a hidden alcove, 'is stuffed to the gunwales with secrets.' Gently he ushered her behind a gilded statue of Bacchus. 'For the price of a kiss, I'll reveal the trick Pylades uses to keep the hall so cool.'

Claudia caught the sharp tang of the alecost on his tunic. 'I'm prepared to live in ignorance,' she said.

'One little kiss,' he cajoled, 'on the lips.'

Claudia freed her arm with a jerk. 'I know that routine, Cal. A kiss on the lips – and then it's all over!'

And yet, caught in the smoky intensity of dark beech-leaf eyes, had she not been tempted? Just a fraction? Had hot blood not surged through her veins when his hand brushed her cheek, stirring up feelings she'd long ago believed buried?

Acknowledging defeat with a click of his tongue, Cal leaned across her, pushed against the side wall and suddenly Claudia found herself outdoors, in the middle of the grove of young walnut trees which surrounded the Temple of Carya.

'There!' He laughed. 'Wasn't that worth a—?'

'No!'

Dear Diana, this boy wouldn't know a refusal if it clocked him round the ear with a haddock. So why was that curiously pleasing?

In the grove, silent and secluded, offerings to the nymph dangled among the flaccid leaves – gaily coloured ribbons, terracotta plaques, wooden figurines, as well as an array of silver votive bells waiting for a breeze to set them dancing. By the gods, shade or no shade, it was hot! Sensing her discomfort, Cal whisked the fan from her hand and flapped the parchment with vigour, his eyes following the ruffle of her hair and the billow of her turquoise cotton gown. It was only when his gaze fixed upon her breasts and didn't waver that Claudia snatched the fan back. Behind them, the door had swung to and, hidden by the painted decorations on the stucco, there was nothing to suggest its existence.

It was like a door to the Underworld, opening into a silent copse where no birds sang and only masculine voices floated out from the temple, one loud and deep, the other high and protesting.

'That's Mosul, the priest,' Cal explained in a voice so oozing with poise that it cut short further imaginings. 'Hates Jews so much you'd think he was a Babylonian, but my word, what a perfectionist! He won't allow Leon – that's who he's railing at now – to go near the spring in case the young acolyte upsets Carya and her holy waters dry up!' Cal's arm found its way round Claudia's waist. 'I'll let you in on another secret.'

Using the closed fan, Claudia swatted him away, though not before they had both registered the five-count delay. It felt good, a man's touch, she reflected. But then it had been a long time . . .

'Come!' His hand closed round her wrist and Claudia found herself spinning between the trunks of the walnuts and into a clump of dank elders before being plunged into a steep, descending darkness. *Cool! It was cool!* She gasped with shock as her back connected with the chill of the rock face. He'd led her to a cave, where the stone was cold but not slimy, to a world which was dark but not damp. And at a time when sheets soaked through in the night and grey mould covered the bread, this was surely the Elysian Fields!

Against the far wall, serpentine lights danced a horizontal shimmy and water plink-plink-plinked into a pool. The spring! Cal had brought her to the sacred spring, where the shadows were the reflections of ripples on water and where the drips were the tears of the nymph.

In the darkness, Cal moved closer and the suddenness overwhelmed her. 'Cal,' she warned.

But a husky voice whispered, 'Come to me, Claudia. Love with me.'

'Cal, I—' Her own voice was as ragged as his. Sweet Jupiter, how long since she'd felt release with a man?

Again he was reading her mind, sensed her desires, her pent-up frustrations. 'I know what you want,' he said, and by all that was holy, she did!

His hands cupped her chin, she could smell the freshness of mint on his breath. Sex with a stranger, wasn't that every woman's fantasy? Who would know? A young man, handsome and confident, in a place hidden by sanctity? Who would ever find out?

'This will be the best ever, I promise,' and she knew it was no idle boast. From the moment she'd set eyes on him, Cal had simply oozed sex.

Claudia fought for control. Her pulse raced, her flesh was on fire. This was no callow youth fumbling his way over her breasts or trying to press up against her. Cal's seduction was moulded. A shudder ran through her body. His touch, when it came, would be light and exploratory. Take its time . . .

'Go with it,' he urged, and still he had not so much as kissed her. 'Don't fight what's inside you.' When his thumbs moved up to caress her cheekbones, she knew he was aware of her trembling. 'Let me give you,' he rasped, 'super sex.'

'In that case, Cal.' Was that strangled voice hers? 'I'll have the soup now and take a raincheck on the sex.'

He laughed, and the laughter was good, and Claudia found herself respecting the man who backed off when he knew the answer was no. In fact, her heart raced that little bit faster—

'Oh, Claudia, there are so many things I must show you,' he whispered. One finger hooked a wayward curl and gently released it. 'But for now, let me impart one more mystery.' He pointed towards the back of the cave. 'Do you see it?'

She blinked at the yawning blackness to the right of the cistern. '*A tunnel?*'

'Apertures have been gouged in the rock to let in light and once you acclimatize to the gloom and that rather steep slope, you'll be fine. Trust me!'

Claudia hesitated. That passageway looked less than inviting . . .

'Chicken!' Grabbing her hand, he raced towards the gaping hole, leaving her no option but to tumble behind him.

The tunnel smelled of mildew and copper and had a faint whiff of fish, but Calvus was right. Once you got used to the punctuations of light then dark, light then dark, the way was smooth, being tamped earth – and it was also exciting! A secret underpass, he explained, a shortcut from the temple down to the lake, passing directly beneath the sun porch and emerging . . .

'Ta-da!' He gave a theatrical flourish of the wrist.

'Ooh, a thicket of alder and willow, how lovely!'

Cal aimed a mock punch and pointed upwards through a gap in the greenery to where, forty feet above, rose the colonnade which surrounded the little domed loggia which in turn led off the famous Athens Canal.

In spite of herself, Claudia was impressed. 'How many secrets have you uncovered here, Cal?'

'Me, I know everything,' he said with exaggerated loudness. 'In fact as long as one understands the golden rule here, one understands everything.'

Claudia tilted her head on one side. 'And what, pray, is this golden rule?'

'That whoever owns the gold, rules! Now.' With the back of his hand, he shooed her away. 'Off you go, Claudia Seferius, get the exploring out of your system and when you return, we'll settle down to some serious flirting.'

Will we, indeed?

'I'll be waiting,' he said, 'right here, on this spot.' He leaned his weight against the rock and crossed his arms over his chest. 'With a picnic of lobsters and mussels, peaches and cherries, which we'll wash down with a jug of chilled hyssop wine, and as the sun sets over the lake I'll tell you why Pylades named this place Atlantis.'

'You'll be wasting your time,' she warned, working her way out of the thicket to where, across a rough patch of grassland, a tethered flotilla of fishing boats bobbed on the lazy blue water.

In the shade of his upturned coracle, a fisherman snored open-mouthed, the net he'd been mending half-submerged in the water, his heather needle slack in his hand. From the reed-beds, a single moorhen croaked, and flies buzzed round a dead fish washed up on the shingle.

The spell had been broken back there in the cave. Claudia was no longer tempted by the touch of Cal's flesh – furtive couplings were not the answer to either her problems or his! But all the same, she knew with full certainty that, despite the numerous paths which led back to Atlantis, Claudia Seferius would return to that tunnel – to share a jug of chilled wine with a young extrovert who knew too many secrets.

Including (who knows?) her own.

IV

Phew, it was hot! You'd think a stretch of water five miles by six would afford at least a modicum of relief, but no. On the foreshore it was as sticky as ever and Claudia's fan turned out to be a waste of seven sesterces. The humidity transformed crisp parchment into limp lettuce and Claudia lobbed the folded fan like a javelin into the lake, but the margins proved shallow and its boxwood frame lodged in the silt, sticking out like a defiant childish tongue.

Still. If one cave had been gouged out of the rocks, by heavens, there'd almost certainly be a number of others!

Unhooking a small grey boat from the jetty, Claudia headed for the island closest to the promontory and whose slopes, like the cliff on which Atlantis was perched, rose almost vertically from the water. According to the man who'd carried her luggage, the island had remained uninhabited until, attracted by Pylades' development, a rich banker decided this would make a perfect place for retirement. Clearing the wooded slopes along the southern shore, he built himself the sumptuous Villa Tuder (modestly named after himself) and systematically indulged the place with riches including a fifty-foot-high statue of a man, his hand outstretched in supplication to the dawn, although from this distance it was impossible to make out more than a hazy glimmer of the villa, let alone any embellishments.

However, Claudia had no desire to mingle with bankers, retired or otherwise. That north shore, she suspected, would be deep in shade right now, and undoubtedly oozing with caverns, cool and dark and running with water.

The blades sucked and slurped as the rowboat cleaved a course across the still, blue waters. Some idiot on the road said the island was dangerous, a place to avoid after a group of yobs set loose a boar a couple of days ago as a joke. Clearly he was winding her up, otherwise he'd know, as she did from experience of the creatures which roamed her own estate, that boar were timid beasts. Granted they got a little humpy when they had a litter to protect, but the only problem Claudia had experienced was keeping them away from the vines, whose tender young shoots appealed so wholeheartedly to their taste-buds. So no. One hairy pig was not a problem. It was this stifling, unbreathable heat.

Across the wide expanse of water, Atlantis shimmered like smoke from a candle, diffusing the landscape so that the building merged with the lake and the sky. There were, she supposed, worse places to lie low, but without dice? Without theatrical performances and dazzling displays in the arena? Atlantis had got off to a promising enough start, but without leopards pitted against tigers or dancing elephants to cheer, it looked like being a bloody long break from civilization.

Tying the little boat to a stem of wild cane, Claudia waded ashore and stripped off her pink cotton robe, draping it over a juniper bush. Now about that babbling brook . . .

Soft sandals made no sound on leaf litter moist from prolonged humidity, it was like walking on sponge, and the woods were eerily still. No birds, no rustle of leaves, no scamper of squirrels, just the incessant sawing of crickets. Even bees would wait until the sun angled low before raiding the brambles and banks of wild mint. Amplified by the heat, the fragrance of white clematis and pines scented the air, and the oaks and the beech wafted out waves of tranquillity.

What was that?

Claudia paused by a poplar and listened. There it was again. A scuffling sound. Like a barrel rolling through scrub. And again!

'Hello?' Her voice sounded thin, even to her own ears. She lowered the pitch. 'Anyone there?'

The shuffle ceased, and then she remembered the boar. Good! Now it had heard her, it would either retreat or stand still and idly she wondered whether it would be lonely out here or whether the yobs, in their ignorance, had released it among a herd of its kind.

Pulling a leaf from a sweet bay, Claudia rubbed its scent into her fingers. How long, she wondered, need she keep clear of Rome? A week? Two? Before the furore over Tullus' money died down? She'd need to return soon, to find out how her vineyards were faring in the drought. Heaven knows, the business her husband bequeathed was not doing well. A poor harvest would finish it off.

The raucous chatter from a magpie made her jump. Goddammit, that's enough! First I suspect Cal of being a military spy, now I'm spooked by the woods. Time to head back to the lake! But Claudia hadn't retraced more than a dozen paces when her ears picked up the sound of heavy breathing. The hairs on her scalp prickled. There was something moving behind her . . .

Oh, grow up! Since when have wild boar begun stalking their victims? The laugh of a woodpecker mirrored her sentiments, and Claudia was ashamed of her mindless stupidity.

Then she smelled it.

'Holy shit!'

For a moment, she couldn't believe what she was seeing. Wild boar be buggered! This was the biggest BEAR she'd ever clapped sight on!

Unable to comprehend the message which her eyes transmitted to her brain, Claudia merely goggled as it reared on to its hind legs, its paws splayed, mesmerizing her with claws which could surely disembowel with one swipe. In the sunlight that slanted through the trees, bright metal glinted off the ring through its nose and off the length of stout chain which swung from the ring.

From deep in its throat, the beast growled.

She retched from fear, then the instinct to run superseded. Sweet Juno. Mighty Queen of Olympus. Don't you think now might be a good time to help? As she sped across the forest floor, the bear lumbering behind, Claudia wished she knew more about them. Should she, for instance, stop and face it down on the principle that, like a dog, Bruno would hesitate to attack a stationary figure? A quick glance over her shoulder suggested that might not be prudent . . .

With sweat blinding her eyes, Claudia skidded on the damp leaves. Nearly there, nearly there, I must be close to the shore! But the stumble had cost precious ground. She could hear every stertorous sound the brute made, smelled the stench of its fur, caught every harsh jangle of chain.

She ducked to the left, and gained five valuable strides. She swerved right, but the bear cut the corner. The precious seconds were lost.

Breathless from fear and weak from exhaustion, she tried to think up a plan. Shin up a tree? Don't be daft, bears can climb! Heft a fallen branch and swing out? Even more stupid. She had neither the strength to offbalance the bear or the time to scurry around for a branch which had not rotted through. Water! Head for the water! Somewhere she had an idea bears could swim—

The ground levelled out. Shrubs and bushes passed by in a blur. Where was this bloody lake? Then a clearing appeared and Claudia felt the chill of the truth. She'd been running parallel to the shore, not towards it!

Her breath was ragged, her limbs disjointed. Yet still the bear shambled behind . . .

Near the edge of the clearing, Claudia's legs finally began to turn traitor. The strength in them failed, her lungs were on fire and one bramble was all that it took.

One tiny bramble, arching over the grass.

Claudia screamed as her ankle became trapped in thorns which tripped her headlong on to her face. The bear reared. She saw its shadow on the grass, smelled its foetid breath on her back, and she curled herself into a ball.

Merciful Jupiter, let death be quick! Don't let it rip me to shreds. Louder it howled. A roar mixed with panting, and Claudia prised open her eyelids. *I must know. I must know how it's going to kill me—*

She blinked the tears and sweat from her eyes. This cannot be! She blinked again. The bear thrashed on the grass and the bellows, she realized, had not been of rage, but of pain.

Small wonder.

From its eye protruded a spear.

Time lost all meaning. As though tracing a sculpted frieze, she watched as if the events had been frozen for ever in marble.

A figure, sprinting across the clearing. A man. His hunting knife drawn.

The bear. Clawing the air, mad with pain and with rage. Blinded, tormented, yet not giving in.

In the speed of slow motion, she had time to take in the swarthiness of the man's skin. His dark hair, falling long over his shoulders. She watched him circle the beast and, when the sun caught the serrated blade of his knife, it blinded her with its brilliance. The bear's yowl chilled her blood, but still the hunter held back. Cascading from a central parting, his long hair concealed his expression, though tight sinews gave him away. Stealthily he circled the bear and the brute's howlings grew pitiful. With a lunge, he brought the knife down. A rumble came from deep within as blood oozed from its muzzle and snout. The bear twitched once, it twitched twice, then with one final growl it expired.

With a satisfied grunt, the young hunter wiped his blade back and forth on the grass. She was shaking, she noticed, from her curls to her blue leather shoes – which, apart from a skimpy breast-band and thong, was all the clothing she wore!

Someone had ripped out her tongue, she was mute. Slipping off a bangle, the gold one set with pearls, Claudia's trembling hand offered it to him in gratitude.

Dark eyes, the darkest she had ever seen, bored into hers. 'Thank you,' growled a voice with a thick, Spanish accent, 'but I doubt it would suit me.' There was a pause. 'Look away,' he said, and it was not so much a suggestion as a command.

Claudia looked away, and when he gave the all-clear, he was cleaning the point of his spear on wild elecampane. She closed her eyes until the waves of nausea had passed.

Suddenly he clamped a hand round Claudia's wrist and in one liquid movement, she was swept upright and on to her feet. For what seemed an eternity, his hand remained clamped and black eyes burrowed into the depths of her mind, reading every last secret, unravelling her past and travelling the route of her fears. The smell of woodshavings and pine drifted between them, then he released her and the moment was gone.

The hunter moved back to the bear. Its fur was dull and unkempt, the weals from a score of savage whippings standing stark and livid, explaining why it ferociously sought revenge on all humankind.

But Claudia fixed on the man. The tunic he wore was no coarse workman's cloth, it was the product of very fine tailoring, cut high above the knee and fastening on the left shoulder only, leaving the right unobstructed for hunting. Gold embroidery rippled round the hem, and it had not escaped her notice that his hands were not calloused and the nails had been manicured on a regular basis. He crouched down, one knee bent, the other touching the ground, and dribbled the chain through his hand. When the links jangled, a shiver ran through Claudia's body. Then, before she realized what was happening, he had collected his spear, sheathed his knife and was loping back to the woodlands.

'Wait!' she called out. 'I haven't thanked you for saving my life.'

Under the umbrella of a gnarled oak tree, the hunter stopped and moved his head half a turn. 'No,' he said, and again his mane veiled his face, 'but you will.'

And with that he was gone. Swallowed up by the forest as though he had never existed.

V

Atlantis was coming back to life as Claudia slung the painter over the mooring post. The fisherman who'd been mending his net was long gone and along the shoreline wildfowl wove in and out of the reed-beds. High above the thicket where Cal would be waiting with his basket of lobsters, merchants on fat profits and artisans on thin stipends hobnobbed in the shade of the cool colonnade. High female laughter rang down from the loggia and further along, the gilded pillars of the twin-storied sun porch shone like molten copper in the glare of Apollo's bright rays. Incredibly, far from dulling her senses, that brush with death had only heightened her lust for life and excitement, and Claudia was whistling to herself as the rough grass swished at her ankles.

Would Cal, she wondered, be able to cast a beam of light on the identity of the mysterious huntsman who'd saved her from ending up a bear's dinner, in the same way he'd sniffed out the sliding panel, the tunnel and the secret of the Great Hall – no doubt a deep underground cellar packed with ice, whose melted output formed a cascade. Probably, but it was the thought of that ice being put in a bucket to chill the hyssop wine which was uppermost on her list of priorities at the moment. Dear Juno, she prayed, don't let all the ice in the bucket have melted. Not all of it! Let there be some left to bury my face in!

'Cal?' He was not at the entrance. 'Are you there?'

She lingered in the mouth of the underpass and frowned. He said he would wait. She'd told him not to, and that would be grist to Calvus' mill. He'll be here. He's just off, fetching the ice. Voices and yawns filtered down from the colonnade above.

'Cal?' Louder she called up the tunnel, and when only a distorted echo answered back, Claudia felt a twinge of misgiving. In the same way she'd misheard 'bear' for 'boar', had she credited Cal with more depth than was actually present? Had he taken off after fresh quarry?

Admittedly their acquaintance was brief, but the relationship had been plunged into immediate intimacy. He would come! Perhaps he was having trouble finding the ice? Yet the longer she waited, the more Claudia realized that, far from bridging the gap between youth and maturity, Cal had merely been acting in type. Bored and seeking to pass the siesta hour, how better than by making love with a stranger? Claudia's cheeks reddened as she recalled the mintiness of his breath on her face . . .

That, my girl, is what you call a narrow squeak. Which makes two this afternoon, if my arithmetic is correct.

In the punctuated gloom of the underpass, Claudia smiled grimly to herself. At least it proved one thing, Cal standing her up. It proved he wasn't a military spy, or he'd be here, keeping an eye on his suspect.

Halfway up the tunnel, a scream cut short Claudia's speculations. It came from directly above, piercing and shrill. Typical. Silly cow wakes up, totters out for a view of the lake, spots a dead dog floating past and it's brought on an attack of the vapours! Claudia strode off up towards the cave. They're all the same, these rich wives. Closeted in isolation, slaves doing this for them, slaves doing that, they're never exposed to real life. Sure, they live in the country, but nature red in tooth and claw? Do me a favour! Yet *still* the silly bitch screamed!

By now, though, curiosity was guiding Claudia towards the next hole in the rock face. What, exactly, was so gruesome that others now joined in the cacophony? She poked her head over the rough sill. Talk about a fuss over nothing! She rolled her eyes in disgust. The only thing floating in Lake Plasimene was water! She was about to withdraw when she heard footsteps on the foreshore. Men. Running. Shouting. Ghoulishly curious, Claudia craned her neck further.

'Oh, no. Sweet Jupiter, please. Say it's not true.'

Tears filled her eyes as she stared at the shingle below. Say there's been a mistake. That I'm wrong. Claudia shook her head again and again. But even by the time she'd shaken it dizzy, there was no mistaking the truth.

The body which sprawled, twisted and bloody, was all too familiar. The blue linen tunic. The corn-coloured hair.

She shivered and hugged her arms to her body, and then, in the pied seclusion of the very tunnel that he'd shown her, Claudia bade a silent farewell to Cal.

VI

Sabbio Tullus surveyed his nephew (the one who was related by marriage to a second cousin of the Emperor's wife), through well disguised distaste. A fleshy man himself, he considered rotundity an encapsulation of all things good, all things healthy both in mind and spirit, yet here he was facing a young blade twenty years his junior with a face like a weasel and dead man's eyes.

'Are you certain of this?' Tullus asked, and when a rivulet of sweat ran down his backbone he was not sure it was entirely due to humidity.

'Positive,' the nephew replied, in that singular grey monotone of his.

Tullus twisted in his chair, and trusted that the creaks were the basketweave, not his discomfort manifesting itself aloud. He reached for his goblet and gulped at the apple juice. Bloody quacks! Putting him on fruit juice and sherbets. What did they think he was, dying? They were only a few chest pains, for gods' sake. Indigestion. Nothing to do with the theft from that bloody depository . . . When a second twinge clawed at his heart, it was the wine that he reached for. Bloody quacks. The liquor glowed inside him like a log fire on a February night and he leaned down to pat the wolfhound panting at his feet, its long, pink tongue lolling from the side of his mouth. And still that bloody nephew of his hadn't moved so much as a muscle. Cold-blooded little toad, thanks to him, I'm *right* in the shit.

'Are you feeling well, Uncle?'

The question was phrased out of courtesy, not concern, and Tullus snorted. How could his plump little pigeon of a sister have produced a desiccated bag of bones such as this? Their father had arranged the marriage, of course, Tullus never even met the husband, but from what his sister had told him, he believed he would have liked the fellow. The second time he snorted, it was from rage. How dare the bastard leave his sister in the lurch. Falling from his horse and breaking his bloody back, what a stupid way to go, and the widow eight months pregnant! Silently, yet with infinite variety, Sabbio Tullus cursed his father for contracting the marriage. His brother-in-law for dying so selfishly. His sister for birthing a reptile. His nephew for landing him in this bloody mess. But most of all, Sabbio Tullus cursed himself. For agreeing to look after that mucking casket in the first place.

He sighed and thought, I should be in Frascati, where the air is fresh and pure and uncontaminated by plague, giving my wife another child and checking my boundary stones haven't been moved by that conniving neighbour of mine, not sitting in this sweatroom of an office, sorting out this little bastard's mess. And Janus bloody Croesus, what a mucking mess it was.

'You ought not have gone to the army,' the boy said.

'You ought to have told me what you kept in that box!' Tullus fired back.

'You would not have agreed to undertake its safe-keeping.'

'Too bloody right!'

But lock it up he had, and now Tullus was as deep in the shit as his nephew. How many times had his poor sister miscarried? They'd lost count after five, and when she was delivered, at last, of a son the whole family rejoiced. *Had they but known!* Tullus rubbed the dull ache in his chest. When this was over . . . By all the gods in Olympus, when this was all over, he'd string that boy up by his tongue and whip him till his gizzard popped out. But until then, of course—

'Has anyone discovered where the bitch is hiding?' the nephew enquired.

Inexplicably Tullus wanted to laugh, and say his bet was on Naples, where she'd be spending his silver on dresses and jewels and placing outrageous bets on charioteers, because there was a whole lot of woman packed into Claudia Seferius, by heavens there was – then he remembered the contents of a certain little box and Tullus steeled his face. 'Not yet.'

'But you are taking steps to recover the . . . contents?'

Why is it, Tullus thought, that sounded just like a threat? 'Of course I bloody am,' he snarled. Did the boy take him for a fool? 'I have agents on the job, up and down the country.'

Holy Mars, he wished the lad had never told him what was in that sodding box!

'Good.' The nephew stood up. 'You will advise me, naturally, the minute you have news of her whereabouts?'

'You can trust me to keep you advised,' Tullus said, barely keeping the grimace from his face.

'Oh, I trust you, Uncle.' Thin lips formed a dead man's smile. 'I trust you implicitly.'

The door clicked silently behind him and inside Tullus' chest, the eagle clawed in earnest.

VII

Claudia was running through the thicket of alders and Cal was crashing behind. 'I remembered the cherries,' he yelled, 'honest I did.' And she shouted back, 'Go away, I don't want the soup or the sex!' And when she looked round, his hands had turned into live lobsters and he had a spear sticking out of his eye . . .

Drenched with perspiration, her teeth chattering like cups in an earthquake, Claudia jerked upright in bed. Disturbed by the jolt, Drusilla wriggled into the crook of her mistress's arm, her tongue rasping Claudia's skin as though she was scrubbing a kitten. Crooning to herself, as much as to the cat, Claudia stroked Drusilla's flattened ears until both sets of eyelids grew heavy.

Dwarfed by the pillars which lined the Great Hall, Cal ran barefoot up the steps of the watercourse. He was laughing, because he'd discovered yet another secret, that he could fly, come and watch, better still, take his hand and fly with him. And Claudia was laughing, too, because the water was cool, icy cool, but then a bear reared out of the stream, snarling with a half-human face, and Cal said, 'We can outrun the beast, we can fly,' and suddenly they were up on the roof, but he wouldn't let go of her wrist and then she was falling . . . falling . . .

This time when Claudia woke up, she knew with

certainty that, unless she saw for herself the point from which Kamar said Cal had fallen, the dreams would torment her for ever. Sluicing water over her face, she calculated there was still an hour before dawn, yet despite the sultry heat of the night, she was shivering. By this time tomorrow, Cal's ashes would be on their way home—

Crackling torches set in motion the ships which sailed the seascapes round the Great Hall and cast diamonds and pearls on the rippling watercourse. Pausing on the central footbridge, Claudia thought, this is madness. What the blazes do I expect to achieve? But just as there was no answer to her question, equally was there no turning back.

Her bare feet slapped the marble floor of the banqueting hall, but the pine doors to the sun porch slid open on silent greased runners. The veranda was not as she'd imagined it. Sure, she'd seen the gilding on the pillars from the lake this afternoon, and certainly the Parian marble on the walls had been used to spectacular and dazzling effect, but that was only part of its splendour. White roses blasted perfume into the torrid night air, climbing between box trees clipped to resemble camels, apes and giraffes. A bronze faun piped a tune in the corner and on the ceiling, six signs of the Zodiac had been picked out in gold.

It was, Claudia thought, a very lovely place to die . . .

With a hammer pounding in her breast, she climbed the wooden staircase to the upper storey. 'How can you be certain he fell?' she'd asked Kamar, as Cal was being laid on the stretcher. There was something about the body which niggled her.

'Because I'm a doctor,' he snarled. 'The boy's neck is broken.'

'Yes, I know.' The angle was hideous. 'Only—'

'Only nothing,' he sniffed, twitching his fingers and making it obvious what he thought of women interfering with his professional judgement. 'The injuries are fully consistent with a fall,' letting his eyes pinpoint the spot from which he calculated Cal had fallen.

As the stretcher party had shuffled away across the shingle, Kamar strode off in the opposite direction and Claudia had had to run to keep up. 'You're not accompanying the corpse?'

'The role of a physician is to tend to the living,' he growled, weaving up the zigzag path towards the bath house. 'Mosul the priest can take over from here.'

'What do you suppose he was doing up on the sun porch that led to his toppling over the rail?'

'Cal was an ungovernable show-off with a third of the sense he was born with!' he snapped. 'How the hell should I know?' And before she could ask anything else, Kamar had collared a fat timber merchant and was enquiring after his bunions.

Cold-blooded son-of-a-bitch, Claudia reflected, lingering on the veranda's darkened staircase. You'll pander to the rich, they pay handsomely to have you oversee their phantom ailments, but when push comes to shove, we see you for what you really are, Kamar. A reptile without an ounce of compassion!

Upstairs were the same gilded columns, the same dazzling white walls, the ceiling studded with the remaining Zodiacal signs, Capricorn to Gemini, but instead of the back wall comprising sliding pine doors, it carried broad arches to light the banqueting hall below, and these arches were filled in with fine alabaster. A lone torch illuminated the balcony and, lifting it free of its sconce, Claudia held the flame over the rail. No one had seen Cal fall to his death, and why should they? They were too busy snoring their heads off. Claudia sighed. Kamar had called the boy reckless and whilst she herself would have preferred the term 'spirited', she had to admit it wasn't impossible to picture him, leaping on to this rail to imitate the skills of the rope walkers. Had he overbalanced while waving to her, as she rowed out to the island?

Since no scuff marks marred the bright rail, Claudia wondered why she'd automatically surmised that he'd slipped from the upper balcony. The drop from the lower storey was still pretty steep! Descending the staircase, she wished she could identify what it was that troubled her about Cal's body. Assuming he was wearing soft shoes, as everyone wore here, not only would they not leave a mark, they'd be all the easier to slip in . . . so what, exactly, made her suspect his death was no accident?

'*Janus!*' Claudia's torch picked out the most amazing blue eyes, which twinkled and shone from a tiny wizened face.

'Did I startle you?' The sparrow of a woman smiled mischievously.

Claudia was on the point of saying you damned well know you did, you venomous bat, when she noticed that the couch upon which the old crone reclined had two wheels nailed to the front. The sparrow followed the direction of her glance.

'I'll bet you've heard my daughter-in-law playing whisper-whisper-whisper with that sourpuss physician – well, indulge them, that's what I say.' From beneath her thin coverlet, she drew out a wineskin. 'Lavinia can dance across this floor any time she fancies.' She chuckled, proffering the liquor.

Close up, Claudia realized Lavinia was younger than she appeared, by ten, maybe even fifteen years, that the wrinkles came from years of exposure to the sun, rather than age. Unexpectedly for Atlantis, the linen she wore was coarse and untailored, simply two widths sewn together and belted with a home-made girdle, and even as she accepted the wineskin, Claudia was wondering how a simple farmer's wife could afford a place like this.

A smoky pink light was spreading over the eastern horizon, and on the sheet of mercury that was Lake Plasimene, a single yellow flame sprang into life. With a thrill of surprise, Claudia saw it came from the Villa Tuder.

'You don't,' Lavinia said, eyeing up Claudia's jewels, 'look like a girl who believes that crap about pine trees filtering the germs. What brings you here, if not to escape the contagion?'

Claudia passed back the wine. 'The same as you, I suspect.'

'I doubt that very much.' Lavinia snorted, patting her one indulgence, a pile of immaculate curls. 'This is the first time in his wastrel life my son has pampered his old mother, but –' she took a long swig from the skin '– it's a beautiful spot, this lake, and you won't hear Lavinia complain.' She wiped her mouth with the back of her hand. 'What a treat, to be free of the olives.'

'You own a grove, then?'

'Near Luca. It's just a smallholding – me, my son and my son's wife, though since neither of them moves without a fire being lit under their tails, Lavinia relies on her field hand, but it's not a bad old life, all things considered. Do you have children?'

'No.'

'Good for you, they're nothing but trouble, especially sons,' Lavinia said, replacing the stopper in the wineskin. 'Take my boy – thinks sesterces grow next to the olives, and in those years we're lucky enough to make a profit, what happens? He blows it on some harebrained venture! I tell you, Lalo my field hand is more like a son – still –' she pulled a face '– my lad's done me proud, treating his old mother to some fancy pandering, though the gossip's as much fun as the treatments. My, my, you should see what goes on! It's like an upper-class bawdy house and talk about scandal!'

'Such as?' Claudia's tone was mild and enticing, and with a smack of her lips, Lavinia rose to the bait.

'There was that woman who died in the mud room, for a start. Lordy, you should have seen Pylades' face when he found out! White as a sheet, poor bugger, scared stiff the scandal would ruin Atlantis! In the end, he got Kamar to hush it up, to say she died in her sleep. Well –' Lavinia cackled like a sea-witch '– that part was true. They just didn't let on where!'

'Anything . . . else?' Claudia kept her eyes on the single yellow light burning like a beacon on the island across the lake.

'Ffff! You wouldn't believe what Lavinia's picked up. That busty redhead from the fishmonger's, palming herself off as nobility to hook herself a rich husband. The blond Adonis-type, having it off with his father's new bride, thinks I don't know. Ha! Because I'm crippled, folk think I'm blind, deaf and dumb – but never underestimate

Lavinia, that's my motto. Folk have tried, and worse they are for it, I can tell you. Not that they all come a cropper like that whippersnapper I was talking to yesterday—'

'What?' Claudia said, and a thousand worms crawled beneath her skin. 'You were talking to Cal? When?'

'Cheeky bugger perched against that rail there just the other night and you know what he said?' The old woman pursed her lips. 'Said he reckoned I was nothing but a fraud! Poetic justice, if you ask me, him falling from that selfsame spot. Told him at the time, I did, mark my words, young fellow, the gods will punish mischief-makers—'

'Did you –' Claudia asked slowly, her nails biting into the palms of her hand '– see him fall?'

'Me?' There was an almost imperceptible pause. 'Too damned hot for Lavinia, this weather.' A gnarled brown hand slipped the wineskin out from beneath the coverlet. 'Like a lazy lioness, she's taken to sleeping through the daytime, only my son mustn't get wind that I let my field hand sleep in my bed at night, he'd go apeshit.' A faraway look came into the startling blue eyes. 'Well, maybe not these days, because I do believe my lad has finally changed his ways. Mind.' She gave a small, self-conscious laugh. 'When I say lad, he's forty-seven, but then some take that long before they grow up, and usually death is the catalyst.'

Claudia watched her take a deep draught of red wine, and thought, Cal was right about you, my girl, you're not what you appear. And you didn't actually answer my question, did you, about whether or not you saw what happened to Cal?

'Whose death?' she coaxed. 'Your husband's?'

'Him? That old miser slipped his anchor when I was

thirty-two, no, no, no.' Lavinia handed the wineskin to Claudia. 'I'm talking about a shipwreck, that's what sobered my son. Every single hand went down, see.'

As the sky began to brighten, Lake Plasimene yawned and stretched and prepared itself for another sticky day. Round the margins waterfowl honked to one another, frogs began to croak and, from the myriad of trees which grew along this promontory, birds called out the daily news – bluetits, blackcaps and siskins, swapping tales of how many eggs they had raised, weren't oak apples prolific this year, and who'd have thought millipedes grew so fat. And Claudia asked herself what it was Lavinia was hiding . . .

'It was the same old story. Every time we made a little profit, he'd invest it in some stupid get-rich scheme and every time we'd end up broke. That's why I refused to remarry, even though it's against the law, but I wasn't going to hand my grove over just –' she snapped her bony fingers '– like that, and my boy wasn't competent! Take this last venture. Two years' profit he invested in grain and what happens? Bloody ship sinks in a storm off Alexandria, fully laden. Mind, it shook him to the core, did that. Set him rethinking all his values, because next thing he's whisking me off for a month of solid pampering and I tell you straight, I'm relishing every single second.'

So how come, thought Claudia, plugging the stopper back in the neck of the wineskin, the son could afford to send his old gossip of a mother here . . .?

'Sadly I'm stuck with my daughter-in-law and her frightful sister—' Lavinia began, then pulled up short, as though catching sight of something over Claudia's shoulder. However, before Claudia could turn to face the sliding doors, Lavinia broke into a cough.

'My . . . medicine,' she croaked. 'In my room. Would you mind?'

Claudia could hardly refuse a sick woman's request, yet she had the strangest feeling Lavinia had contrived to get her out of the way. That cough was pretty unconvincing! But why? Why should an impecunious, weather-beaten olive grower want her out of the way?

So busy was she conjuring up a list of possibilities that Claudia was completely unprepared for the sight which greeted her when she flung wide Lavinia's door. On the couch, their limbs naked and entwined, a dark-haired girl and a negro were worshipping Eros with uninhibited abandon!

'Who the blazes are you?' the man demanded, hauling up the sheet as they sprang apart.

'The medicine!' Claudia barked. 'Where's Lavinia's medicine?'

'Merciful Jehovah, is she all right?' It was the girl who sprang off the bed and grabbed a small phial from the table.

'How the hell do I know?' Claudia snapped, whipping the draught from her hand and racing back to the sun porch where, surprise, surprise, Lavinia had stopped coughing. 'Shall I fetch Kamar?' Claudia asked sweetly.

'That useless fool!' the old woman retorted. 'Couldn't tell a fracture from a freckle! No, no,' she waved away the phial, 'I'm all right.'

And Claudia thought, I bet you are!

'Ah, Ruth! Lalo!' Lavinia addressed the amorous couple. The negro, his skin still glistening from his aerobic endeavours, had pulled on a tunic of such rough quality it would have curled Pylades' lip, while the girl was wearing a fringed skirt below a tight high bodice which revealed her ancestry as much as her midriff. 'You three have met, then?' Lavinia asked, her blue eyes shining with mischief.

The Judaean girl ignored her mistress to put her hand on Lavinia's forehead, then studied the whites of her eyes. 'You've been drinking again,' she said. 'You know what happens when you mix your drugs with the wine.'

'Never touched a drop,' Lavinia said, pulling the coverlet over the wineskin, then turned to Lalo and said, 'For heaven's sake, stop fussing.'

'I'm not fussing,' the field hand said, scooping her into his arms, and Claudia noticed that his knuckles were bleeding and raw, as though he'd been in a fight. 'Merely taking precautions, and it's bed for you, my lady.'

Leaving Ruth to wheel out her day couch, Lavinia clasped her wizened hands round the outworker's neck and shot Claudia a vulgar wink before the trio disappeared.

Claudia rested her elbows on the gold-painted rail and gazed out over the water as she wondered again what the old woman was concealing. Had someone appeared in the doorway? Overheard the discussion about Cal? Or was Claudia's overworked imagination running away with itself? Other islands were popping up now, smaller, rockier outcrops close to the north shore of the lake. The flame on Tuder's island, she noticed, had been extinguished. A heron stalked the shallows for tadpoles and eels, and an osprey scooped a fish in its talons.

About twenty strokes out, a lone rowboat cleaved a

path through the opalescent water, leaving ripples which reflected the misty mauve of the dawn. Claudia frowned. That boat. Where had she seen it before? As though her head was befuddled by a heavy cold, she couldn't seem to think straight.

Then it came to her.

Yesterday. It was the boat she had taken out to the island.

His hair still hung like drapes from that same central parting, and in the clarity of Aurora's rosy rays, his muscles showed stark and rounded as he hauled on the oars.

Then the movement stopped abruptly, and Claudia knew then that he'd been aware of her presence all along. For maybe thirty seconds he sat motionless before pushing the oars once more through the water, and in the pellucid light she saw a flash of white which could have been a smile, or then again might have been nothing more than a grimace of exertion.

I'm tired, she thought. Weary. I need to lie down. But she made no move to leave, and the V of the grey rowboat's wake grew fainter and fainter.

Fifty feet below this spot, Cal's twisted body had lain for how long before somebody noticed? An hour? Three? A stone dropped in Claudia's stomach. Suppose he'd been trying to attract her attention? To warn her, say, about the bear? Might the accident have been avoided, had she stayed with him, or would he still have been tempted to leap on to the rail to show off?

A frown puckered her brow. Surely if Cal had been treating this as a tightrope, he'd have wanted an audience . . .? *Wait!*

The tiredness evaporated as Claudia grabbed the torch and, running now, retraced yesterday's route. The secret doorway . . . Through the cave . . . Down the tunnel . . . Her bare feet crunched on the shingle as she sprinted to the spot where Cal's body had lain. Now she knew what was so odd about it.

Cal had not died here.

With daylight supplementing the light from her torch, her suspicions were confirmed. There was no trace of blood on the stones. Of course not. The body had been brought here and arranged as though it had fallen, although the limbs had been rather too artistically placed for her liking. Someone had killed him by snapping his neck, and as an afterthought tried to make it look like an accident by smashing the bones of his face.

Someone who knew the only person they had to fool was a doctor used to corns, rather than tumours. Someone familiar enough with Kamar to know he was too bone-idle to examine a corpse once life was extinct . . .

Slowly this time, scouring the ground with her eyes, Claudia returned to the mouth of the tunnel and tears stung in her eyes. Cal *had* waited here, just as he promised, and she didn't need to bend down to see that the rusty brown patch which discoloured the rock was his blood.

'Damn you!' She hurled the burning brand into the lake and heard the flame sizzle as it died. 'Damn you, you murdering son-of-a-bitch!'

She didn't know who had killed Cal, she didn't know why, and what's more, she didn't give a toss for the reason.

All Claudia knew, so help her, was that she'd unearth the bastard who murdered this boy and, by the gods, she'd make him pay for his crime!

VIII

As dawn broke across the seven hills of Rome, its residents braced themselves for revelations of an altogether different kind. Are those spots, or just a bruise where she fell over? Are you off your food from fever, or was it curdled milk which made you queer? In every household, from the richest to the squalid, families lined up to inspect one another for the symptoms of the plague, because with seventy more souls ferried over the Styx every day, they needed reassurance they weren't going to be on the next boat.

For Marcus Cornelius Orbilio, trudging down from the Capitol, he was simply too bone weary to care. His eyelids, he was sure, could double as scouring pads, every muscle he owned cried out for rest. Forty-two hours had passed since his last proper sleep, his stubble itched and the soles of his feet felt like they'd been beaten with paddles. He needed a drink. He knew that he shouldn't, that his brain and digestion were shot all to hell, but Mother of Tarquin, what he wouldn't give for a drink!

In the shadow of the Temple of Concord, he glanced across to the Imperial Palace and cursed his boss under his breath. Bastard! Simply because Orbilio had dined with a select group of senators, two of them personal friends of the Emperor, and his superior officer hadn't been invited! Never mind these were Orbilio's relatives, that he had no say in who was or wasn't asked. In his boss's eyes this was a snub, a sharp reminder that, in class terms, the Head of the Security Police ranked lower than his patrician employee and thus, to keep the upstart in his place, he'd hauled Marcus Cornelius away from the murder he was investigating and assigned him instead to round-the-clock guard duty outside the Imperial Palace.

That he could justify the humiliation by citing the dire consequences of the plague entering the imperial blood-stream made it doubly hard for Orbilio to swallow, because on that particular issue at least he backed his boss to the hilt. Rome had enough on her plate, she daren't lose Augustus!

It was only seven weeks back, remember, that Agrippa died so unexpectedly, depriving the Emperor in one single blow of best friend, son-in-law, his finest general – and, most importantly, his heir. Rome had become a bucking bronco with revolution, anarchy and sedition jostling to jump in the saddle, and with no one left to hold the reins. Jupiter alone knows what backlash might unfold! No, Augustus' life needed careful guarding at the moment, that went without saying, but the Palace watch was a job for the Praetorian Guard and, unlike the Head of the Security Police, Augustus was no snob. He wouldn't give a toss who kept the plague out!

Rather, Orbilio felt, being a red-blooded bloke himself, the Emperor might be sympathetic towards what Marcus' boss would undoubtedly call deserting his post . . .

Glancing across to the Senate House, Marcus felt a sour taste in his mouth. Accusations of desertion would not sit well with his ambitions to take a seat one day, so he had to play this right. One step wrong and it's no use shouting about the double standards of putting the Senate in unofficial recess until May, so the politicians can escape the plague! The mud would stick and Orbilio's chances of crossing that most illustrious of thresholds would be squashed for ever. On the other hand. His step quickened. Minor slurs could be forgiven, providing he solved enough cases – and naturally, the higher their profile, the higher the odds. Well, the profile of what he'd been working on (leastways until his boss got the hump) could outstrip the Great Pyramid of Egypt! And murder was just the tip of the pyramid . . .

Once across the Forum, Marcus kept to the diminishing shade of the Via Sacra. The beads of sweat which had linked hands round his belt told him today would be another stinking inferno and already, even at this early hour, fumigatory fires burned the length and breadth of the city. Orbilio did not think that, in this heat, they helped.

How long, he wondered, before the contagion ran its course and the Forum could reflect a different mood? Lately, in place of strings of roped ostriches kicking up mayhem, scrawny pigeons pecked in the dust, with no children to chase them away. Gone were the dancers, the acrobats, the fire-eaters in their gaily coloured costumes. Silent were the taunts of the bare-knuckle fighters, the strident cries of the hucksters, the hup-hup-hup of the litter bearers. For the past week, heads wagged low in sombre consultations with fortune-tellers while augurs studied the stars, the entrails of sheep, even the flight patterns of owls in search of encouraging auspices. The sun might shine, thought Orbilio, but the light had gone out in the city.

Swerving past a man up a ladder fixing his gutterspout, he glanced down a sidestreet and saw yet another handcart wheeling away a tiny body concealed by a sheet and heard that most heartrending of sounds – the muted sobs of a father bereaved.

'Shit!'

As Orbilio pressed on up the Velian slope, the lump in his throat refused to subside. Death he was used to. He was twenty-five, for gods' sake, he'd seen men die – good men, bullies, bigots and cowards, he'd watched them expire on the battlefield and from public execution – *but a child?* Its soul stolen away in the night? That can't be right. And whilst his objective in visiting Jupiter's temple had been to gain ammunition to fight his boss rather than to offer up prayers, Marcus couldn't help wondering when the King of Olympus intended to tear himself away from his drinking and his whoring and send a thunderbolt to put paid to this murderous heat.

People were dying, and Jupiter did not care. Orbilio snorted. Who did *that* remind him of! Three painstaking weeks he'd spent gathering evidence on that damned murder and, snap, just like that, his boss suspends further enquiries! Well, the case was too important to walk away from, both from the victim's point of view, as well as Orbilio's. He needed a weapon to fight back with and this morning he had found it.

A personal application from his boss for his brother to fill the role of Jupiter's priest. Brilliant! Just what Orbilio needed!

For the last seventy-five years the job had not so much been vacant, more covered by the collegiate as a group, but lately, to emphasize the importance the king of the gods played in Augustus' golden age of peace, the Emperor decided to entrust the task once more to a single individual. Heaven knows, the list of applicants would be tremendous (what a feather in their cap, whoever got the job) but the post would not be as easy to fill as some might imagine. Few people in living memory had ever seen the original functions performed, but only a foreigner could not be aware of hundreds of taboos by which Jupiter's special priest was bound and the job would only go to a man who could recite the rules and regulations.

Well, Orbilio knew. The whole list lay in his family vault.

And with this information, he could trade with his superior officer, for the man's ambitions knew no bounds. His brother, as weak and clumsy as he was strong and shrewd, would not care a jot. But for the Head of the Security Police to boast a sibling in this prestigious role . . . Oh, yes. Orbilio was in an excellent position to bargain.

He paused in the street to stroke the ginger tomcat which came rubbing round his ankles, and vowed he would not bargain with his boss unless pushed to the limit. Scrubbing the cat's ears, Marcus was keenly aware that, if he could solve this outstanding murder case – correction, this Giant Pyramid of a case – there'd be no need for horsetrading at all. His skills would see him through. Hadn't those selfsame skills put him on to it? Long, weary legs began the long, slow haul up the Esquiline Hill.

It had all started with a bit of gossip. One man in the steamy atmosphere of the public bath house bragging to another how he planned to spend the fortune he'd inherited from his wife. The voice was not that of an old man, and Marcus' investigative ears twitched, albeit idly.

'Didn't she keep cats or something, your late wife?' the friend asked.

'Twelve of the fuckers,' the husband spat. 'Got rid of them *straight* away!'

That was all. A snippet of overheard conversation, but somehow it stuck in his mind. Twelve cats, the man said. Twelve's a lot, an awful lot, but perhaps Orbilio would have thought no more of it, had the husband not sounded so bitter when he snarled out the number. Plus, he didn't like the way the man laughed when he said 'straight away'. In fact, the whole tone of it stuck in Orbilio's craw, and it was more to put his own mind at rest that he checked out the fellow's history. Which was shabby, to say the least. A wastrel, a womanizer, a professional sponger, but he could not have killed his wife. He had an alibi, his wife was a hundred miles away, and she died of natural causes—

Except healthy women do not die of natural causes. Uneasy now, Marcus delved deeper, and what he found made his blood turn to ice.

At which point, his boss got the hump.

'The woman's been dead three fucking months,' he had snapped. 'What difference does another month make? Just get your arse up to the Palace and keep the fucking plague out!'

Well, sorry, but Orbilio had no intention of dropping this case. Not this one! Solving it would propel him through the Senate House doors faster than a tornado and since there's more than one way to snare a song thrush, even when his brain felt like porridge and every muscle screamed, Marcus Cornelius trekked all the way across town at the end of his shift to verify his boss's application regarding the role of Jupiter's priest.

Success. Whichever way it swung now, Orbilio would be a hero!

First, though, a hero needs his beauty sleep. Three or four hours should suffice, and the kudos of scaling his criminal pyramid buoyed his aching feet. In three or four hours, he'd be turning his back on these dark alleyways, the towering tenements, on mournful, plague-ridden wails. He'd be heading for the country, to a place with views of hills across a lake. Where birds sang in untrammelled bliss. Where fish leapt out of the water at sunset. A place, he mused, which offered health-giving springs and baths of hot, energizing mud.

A place, in short, which contained Claudia Seferius!

A python coiled round his innards and undertook serious constriction work. *Claudia*. The appearance of a goddess, the temperament of a tigress, there were strands of molten metal in her hair. *Claudia*. Eyes which flashed like sparks off an anvil, she lived life with the wind in her hair. Like lightning in a tempest, the electricity between the two of them was as terrifying as it was rousing. Wild. Unpredictable. He would follow her, he knew, Orpheus-fashion to Hades if she so much as crooked her finger . . .

Except Marcus was no gentle musician – and Claudia, certainly, no sweet Eurydice!

But such was her pull on him, stronger even than the moon on the tides, that wherever she left her footprints, he'd be there.

Not in front. Not behind.

Alongside.

As equals.

The thought of her made his gut lurch. Janus, he really needed that drink!

For all that the sun was beginning to rise, the hour was still early and Orbilio's house was in darkness as he let himself in. A whiff of proving bread escaped from the kitchens, but his stomach recoiled at the prospect of food. Sleep! He needed sleep. Urgent, replenishing sleep. And then . . .

Love or lust, who gives a damn? Like a drug, he was addicted to the woman. Try as he might, he could not live without her.

Marcus staggered across the atrium like a drunkard. The bedroom, too, was in darkness. He unbuckled his belt and it clattered as it fell to the floor. Sleep, yes, but surely a drink? To settle the flutters Claudia invariably brought on. By touch he fumbled for the jug beside his bed and without reaching for a goblet drank straight from the jar. The wine hit his stomach like a punch and too late he realized he should have sipped rather than gulped, but the damage was done and in this stifling heat, what difference did one more hangover make?

He was wiping a damp cloth over his face when the crack of a whip made him jump. What the hell . . .?

Again, the snap of rawhide rang out in his room, accompanied by rich, female laughter. Croesus, what was in that bloody jug?

'I thought you were never coming home.' She laughed, and he realized this was no hallucination. This was what-sername. Thingy. *Barbia*. That's right. And Barbia, he remembered, had a penchant for whips. And for manacles. And chains . . .

'I—'

The wine made his brain fuzzy, he couldn't think straight. How did she end up here? In his bed? He'd flirted with her in the Palatine Gardens. She'd been a real laugh, earthy and vibrant, and they'd passed two jubilant hours rustling the laurels. But here?

'I . . . can't stop,' he muttered. 'Just called in to change my tunic – *youch*!' The whip stung his flesh. Mother of Tarquin, she thought he was larking about!

'Not playing hard to get, are we?' Her breathing was heavy and scented with wine. 'Or else Barbie will have to get rough!'

'No!' It came out more terrified yelp than manly denial, but in any case it came out too late. Metal clamped round his right ankle and a second click fastened it firm to the bed. Orbilio let out a shaky laugh. 'Barbia, look—'

Before he could clarify the misunderstanding that he'd given his address as a joke, a loud rip cut through the air and, whoosh, his tunic was gone. Thanks to glimmers of sunlight beginning to penetrate the cracks in the shutters, he could make out Barbia's figure. It seemed to be encased in some form of harness . . .

In the blackness, he heard the jangle of handcuffs and lunged at where he thought they would be. But Barbia had been teasing. A diversion for the chainlink which snapped round his wrist and, shit! He was spreadeagled on his own couch, right ankle, left wrist, and there was not a damned thing he could do!

Orbilio considered the one thin sheet of inadequate linen which concealed his sad lack of enthusiasm and knew that if his boss walked in right now, he'd strangle the oily bastard with this bloody chain, purely for exposing him to the siren from hell!

As Barbia whisked a knife through his loincloth, Orbilio prayed to Priapus to help him in this, his hour of need—

Somehow the misty shores of Lake Plasimene belonged to a different incarnation, and instead of the quacking of ducks and the croaking of frogs in the bulrushes, he was stuck with Barbia's fruity laughter and the acid smell of her leather gear. In fact, as the bullwhip stung his thigh, Orbilio's final thought, as Barbia pressed her ample breasts into his face, was that, sleep or no sleep, by Croesus, he'd be on the first horse out of town the instant this harpy untied him.

Assuming, of course, he survived.

IX

Tradition demanded Cal's body lie in state, his feet facing the door, for several days.

The heat, alas, decreed otherwise.

With oak leaves wreathed around his shattered skull and less than eighteen hours after he had met his violent end, Cal set off from Atlantis on this, his ultimate journey. In deference to his youth, flute players rather than trumpeters led the procession as eight bearers shouldered the funeral bed on poles of sacred oak. With his face washed clean and his hair combed low, Calvus resembled more a dashing blade knocked out cold in a drunken brawl and it seemed to Claudia quite impossible that he wouldn't bounce up any second, yelling, 'Which of you bastards wants more?'

But he wouldn't.

Those beech-leaf eyes would never sparkle in fun. Battered lips could never again beg kisses in exchange for a secret.

This was not a practical joke.

Swinging censers of smoking cinnamon accompanied the bier, barely masking the sulphurous stench of the torches which purified its four corners. Cal had no relatives in Atlantis, no close friends, so the mourners were hired, wailing women, beating ash-covered breasts and howling with such conviction, few would suspect it was not their own son or brother they were burning today.

Slowly, the cortège made its way down the slope of the promontory, the black-clad undertakers setting the pace as the sun beat down on a landscape which, until Pylades arrived, had remained untouched for eight generations. Usually two centuries is time enough to regroup and rebuild after battle, but the fighting left behind a sinister legacy. 'The Place of Blood'. 'The Place of Bones'. Graphic names which not only immortalized the twenty thousand men killed in that fateful Battle of the Lake, but which had served to deter settlers, wary of the restless ghosts of the warriors. Only fishermen doggedly continued to ply their trade, their base a small village unsullied by the ferocious spilling of blood on the eastern rim of the lake.

Then a visitor from Greece discovered a mineral spring on the cliff-like projectory, and the augurs said, 'This is a miracle!'

And it was! Not only Atlantis, with its shining opulence and hedonistic splendour, rose from obscurity. Attracted by the influx of visitors, a whole host of shops, houses and businesses sprang up, and in the five years since Pylades arrived, a whole town had evolved, with its central Forum and its main street and its taverns and brickworks and lawcourts. There were blacksmiths, dentists, barbers, potters, barrelmakers, herbalists – you name it, they were here in their droves – and they called their town Spesium, 'Place of Hope'.

To the sounds of trumpets, horns and cymbals loud enough to scare every spirit, not just the bad ones, the funeral procession rumbled past leadbeaters and coppersmiths, bakers and glassblowers, apprentices and matrons. For a moment, Claudia thought she glimpsed a familiar face in the crowd, someone from Rome, but maybe she was wrong, because when she lifted her mourning veil for a better view, there was no one she recognized after all. Bugger.

Finally, on the far side of the newly constructed triple-arch gateway, the parade ground to a halt, silver censers blinding in the sunlight. With professional ease, Cal's final wooden bed was hefted on to the pyre and Claudia noticed that the immense Oriental she'd seen yesterday on her arrival had also latched on to the party. His posture was identical – feet squarely apart, arms crossed – and he still wore that tight leather vest and strange kilt. Today, though, the long tuft of hair was tied in a thong like a mare's tail on parade day. Somehow it looked like a weapon, as deadly as the curved blade at his hip. Despite the heat, Claudia shivered.

Then the bruiser slid from her mind as Pylades stepped forward to deliver the oration, and to hear him list the achievements of a young man he probably never knew to a crowd of people who'd never heard of him, you had to admire the professionalism of this stocky hillsman, so glowing were the tributes, so touching the anecdotes. As a young acolyte swung a censer with clumsy abandon, a priest in long flowing robes sprinkled the bier with wine. These two, Claudia deduced, must be Leon and Mosul. Spluttering from incense overdose, the priest snapped for Leon to withdraw, and as his little black eyes met with Kamar's, so he shrugged in a mixture of irritation and despair. This, then, was the perfectionist who tended the shrine of the water nymph all by himself? A tub of a man with the eyes of a mole.

As Pylades began to quote a few lines of Virgil, appropriate to the occasion, Claudia noticed the hint of fluff on Leon's upper lip and sympathized with Mosul. Already the lad's concentration had veered towards a shapely ankle protruding from the long, white tunic of a flautist, although from this angle, Claudia could not tell whether the joint belonged to a youth or a girl.

Mosul completed his purification procedure and resumed his place next to Kamar. Pylades, keen to give Cal a good send-off, was now quoting Sappho and Claudia glanced round the crowd. Strange. Not a military uniform in sight. Not that she minded, of course! The greater the distance between the army and Mistress Seferius the better at the moment, but all the same, it struck her as odd, no official attendance at a funeral. The Oriental, she noticed, had melted away as invisibly as he had appeared, but right at the back, Lavinia's tall field hand had appeared, his ebony skin shining in the sunlight. At his shoulder, the young Jewish girl appeared to be pleading with him, and Lalo spread his weathered outdoor hands in silent pacification, as though to say 'not now', and Claudia made a mental note to find out how long Ruth had been with Lavinia and where she had come from before. Her Latin was perfect, barely a hint of a Judaean accent, but it was strange she hadn't adapted to Roman attire, and equally strange that Lavinia didn't object. If only to spare her servant from Mosul's cold and contemptuous stare.

Observing the nimbleness of Lalo's olive-picking fingers and the raw, damaged knuckles, Claudia decided that it wouldn't hurt to enquire how long *he'd* been in the old woman's employ, either. What exactly was his role within her smallholding? For a field hand, he was exceptionally familiar with his mistress, even to sleeping in her bed. Did he bully her? That seemed unlikely, but why should he be here today? Had Lavinia sent him to watch and report back? Or was he paying his own last respects?

As Pylades wound up his oration, the pre-paid sobbing took over and branches of cypress were solemnly laid over Cal's body, covering for ever that mop of corn-coloured hair. With a lump in her throat, Claudia inched through the crowd. Lecher or not, the Greek ought to know his efforts in ensuring Cal didn't journey alone on this tragic morning were appreciated. When she saw him turn to Kamar and mutter, 'I can't take much more of this,' under his breath, Claudia froze.

'Be patient,' the physician replied. 'It'll be over soon enough.'

Pylades snorted. 'That's fine for you to say,' he flashed back, 'you're a doctor, but me! I have a business to run!'

The hiss of the flames sweeping over the pyre drowned the rest of the interchange, but in any case Claudia could stomach no more. Sickened by the callousness, she reeled away from the congregation, to be swallowed up amongst the basketweavers and the moneychangers, the fishmongers and the wheelwrights.

Did no one care? A boy dies, and nobody here gives a damn?

Forget Kamar. He'd pronounced death by falling and nothing would sway him from that conclusion, and in any case who's to call him a liar? The evidence was literally going up in smoke, and as to a few bloodstains on the rock, why, you're overwrought, my dear, those could be anything – fishguts, a cracked shin, in fact are you sure that it's blood? It looks very like paint, you know... Turtleface's stock would probably soar as a result of the calm and professional way he dealt with another neurotic attention seeker!

By the basilica, she pulled close to the wall to let past a bloodied carcass of beef. Bluebottles swarmed over the meat and a mongrel trotted behind, pausing to lick the odd drip of blood.

If the priest with the shiny black eyes won't let even his own acolyte near the spring, he'd not wish to become embroiled in a scandal which might cast a cloud over his nymph.

Leon was too clumsy, too obsessed with galloping hormones to care, which only left Pylades – and far from being the high-minded deliverer of Lake Plasimene, bringer of trade and prosperity and cures for the sick, Pylades turned out to be just another shallow, self-seeking money-grubber, concerned more with his daily schedule than the boy who had died!

When it came to matters of conscience, it was clearly a case of the bland leading the bland.

'You wish to steal my boat again, yes?'

The voice in her ear made her jump, causing Claudia to stub her toe on the kerbstone. What else could account for the colour flooding her face? 'Ah.' The grey rowboat. 'Um—'

He was leaning against the side of a barber's shop, the sole of one foot flat against the stonework as he carved a small piece of wood with a knife. Today his long hair was tied back at the nape, though there was no change in the depth of the accent.

'Is "ah-um" Latin for yes or for no?' the Spaniard enquired and despite his dark, dark eyes being hidden in the shadows, Claudia knew they were laughing.

'I assumed the boat was the property of Atlantis,' she said stiffly. Dammit, he had no right to creep up on her like that! 'However, I wish to thank you for saving my life yesterday.'

'No need,' he replied, flashing a sharp glance. 'The bear, also, was trespassing.'

Also?

'You know, this man Tuder –' he shrugged expressively '– for a banker, he have very good taste. Maybe I show you around? The villa, the grounds. You wish to see, yes?'

Above the hum of conversation from the barber's came the sound of iron scissors snipping at hair, bronze knives being stropped, the sizzle of curling tongs heated in charcoals and whetstones being lubricated by spitting.

'I wish to see, no.'

The Spaniard grunted, and the grunt could have meant anything.

Funny, but despite the lane reeking with the wolf's grease used to cure baldness, with steam and the dust from the scrape of their stools, Claudia could smell only a subtle blend of woodshavings and pine . . .

'I come anyway,' he insisted. 'Three hours from now. I wait by the jetty and –' he cut short her protest with a flash of white teeth '– I let you row, if you want.'

Claudia willed her feet to start walking, because the Spaniard made no effort to prise himself away from the wall.

'You know,' he was addressing her retreating back – so she might have misheard, what with the babble of gossip from inside the barber's and a chariot rattling past – but it sounded for all the world as though he said, 'you look just as good with your clothes on.'

Accompanied, perhaps, by a chuckle.

Who was he? Her mind whirling like a mill-race, Claudia elbowed her way down the street, careless of a packmule loaded with grain. The owner cursed roundly as he bent to scoop up the trail of spilled corn, but Claudia didn't hear. Who the hell was the stranger who, with the utmost calm and composure, circled a blood-crazed bear with a spear in its eye? The same man who issues veiled warnings against trespassers on the island, yet conversely offers to show her around? Who mocks her state of near nudity without enquiring as to her health after so narrow an escape?

Who was the stranger who, let's be honest, had strip-searched her soul yesterday?

A picture flashed into her mind. Of him standing at the edge of the clearing, one shoulder bare as he leaned on his lance. Today he wore a tunic of watercress green and the gold had not been restricted to the hem, but was embroidered into oak leaves and acorns. What job, she wondered, swerving past a pedlar, what job on Tuder's estate would befit a man of twenty-five, twenty-six with broad shoulders and strong, corded muscles? She exchanged five sesterces for an ostrich-feather fan from the pedlar. Tuder had a wife, had he not? Lais, someone said her name was. Closer to sixty than fifty they said. Would Lais have need of a slave with smouldering good looks? To explain the gold thread in his cloth?

Pausing to drink from a fountain, Claudia decided that Lais would be living dangerously were that the case – the Emperor's reforms were exacting in the extreme! Nowadays, not only a cuckolded husband had the right to instigate a divorce against an adulterous wife. Recent legislation gave others an incentive to shop her, because if the husband, for whatever motive, decided against prosecution, the informant himself could indict – with the added inducement that, should the erring wife be proved guilty, said accuser could claim half her dowry.

Bound by the stifling, almost incestuous, isolation of an island, petty jealousies would escalate, imaginary scores would need settling. Lais and her lover would need to watch out!

Assuming, of course, the supposition was correct. Claudia trickled lukewarm water from the fountain over her face. There might be a perfectly innocent explanation for all this. Lais, for instance, could turn out to be a nagging shrew, a middle-aged cripple or some kissy socialite. Who knows, she might be all three, with not a thought to romancing some drop-dead sexy slave which, if the affair came to light, could result in her being cast out and sold into slavery, and for him would mean certain death.

Was he worth it? Claudia wondered. Was the Spaniard worth risking the auction block for?

She was heartily relieved that the triple arch loomed before the question required an answer!

Cal's pyre had burned through and, to the piping of flautists, attendants swept the smouldering debris into a pile, sprinkling it with a purifying mix of wine and water before sifting it into the urn. Flapping the ostrich feathers brought on a tight constriction inside Claudia's ribs. Was it really only yesterday Cal had grabbed that parchment fan from her hand in the sizzling heat of the walnut grove and whipped up, not just a breeze, but a whole storm of passion? As the lid closed for ever on the pottery urn, her vision clouded at the memory of chiselled features which would never again break into a self-mocking grin, of hands stilled for ever from turning somersaults.

'I'll be waiting.'

The words echoed in her head and Claudia bit deep into her lower lip. From now on, whenever she inhaled the astringency of alecost she would think of Cal, and more than ever she was glad she hadn't succumbed to her desires in the clandestine anonymity of the cave. *Who would know?* Claudia would know. Now, at least, his shade could walk the Elysian Fields with one less stain on its soul.

Claudia blew into her handkerchief. It was so bloody unfair. Cal was too young to die, to be murdered! He'd been in the prime of his life, guzzling every opportunity which presented itself before maturity took a hold of his character and twisted it out of all recognition. Beside one of the tombs, a freckle-faced girl of maybe seven or eight rolled a hoop with a bone. For her, the world was a blank stucco wall upon which she could paint out her destiny, and whether the child turned out a thin-lipped virago, a brow-beaten doormat or a drink-raddled jade, only time or a clairvoyant could tell. But at least the future was hers to chart out.

Cal had been denied that opportunity.

A fat tear trickled down Claudia's cheek and angrily she brushed it away. Our characters are the product of the decisions we make, and Cal ought at least to have been given a fighting chance. To die nobly in battle, perhaps, or face down disease with some dignity. Even hand-to-hand combat with his killer would have been preferable to having his neck wrung like a chicken's!

It was too soon, the emotions still too raw, for Claudia to set her mind to considering who might have murdered Cal, or even why.

Yet, if only she had turned around, Claudia Seferius would have seen his killer standing behind her, deep in the shadows of the triple-arch gateway.

Watching intently.

X

Under the circumstances – heat which sweat-stained their clothes and attracted ravenous insects, the funeral going on all around them – you'd expect the citizens of Spesium to ease up a bit, but no. If anything, people seemed more careworn, more anxious. Farmers had fetched their cheeses, eggs and cattle in for market day, they were damned well going to sell them, and the Corn Measurer doled out the grain, flanked by two solid henchmen who put paid to all thoughts of pilfering. Rich men and poor, artists and administrators frantically thrust and jostled through the crush, shouting and squeezing and gripping their purses amid the clatter of wheelwrights and the grinding of shovels mixing cement as more and more apartment blocks were thrown up. So much brick dust, thought Claudia, so much construction, I could almost be back in Rome!

Then she saw him, standing head and shoulders above the crowd, a whopping great bear of a man with a black bushy beard and hair spiking out in a thousand directions, shaded by a scarlet awning over his stall. He was, at that moment, offering half-price enemas to a portly magistrate.

'Dorcan, you old fraud!' Claudia waited until the lardball waddled off before approaching the giant. 'I thought I caught a glimpse of your ugly mug earlier!' She examined the array of potions laid out on the counter. 'What brings you so far north?'

Dorcan, whose ancestry could only be guessed at, exhibited a row of perfect white teeth and it was only when he tipped his head back and roared, like he did now, that you could see they were someone else's, held together by strands of gold wire. 'Remember my instant cure for hangover?'

'Not personally.' Claudia ran her finger over a thin plait billed as the original thread from the Minotaur's labyrinth. 'Although if I recall, it was a gruesome mix of goat dung and rennet, was it not?'

'That's the one! Got me into a real spot of bother, I tell you.' His was not so much a laugh, more the bellow of a bull. 'See, I never expected the silly sods to eat the ruddy stuff, they was supposed to rub it on their foreheads!'

Claudia picked up a dried snake purporting to be a clipping of Medusa the Gorgon's hair. 'Is that why you had to grow the beard?'

'That come about after a misunderstanding over my fertility ointment when it appears I was somewhat heavy-handed with the mustard.' Dorcan leaned over the counter and lowered his voice to a whisper. 'Made their dicks glow like embers, it did!'

Claudia's eyes were beginning to stream. 'How many times have you been run out of town?'

The giant counted them off on his fingers. 'Well, there was that incident over the toothache cure, which I sold as black chameleon and they caught me grinding chicken bones. My ointment for nappy rash went down none too well, owing to the fact it made their little bums go green—'

'Stop!' she wailed, fearing she might stay permanently doubled up, when a child ran over, making such a screech on a whistle made of wood that she was forced to stick her fingers in her ears.

'Put it away, lad, until you've learned how to play it,' Dorcan chided, but the child's mother did not see the jest.

'I say,' she asked stiffly, 'do you have a cure for moths?'

Claudia, who had no idea moths got sick, stuffed her fist into her mouth when Dorcan smoothly knocked over the sign which read 'Reduces Fever' and handed over the small clay pot it rested against. The woman counted out three bronze coins and she and her unmusical offspring moved on.

'So then, my lovely,' the burly bear pocketed the money and propped the sign against a thin blue phial, 'I presume you haven't travelled one hundred miles of met-alled road just to sample my world-famous remedies. What brings you to Atlantis?'

Claudia ignored the question. 'You're a chap who hears things, Dorcan. I'm looking for a man.'

Another day aren't-we-all would have tripped off his tongue, but suddenly he scowled and dragged her underneath his scarlet awning. 'Don't have no truck with them,' he growled, and for a second she was bewildered.

'No, Dorcan,' she patted his arm, 'I appreciate your concern, but it's not an abortionist I'm after!'

His face dropped back into its amiable position. 'That's a bloody relief,' he said. 'You won't believe what them backstreet quacks gets up to. Now that, ma'am –' he turned to address an elderly matron '– is a string from the lyre of Orpheus himself, the only one in existence and a snip at three gold pieces.'

'Ooh, I don't know—'

'Strum on this, you'll charm the feathers off a bird and have creditors eating out of your hand.' He gave a wicked wink. 'Works a treat on daughters-in-law, too! Why, thank you, ma'am, and may the gods smile upon you.' Stashing the gold, he brought another lyre string out from under the counter and beamed at Claudia. 'What man are you after, my lovely?'

Claudia described the Spaniard and Dorcan said, yes, he knew the bloke, though not to speak to, mind. Tarraco his name was. Not what you'd call social, keeps himself very much to himself, steering clear of the drinking dens and that, and he never takes parts in the local athletics, the discus, foot races and the like, although whether he'll attend the new theatre when it's finished Dorcan couldn't say. But Tarraco was a rum bird, in his opinion. A real dark horse.

'What does he do out on Tuder's island, do you know?'

'Do?' The big, black bushy eyebrows shot straight up. 'Tarraco don't *do* nothing, lovely. Tarraco owns the bloody place!'

'But . . . What about Tuder? I thought—'

'Tuder!' Dorcan threw his head back and roared again. 'If you'd kept them pretty eyes of yours open, you'd have seen the banker's tomb right beside where they was burning Cal.'

This time it was Claudia's turn to be surprised. 'You knew Cal?'

Dorcan shrugged his massive shoulders and began straightening the jars and pots. 'Not really, no.'

Since he refused to meet her eye, Claudia fired off a different arrow. 'Who's that chap?' she asked, indicating the kilted Oriental standing on the temple steps, fingering his walrus moustache.

Dorcan puffed out his cheeks and rolled his eyes. 'Now that is a man you *should* avoid,' he said soberly. 'His name is Pul, and he's not so much an Oriental as a half-caste. His father was a Bessian tribesman, his mother came from far beyond the Caucasus, that's all anyone really knows of Pul. Except –' he spoke from one side of his mouth '– he's the law around here.'

'Don't give me that,' Claudia scoffed. 'What about the military?'

'You see any hammered breastplates here? Any feathered helmets?'

'There's a barracks, I passed it on the way in yesterday.'

'Sssh.' The charlatan held up a cautionary finger as a goldsmith approached the booth, his apron sparkling with precious dust. 'Colic, sir? I have the very remedy.' He passed across a brew of myrtleberries crushed in white wine. 'Drink this with every meal and in two days you'll be fine.'

Around them, the Forum buzzed like any other town on market day, with the squeal of fretful children, the protesting bleat of goats, the aromas of pepper, cumin and nutmeg in the air. Surveyors with their rods and lines pushed through the crowd, wagoners and carters spilled out of taverns, clapping one another on the back. How could it be possible, in a society run by an army which prized itself on discipline, that a civilian such as Pul could control a lively commercial centre?

A distant echo rumbled inside Claudia's head. Cal, laughing in the alder thicket. *Remember the golden rule*, he said. Whoever possesses the gold, rules.

'You haven't explained why Walruschops makes the law and not Pylades,' she said.

'Did I give you that impression? No, no, no.' Again, Dorcan seemed intent on rearranging his relics. 'I just meant Pul's not a man to be crossed.' His eyes alighted on the temple steps where Pul had been – but was no longer – standing. 'That was all.'

The hell it was! But Claudia sensed she'd got all she could out of the big man this morning and, purchasing an alabaster pot containing a cream which he swore was the selfsame recipe used by Cleopatra to maintain her own flawless complexion, she set off back to Atlantis.

Down on the lakeshore, a group of fowlers wearing wide-brimmed hats against the sun strode towards the town across the grass, the sacks on their backs bulging with the morning's endeavours, their dogs splashing in the shallows, but siesta time held Atlantis in its thrall. The ramp was all but deserted when, from the bath house, Ruth emerged, her skin red and glowing from either fluster or the sweatroom, with a pile of towels in her arms. She was halfway up the red marble steps when Mosul came barrelling down, his face like thunder, knocking her to the ground. This time his head was no longer covered in ritual, and Claudia could see he was bald, apart from a horseshoe of grizzled grey hair. She watched as one by one Ruth picked up the towels, shook and refolded them, but her eyes, Claudia noticed, never left the priest's back. The expression in them was of undiluted hatred.

Pausing to pluck a sprig of lavender, Claudia considered the curious events unfolding around her. Lavinia. Could she walk or not? Why were Lalo's knuckles fighting raw? How come Dorcan had suddenly popped up in

Spesium? Individually these things were minor, meant nothing. But collectively . . .? Engulfed by the coolness and tranquillity of the Great Hall, Claudia questioned whether she was overreacting. So what if Pul threw his weight around this brand-new town? Damn, it was like a haunted villa. Once you hear there's ghosts around, you start to jump at shadows. And without doubt, she'd been spooked by Tullus and the fact that he'd brought the army breathing down her neck!

Hell, you met Cal, she thought, sweeping down the corridor towards her bedchamber. In the end he probably seduced one wife too many and a bitter husband took his revenge. It is not, Claudia told herself, your problem!

Oh, but it is, a little voice answered. I made a promise.

You were tired and emotional and stressed to the eye-balls, she barked back, now forget it.

A dip in the plunge pool followed by a long massage with spicy oil of basil will soon put matters in perspective. So whilst her spirits might not actually have been brushing the ceiling, they were far from earthbound as she flung wide the door. They did not remain airborne for long. Claudia Seferius was about to discover there were yet more surprises in store in Atlantis.

Sprawled on his back across the wide double couch lay a man, arms outstretched in sleep. He was in desperate need of a shave and looked as though he'd ridden to Hades and back to judge from the lines etched deep in his cheeks, but other than that, she decided, for a Security Policeman he looked fit and healthy enough.

She remained in the doorway until her heartbeat was back on an even keel, watching the rise and fall of his chest as she took in the long, patrician tunic and trademark high boots, the dark shadows underneath his eyes and the darker curls of his hair on the counterpane. Despite a layer of brown dust which clung to his clothes, Claudia picked up a strong hint of sandalwood, and possibly rosemary too.

Stroking her chin, she considered her next move, but really, when it came down to it, the answer was staring her right in the face.

Atlantis was on a lake, for gods' sake!

XI

Marcus Cornelius gasped as the tidal wave swept over him. One minute he'd been sitting on the edge of the couch with the dust from the road still sour in his mouth. The next he was caught in a flash flood. What happened? His thoughts tumbled like the water which engulfed him. Barbia's whip-cracking demands . . . the hundred-mile ride . . . him collapsing with exhaustion . . . Through the whirlpool, he heard a female voice warning him he had until the count of ten to get out of her room or she'd have him bodily evicted.

'Claudia,' he spluttered, 'you don't understand—'

'Nine.'

'Hell, woman, at least give me a chance to explain.'

'You think I accepted this holiday without first checking that the goodies had been paid for?' A brittle laugh rang round the room. 'Wouldn't you know it was no long-lost friend of my late husband who reserved this haven of luxury, but a patrician, name of Marcus Makes Me Quite Bilious. Eight.'

The smile which had the temerity to flit across his face dived for cover when it came into contact with Claudia's glare. 'It's not what you think,' he protested.

'Men always say that,' she smiled, and the smile could

have concertinaed steel, 'when the girl doesn't swoon at the sight of their wide double couch. Seven.'

Orbilio lifted his shoulders off the soggy bedspread and leaned back on his elbows. 'That,' he grinned at the woman with strands of molten metal in her hair and a leather bucket in her hands, 'is because girls never learn that if they want to see a chap again, they shouldn't sleep with him. Six?'

Had looks been earthquakes, Claudia's would have flattened Byzantium. Marcus simply squelched off the bed and proceeded to wring out his tunic. 'Would you have come here, if you'd known the letter was from me?'

The bucket ricocheted off the wall, chipping the plaster. '*Five!*'

'Exactly.' A muddy puddle began to spread across the dolphin mosaic. 'So for once in his life, your hero stopped to think things through—'

'Pity he forgot to start again. Four.'

The feathers in the mattress were sagging from the weight of the water. He couldn't know about Tullus. Of course not. How could he? That couldn't be why he was here.

'Claudia, why do we fight every time we get together?'

'Because you refuse to agree to my terms. Three.'

'And a half,' he said quickly. 'What terms?'

'Unconditional surrender. Two.'

'And three-quarters. Surrender to what?'

'Getting lost once and for all. Time's up, I'm calling the bouncers.'

'All right.' He held up a placatory hand and squelched his way to the door. 'I haven't picked the best time to set out my stall, I admit that—'

'Hey!' Claudia's hands clamped upon her hips. 'Just where the hell do you think you're sloping off to?'

'To get myself a much-needed drink.'

'Listen, if anyone here's communing with the wine jug, that person's me,' she said. At least when you have a relationship with alcohol, you're both clear about the objectives. You know you won't come home and find a jug of wine lying unshaven on the bed, and, whatever else its faults, a jug of wine will never tell you lies. 'You made this mess, Orbilio—'

'*Me?*'

'—you can bloody well clear it up!'

No way could he know her connection with Tullus. It was a serious offence she was involved in, but not so bad it warranted the attentions of the Security Police. No, no, no. Arrogant son-of-a-bitch simply booked a room – a double room – then lures her here for a spot of hanky-panky.

'I suppose this is your idea of foreplay,' she steamed, 'lying spreadeagled on my bed with the words "take me now, you know you can't resist me" all but plastered over your chest!'

'Why change a technique which works?' He ducked as an inkwell whizzed past his ear. 'Claudia.' Suddenly there was a serious frown on his face. 'It pains me to mention it, but we have to talk.'

'The only pain around here is from you. In the neck.'

'We have to discuss official business sometime,' he said quietly, and she felt sure he heard the thump of her stomach flipping over, 'but maybe this is not the time. Er, before you go.' He paused, and when he spoke his voice was barely a whisper. 'You don't really think I'm a pain in the neck, do you?'

Caught offguard, the breath lodged in Claudia's throat. She paused by the window, fixing her eye on the distant blue shore, listening to the rasp of the crickets and the drip, drip, drip of the mattress. Deep in the shade of the laurels, Drusilla washed her back paw and just to the left of Claudia's breastbone, something heavy began to swell up. Him? A pain in the neck?

'No, Marcus,' she said sweetly, 'my opinion is lower than that.'

In his town house on the Quirinal Hill, close to the gate on the north-western slope, Sabbio Tullus sat in the shade of his peristyle and watched a bluebottle settle on his lunch. Bugger's laying its eggs, he thought. I'll bet it's laying its mucking eggs on that piece of cheese! He pushed his plate to one side and concentrated on hacking off a lump of mutton from the bone as the fountain made music in the corner. He'd have expected to lose weight, if anything, with this wretched cloud hanging over him, yet he could hardly stop stuffing. No sooner had he finished one meal, he was planning the next, not to mention the candied sweets and titbits in between.

His wife would undoubtedly put a stop to that, but his wife was in Frascati, where his bloody neighbour would be sweet-talking her and winning her over with lilies from his garden while his men were out shifting the boundary stones. Well, he'd not get away with it! Tullus would measure up when he went down there, the bastard tried it twice before, he'd try again, but by Croesus, he'd not get away with it this time, either.

At the thought of his wife, Tullus groaned. So young, so pretty, he hated being absent from her, missed hearing her laugh in the mornings, the softness of her skin in the night. Never mind; they should be reunited shortly, and as he speared a hard-boiled egg on his knife, he debated whether he ought to tell her about this business with his nephew. His wife, he knew, had never taken to the boy, said even as a child he was cold and self-obsessed. Tullus had put it down to resentment (his wife had never taken to his plump pigeon of a sister, either!), but as the years rolled by, especially more recent years, he, too, began to feel an uneasiness whenever he breathed the same air as his sister's son. Perhaps those expressionless eyes? The monotone voice? Either way, these days the boy gave him the creeps and to confide to his wife that he'd been duped by his own kith and kin would only induce a smug 'told you so'.

Besides, why worry her? There were better things to do when they got together, making more babies for a start, and checking on his neighbour – and before he left for Frascati he intended to have a word with that bloody architect and find out what the mucking hell he was playing at, not checking the mortar work on the depository. Munching on a bun, Tullus called for his secretary.

'Any news on the Seferius chit?' he asked through a spray of yellow crumbs.

'Not a whisper, sir. Wherever she's gone, she's taken no servants and left no forwarding address.'

'What about word from our agents?'

The secretary spread apologetic hands and Tullus

grunted. Bloody saffron buns, bloody heavy-handed cook, he'd got bloody indigestion. He rubbed at the ache in his chest. 'Heartburn,' he mumbled. 'Bloody heartburn from those bloody cakes.'

Reaching for a second bun, he ordered the clerk to make an urgent appointment to meet with the architect who built that strongroom and also to send a letter to his wife, informing her he'd be down by Tuesday next.

After all, Claudia Seferius can't be that hard to track down, now can she?

Across the other side of Rome, in the warehouse district on the Aventine, the object of Tullus' revulsion held a sprig of chamomile to his nostrils to counteract the putrid stench rising from the river and studied the flab around his visitor's jowls, the overlap of his huge belly. He certainly didn't look like the best, but then, as he knew himself, looks could be very deceptive.

'Your wine, sir.' An unctuous dwarf arrived to set a silver tray down on the desk and poured two glasses of the tepid wine, one for his master and one for the fat man who stank of cardamom.

'Is he trustworthy?' the fat man asked, crinkling his nose at the attendant.

Tullus' nephew sniffed at the chamomile. With the plague ravaging the city, servants were thin on the ground, thanks to jittery slave traders who refused to come within twenty miles of the Forum. The opportunity to snap up a free man with impeccable references as well as a flair for discretion was not to be sneezed at. In fact, the young man decided smugly, the dwarf was proving something of a bargain.

'The minion is eminently trustworthy,' he murmured, fixing his chubby visitor with his cold, fish eyes. 'The question, my friend, is – *are you?*'

XII

So soon, thought Claudia. She hadn't expected Orbilio to pop up so soon. Ordinarily, of course, she'd have mapped out a strategy for dealing with him, but too many events had intruded – Cal, the bear, that wretched funeral – in too little time, with too many sidetracks. And now he was here. The thief-taker, goddammit, was here.

In the Great Hall, she cannoned into a middle-aged woman with a snub nose and hard eyes and the pair of them went tumbling. Stony-faced cow didn't even apologize, thought Claudia, stepping over the woman's tangled legs and blind to the venomous glare.

You should have anticipated his arrival, she told herself. You should not have assumed he'd turn up at some unspecified time in the future. You should have thought this through – dear Diana, you've encountered him often enough. For a start, there was the investigation into your husband's death. Then Sicily. Umbria. Plus he was around that time – Jupiter, Juno and Mars, what is this? Some kind of maths test? Who cares how many times their paths had crossed, who gives a damn the way his hair falls across his forehead when he's tired, and come off it, she'd hardly noticed that little scar underneath his collarbone as he lay sprawled on the couch!

Outdoors, the air pulsated, the crickets rasped as she

skipped down the steps towards the shoreline, where two red dogs chased and tumbled in the long rough grass. Across the marshes, cranes trumpeted to one another and smells of roasting goose wafted down from the kitchens. A horse whinnied far in the distance.

Official business, he said . . .

Arbutes, tree spurge and straggly capers clung to the rock which thrust its way out of the water. Atlantis. Perched on top of this cliff. Atlantis. A triumph of marble and porphyry and cool colonnades. Where a glass of cloudy water can cure anything from gout to an ingrowing toenail. Where fortunes change hands for the privilege of being pummelled with oils and lolling in tubs of foul-smelling mud.

A miracle, the augurs pronounced, when Pylades discovered Carya's sweet spring. Really? Claudia watched a lazy heron flap across the lake. Was Atlantis truly a place of miracles? Or mirages?

Of high standards? Or just double standards?

As a lone curlew let free its bubbling call, her mind considered the anomalies. The cave, the tunnel, Mosul the priest – as incongruous as they were linked. Because why should Pylades go to the substantial expense of gouging out an underpass and not show off this feat of civil engineering? Why not allow guests direct access to the spring? Surely not to keep sick pilgrims at a distance? That was unheard of! And yet Pylades had certainly segregated the classes here. Members of the aristocracy, alternating between their vast country estates and this spa. Merchants, flaunting their wealth as they indulged in long mudbaths and canoodled with women who in no way resembled their wives. Rich hypochondriacs, attracted to the waters for their chest/kidney/liver problems, oh yes, the wily Greek had separated the wine from the vinegar all right! Of course, there were always the artisans, gambling on wheedling noteworthy commissions from the relaxed holidaymakers, but by and large his clientele were the very cream of society.

Except for Lavinia.

See what I mean? Claudia paused to watch a two-tailed pasha flutter round the arbutes, to be joined by a second butterfly, this time an early grayling. Every time I turn my mind to Supersnoop and his wretched official business, another diversion leads me astray!

Without realizing where her steps had been leading, Claudia found herself down on the point where, perched on the jetty with one foot swinging free and his hair still tied back in a fillet, Tarraco whittled away at his woodcarving, undeterred by heat which could have fried oysters to a crisp.

'I knew you would come.' He did not look up.

'Actually—' She'd never even considered keeping the appointment.

'Here!' He blew the sawdust off the carving and tossed it across with a lopsided grin. 'The only bear you encounter today.' He turned to unhook the rowboat Claudia was so familiar with.

'Sorry—' she began, and then thought, what the hell? I've had it up to here with is-it-murder-is-it-not, of suspecting everyone I meet, of being petrified the army will clap me in irons any minute. At least there's one place which offers a refuge outside the messy muddle of my life. One man who is not involved or under suspicion.

As Tarraco began to turn the boat around in the water,

her eye was drawn to a figure watching from the sun porch and despite the searing heat, she shivered. Coincidence? That that just happened to be the spot from which Cal was supposed to have fallen?

Fluttering her fingers in a wave, Claudia smiled a cheesy smile at the man who leaned his weight against a glistening, gilded column.

Marcus Cornelius did not wave back.

The dispatch rider felt sure he must have put Pegasus to shame, the speed with which he covered the distance from Rome. The seal of the heron was sufficient to appease the most officious of post-station bureaucrats, and in the one instance where it was not and some pompous little twit had demanded to check the documents in full, the rider had ignored the silly sod and simply helped himself to a fresh horse. Let others set him right regarding the seal of the Security Police!

'Will there be an answer, sir?'

He had delivered the letter, personally as instructed, to the tall patrician standing in the scorching heat of the sun porch, and the recipient had merely grunted his thanks as he maintained a tight-lipped watch on a rowboat cleaving a path across the silvery lake. Considering the contents were so urgent they'd brought the sparks flying from the hoofs of his horses and had jammed every joint of his backbone, the least he could do, the rider felt, was open the bloody thing!

Orbilio tapped the scroll against the gilded pillar. 'Why don't you get something to eat?' he suggested, leaving the exhausted rider to make what he could of the answer.

Marcus stared at the shingle beach fifty feet below, then squinted towards the boat, practically swallowed by the heat haze. He exhaled slowly and with a shrug of resignation, finally broke the heron seal. Even before he started reading, he tasted bile in his mouth.

'*The choice*,' wrote his boss, '*is simple. Either you ride back to Rome this instant, or you don't come back at all.*'

Shit! He knew his boss would go ballistic, but he didn't expect to be sacked! Orbilio took three deep breaths as he stared across the hazy blue hills, then read on. There was only another line.

'*You aren't the only one who doesn't like the plague.*'

Bastard! Orbilio's knuckles were white where he gripped the golden rail. The dirty rotten little bastard! His teeth clamped together in white-hot anger as he visualized the scene in an office stuffed with lackeys hanging on to every word the master dictated – and his boss would be sure to have dictated this loving missive in his very loudest voice! Let no man miss the fact that Marcus Cornelius Orbilio is a coward. That whilst patricians have blue blood in their veins, it's the yellow streak down their backbone folk should be wary of.

At that moment, had Orbilio dipped his finger in a bowl of ice, steam would have risen from the surface, he was so damned mad. Him! A man who only ever sought for justice, being accused of cowardice! The stinking, oily little bastard!

For another quarter hour Marcus let the anger flow, releasing every pent-up gripe he held against the worm who he reported to. The same worm who had not worked for his position, but had bought it. The very creep who had no idea what was involved in catching murderers and fraudsters, yet basked in the reflected glory like a lizard in the sun . . . Finally, when he'd luxuriated in his rage for long enough, Orbilio took himself off to the bath house, where the scraping and the pummelling, the oiling and the unguents drained the remaining tension in his flesh. Cracking his knuckles in cheerful anticipation, he then called for a scribe.

In the end it took five drafts, but when the rested rider set off back for Rome, Orbilio was confident that not only would his superior officer rescind any threat of dismissal, but that to get his hands on the list of taboos surrounding Jupiter's priest, the smarmy toad would actually send an apology by return!

Orbilio had not trekked all the way up to the Capitol and back yesterday morning for nothing!

With the sun sinking fast behind the hills which cradled Plasimene, he worked his way round to the shrine of Carya, where a corpulent priest gathered hyssop in the dusky pink rays to purify the altar, growling at his lanky novice to put some effing elbow grease behind his effing broom, or the boy would be working in the effing dark. At the edge of the walnut grove, Marcus leaned his hands on the low wall which surrounded it. The stone was warm upon his palms, purple from the glow of the sunset. All around, hills tamed into providing wood for hurdles, yokes and charcoal sank into the gentle, smoky twilight. Sheep grazed contentedly on the marshy plains and cattle chewed the cud, lowing softly now and then to rein in their boisterous calves. Lowering his gaze, he watched coracles and fishing boats, homeward bound and heavy, studding the surface of a lake which rippled with nibbling fish.

Finally his meandering eyes found what they had, of course, set out to find from the beginning, and Orbilio could fool himself no longer. One of the fishermen's hooks must have got left behind by mistake, it pulled in his gut as he watched lights far across the water twinkle in the darkening sky. There was no mistaking the island that they came from and he swallowed the lump in his throat. So many lights, they danced like fireflies out on that wooded lump of rock developed by a banker and his wife into a villa of great luxury and grounds which were, he understood, a beauty to behold. Then the banker died, and not so many months ago. And earlier this afternoon, his successor had rowed a certain party over to the island.

But had not yet rowed her home.

Out where those torches burned like fireflies, a man and a woman walked side by side, one unaccustomedly voluble, the other unaccustomedly quiet.

This island, Tarraco told her, was once a sacred Etruscan burial site and though the tombs had been robbed long ago, probably at the time of the Battle of the Lake, the paintings inside could rival the artists of Rome. One day, maybe tomorrow, maybe next day, he would show her.

'But they are nothing compared to what I show you. Come.' He led her to the eastern tip of the island. 'My colossus! Fifty feet high, it takes your breath away, no? Is Memnon, son of the Dawn, and at daybreak he calls to his mother. Oh, you scoff, but is true. Memnon sings. You wait and you see. Memnon sings!'

Let me show you the gardens, magnificent gardens,

with the peabirds who spread out their fan of fine feathers and the cote of white doves. Listen with me to the murmuring fountains; we feed the fish in the ponds. You like the villa? This marble here comes from the high Pyrenees, the doors are cedar from the forests of Lebanon.

Like a gentle tide, his words went in, his words went out, and Claudia's mind was the beach they left no trace on. For her, this offered the perfect breathing space. Cold-blooded murder could not intrude on this island. Strong-room robberies did not exist. The tentacles of the Security Police could not reach this far out. As the sun turned the banker's villa salmon pink, stress floated away like a leaf on the water. Pressure flew home with the geese.

Leaving his guest in a portico planted with basil to counteract the clouds of midges, Tarraco returned a few minutes later with a magnificent gown in his hands – harebell blue, vivid rather than flamboyant, daring, yet anything but flashy. Claudia gasped with surprise. It was exquisite, true, but more than that, the gift revealed so much about the Spaniard. Perhaps it smacked of arrogance, that Claudia would show at the jetty, but it betrayed what she had suspected yesterday. That Tarraco could read her thoughts, because this was a gown she'd have chosen herself! In the setting sun, she smiled inwardly. In her experience, the only men who have such taste and comprehension are inclined towards their own sex, but not Tarraco! His dark eyes were compelling, his movements lithe and beguiling and she did not need to hear his sharp intake of breath to appreciate the effect of his gift when she changed into it. Without a word he led her between a line of tall cypress to a white marble seat which looked out over the lake. Laid out in the centre were platters piled high with oysters and stuffed eggs, asparagus and wild mushrooms.

'The shadows lengthen,' he said as they pushed their plates away. 'Come.'

With the flat of his hand on her back as a guide, he led her to the dining terrace, where spiky palms flanked the marble steps and garlands of flowers – roses, lilies, valerian – hung from the capitals of deeply fluted pillars. Two couches upholstered in Tyrian purple and cast in bronze gleamed in the light of a score of burning torches and Claudia knew, as she stretched out, that the colour of her gown set off the scene to perfection. Tarraco, she reflected happily, was not just rich, he was an artist!

Crab and lobster, venison and quail sizzled under silver-lidded platters and the silence was broken only by the rasping of cicadas and an occasional mew from the peacocks. Across the lake, the lights of Atlantis reflected like stars in the water.

'Your—' Claudia cleared her throat and started again. 'Your servants. Are they invisible?'

'You wish for a crowd?' he asked, stroking his long, dark mane out of his eyes.

She remembered the clearing. Him standing there, veiled by his hair, and her nearly naked, and despite the warmth of the evening, a shudder ran through her body. 'How long have you lived here?' she asked, gulping the heavy red wine.

He spread expressive hands and shrugged. 'I lose track of time,' he replied, and Claudia could believe him. Was this what happened to Odysseus, when he stopped on Circe's island? Perhaps time stood still for him also? But then Circe, she recalled, was an enchantress . . .

Inside her chest, a blacksmith hammered on the anvil of her ribs. 'Where were you before that?' she asked.

'Iberia, you mean?'

Whatever.

'From the hills above the coast on the east.' His mouth twitched downwards briefly and, she felt, involuntarily. 'I was slave originally. Prisoner of war.'

'What happened?'

'You,' he grinned and picked up a lyre, 'talk too much.' Softly Tarraco began to strum. 'Just lie back. Listen to the music and the night.'

Sod it, why not? There were demons enough waiting when she returned! Thus Claudia abandoned herself to the marriage of chords which she never imagined existed. Haunting, aching melodies of sun-drenched Spanish hills filled the air, wordless songs of broken hearts and unrequited love, and they echoed across the terrace and far into the night. The level in the wine jug dropped, and the scent of the roses and the lilies intensified in the heat of the torches.

'Now,' he said at length, laying down his lyre, 'let us eat honeycombs fresh from the hive.'

'What is this?' She laughed. 'Like our festival of Beating the Bounds, have you laid on a moveable feast?'

Tarraco made no reply, but silently ushered her through an atrium resplendent with golden rafters and redolent of myrrh, past a fountain chattering in a diamond pool. Finally he pulled aside a heavy tapestry curtain, the entrance to a small office, from which a large door opened inwards.

'I think,' Claudia said slowly, 'I've eaten enough for one meal.'

'You do not like honeycomb?' He was mortified. 'I fetch candied fruits, yes? Maybe nuts.'

Damn right I am!

Claudia cast an appreciative eye over the bronze lamps guzzling up the finest olive oil, the painted stucco ceiling, the gaily patterned frescoes. On a tapestry which covered the far wall, Jason and his Argonauts searched for an embroidered golden fleece. So much, she thought, for breathing space . . .

Tarraco placed the flat of his hands together. 'You think I take liberties, serving honey in my bed? That I move too fast?' He strained a grin. 'I-I thought—'

'A bolt of blue cotton could buy me?'

'No, no. Claudia, no. You and I . . . I thought . . . there was—' The frown on his face was like pain. 'Claudia, there is something between us.'

Claudia leaned close enough to catch the familiar scent of pine. 'How right you are, Tarraco,' she said. 'And it's called your ego.'

XIII

Around Atlantis, torches burned low and Claudia's footsteps echoed down the wooden jetty. Three men, she thought, each with a single objective. One younger than her, full of fun, full of life, with his corn-coloured hair and his secrets, who believed he could cartwheel her into his bed. The second the same age as herself, a dark horse according to Dorcan, believing he could charm her into his bed with his gifts and his magical lyre. And a third, considerably older – and this one didn't even imagine he'd have to work for results, the fact that he'd turned rock into gold quite sufficient.

Three men. One objective.

One dead.

The lights might be low, but they weren't muted enough to conceal a figure flitting back into the shadows. Claudia frowned. Not Tarraco, he was already halfway back to his island and, since the gates were locked at dusk, this could be no common criminal creeping around. Orbilio, of course, would never give himself away, he'd learn to walk on water before he allowed a trace of himself to be seen, besides this shadow seemed taller, broader, of far greater bulk. So who, then? Who might wish to spy on her?

Silly bitch. Claudia swept up the steep, stone steps.

Imagine you're the only one keeping late hours? They don't all come here for Carya's healing waters and to listen to the choirs! Your problem, she told herself, watching bats forage for insects on the wing, is an overactive imagination. Cal has been murdered, his killer walks free – and what's driving you daft is that despite a list of curious characters lurking in the background, there's no tangible suspect and not so much as a whiff of a motive.

I have a solution, squeaked a little horseshoe bat. You could enlist the help of Supersnoop. (Whatever his motives for fetching her here, he'd never turn away a chance to solve a killing.)

No way, piped a pipistrelle. His involvement would mean him tucking his feet under the table indefinitely.

Quite right, said a noctule, its mouth full of moth. She needs to get rid of Orbilio fast.

But since the bats could not come up with a strategy for disposing of this hotshot investigator, Claudia left them to their supper and slipped through the doors of the Great Hall. Hello, hello, hello. She paused on the threshold. What's old Kamar up to, then, canoodling behind a statue? And him a married man with a disfigured wife, who everybody talks about, poor bitch. Claudia allowed the door to close silently behind her as Lavinia's voice echoed down the corridor of her memory. 'I'll bet you've heard my daughter-in-law playing whisper-whisper-whisper with that sourpuss physician . . .'

That could not, of course, be Lavinia's daughter-in-law. Despite hair curled to within an inch of its life and a face pancaked with cosmetics, this woman would be close to the olive grower's age. And now Claudia peered closer, she could see they weren't actually canoodling, but all the same, Lavinia had Kamar to a T. Amongst his own sex it was hail-fellow-well-met, a man among men, whereas with women he employed subtler tactics, conspiring in secret to add a frisson of excitement to their phantom ailments. Watching a small phial pass between them, Claudia couldn't decide which was worse: society women who gorged on pandering or physicians who were little more than gigolos, servicing their needs in exchange for a coin.

They broke off when they became aware of her presence, exchanged glances, and Claudia recognized the woman as the stony-faced old boiler she'd bumped into earlier, after her countdown with Orbilio. Worse, the harridan was bearing down like a trireme in full sail.

'Forgive my impertinence.' Stoneyface daren't smile for fear of cracking the mask and the voice went with the eyes. 'But that robe is simply sublime. Might I trouble you for the name of your seamstress?'

Her hair had been dyed with the juice of walnuts, her complexion was not holding up well, yet, despite rising to every cosmetic challenge with her plucked and painted eyebrows and the plethora of moleskin patches plastered over her liver spots, she still played up her little snub nose as though it were some girlish attribute by sticking it high in the air. Sad, really. Deluded cow thought she turned heads, but in practice it was stomachs she turned.

'Oh, you know Atlantis!' Claudia quipped, speeding up to escape the frightful creature. 'Everything's done for you round here!'

'Off the peg?' A variety of expressions skated across the plasterwork of her face, and hard eyes narrowed to slits. 'Then I'd be obliged if you'd point out the shop.'

Behind her, Kamar was hopping from one foot to the other. Cramp? Or agitation?

'First on the left past the basilica,' Claudia invented. Anything to break free of this ghastly woman's clutches. What a horror! In the corridor, her mind skipped back to Cal's funeral, to the freckle-faced girl rolling the hoop. Would she, one day, become a hard-eyed ravaged harpy, hankering for her old salad days? Skulking round at night to consult a physician? Perish the thought! But the point was, that child should have the choice.

Within the dark seclusion of her bedroom, Claudia kicked off her sandals. First she must establish the motive for Cal's murder. Only through that could she unmask the killer, and then maybe – just maybe – she'd have something to trade with Orbilio when it came (as it would) to discussing Sabbio Tullus . . .

Outside frogs croaked to one another and an owl hooted far across the lake as she collapsed on the bed. Somewhere, just before sleep and exhaustion overwhelmed her, she thought she heard a woman scream.

Dawn was casting silver shadows on the bath house's limestone walls and a coil of blue woodsmoke writhed up from its vent as the agent of Sabbio Tullus pursed his lips and estimated that any time within the next half-hour his message would be arriving in Rome. Dispatch runners cared not a jot that they travelled through the night, money was money, and let me see, ten miles per runner, ten runners – yup, the last one should be arriving very soon. Very soon. Delving into his satchel, to deliver a sealed and secret letter to Rome.

A letter which read: '*The jewel that you are seeking, master, has been discovered in Atlantis.*'

Now that, thought Tullus' agent, rubbing his hands with satisfaction, should earn a fat reward!

One which would not, however, come from the treasure chests of Sabbio Tullus.

The letter was winging its way to the nephew.

Claudia was whistling when she waltzed into breakfast, though since the hour was late, only a few diehards remained at the trough. That loudmouthed general, for one, the chap whose paunch stuck out like a packmule, and the woman who walked like a camel, right now gulping down the general's raisin troops the instant he'd positioned them on the flank. Lounging on a couch in the corner, a famous wrestler – a dapper dandy with the body of an ox – recounted exploits to a dull-eyed nymphet, who'd patently prefer just to go to his room and get it over with. It was a screw he was paying for, not a bore.

Which left one other individual in the banqueting hall. And Claudia had a feeling he'd been there some time.

Sweeping past, she plumped down on a couch close to the sun porch with a fine view of the lake. Almost immediately, the opposite recliner was occupied.

'Sleep well?' Orbilio asked, framing stiff lips into a smile.

'Hardly a wink.' Claudia heaped her plate with cheese and shrimps and ignored the fact that she'd slept like a baby. 'You?'

'Terrific.' He saw no reason to mention the cockroaches in the pawnbroker's attic which he'd been forced to rent since Atlantis was full.

Behind them the general reminisced about some ancient campaign in Galatia and the fat woman picked her teeth.

'Business first,' Orbilio began, lacing his fingers and leaning forward, but he was interrupted by the arrival of a brunette practically bursting the seams of her tunic as she sashayed up the banqueting hall, surveying the breakfasters through kohled lashes.

Claudia could not resist a smile. In Rome – indeed anywhere within the paid eyes of the Emperor – standards these days were close to puritanical. In return for bestowing stability and peace on his people, Augustus demanded purity of mind as well as body, family values to reflect this Golden Age, an example to the conquered masses. No gambling, no spinsters, no sex outside marriage. As a law, Claudia felt it didn't have a lot going for it. For one thing, the rules patently did not apply to him, the Emperor's infidelities were legendary, and, for another, whilst he bestowed privileges on men fathering endless baby Romans, there were few crackdowns on those who clung to their bachelor freedom, and certainly his vision failed when it came to philandering husbands. But Augustus was a man, and men will have their little jokes, now, won't they? Like making marriage compulsory for women. Like not letting them speak in the law courts. Like imposing bitter penalties on adulterous wives.

Like forcing widows to remarry within two years of the death of their husband . . .

For the brunette, filling out her sails both fore and aft,

it was unlikely she'd ever heard of moral reforms, let alone put one into practice. Claudia beckoned her over.

'Do meet Marcus,' she said, pointing to his couch in invitation. 'He likes women with big chests and small drawers.'

'You'll have to speak up,' Phoebe trilled. 'I missed that.'

'Orbilio here,' Claudia shouted, 'said he's been dying to meet you.'

She thought she heard the girl purr. Then again, it could have been a deep Security Police growl.

Phoebe snuggled against him and pouted when he shuffled along. 'Is he shy?' she asked, as though Marcus wasn't present.

'Merely stodgy,' Claudia explained. 'Poor chap thinks getting a little action means his prunes have started to work.' She smiled sweetly at Orbilio, who had sucked in his cheeks. 'In fact, these days his back goes out more than he does.'

Marcus turned a laugh into a cough, but Phoebe's attention had been caught by Claudia's gown. 'That is beautiful,' she gushed. 'Harebell blue, so elegant. Goes with absolutely anything.'

'And there speaks an expert,' Claudia murmured, fluttering her eyelashes at a man who had all but disappeared into his handkerchief. Louder, she said, 'As a matter of fact, this gown was a gift.'

Across the table, Marcus stiffened. 'The Spaniard?'

'However did you guess?'

To emphasize her point, she stroked the silver pendant at her neck, suggesting this, too, was a present from Tarraco, even though she'd won the thing last week in a game of knucklebones behind the Rostrum. As Phoebe helped herself to chestnut bread, Claudia heard Orbilio mutter underneath his breath, although she failed to catch the definition.

'Now, now, Marcus,' she chided cheerfully. 'Tarraco is handsome, rich and generous, there's nothing to dislike about him, surely?' And thought she heard him mumble, 'No, but give me time,' as she slipped into her sandals.

Phoebe, straining every stitch, sidled up to her conquest, running her hand along his thigh as she tried to feed him a grape.

'You two lovebirds must excuse me.' As Claudia stood up she heard Phoebe entreat Marcus to come with her, she knew exactly how to please a man in bed, and Claudia thought, no you don't. Phoebe, despite her outward appearance, was no casual conquest. What she sought was love and affection, and certainly what pleases men in bed is none of those you-still-respect-me-don't-you recriminating conversations, it's to roll over and drift off to sleep without hearing either the word 'love' or its companion, 'commitment'.

No doubt this voluptuous creature would cotton on one day, but until then a lot of men would have a lot of fun bouncing on her well-upholstered charms.

Orbilio did not look as though he might be one of them. The only man, Claudia reflected cheerfully, who won't take yes for an answer!

With a radiant smile, Claudia fluffed the frills and ostentatiously smoothed the pleats of this fabulous harebell gown and, just on the offchance that Hotshot hadn't quite got the message, made her way very, very slowly up the banqueting hall.

Now, with luck, he might sod off back to Rome – and take his official bloody business with him.

In fact, the sun was considerably higher than Tullus' agent had calculated by the time the courier made his way through the twisting alleys of the Aventine Hill to the house next door to the marble merchant's warehouse. Lean, tough and muscular, he barely panted, though his throat burned dry and dusty as he handed over the letter to a thin-faced individual bizarrely devoid of character. When he ripped open the seal, only the appearance of two high spots of colour on otherwise colourless cheeks hinted that the news he'd received was the best.

'No reply,' a monotone voice told the messenger.

Tullus' nephew waited for him to leave before reaching for his goblet. It was empty, and so was the jug. He clapped hands for a refill. Wine, godammit, was out of the question. In this searing heat, it made his throat drier than ever, even watered, so now he was reduced to gulping fruit juice like that bloated bladder of an uncle. Bloody hell, his bowels were on overtime, yet his windpipe grated like an ungreased hinge.

It was his uncle's fault he was stuck in this sweatbox! Tullus had assured him that sodding strongroom was secure – 'safe as the State Treasury' were his words – when in reality he might as well have kept that casket under his bed for all the protection it had been given!

Well. He sipped at the apple juice the dwarf set down and grimaced. There was no point in going over old ground, the damage was done, and with luck the damage was small. He glanced down at the letter from the agent up in Plasimene. The bitch was holing up in Atlantis, was she?

'Not for long, sweetheart,' the nephew said softly, steepling his long, skinny fingers. 'Not for bloody much longer.'

What's mine is mine, he vowed, and I will have it back, but there's bugger all time to play with. Already twenty days into May, the bloody Senate sits on the first of next month. His thin lips pinched tight together. For years, I've worked towards this goal. Every move, every action has been designed to bring me that little step closer – and I am so close, Claudia Seferius, so very, very close to fulfilling my self-appointed destiny that I can almost reach out and touch it.

'The fate of the whole fucking *Empire* is in my hands,' he breathed. 'No meddling bitch can be allowed to inter-. fere with my plans.'

His pen scratched across a sheet of parchment and, sealing the scroll, he rang for his new servant. What a find! Solicitous for his master's welfare, discreet at all times, willing to undertake a few unusual tasks – what a treasure, this ugly mutant!

'This letter,' he said, cursing the dryness in his throat. 'Deliver it personally, will you, to the visitor who called here yesterday.'

'Very good, sir.' The dwarf withdrew, slipped on his outdoor shoes and with a tuneless whistle set off for the apartment house of the fat man who stank of cardamom.

On the principle that no matter what goes wrong, it can always be made to look right, Claudia rapped on Lavinia's door. To think she considered her own room luxurious! The old woman's son had really done his mother proud, and again she wondered how an impoverished smallholder could afford such a treat. Ivory and tortoiseshell, maple-wood inlaid with silver, couches, chairs and tables, silver salvers bursting with hot hams and sausages, bowls piled high with fruit and a basket of steaming, crusty rolls. Maybe his hare-brained ventures weren't so irresponsible after all? Maybe Lavinia, being a simple country woman, didn't really understand the wheelings and dealings of commerce? Or perhaps she'd just bred a son with the instinct of an Arab horsetrader! On a table by the window, blue and red counters were set out in a half-finished game of Twelve Lines and Lalo, despite his coarse linen tunic, looked bigger and more handsome as he flapped an ostrich fan dyed green. Ruth, on the other hand, appeared to be moulded into a niche on the wall in an unsuccessful attempt to render herself invisible and the reason, Claudia suspected, were the two harridans breathing over the couch.

'You've got to drink it.'

'Got to.'

'How on earth will you get better otherwise?'

'Never get better.'

When they saw Claudia one of the women straightened up, a signal for the other to copy, as surely she had done all her life. They had to be sisters. There was an age difference, six, maybe five years, but the similarities were not confined to mere dress or hairstyles. Both sported matching double chins and piggy eyes and flesh that knew better than dare wobble, but never had the incongruity of their simple, rustic lives clashed more violently with the luxury of Atlantis. Cheap cottons stood out against slinky damasks, natural fibres screamed beside rich, expensive dyes.

'Fabella and Sabella,' Lavinia said coldly. 'Fabella is married to my son.'

Claudia felt a sudden rush of sympathy for the son.

'It's this medicine,' Fabella said. 'She won't drink it.'

'Won't,' echoed Sabella, with a sad shake of her head. 'And she's hardly touched her breakfast.'

'Heaven knows what my hubby'll say, when he finds out his money's been wasted.'

Try not mentioning it.

'And we're due for our massage any minute!'

Claudia beckoned the sisters towards her. 'It's this pampering,' she whispered. 'Gone to Lavinia's head.' She clucked her tongue sympathetically. 'Won't touch a thing unless it's served off gold.'

'Never!' they chorused, tutting their joint disapproval.

'Look, why don't you two trot off to your massage and I'll arrange the necessary plates and goblet?'

Not so much trot off, she thought, more off on their trotters.

Behind her, Lavinia let out a sigh of relief. 'I don't know what you said to them,' she cackled, 'but I'm indebted! Frightful pair!'

Claudia drew up a chair and by the time she'd turned round, Lavinia's elegant coiffure had turned into a fluffy white fleece. 'You old phoney!'

'We're all frauds here, dear.' As though it was a cat, the old woman stroked the wig in her lap. 'Every single one of us.' She cast a knowing glance at her visitor, who found that for once in her life she couldn't stare someone out.

Instead, Claudia reached for a pomegranate with a studied show of nonchalance. 'I don't suppose you heard any strange sounds in the night? Screaming, for instance?'

Lalo and Ruth exchanged glances. 'Nothing,' they said.

'Liars, the pair of you,' Lavinia snapped back. 'Where were you two, eh? Out with it, because neither of you was in Atlantis last night!'

'I—' Lalo began to fidget with the handle of the fan, and Claudia noted that his knuckles were bruised and swollen again. 'I spent the night in Spesium,' he said.

'More fool me, I went looking for him,' Ruth flashed back. 'And never found him, either!'

'We'll talk about this later,' Lavinia said, dismissing them with a curt nod. 'So, then.' The wizened face broke into a smile. 'What can I do for you this fine, sunny morn?'

'Oh,' Claudia breezed, 'I just dropped in to ask whether you plan to attend the Agonalia in town.' The spring festival of lambs was a highlight on most rural calendars, particularly in a month devoid of celebrations.

Lavinia put aside the wig and scratched the side of her nose. 'I think you know the answer to that,' she said pointedly. 'So why don't you dispense with the formalities and tell me the real reason why you came?'

Claudia grinned and curled her legs up in the chair. 'I want to know how you managed to avoid compulsory remarriage when you were widowed at the tender age of thirty-two.'

Lavinia's sigh was like water trickling through a sluice gate. 'So that's how the land lies!' She nodded slowly several times as though wrestling with a decision, then finally cleared her throat. 'My husband was an old man, but do you know, in seventeen years of marriage he never showed Lavinia a single scrap of kindness. Who'd have thought that, in dying, the old sod would do so well by her?'

A gnarled finger beckoned Claudia closer. 'My sweat went into that land and I tell you straight, I wasn't prepared to let the grove pass to another slave-driving bastard. So,' she lowered her voice to a whisper, 'Lavinia surrounds herself with busts of the dear departed, commissions several portraits of the old goat, says prayers for him several times a day . . .'

'In public, of course.'

Lavinia wetted her lips with the tip of her tongue. 'It's a hard man who would force a grieving widow into his bed and even the Prefect –' one sparkling blue eye closed in a wink '– even the Prefect of Luca agreed that, under such harrowing circumstances, the rules ought to be waived.'

She paused to let the impact of her words sink in, then added airily, 'I hear there's an excellent portrait painter staying in Atlantis at the moment. Now run along, there's a good girl, Lavinia's getting tired.'

The hell she was!

'But be sure to tell me everything that happens in the town,' the old woman called after her. 'Lavinia likes to keep abreast of what goes on.'

XIV

The origins of the Agonalia, like so many rustic festivals, had become blurred with the passage of time. Undoubtedly its roots were entrenched in some ancient thanksgiving ceremony for flocks which had not only survived, but procreated to boot, therefore what better time to display newly shorn wool and for priests to bless lambs – but quite why a ram, the bringer of said good fortune, should fall to the sacrificial knife, no one was sure. Indeed, until recently, the festival had been confined to private rituals conducted by smallholders clubbing together to propitiate their local deity . . . in the old days, before that arch revivalist Augustus stepped in.

He had conquered Rome's enemies without and within, the dark days of war and civil war were now over for good. He had disbanded his part-time peasant army in favour of hand-picked professionals and since that meant the land was no longer abandoned for months on end, agriculture prospered with a vengeance, inspiring Augustus to resurrect firstly the old celebration of May Day and then raise the profile of the Agonalia, thus doubling the number of jollies in an otherwise dull and unlucky month. Romans throughout the Empire embraced the addition of two more state holidays, and Spesium was right at the fore.

Flowers decorated walls, balconies, statues and columns, they were woven into chaplets and garlands and wreaths. Tumblers in gem-bright tunics entertained swelling crowds to a backdrop of flutes and castanets, rope walkers drew gasps, beggars drew alms, artists drew scenes on the pavements – of shipwrecks they had seen off the coast of Achaea, of a three-legged dwarf in Damascus.

Claudia's audience with Lavinia meant that although she missed the sacrifice itself, her arrival coincided with the point where the haruspex was examining the ram's vital organs in order to pronounce good or bad auspices. Because the area around Lake Plasimene had been deserted for two hundred years, there were no obvious indications as to who should receive this noble offering, so the obvious candidate was Spes, Goddess of Hope, after whom the town was named. And as befitted her status, Spes had a temple approached by fifteen marble steps, two rows of Corinthian columns at the front, and a storehouse of gold and silverware inside. As Claudia inched her way into the crowd, a hush had descended and even the dancers and acrobats broke off their shows to await the announcement.

'Hmmm,' said the gut-gazer. Men with their hair garlanded and women with theirs streaming free shuffled forward. 'Hmmm,' he said again, nodding with practised ambiguity. 'Hm, hm.' Solemnly he picked up the dripping liver and weighed it in his hands from left to right. He peered, he prodded, he even smelled the wretched thing, then he harrumphed a little more, re-examined the heart and kidneys, and muttered dolefully, 'This bodes well. Spes has favoured us.'

Heaven knows what the man was like when he encountered a bout of the miseries, but the proclamation was enough for the crowd. Roars broke out, cheering and clapping, and the music started up again, with a trumpet thrown in for good measure, and then the lambs were set loose, scores of bleating, silly, bright-eyed creatures skipping down the street, unaware their dad was being roasted on the fire. Ropes had been stretched across the upper storeys of buildings along the main thoroughfares from which sheets of every hue were hung to provide rainbows of shade—

'If you suffer from insomnia,' Kamar whispered, chomping on a piece of sacrificial mutton, 'I can prescribe a poppy draught.'

Claudia looked up at him, his turtle face as lugubrious as ever. Was it her imagination, or was there steel inside that silky offer? Beside him stood a mouse of a woman, his wife, whose badly disfigured face, rumour had it, resulted from falling into the fire as a child. One rather had the impression that the burns had been the first, rather than the last, of this woman's burdens. 'Insomnia?' Claudia asked.

'Chronic sleeplessness,' he said. 'The inability to fall asleep; waking and being unable to get back to sleep.'

I know what it means, you sour-faced oaf!

'Only one couldn't help noting you do not siesta and were abroad in the early hours of the morning,' he explained.

Claudia pictured Kamar again whispering behind the statue with old Stonypuss. 'Does it bother you I keep late hours? Has –' she tilted her head towards Pylades, conferring with Mosul and the temple warden '– someone complained about my activities?'

'Of course not,' Turtleface said quickly. 'Not at all.

Certainly not. My concern is purely for the residents' welfare.'

'Then you must have had a busy night,' she said silkily.

'Busy?' he growled. Beside him, the dormouse pulled nervously at the hem of her sleeve.

'Yes, I –' Claudia loaded sympathy into her voice '– thought I heard screaming.'

The big Etruscan's mouth pinched even further inwards so that now no lips were showing. 'It's the midwife's job to deliver babies,' he snarled, 'not mine. By the time they called me in, it was over bar the shouting, the woman had haemorrhaged too long.'

Claudia felt a punch in the pit of her stomach. Those screams were a young mother *dying*?

Kamar sniffed. 'I daresay you'll find she'd not taken sufficient care to preserve the seed during the early stages of gestation. In my professional opinion, haemorrhaging at birth occurs because some women are foolish enough and irresponsible enough to imagine they can live a normal life when they carry a child in their womb.'

Is that a fact? 'Then how do you account for so many healthy births among women in the fields?' Or don't the poor count, in your fine *professional* opinion?

'What's that you say?' Kamar stooped closer to hear. 'I didn't catch that.'

You couldn't catch crabs in your loin cloth, you cold-blooded rodent. 'I was merely enquiring after the health of the infant,' Claudia replied, accepting a sliver of roast from the sacrificial platter.

'The child?' Kamar jumped backwards as though burned. 'My dear girl, the child was the least of my worries. When I saw the state of the mother, I simply hooked the foetus out and got on with the job I was paid for!'

The mutton in her mouth turned to lard. *He what?* Claudia fought against the rising nausea in her stomach. This callous son-of-a-bitch killed a child at the moment of its birth, simply because he'd been paid to attend the mother, not her baby? For a second, she feared she might throw up all over him, but Claudia was a past master at the concealment of feelings. She merely prayed to Jupiter, god of justice, that Kamar was the one who'd snapped Cal's neck, she wanted to see this man trampled by elephants, torn apart by wild asses, flayed alive. Preferably all at once.

'I'm wondering whether that cross-eyed little pedlar didn't have a point, dear,' piped up Kamar's little peahen of a wife. 'He,' she gave a wan smile, 'said he'd rather take his bonework back to Rome and take his chances with the plague. He . . . well, implied there was a jinx on this place.'

'I've warned you before about mixing with the common rabble,' Kamar snapped. 'One day you'll pick up something more than malicious gossip, which medicines might not be able to cure.'

Was that a threat?

'Honestly!' he tutted, rolling his eyes as, with reddened cheeks, his wife mumbled an apology. Then he pulled his lips back into what Claudia supposed was a smile as Pylades strolled up to join the party.

'Enjoying the festival?' he beamed, his gaze roaming over the curves of Claudia's figure, and again it flashed through her mind. Three men. One objective. *One dead.* 'This year's Agonalia is the best to date,' the stocky hillsman was saying, 'but then the town grows stronger by the month. Down there.' A richly embroidered sleeve pointed towards a group of merchants milling around their terracotta vats, though his gaze was fixed on the swell of Claudia's breasts. 'Down there you can buy olive oil of every quality and colour – local produce, Spanish, African, even,' he bowed modestly, 'Greek. Another year and Spesium, I'll wager, will boast its own oil market like any other fine and prospering town.'

'A commendable rate of expansion,' murmured Claudia, her eyes alighting on his loins.

A rumble came from deep within the Greek's throat and colour suffused his cheeks as he clasped his hands across his body.

'I notice another hulking great warehouse is nearly complete,' she continued, because this town, this strange town, had sharpened its interest for her. Look at it! There were few signs that the town was built on anything other than private investment and only the arena, still in its foundation stages, and the half-built theatre smacked of imperial backing.

'Ah, well—' Happy to be back on firm ground, Pylades launched into a great discourse on commerce and the value of attracting trade guilds, but it was those tortoise eyes which bothered Claudia. As the founding father of this town pontificated on the merits of private investment, Kamar's gaze flickered back and forth in the direction of the sacrificial fire at the steps of the temple. Strange. Shifting her position for a better view, Claudia saw his scrutiny was directed at Pul, adopting the usual stance, and idly she wondered whether he ever peeled that leather vest off, and if not, what he and it must stink like.

'Now if you'll excuse me,' Pylades said, 'duty calls.' A smug look descended on his swarthy face. 'Atlantis, I'm pleased to say, has never been busier.'

'So the plague isn't all bad, then?' Claudia said sweetly.

Grunting, he offered a stiff arm to the doormat, who, at a nod from her husband, accepted with yet another watery smile.

Leaving just Kamar and Claudia under the cold, almond eyes of big Pul.

'I thought I caught the smell of hokum in the air!'

Dorcan looked up from placing an Argonaut's oar on the counter. 'Bless my chilblains! Marcus Cornelius! My, it's been a while!'

'Are you surprised?' Orbilio asked. 'After the way you dosed my uncle?'

'He was constipated, poor sod. I was only trying to help.'

'Whatever you put in that pessary,' Orbilio fought to keep his face straight, 'he missed a vital vote in the Senate.'

'I never made no promises,' protested Dorcan, his massive shoulders starting to heave.

'I know, but when you said he'd be well enough to take his seat, my uncle thought you meant in the Senate House, not a marble one in the latrines! So, what brings you so far north, big fellow?'

Dorcan showed his full set of false teeth. 'This . . .' he said, 'and that . . .'

'With you, Dorcan, it's usually the other! Who was she this time?'

The giant clenched his fists in excitement. 'Oh,

Marcus, you should've seen her, the sweetest little whore that ever plied her trade in Rome.' He held one flattened hand up to his armpit. 'Tiny little thing, only come up to here, she did.' He made a circle with his hands. 'Waist this thin.' He spread his fingers and rounded them. 'Tits—'

'Thank you, Dorcan, I've got the message! What went wrong?'

'What ever goes wrong with women? As soon as you gets cosy, they wants you to marry them.'

Orbilio examined a desiccated two-headed tortoise. 'Why didn't you?'

''Cos I've already got three wives, I can't keep tally as it is!' the giant bellowed, and in his mirth Orbilio dropped the dead freak, which promptly shattered into pieces. He kicked the pottery shards under the stall as Dorcan leaned over. 'Do you good, lad, to get yourself wedded and bedded again. Can't be much fun since your wife up and left – ran off with a rich merchant, didn't she? To Alexandria?'

'Lusitania,' Orbilio corrected, 'with an impecunious sea captain.'

The bristly bear dismissed it with a slicing motion of his hand. 'The point is, son, that bloke she run off with puts a smile on her face every bloody night while you ain't getting any. A man needs his comforts, Marcus, my lad, take my word for it, and it's a funny thing, but I have—'

'No way!' Orbilio took a step backwards. 'You're not palming me off with your pseudo-magic potions. I'll be impotent for years!'

'No, no, no,' Dorcan bellowed. 'I'm talking about marriage, boy, marriage. That exquisite meeting of two minds that feeds a man's soul, nourishes his inner core and gives him a chance to get his leg over morning, noon and night. Now it happens, I know just the girl for you, sparky piece of goods – hey, don't look at me like that. You'd like this one, I swear!'

'Forget it.' Marcus laughed. 'Marriage is like liquor, Dorcan. First you lose your head, then you lose your senses, and finally you lose your fortune, only with women it goes on frocks and fripperies and ghastly figurines. I tell you, big man, I'm done with playing harpy families.'

'Don't you mean happy families?'

'That's a contradiction in terms.'

The giant scratched his thick, black mop. 'You're making a mistake, lad,' he said sadly. 'A man needs to settle – *here*!' His mood changed instantly and his voice became a harsh whisper. 'You ain't in Spesium on official business, are you, lad?'

'Why?' Professional eyes followed salt sellers, tumbling acrobats and shepherds rounding up lambs.

'If you is, you'd best tread careful. It's a funny situation here and no mistake.'

The bleating flock was instantly forgotten. 'In what way?' Marcus asked sharply.

'Well,' Dorcan tapped the side of his nose, 'it all depends on whether you're prepared to pay for information.'

'Aren't I always?'

'Then let's meet after dark behind Tuder's tomb. You can't miss a monument that size and I tell you what. Tomorrow I'll introduce you to that sprightly filly – and tell me then you don't fancy bouncing on her swansdown mattress till you're both too old to romp!'

*

In the necropolis beyond the triple-arch gateway, only a patch of scorched grass lay testimony to Cal's cremation. Was it really only yesterday? Remus, his ashes wouldn't be home yet! Settling herself on the step of one of the tombs, Claudia watched soldiers and townsmen guzzling wine which flowed straight from a fountain, clapping their hands to the rhythm of girls dancing to the beat of their own tambourines, and in the short while since Claudia arrived, the men grew drunker and the music grew louder and the girls whirled faster and streamers twirled passed her, until the whole scene became blurred. So much revelry. So early in the day . . .

Turning away, she realized with a start that this square, capacious tomb faced with fine travertine boasted a frieze depicting a man sitting beside a pair of balances. Tuder! Claudia sprang up and with her finger traced the life of the banker which had been so painstakingly cast in stone, pausing at the section where a tall angular man betrothed himself to a tall angular woman. Further round the frieze, three small sons played with their father under their mother's watchful eye, but by the time Claudia reached the part which celebrated Tuder's achievements, the children had gone and only Lais remained at the banker's side. There was no mention of what might have brought about his death.

Let alone how it might be possible for an ex-slave to become master of Tuder's island.

Unfortunately, the sight of the banker's balances had conjured another, this time invisible, scene. Claudia, stuffing coins into her satchel. A key rattling in the lock. The look of utter stupefaction on Tullus' face. A centurion pacing her garden, casually pointing out that part of the property in the strongroom belonged to a person who was related by marriage to a second cousin of the Emperor's wife . . .

Didn't that pea-brained footslogger also happen to slip in the word 'treason' somewhere between the rose bush and the laurel?

Jupiter, Juno and Mars, if the prospect of being thrown penniless into exile wasn't bad enough, it paled into insignificance compared with her falling for that old friend-of-the-husband trick. Good move, Claudia. Put yourself right in the spotlight of the law. Never mind lying low, you embroil yourself in a murder case while you're about it, draw even more attention to yourself!

She glanced across at the blackened patch of grass. For the price of a kiss, Cal, I'd let you show me a way out of this mess, that's for sure!

Yet, as the townspeople roared with manic laughter, a germ of a motive behind his murder began to take hold. By his own mouth, Cal admitted to looking up her registration – in which case, he must have discovered neither she, or the mythical friend of her husband's, had paid for her stay. Was it also recorded in Pylades' accounts that Marcus Cornelius Orbilio was attached to the Security Police? Logically, then, it was not beyond the realms of possibility that Cal had rooted out a criminal secret and was threatening to turn that person over to the authorities unless—

Unless what? Claudia slumped back against Tuder's memorial and watched a family of jackdaws in the triple-arch gateway. I need more than a wild supposition to worm my way into the army's good books. I need something I believe they call proof . . .

'Mead!' a voice bellowed. 'Nectar of Olympus!'

Well, well, well. We may have an opening . . .

'Drink this, sir, for Jupiter's virility and the stamina of Mars. Madam, after just two glassfuls, you'll possess the beauty of Venus herself as well as the wisdom of Minerva. Mead! Nectar of the gods! Who's next?'

'Dorcan,' Claudia slipped her arm through the giant's, 'I'd like a quiet word with you.'

She felt his muscles stiffen. 'I meant no harm,' he protested. 'The pay was good—'

Talk about a guilty conscience! 'Actually, I want to ask you about Spesium. There's something distinctly odd about this town.'

'Odd?' he asked, handing out goblets filled not so much with divine liquor as honey mixed with milk and cinnamon.

'Don't pretend with me, Dorcan. There's an almost manic quality about the way they've thrown themselves into this festival, and yesterday, market day, there was a dogged, one might say obsessive, air about the way they conducted business, and that is eccentric by any standards.'

'When you've been run out of as many towns as I have, nothing strikes you as odd any more,' the giant replied, but the laugh in his voice was forced.

'Dorcan, the townspeople are interacting like strangers, rather than—'

'Look.' The charlatan swung round and led her under the shade of a lotus tree. 'It's the plague,' he said gruffly. 'Makes people act kind of funny, knowing death's just down the road and that anyone might bring it in any moment. This –' his arm embraced the Forum – 'is their way of coping.'

'Right. And next they'll put up six-foot-high fences to stop the pigs flying off.'

'Hey!' the giant called after her flouncing back. 'You will be staying in Atlantis for a while longer, won't you?'

Claudia pulled up short and carefully masked the unease which fluttered inside her. 'Of course,' she said steadily. 'Why?' At least one issue was solved. The big man who had been keeping tabs on her by the lakeshore last night . . .

'No reason.' Dorcan shrugged, shuffling the glasses on his tray. 'Just curious. That's all.'

Pushing open the doors which led to the Athens Canal, Claudia could see now why it was famous. What a place! Open to the sky, it nevertheless formed a tranquil and private retreat, surrounded on all four sides by a colonnade of caryatids. Caryatids! What a masterstroke! In place of straight, fluted columns, sculptured water nymphs supported the entablature – and who had Pylades named his spring after? None other than Carya herself! Self-serving moneygrubber or not, you had to hand it to the stocky architect. Pylades knew what he was doing when he created Atlantis!

Out on the water, swans arched graceful necks and puffed their wings like clouds as water from the jugs of half a dozen marble nymphs cascaded into the clear blue basin.

'Spring lamb not to your taste?' a familiar voice asked, and Claudia spun round.

'You're an evil old witch, you know that, Lavinia!'

Blue eyes twinkled as brightly as the water in the pool.

'I wish my hex would work on the two ugly sisters,' she said. 'Faced with the choice of sharing luxury with Fab and Sab or austerity at home, I'm starting to hanker after my old sagging mattress and a bedside lamp which perpetually splutters. Still,' she made a moue with her mouth, 'he means well, my lad.'

Does he? Or was the price small, compared with being rid of his wife and her echoing sister? Claudia dragged a basketweave chair into the shade beside the wheeled daybed. 'Is there a jinx on this place?' she asked, frowning at a spot on the hem of her harebell-blue gown.

'You've been talking to that skelly-eyed hawker, haven't you?' the old woman chuckled. 'I bought a bone needle off him and before he'd even counted out my change, he was all gloom and doom about death and failed marriages, bankruptcy and so on.' She tapped her temple with her forefinger. 'Decent carver, but . . .' Lavinia left the sentence hanging.

'He knew about the pregnant mother who died in the night.'

'The fight she put up, everyone from Atlantis to Alexandria heard what happened to that poor cow. But,' Lavinia's thin shoulders shrugged, 'what can you expect of a charlatan who doesn't know a hernia from a heart attack? Like I told the pedlar, whenever you put men and women together under a roof, the one in loin cloths, the other in skimpy gowns, the two sets of garments are bound to end up on the same floor. It's only natural. The same way that when sick people bunch together morbidity's higher than average, but only because the statistics are out of proportion. You'd best help me eat these dates, before Fabella force-feeds me the bloody things!'

'Only if you share that jug of wine.'

Slowly the pile of date stones grew higher and higher, and the level in the jar grew lower and lower, and as the swans and the nymphs cast white reflections in the water, the only sounds in the Athens Canal were the creaks of the basketweave chair when Claudia shifted position and the hypnotic gurgle of fountains.

'Too many idle hours,' Lavinia said out of nowhere, 'are passed by individuals with narrow lives and with minds narrower still. Atlantis is like that game of Gaulish Whispers, where you say a few words to one child, they repeat what they think you said to another and by the time it's gone down the chain, the meaning is totally changed.'

Slowly Claudia laid down her glass. 'But there's substance behind the stories, is that what you're saying?'

'Lavinia's a crippled old olive grower with time on her hands, she likes to gossip,' she cackled. 'That is a very striking gown, if I may say so.'

'I'm glad you approve. You were saying?'

'I always approve the understated,' Lavinia flashed back. 'Is there something wrong with the hem, you keep rubbing it? Oh, Ruth. I told you to take the day off, enjoy the Agonalia.'

The young Judaean girl rolled her eyes to heaven. 'There's no pleasing the old bat,' she laughed to Claudia. 'One minute she's desperate for company, the next she can't wait to be rid of me. Here!' She thrust a small copper beaker towards her mistress. 'You forgot to take your medicine.'

'Forget didn't come into it,' snapped Lavinia. 'It stinks like death and is as bitter as bile. Now get to town, girl, before the ox that they're roasting's nothing but bones.'

She shooed her away with her hand. 'And don't come home before the stars are high, either.'

'I don't mind staying,' Ruth offered. 'Honestly.'

'Tch! Think Lavinia can't manage on her own for a couple of hours? Go and find Lalo, have a good time. Besides,' one blue eye winked wickedly, 'I'm gossiping.'

'Not again.' Ruth's mouth twisted as she turned to Claudia. 'Pay no attention,' she said. 'Half the time the old crow makes it up and the rest she embroiders—'

'—as elaborately as a seamstress with gold thread,' Lavinia finished. 'You're repeating yourself, Ruth, it's a sign of old age.'

'So's *forgetting* your medicine!' She thrust the beaker in the old woman's wrinkled hand. 'Don't believe,' Ruth told Claudia, 'a word about the woman who kept cats.'

'Nonsense, that was scandalous!' Lavinia set the goblet down and leaned across to Claudia. 'Just as well the poor woman's heart gave out when it did, heaven knows what her reaction would have been when she found out her husband had all twelve moggies strangled!'

'See what I mean?' laughed Ruth, stuffing the beaker back into her mistress's hands. 'Makes it up as she goes along. Now will you drink this, you stubborn old bag, or do I have to pinch your nose?'

'That—' Lavinia threw the liquid over an undeserving fern '– solves both our dilemmas, so why don't you join the Agonalia and leave me to tell Claudia about the silversmith?'

'Lavinia, please! I insist you stop this tittletattle at once,' Ruth wailed. 'He was in tremendous pain, poor man, there was a canker eating at his belly from the inside, he could have gone at any time, and the same, I'm sure, was true of the woman who wore red, so don't you bring that up, either.'

Lavinia pulled a face and said, 'You wouldn't think she was my servant, would you? Very well, Ruth, you win. I give you my solemn promise to stick to politics this afternoon and before you nag, no wine, either, you have my word. Now do stop fussing, child, and run along.'

She watched the girl out of sight before reaching behind a pillar to drag out another full jug. 'Terrible thing about that little orphan boy,' she chirruped, pouring the thick, vintage wine. 'Ten years of age and he was killed in a hunting accident right –' she pointed to the woods up on the hill '– there. Fortuitous for the kid's cousin, mind. Inheriting his fortune.'

Holy Jupiter! 'Are you suggesting—?'

'Lavinia simply repeats what she's heard, and she heard it was an accident, same as the woman in red that Ruth mentioned just now. Died in her honeymoon bed, poor cow, two doors along from me, as a matter of fact, and ho, did the tongues wag over that! Just because she was thirty years older than her man and had a few bob stashed by. But then they said the same about your young man, when his first wife died.'

'Excuse me?' Claudia rubbed at her temple. She must have drunk too much wine. 'I don't—'

'Think I haven't seen the two of you together?' Lavinia shot her a shrewd look. 'Noticed the way those dark eyes follow you around? Are you sure there's nothing wrong with the hem of your robe?'

'Lavinia,' Claudia said carefully, 'are we talking about Tarraco, by any chance?'

'Married or not, that boy is keen on you, and I'm—'

'Whoa!' Claudia tried to hang on to Lavinia's thread. 'You did say *married*?'

Lavinia's chuckle bordered on evil. 'Forgot to mention his wife, eh? Well, Lais isn't the first middle-aged woman he married, only let's hope this doesn't end in tragedy like his previous union.'

Lais?

Tarraco?

Suddenly it made sense. The slave who rose to riches . . . 'Don't tell me,' Claudia said slowly. 'Tuder bought a Spanish slave at auction, Lais was smitten—?'

She rose unsteadily to her feet and began to pace the colonnade. Wrong, she thought. Lais wasn't smitten. Lais had been seduced in a cold and calculating campaign. Then when Tuder died, Tarraco had made his move – *and now look who's master of the island!*

Hang on! 'Did you say second wife? What do you mean, the first marriage ended in tragedy?'

But the effort of so much gossip on top of too much wine had exhausted the old woman. Slumped on her daybed, Lavinia snored softly beneath her coiffured wig, her wrinkled face turned up towards the sun and with an indigestible ball inside her stomach (the dates, what else?) Claudia retreated indoors.

No wonder Tarraco knew so much about women. Their sizes, their tastes, what gifts would make the most impact. Tarraco was not an artist, after all.

Tarraco was a bloody gigolo.

His first wife was dead, Tuder was dead, and considerable wealth was involved. She recalled him strutting round the island. Marble come from high Pyrenees, cedar only from Lebanon. This bust? Pff, is nothing, wait till you see the colossus. What she had taken as pride in his possessions was nothing more than pompous boasting and the ball of dates (what else?) solidified further. In her bedchamber, Claudia jerked off the harebell gown and hurled it into a corner.

'Bastard!'

He hadn't got the robe made up, the bloody thing belonged to Lais! It wasn't even clean, there were spots around the hem!

'Dirty, double-dealing dago!'

With a fruit knife, Claudia hacked at the cotton until it hung in shreds, the sweat pouring down her forehead and leaving dark drips on the pale harebell blue. No wonder he'd dismissed the servants! With him still married to the master's wife, he daren't risk the scandal of adultery.

'Bastard, bastard, bastard!'

Wait. Claudia leaned back on her knees and tapped her finger against her lower lip. Where exactly was Lais while all this was going on? With the plague in Rome, she'd hardly have headed for the capital! Claudia straightened up and stared across the shimmering lake, her face puckered in thought. For the question of Lais had raised another, more deadly, issue.

Because, if Claudia had rowed the Spaniard's boat *out* to the island, Tarraco must have been ashore in Atlantis.

The afternoon Cal had been killed.

XV

Ankles puffed up in heat as merciless as it was unrelenting, bones felt like lead and hair hung in damp ropes. In Rome, the chaos was worsening as more and more roads became clogged with locked spokes or carts tipping over in the rush to exit the capital. The military were working round the clock, but as verges piled higher and higher with everything from crockpots to copper, saltfish to spoons, the smell of oxen and asses attracted bluebottles by the billion, and the dispirited legionaries likened their task to that of Hercules tackling the Augean stables. They ferried in water, beans and bread, they dug makeshift latrines and erected temporary awnings for the trapped stew of humanity, but, when a man's livelihood rots by the roadside and his children are in danger from dirt and disease, the soldiers were on a hiding to nowhere.

Morale hit rock bottom.

And while the army battled with the congestion, a dark shape formed in the void, and the name of the dark shape was Anarchy.

For safety, pedestrian travellers either postponed their trips or journeyed in groups. Empty houses were looted, horses stolen; women feared for their lives. At nightfall, shutters were bolted, doors locked and then barred – for who was left to patrol the streets and keep them safe?

Gradually a million people became trapped in their homes, scared to go out for fear of bandits. Maggots infested the foodstuffs. Rats multiplied too fast to keep count.

The death toll was rising.

And not all the symptoms tallied with plague

'*Ouch!*'

Marcus Cornelius flinched when the wooden bear bounced off the crown of his head, although it was with no mean deftness that he caught the second carving before further damage was inflicted. Gingerly his fingers explored the tender swelling and, despite the pain, he grinned. Since his conversation with Dorcan, he'd been wandering aimlessly with just his thoughts and suspicions for company, yet of the fifty or so bedchambers in Atlantis, he was not so disorientated that he couldn't work out whose open window ejected such a treasure trove of goodies.

'We're making progress, then?' he called up. 'When you shower me with gifts!'

'Orbilio?' A head thrust itself through the gap, and he couldn't fail to notice that several elegant curls had slipped their leash. Or that they rested on perfect, naked shoulders. 'What the hell do you think you're doing, prowling underneath my bedroom window, you filthy pervert, you!'

'Flattery, as well as gifts! Now I know you love me!'

'I'd love a suppurating sore more than I'd love you!'

Oh yes, he sighed. He was definitely making progress. 'Claudia,' he said, 'we do need to talk.'

'Talk?' A finely tooled sandal came winging through

the air. Green. 'You call yourself a criminal investigator and all you want to do is talk? I don't suppose it occurred to you to consider earning your crust for a change?'

'My business with you is official,' he answered mildly, lobbing back the shoe.

There was a long silence, which he savoured.

Followed by a longer silence, which he did not.

Finally, when he craned his neck upwards again, he saw that the shutters had been snapped shut and to salvage the remains of his dignity, Orbilio stuffed his thumbs in his belt and sauntered on down the path praying that his tiddly-om-pom whistle was as jaunty as he hoped. Round the promontory his footsteps took him, beneath the domed loggia and past a thicket of alders. He glanced up at the sun porch and thought he caught a movement halfway up the cliff face. Surely not . . .? But there it was again. A shadow on – or rather inside – the rock. Frowning, he stared at the impenetrable grey wall, at the straggly shrubs which clung to the rock, at the strange shadows they threw. Then a sapphire-blue dragonfly whizzed, breaking the spell, and Marcus continued his stroll.

At the foot of the zigzag steps which led up to the walnut grove surrounding Carya's shrine, a man with shoulder-length hair and a sharp taste in dress was being approached by a small boy with a package under his arm. Marcus melted into the shadow of the cliff. The boy, nut-brown and naked, proceeded to hand over the parcel. The Spaniard unwrapped the sacking and Orbilio watched a thousand ribbons scatter over the path. Tarraco fired off a succession of questions, the boy pointed up to Atlantis and, in his private hiding place, Orbilio grinned to himself.

The shreds were the unmistakable hue of summer harebells . . .

A flash of bronze caught the sun as it spun through the air before being clasped in the fist of the boy, who scampered away, testing the coin in his teeth as Tarraco glowered at the heap of blue cotton. Then, with fists clenched and a face like thunder, the Spaniard ran up the steps. Orbilio waited until he'd disappeared into the walnut grove before retracing his route round the promontory, and this time there were no strange shadows flitting in a descending line down the rock face and his whistle was slick and robust. He paused to watch an osprey cruise the shimmering waters and a trickle of sweat wriggled down his backbone to join a party of its cousins. His meeting with Dorcan this evening should eliminate one or two—

'Tuder,' a voice said and, startled, Orbilio peered round a protruding tongue of rock to where Claudia Seferius was perched on a tree stump, her knees drawn up to her chin.

'Chewed a what?' he said. 'Oh, by the way.' He tossed across the wooden carvings. 'You dropped these.'

'Correction.' Claudia weighed the figures in each hand. 'I rather think I threw them. Like this.' At the second plop, a screeching moorhen shot out of the reed-bed, its wings beating the surface of the water.

'That's not nice,' Marcus said, settling his back against the rock face as the ripples in the lake began to settle. 'You'll give the tadpoles headaches. Why do you want to talk about Tuder? He's dead.'

'Exactly! And how did he die?'

'I'm afraid you have me there.'

'You, Orbilio, are not that lucky.' Claudia stood up and shook the splinters from her skirt. 'However, I think that, as a detective, you could start to earn the exorbitant salary they pay you—'

'Actually, it's a pittance—'

'—and set the tiny bean inside your thick skull to finding out what happened to our wealthy banker.'

Swallowing a laugh, Orbilio noted with a tinge of disappointment that, whilst the curls ran free, those perfect shoulders had disappeared beneath a blaze of jade-coloured cotton, and jade, he decided, suited her better than that wishy-washy blue. 'I'm sure you have a theory or two as to his demise, though?'

Beside him in the shade, Claudia snorted disdainfully. 'How typical of the army to stick to single figures! Any number of things could have happened to poor old Tuder with what was going on out there! Maybe he burst in on Lais and her tacky love-slave and, mortified by her betrayal, plunged a knife deep into his broken heart, or—'

'A progressive illness snuffed out the last, faint flame of life?'

'Or,' she glared, 'he took a gallop round his island, discovering too late the strap on his saddle had been cut, or—'

'Suffered a massive stroke?'

'Or,' she spat through clenched teeth, 'he takes a deep draught of Falernian wine, only to find it was poisoned. *Or*—'

'He died of the pox after a lifetime of debauchery and couldn't give a toss whether his middle-aged wife remained chaste or slept with an entire legion every night. Claudia, he's dead,' Marcus pointed out, 'and it's unlikely the truth will ever come to light, because there are only two people who could tell us. One is Tarraco, and I don't see him soiling his pretty nest somehow, and the second person is his dear, sweet wife.'

Orbilio paused to buff his bronze buckle.

'And Lais,' he said quietly, 'surprise, surprise, has disappeared.'

XVI

Dead to the world, drunks sprawled under horse troughs as a thief relieved them of their bootlaces and sparrows squabbled over piecrusts. The Forum was deserted in the throbbing midday heat and amid the smashed pots and mussel shells, dogs snarled over meat bones and the glassy-eyed mother swaying with a baby on her shoulder to music inside her head did not see six well-built men slip down the side street, wielding clubs and staves and axes.

The leader, a hard-faced thug with one empty eye socket, paused to check his bearings before signalling the group to turn right at the basilica. The street began to narrow. They passed gaily painted apartment blocks, smart but not posh, so these would be for the scribes and the clerks and their families. The tenements became smaller, packed closer together, homes for freed slaves or tradesmen on the first rung of the ladder, then the buildings ran out altogether and soon the men were trudging down a stony path towards the lake.

The grass was dry and crisp and yellow, lined with firethorns and fig trees. They passed a small but unattended olive grove, an umbrella pine with newly shorn sheep and their lambs nestling down in its shadow. One bleated softly, but the men paid no heed. At a signal from One Eye, they checked their weapons, then nodded brusquely to one another before approaching the wooden shack which stood on its own. Blue smoke coiled from the roof, and a buzzard mewed in the distance as the thugs circled the building.

'Right!' growled the leader, grasping his club in his hand as he kicked open the door.

A woman screamed, a man jumped up from his pallet.

'You!' One Eye snarled, pointing to the woman as he raised his weapon high above his head. 'Shut it!'

The woman, seeing the vicious nails which protruded from the head of the club, merely screamed louder.

'I mean it, you bitch!' He grabbed her by the scruff of her tunic and stuck his dead eye into hers. 'One more squeak and Loverboy ends up like me.'

The woman, swelling with her second child, gulped back her hysteria and forced her head to nod up and down. So far, her man had not moved.

'You were warned,' One Eye growled, 'what would happen if you didn't pay.'

'I have paid,' the young man retorted. His face was white, but his voice was steady and clear. 'On the Ides of every month, I've handed over forty bronze pieces and I've never been late.'

'The price went up, remember? To fifty sesterces.'

'By the gods, man, I can't afford that! We barely scrape by as it is!'

'So you're refusing?' A sly smile twitched at the thug's mouth.

The young man spread his hands in helplessness. 'We can't afford more than forty,' he protested. 'I cure fish for a living, you can see how it is—'

From a cradle in the corner, a baby began to bawl, setting off a dog out the back.

'Shut that brat up,' the thug shouted to its mother.

The woman stumbled over to the cot, but the child was not comforted and as it cried harder, so the dog's barking increased.

'Silence that fucking mutt!' One Eye yelled through the open doorway. For maybe twenty seconds the dog snarled and thrashed on its chain, then, with a pitiful whimper, fell quiet. The woman collapsed, sobbing convulsively into her infant bundle and muffling the sound of its screams. The leader of the gang glanced up the path to check no one had been alerted to the racket, then turned back to the man.

'You had fair warning,' he said.

'For gods' sakes,' there was a rising note of panic in the youth's voice, 'we're barely surviving as it is.' He wiped his hand with his face. 'It started off at ten a month, then twenty, thirty, forty – where will it end? I'm only a smoker of fish, have some pity!'

'I'm not paid for pity,' and for a moment the woman thought she detected a note of sympathy in the thug's voice, but she was mistaken, because she knew without looking again into that single, cold eye that he had been born without warmth or compassion. And when he said, 'Right, boys, you know what to do,' she hugged her daughter tight to her chest and buried her face in the silky, soft hair, crooning to the child to block out the splintering and crashing around her.

The smoke-house door was the first casualty. Then rack upon rack of hanging fish were hurled on to the grass to be pulped with staves as the bullies kicked over fires, drenched the wood piles with water and trashed the living quarters, even grinding the baby's clay rattle under a heel, and she heard her man spit 'Bastard!' at the leader of the gang.

'Well,' One Eye brushed his hands together and wiped them down his tunic, 'we all have some trade we're good at.' He laughed. 'And I'm damned good at being a bastard, right, lads?'

The others guffawed at the joke, then One Eye pulled at his ear lobe.

'You're still in arrears,' he said, shrewdly surveying the mess, 'by fifty sesterces, don't forget.'

'You've destroyed my stock, my equipment, my shed,' the fish smoker whispered. 'You've left me with nothing, not even our baby's birthday dinner.'

The woman looked round, to see jars of beans smashed and trampled, oil jars kicked over, even the bread that she'd baked bore a footprint. Her daughter was one year old today and even her honey cake had been scoffed by the thugs. Then without warning her own face was pinched in the thug's hand and she screamed.

'Pretty piece,' he leered. 'Can't be more than seventeen. I'm sure you'll find ways of settling the debt.'

'Leave her alone!' her man yelled. 'Take your filthy hands off her, you hear!'

'Me?' sneered One Eye, brushing him off. 'I've no use for a pregnant sow, but I tell you, boy, there's men who likes 'em like that.'

'You dirty bastard—'

'Now, now,' the thug laughed, crunching over the debris and deaf to the young woman's whimpers, 'I'm merely opening your mind as to different ways of raising the cash you owe. Don't be too hasty to dismiss the idea.'

And with that, he and his gang strode back up the path towards Spesium as silently as they came. The young man staggered outside to inspect the damage.

The smoke house had gaping holes in the wall. They could be patched.

The doors were smashed, their hinges thrown in the lake. New could be bought.

The dog had been clubbed, but it was a mastiff with a head like a stone. It would recover.

Slowly, he nodded to himself. He'd worked hard to establish a reputation for plump, juicy smokies and for that reason he hadn't minded handing over a small part of his income to nameless individuals for what was known as 'protection'. In time he hoped to sell to Atlantis, so he didn't complain, even when the price for protection crept up. So what, if it meant postponing building a proper house for a while? Life was sweet. He wore no man's shackles, ran his own business, had the love of a good woman, one child and a second on the way, this time maybe a son? It would happen, he felt, in good time, the house and cart and the smallholding.

But not at fifty sesterces a month. That was over half his income.

The bastards were bleeding him dry.

He was not alone, of course. The baker – they put weevils in his flour, killed his donkey until in the end he found it easier to succumb. Now he received chicken-feed to manage the very business he'd set up, his own profits siphoned off. The wheelwright, too – his solution was to take his boys out of school to earn the extra money, and the fish curer knew there were more, many more. Shops changing hands for a pittance, families weeping as they packed up and left town . . .

Well, humble fish smoker or not, he would not be driven away like the others. He was not a fighting man, but if that's what he had to do, so be it, he would learn to use a bow and swing a sword. His woman, child and unborn son were worth fighting for and when he found the bastard who was masterminding this, he'd kill him. So help him, he would gut him like a mullet and smoke him for days over oakwood.

'We must leave.' Her whisper was so faint that at first he did not catch the words. 'Did you hear me? We must leave now.'

'Never,' he said firmly, kicking at the mangled fish with his bare toe. 'We're young, we can rebuild and I swear on the life of my daughter you won't be driven to prostitution to pay off this so-called protection. But I must make a stand.'

'I've put our clothes in a bundle, let's go.' She tugged like a mouse at his sleeve, and forcing a smile, he turned to put his arm round her and draw her towards him.

Instead his arm froze.

'What is it?' he rasped. Her face was grey, she looked thirty years older, and something had died in her eyes. Involuntarily he shivered.

'Come,' she said, and he saw she was clutching an old towel rolled into a ball and a beaker whose handle had just been smashed off.

A thousand leeches sucked at his blood, draining every single drop. 'Where is she?' The words became snagged on his lip. 'Where's the baby?'

Skidding in his panic, he raced back into the tiny hovel, where feathers from the ripped bolster floated in the smoke-filled air as his feet crunched over the shattered furniture. In her cot, sleeping, lay his baby daughter, one white feather on her chest, and the young man scolded himself for being so jumpy. Gently he leaned over the cradle, inhaling the milky soft smell of her and smiling at the pink, button nose.

'It's all right, pumpkin,' he crooned. 'Daddy's here, it's all right.'

But it was not all right.

As he lifted his child, the tiny blonde head lolled backwards and her little arms fell limp – and he knew, then, what he had known the second he had looked at his woman.

His baby was dead.

Suffocated in her mother's terrified embrace.

For several long seconds, he stared at his child, before laying her back in the cot and tenderly tucking her in. After several long minutes, he leaned over and kissed her rosebud lips.

When the revellers in Spesium finally stumbled back to consciousness, they awoke to an animal howl from the lake end of town.

XVII

In the dark, dry serenity of Carya's grotto, Claudia munched on a hunk of Sarsina cheese, redolent of the lush Umbrian fields of its homeland, and paused from time to time to pour water down her throat, either inside or out, it didn't matter, both were sensational. Here, the slope of the cave muffled any eerie howlings which came from over the lake, filling the void with the hypnotic drip-drip-drip of the water nymph's tears, and soon Claudia's eyelids became weighted . . . weighted with lead . . .

'Are you deaf as well as stupid, boy?'

The nasal whine, shriller still in anger, jolted her into wakefulness and instinct made her retreat into the corner where it was too dark to make out much more than reflected ripples on the wall and the white blur of Mosul's priestly garb, but the slap did not need to be seen. Neither was it necessary to see Leon's face to appreciate the impact of Mosul's wrath, the lad's groans were expressive enough.

'How dare you' – thwack – 'come down here' – thwack – 'when I have forbidden it!' Mosul was puffing from effort, Leon was gulping back sobs. 'Out, you little shit, before I take the buckle end of this belt to your hide!'

'I only wanted to help—'

'Out! You hear me!' Another octave higher and Mosul's voice would have shattered glass. 'Out!'

Memories blasted back, crushing hearing, sight, every known sense. Bitter memories. Of a leather strap biting in flesh. Of pain. White-hot pain. And an uncle, her mother's brother, beating obedience into a small, orphaned child . . .

In the darkness, Claudia cringed and curled herself into a ball. *Go away. Go away.* But the uncle would not go away, not until his arm tired, although if she made herself small, she could hide. Hide inside herself and seek refuge against the bristly cheek of her father and it didn't matter he was dead. Tight in a ball, she was his again. Safe and protected . . .

Through the tears – stinging tears, salty tears, not the make-believe tears of a nymph – Claudia became aware of Leon, stumbling out of the cave, whimpering like a whipped mongrel. Of the mole-eyed priest, glancing several times over his shoulder before leaning into the cistern. Finally, his hands swished the water, then he, too, was gone and soon the dancing ripples moderated their rhythm and Carya's grotto was calm once again.

Scrubbing her face with the back of her hand, Claudia crawled out of her hiding place and cupped trembling hands in the water, but the water was sour and the darkness no longer a haven. Nevertheless she counted to twenty before striding out of the cave, and when the tub of a priest glanced up from the shrine, he saw a young woman skipping up the red marble steps without a care in the world, tossing back her curls as she improvised silly words to a popular festival tune.

'You've got a bloody sauce!'

He was leaning with one shoulder against the window

embrasure, his arms loosely crossed, staring towards the orchard of cherry trees and damsons, where pink piglets squealed over fat, contented sows and where blossoms fell like snow on the grass, and he did not look round when she entered, though the rush of air must have alerted him, even if the door slamming on its hinges did not.

'Well, let me tell you now, you duplicitous son-of-a-bitch, you can stick your apologies where the sun—'

'Uh-uh.' Still he did not turn his head, and just like on the island the day before yesterday, his expression was veiled by the mane of dark hair. 'I am not here to apologize, merely to explain.'

'Forget it, Tarraco,' Claudia said coldly, 'the game's over.'

'Game?'

Sorry, I was forgetting. For you, this is deadly serious, isn't it? 'Allow me spell it out in words even a simple Spaniard can understand. You've lost, Tarraco. Give in gracefully, because,' she flashed a wicked smile, 'I'm nowhere near as wealthy as I make out.'

His head snapped round so fast, Claudia wondered whether it would spin off altogether. 'Is that what you think?' he hissed, and the sinews in his neck stood out like clewlines. 'You think I am after your money? Tcha!' He flicked his thumbnail against his front tooth. 'You have seen my island, do I look poor?'

'But how much is enough for you, Tarraco?' she fired back. 'Where does greed draw the line?'

'You sneer at me, because I pursue rich, lonely women, yes? Is better to slog from dawn to dusk in the wheatfields, to spend a life underground in the silver mines? Which would you do, my so-upstanding maiden, when uprooted from your home and family and shipped in chains to foreign land? Stoke furnaces? Scrub pots? Pour wine yes-sir-no-sir for the scum who put manacles around your ankles and sell you as slave?'

Fury had distorted his features, colouring his skin and blazing bolts of white lightning from those charcoal-dark eyes.

'I am eighteen, have no skill, only muscles to be sold by the pound at an auction! Then I catch eye of rich lady and wonder, hmm . . . So I flirt with her from the block, rich lady buys me, all is fine until her husband finds out, then – rich lady stripped of her status, thrown into the gutter and spat on by those who once called themselves friends. But Tarraco?' He let out a bitter laugh. 'Suddenly this ignorant Spaniard is in great demand, for what does he have, the fine ladies wonder, that is worth losing everything for?'

Outside the crickets buzzed with irritating regularity, and inside the room, the sweltering heat threatened to squeeze the breath from Claudia's body. That, surely, was her reason for holding it in? A heady blend of pine and woodshavings drifted across on the air and the gold on his tunic, fish, leaping round a navy-blue hem, shimmered in the sunlight.

'So they had an itch and you scratched it?' she snapped. 'Think I give a damn?'

Tarraco turned back to gaze out of the window, where the hills had disappeared in a blue smoky haze, hiding pines grown to tap for their resin and myrtles grown for sweet-smelling garlands.

'You look down on me because I am gigolo, but what–'

he paused to spike his mane out of his face with his fingers '– if I am woman in same situation?'

Carefully (very carefully) Claudia poured herself a glass of wine.

'My husband, I admit, might have been one or two years older than myself.' Thirty, if you're picking nits. 'However, I married him because he was a witty and entertaining man –' this was not the time to mention he'd been an ageing lardball with poisonous bad breath '– and good points too numerous to mention.' All of them inside his moneybox. 'I was utterly bereft when he passed away.'

Her voice dared him to call her a liar, yet when the Spaniard turned to face her, the blood pounded at Claudia's temples as dark, demanding eyes peeled back the layers of her past, laying bare memories only she could possibly know . . .

It was no mean feat, staring him out! 'At least I didn't kill him to get my hands on his money.'

Tarraco's laughter came out as a snort through his nose. 'Is that what the gossips put out? Because Virginia drowned in the lake? It was dark, there was a thunderstorm, I told her not to row out alone, but like you,' he flashed her a glance, 'she is stubborn.' Suddenly he grinned. 'Knows it all.' Then the grin slipped away. 'Next morning, her boat was in pieces and Virginia floated face down on the water.'

'Rich, was she?'

'Comfortable enough to afford long and regular visits to Atlantis,' he conceded. 'Is how she became friendly with Lais, and when Tuder died, it seemed natural for me to . . . comfort the grieving widow.'

'As only you knew how!'

In a flash the Spaniard leapt over the room, grabbing Claudia's wrists in his hands and jerking her round. With a crash, her goblet smashed into a thousand sparkling smithereens and the strange thing was, neither of them noticed.

'I have worked hard to achieve my ambitions,' he spat. 'The gold and the marble, lush grounds, a big house. But I have done nothing without honour, you hear? Nothing I am ashamed of!'

He released her and pushed her away.

'First you believed I was a slave, who ingratiated himself with Lais and Tuder. I tell you otherwise, but still you suspect me of wrongdoing. I know nothing about the banker, how he came to die, and I do not think it is any of your business, either, but if you really want to know, why don't you ask Lais?'

Congratulations. I thought you'd never get round to her!

'Lais of the harebell-blue gown, you mean?'

Tarraco's chin jutted out, but it was his only reaction. There was a pause, then, 'I wanted,' he said simply, 'to give you a present. Was spontaneous, and that robe was – oh, Claudia, that gown was –' his eyes closed in pleasure '– just perfect on you.'

Silver-tongued bastard!

'It was probably perfect on Lais, as well.'

'No, no, no. Lais is a fine woman, but she is fifty-six. Of course,' he spread his hands, 'she thinks herself twenty years younger, never allowed me to see her without her cosmetics, but when a man makes love to a woman . . .'

Unable to meet his smoky gaze, Claudia reached for

another glass to fill with thick, heavy wine. 'Don't tell me. You found it a chore.'

'I tell you the truth, Claudia, as I have told no living soul. It was bloody hard work.' There was no anger in Tarraco's voice, only sadness. 'Desiccated flesh, sagging breasts, face whitened with a ton of chalk. Every day you live with her eyebrows painted on, the brow itself long since fallen out, you steel yourself to put your tongue in a mouth where it probes round missing teeth. Do you start to get the picture?'

Claudia recalled the pinched and petulant middle-aged woman conferring with Kamar in the early hours of this morning and thought, yes, that's the type he means. Self-obsessed and self-absorbed, the likes of Stonypuss couldn't understand why a dashing blade *wouldn't* want to court them!

'Can you imagine making up to old women as though they were virgins? Playing day in and day out the role of their pleasure boy? Flattering, cajoling, learning to lie with the utmost conviction, yet knowing all the while your livelihood depends on the size of your muscles and the strength of your stamina in bed?' His voice was little more than a whisper, and it seemed to be addressing Lake Plasimene. 'I defy you to tell me I haven't earned what I own!'

A long silence followed, and when Claudia finally broke it, her voice was as soft as a breeze in a poplar. 'How, exactly, is it that you come to own Tuder's island, Tarraco?'

'I am Lais' husband,' he huffed. 'Is mine by right.'

Really? Claudia drained her glass and refilled it. Of course, the law was unequivocal. A woman's property automatically transfers to her husband upon marriage; that was Lavinia's point. On the other hand, it was a naïve Senate which imagined it could outwit a wealthy woman and virtually unimaginable that a rich banker's wife would not be cognisant of loopholes! Rather, Claudia imagined, rolls and rolls of legal parchment would have been invested to ensure wealth on that scale remained in Lais' title . . . unless . . . unless . . .

Claudia phrased her next question carefully. 'How long since Lais left you?' she asked, with almost indecent politeness.

'Wednesday. Why? You imagine I take you to my bed, while the marriage still stands?'

No. I am just remembering that Cal was killed the following afternoon . . .

'You did not take me to your bed,' she reminded him. 'But I'd be intrigued to hear what happened on Wednesday.'

Tarraco threw his hands in the air in what Claudia had, until then, assumed to be a purely Gallic gesture. 'We have row, she walk out. End of marriage, end of story. Claudia, this took place before you arrived.' He crouched at her feet, one knee bent, the other touching the ground, the way he'd knelt before the dead bear. 'I swear this is not adultery, I am not after money, you must believe this.' He closed his eyes and inhaled deeply. 'On the island, when I see the bear chasing you, I knew—' He broke off and stood up, and as so many times in the past, let his hair hide his face. 'You saw it,' he said thickly. 'When I lifted you up, you saw how I felt. There was nothing I could do, neither,' he added slowly, 'did I wish to fight what I have never before felt in my life. Claudia.'

149

He turned round to face her, his face twisted in pain.

'I must know,' he rasped. 'Do you believe me?'

Claudia stood up and there were white water rapids coursing her veins. 'Not one single word.'

He was a liar, a cheat, but worse, here was a very dangerous man.

'And this,' she hurled the contents of her glass in his face, 'is for presuming a soiled frock would get me into your bed.'

Down by the jetty, Marcus Cornelius watched the dandified Spaniard bound down the steps from Atlantis. By his reckoning, the sun had moved fifteen degrees in the sky, and that, in his opinion, was a bloody long time to pass in a lady's bedroom simply playing chequers.

A lion clawed his stomach from the inside, and the pain was the worst that he'd known.

Then he noticed, as the Spaniard drew closer, that a scowl disfigured his face almost as badly as the stain which disfigured his shirt. As Tarraco approached the jetty, there was a distinct spring in Orbilio's step as he reached over to untie the rope to Tarraco's boat.

'Allow me,' he said cheerfully.

The Spaniard accepted the favour with a grunt and, as he did so, Marcus leaned over and sniffed.

'Let me guess.' He sniffed again. 'Vintage – eight, possibly nine years old. Fine, rich bouquet, with a hint of wild blackberries –' (sniff) '– ripe figs –' (sniff) '–and, yes, I do believe oak.' He straightened up and passed the rope across. 'At a stab, I'd say that's an amusing little Campanian soaking into the cotton.'

'Actually, it's Falernian,' the Spaniard growled, snatching at the oars.

'Well, whatever,' Marcus acknowledged. 'Either way, it's still amusing.'

XVIII

With more riveting entertainments offered by the Agonalia, Claudia had the bath house to herself. Well, almost. The plumes of steam coiling their way up the columns to fill the arches didn't count, neither did the squad of yawning female attendants perched on their high stools, filing their nails as they waited.

'This beauty treatment will make you feel a million sesterces,' the supervisor promised in a lilting Sarmatian accent.

'Uh-uh.' Claudia indicated her chin with the flat of her hand. 'I've had it up to here with millionaires.' Greeks, Spaniards, patricians – they think they can buy anyone!

'Yes, yes,' the supervisor nodded, pointing to her own chin. 'The mud comes right up to here. Wonderful therapy, based on a marvellous Scythian preparation.' She eased Claudia out of her clothes and secured the voluminous towel with a pin. 'Your skin will remain glossy and fragrant for a fortnight or more.'

'A fortnight?'

'Minimum.'

I ask you, who could resist? Across the empty exercise yard and through a high vaulted archway Claudia entered an area divided into sections by heavy tapestry drapes and here the homely Sarmatian supervisor pulled aside a blue curtain to reveal a cubicle containing one marble slab and a dozen buckets of mud, before handing her over to a slave girl with an aureole of bright red curls and the broadest smile this side of the Caucasus. Unfortunately, even the camphor burning in a brazier couldn't mask the ghastly pong of the sludge, but this, the redhead assured her, emptying the first bucket over the slab, was every bit as beneficial as the treatment itself.

Unconvinced, Claudia watched as a second followed by a third bucket was upended, the girl spreading the black slime into a nice even layer before helping Claudia on to the squidge.

'You'll feel a whole new woman after this,' she trilled, slapping another bucket over Claudia's thighs, her torso, her arms. 'The mud dries on you like an Egyptian sarcophagus, but oh! once I crack it off and the impurities in your skin come away with it, your skin will feel like liquid gold all over.' She plumped the pillow under Claudia's head. 'Comfy?' she asked, not waiting for an answer before drawing the curtain and clip-clopping over the tiles like a filly in a stable yard.

Then came nothing but silence.

Maybe a distant knock in the hypocaust, a hiss of steam from the bellows. A few muffled words from the attendants as they passed the pillared arch. But mostly nothing.

Twenty feet above, the paintings on the ceiling appeared and dissolved in the swirling vapour and gradually, as the mud began to harden, the smell of camphor gained the upper hand and Claudia felt the tension in her bones begin to dissipate. At last, she thought. At last, a place to unwind and think things through.

And plan.

To her left, the tapestry curtain proclaimed grand Homeric scenes, red and vivid like the blood which had been shed so freely on those windy plains of Troy, whilst to her right, greens predominated, with Arcadian scenes so lifelike, you could almost hear Pan's pipes whistle round the woodlands and the goats bleat on the hills.

Inside her mud coffin, Claudia let out her breath.

It was as though those two curtains summed up her dilemma. Her life, even. Red for passion, for feet-first hot-headedness. Grey-green for logic, for stepping back and listening to good, old-fashioned reason.

All right, then. Let's see where this takes us. Focusing on the green tapestry, Claudia laid out her thoughts one by one and set Logic upon them.

Cal first. She had barely known him and perhaps it was time she questioned her motives for wanting to find his killer. Could it (dare she admit) be to divert attention from her own predicament? To neutralize her fears and troubles by transferring them on to a disinterested party? Suppose it had truly been an accident? Cal has one affair too many. The husband confronts him. Cal laughs it off as another casual conquest. The husband is incensed. He lunges. They fight. And suddenly, unintentionally, Cal falls dead. What now? The husband panics. He smashes Cal's face against the rock and arranges the body to look like a fall.

Claudia stared beyond the green-embroidered wood-lands to a voluble trial by jurists. Who would benefit? It couldn't bring Cal back. Would cause further unhappiness to his family. Would punish a man already facing a lifetime of guilt, and what if there were children involved? Who was Claudia to tear apart a family?

Her eyes traced a flock of sheep and their shepherd, and she almost smelled the thyme which covered those same Arcadian hills which abutted Pylades' homeland, Laconia. Ah, Pylades. He visits Plasimene and in no time Atlantis rises out of the rock, a glamorous palace of fun, and with the plague ushering those who could afford it out of Rome, what was so wrong with Pylades bitching about the smooth running of his business? Agreed such remarks at a funeral were callous and crass, but when all's said and done, Cal was a fee-paying customer who, from Pylades' point of view, had left a precious vacancy to fill.

Towards the top of the Arcadian tapestry, nymphs bathed naked in a crystal-clear pool, leaving Claudia to consider Carya, the spirit after whom Pylades named the sacred spring he discovered. The nymph tended so possessively by Mosul the priest that he drove away every acolyte who came here, because Leon wasn't the first lad he'd beaten black and blue, a dozen others had left Atlantis, their heads hung in shame because they couldn't meet his exacting requirements. So what, he'd had a run of bad experiences with his novices? Which, combined with his hot temper, had made him unnecessarily perfectionist? For all his faults (and anti-Semitism ranked pretty high), Mosul was devoted to the shrine, the altar was purified twice daily, you'd see no cobwebs in the corners, no dust on the steps, no stale offerings in the grounds and he never turned away a single sick pilgrim.

Satisfied with progress so far, Claudia allowed logic to move along her row of thoughts until it stopped at Kamar. The most you could level at him, Logic said, was incompetence and let's face it, there are far worse quacks than Turtleface dotted round the Empire. After twenty years of peace, the population was expanding, and what's more, expanding fast. As more and more people fell sick, the call on doctors' time became greater, there were simply not enough to go round . . . and in any case, no physician worth his salt would linger in Atlantis! A special breed was required to toady day in, day out to rich hypochondriacs and here, for all his faults, Kamar came into his own.

Even charlatans prospered, she thought, recalling her surprise at seeing the giant, but then again, why shouldn't Dorcan come here? A chap who can smell gullible souls like a shark senses blood in the water, a new town like Spesium, right next door to Atlantis, was perfect for business – and Dorcan wasn't a man who hoarded his takings. He was a born fritterer, his whole philosophy being that life is for living and hell, Claudia could identify with that!

She moved on to Lavinia. Sure, the old girl had a secret, but considering she'd been widowed for thirty years whilst avoiding compulsory remarriage, Lavinia struck Claudia as the sort of woman who'd nurtured secrets all her life, the way some folk collected faience or inkpots. Was it any surprise her servants didn't conform?

Finally Logic arrived, as it had to eventually, at Tarraco and she was curious. What would Logic make of this handsome chancer, who used his muscles in the bedroom instead of the fields? Well, as a matter of fact, Logic said there was no disgrace in a career which paid in gold, provided him with soft boots and jewels and servants of his own. The choice was his, and if he didn't mind sucking up to the likes of that stony-faced old boiler who'd so admired Claudia's harebell gown, who was anyone else to complain?

Inhaling the camphor oil, Claudia closed her eyes. The green tapestry had clarified her thoughts and calmed her fears. Sabbio Tullus? Tch! Such a skitchy-witchy loan, nothing to get steamed up about, she'd have that repaid before too long. A hiccup in the cash flow, that was all, dependent upon sales which would liquidate shortly. Now all she had to do was close her mind. Relax. Unwind with those watery gurgles coming up through the piping. Drift off with those distant, hollow voices floating under the floor from the furnace room.

Claudia's eyelids grew heavy. In her dream, she was alone in the great banqueting hall and filtered sunlight was streaming in through the upper arches of the sun porch. Claudia was stepping out on to the balcony, plucking a rose and stroking the clipped box giraffes. Her eyes were wandering upwards, to the zodiac ceiling. Where twelve cats hung from twelve nooses—

Gasping, gulping, Claudia's eyelids shot open, but when she tried to move, she could not. Except this wasn't a dream. She was trapped – what the . . .?

Then she remembered. The Scythian mud preparation. Sweat poured down her face, but the nightmare was only illusion and she listened to the reassuring hiss of the steam, the eerie echoes, the resonance of clogs on red-hot tiles.

But something had changed. Now the green tapestry was no longer suggestive of hazy spring meadows, of waterside ferns and lacewings dancing in the air. The monstrous vision of twelve cats dangling from ropes brought the colour red thundering through her thoughts. Brilliant poppy red, conjuring up visions of battle, blood-drenched soil, of surgeons staunching wounds and stitching flesh.

Of one physician in particular, whose Etruscan forebears painted themselves that same poppy red for their rituals, prayers and sacrifice, and who buried their dead on an island out in the lake. He was a tall man, was Kamar, with hands strong enough to set broken limbs, realign joints – and snap a man's neck cleanly in two!

Wasn't scarlet the colour of the awning which sheltered Dorcan's potions from the sun? He had lied once to her, twice, maybe a third time and affable though he was, let's not forget every move that big bear made had financial motivation. The figure flitting in the shadows in the early hours as she returned from Tuder's island was undeniably him, but why? Who had paid Dorcan to spy on her?

Claudia chewed her lower lip. An hour ago, in the dark seclusion of the grotto, a beady-eyed priest had sluiced his hands around in the cistern of a spring discovered on a promontory, which the augurs proclaimed as a miracle. Was it truly visionary – or simply vision? Mosul and Pylades. Both obsessive individuals, both perfectionists, both workaholics. Add a man-made tunnel and cave, what do you have?

One person who knew the answer now lay dead, and somehow the idea of a convenient husband exacting revenge just didn't ring true, no matter how hard one tried to make the pieces fit. Was Cal a blackmailer? Trading in sex, maybe information, rather than coins?

Damn you, scarlet curtain, damn you! Thanks to a few strands of dyed thread, you've twisted my thoughts like those twisted, dead warriors embroidered the length and the breadth of your drapes. You've stirred up a blood-red imagination, distorting pictures of a young man cart-wheeling down the aisle into a spy listening at keyholes, creeping round caves and skulking down tunnels.

To whom might he have confided his findings? Dorcan? Pylades? Lavinia . . .?

What the hell is that woman hiding? She's an olive grower, for gods' sake, how can her son afford this? From a homestead which boasts just the one field hand and maid, where tallows splutter and mattresses sag? What's she lying about? Did she, after all, see what happened to Cal? And Lalo. How far would the loyal hand go to protect his mistress's secret? *How far would he go to obey orders?* Why had he taken to disappearing for hours on end since he arrived in Atlantis, and where was he, the afternoon Cal was killed? Claudia had already checked with Ruth – she was alone.

'Hey!' Claudia called out. 'HEY!'

After the twentieth bellow, the redhead finally put in an appearance. 'Is there a problem, madam?' she asked, casting a professional eye over the mud pie congealing on the slab.

'I want to come out.'

'No, no, no, no!' squealed the horrified attendant. 'It'll undo all the good work, the mud inside won't be set!'

'Absolutely correct!' A strong Sarmatian accent threw her weight behind the argument. 'The mud needs to dry completely on your skin.' The senior attendant tapped the sarcophagus. 'About halfway,' she calculated. 'Well worth the wait, I assure you.'

'I have no intention of waiting,' Claudia snapped. 'I want—' Suddenly she recalled something Lavinia had said, and it was as though she'd been transported to the very highest Alps, so cold was the blood in her veins. 'A woman died having a mud treatment. Was it *here*?'

The spatula in the redhead's hands clattered on to the tiles and for the first time the broad smile disappeared. It was left to the supervisor to explain.

'Ah, now that.' She exchanged sober glances with her assistant, who began to twist her finger in her fist as she stared at her feet. 'We um . . .' The Sarmatian accent grew more pronounced. 'We didn't think anyone knew—'

'It was terrible,' cut in the redhead. 'My best friend was in charge, and she got the sack over that, but, honestly, it wasn't her fault—'

'It wasn't *any* of our faults,' the overseer corrected sternly. 'When the girl left, the client was laughing and joking—'

'Teasing her about her freckles, my friend said—'

'Exactly. And when the girl returned two hours later . . . well, it was just one of those things. However,' the Sarmatian woman sniffed, 'you mustn't blame the treatment, her heart simply stopped beating.'

'It happens,' the redhead added with a philosophical shrug.

'Just not here?'

'Pylades felt the tragedy could only damage Atlantis,' the supervisor sniffed, 'and I for one believe he was absolutely right to hush it up – look what effect it's had on you, for a start! Wanting to come out halfway through – imagine!'

'I still do,' Claudia replied through gritted teeth. 'Would you fetch the nutcracker?'

'Nonsense, dear,' the Sarmatian woman tutted. 'Another hour and you'll laugh about this. Come along.'

Taking the redhead by the elbow, the pair of them departed deaf to Claudia's impassioned pleas, her threats, her curses.

Finally, with only swirling steam for company and a few ghostly gurgles from the pipes, Claudia felt the first faint flutterings of panic.

Dammit, I have to get out. She elbowed, she kicked, she used her shoulders, knees, she squirmed, she heaved, but the bloody mud wouldn't shift. Not one tiny crack had appeared. For the first time since she'd slipped from her mother's womb, Claudia Seferius lay absolutely helpless.

Except that here, in the cubicle, there were no warm and loving arms to scoop her into, no reassuring breast to suckle, no mother's voice to soothe.

Claudia was entirely alone.

Her heart pounded erratically, her breathing quickened. In desperation, she turned to the green curtain, but it was no longer Arcadia, where the sun always shone and goats chomped as the goatherd blew on a flute. It was a piece of cloth upon which some clever madam had stitched a scene or two, that was all. There was nothing restful about it, nothing reassuring, it was merely a sheet.

So why then, thumped her heart, wasn't the red curtain the same? Why not a two-dimensional portrayal of the siege of Troy on a single bolt of fabric? Look, there are the battlements, with Priam and his sons. There's the wooden horse, and down there the warships, while a dozen brave heroes slugged it out, she recognized Hector and Achilles, Ajax and Lysander. That, too, is simply a curtain!

But it wasn't. It was a reflection of the wrath of Sabbio

Tullus. Of some terrible, unnamed repercussion. Of Tarraco, whose boat was moored here the day young Cal was killed. Beads of sweat broke out on her forehead. Tarraco already had one tragedy behind him and now his second wife had disappeared. His second rich, middle-aged wife, to be precise. Lais, who had inherited all of Tuder's wealth with or without a certain Spaniard's connivance . . .

With a shudder, Claudia realized she knew absolutely nothing about this place or the people in it, yet in the space of three short days she had become aware of a huge and deadly shadow hovering over Atlantis. Cal was dead and so, according to Lavinia's gossip, were others.

A young mother last night in childbirth. The silversmith with the tumour. An orphan boy, whose cousin, as Lavinia pointed out, so fortuitously inherited. The woman who kept cats. The nightmare vision in Claudia's dream came back to haunt her. And then there was the woman who died, lying on one of these very slabs . . .

This is madness, she told herself. Wild imaginings born of helplessness! But instinct fought back. And instinct told her that, by meddling, her own life might be in jeopardy . . .

What was that?

The hairs on her scalp began to prickle. Footsteps. Heavy. Male. Like drumbeats in a sinister play, they grew louder with each rhythmic beat. Closer. Closer . . .

Claudia stopped breathing. Please pass by. Sweet Jupiter in heaven, make them pass by.

The footsteps grew louder, and Claudia thought of Pul, his bulging pectorals, his shining skull with just that stupid topknot on the poll. She pictured that tight leather vest, straining from heavy musculature. The curved blade on his hip—

Holy shit, Pul wouldn't need a weapon. He'd use a pillow, to hold over her face. No screams, no struggles. Just – what was the phrase that oh-so-homely Sarmatian woman used? *Her heart would stop beating.*

Like a white heifer to the sacrificial block, Claudia had allowed herself to be led to this chamber and imprisoned in a rigid coffin . . . and now she might pay the ultimate price for stupidity. Panic beat in her chest. I don't want to die. Mighty Mars, help me! Please don't let me die. She remembered how Pul's almond eyes had followed her as she conversed with Dorcan after Cal's funeral, had pinpointed her with hostility as she talked with Kamar at the Agonalia. Always around, always watchful. From the moment she'd first clapped eyes on him, Claudia had known Pul was evil . . .

The footsteps stopped, and now Claudia could only hear the terrible pounding of her blood in her ears. He was outside her cubicle. Waiting. For what? In her mind, she saw his monstrous walrus moustache lifting in a blood-thinning smile as he plumped the pillow he'd pulled from under her head . . .

Sweet Jupiter.

A brown hand closed round the curtain at the end of the cubicle. Brown on blue. They would be the last colours she ever saw in this life—

Slowly the hand drew back the drape.

XIX

Claudia opened her mouth and screamed. There was nothing subtle about the sound, it was a bug-scrunching, ear-splitting, milk-curdling yell which would have reached as far south as the Libyan deserts and north to the rugged homelands of the Scythians who'd invented this bloody treatment, may they rot with scrofulous sores. She squinted up her eyes, her nose, her entire face and she screamed. She screamed until her lungs were on fire. Until her tonsils were raw. Until, in fact, a whole platoon of attendants came running.

'Mighty Earth Mother, what's wrong?' gasped the Sarmatian supervisor. 'Are you in pain, dear?'

'It was a spider,' an amused baritone explained. 'A big, hairy black thing which scuttled over her neck, but she's fine now. I er –' he lowered his voice to confide '– squashed it.'

Tittering broke out behind the curtains and Claudia dared not unscrew her eyes. She knew – she bloody knew – that Sarmatian cow would be laughing at her. Her and a dozen others! She waited until the women clopped off.

'Orbilio, you bastard!' Her lungs were down to a burning wheeze. 'What the hell are you doing here?'

'There's no segregation in the treatment area,' he said amiably. 'I mean, who could make improper advances to a sarcophagus? Indeed,' narrowed eyes capered the length of her mudpack and his mouth turned down at the edges, 'who'd want to?'

She'd skin him. Flay him alive and then fly his hide as a kite.

'I was not crying rape!' she protested through tightly gritted teeth – and immediately realized her error. Perhaps, with luck, he was too busy sniggering to notice?

'You weren't, were you?'

Damn.

Orbilio leaned over, leaving her in no doubt that he had not misread the terror etched on her face when he pulled back the drapes. Watching a pulse beat at his neck and with the smell of his sandalwood unguent tingling down her throat, she waited for him to ask, 'Who were you scared of, Claudia? Who did you think I was just now?'

Goes to show the scrambled state of your brains, you silly bitch! It sounded utterly preposterous, even to herself, to admit that she'd cowered in fear of her life from a total stranger with whom she'd exchanged not so much as a nod! Claudia sent a silent prayer of thanks to Jupiter that thoughts weren't as easily communicated as words put down on parchment.

Marcus straightened up and hooked a stool across with his toe. Another time, the scrape of wood on tile would have set Claudia's teeth on edge. Right now, she didn't even notice.

'Why won't you trust me?' he asked quietly.

'Who says I don't?' she said. 'Last night I slept in that wide double couch you so magnanimously paid for and you made no assault on my virtue.'

Orbilio rested one booted foot on the stool and grinned. 'If that's a complaint . . .'

Claudia's mouth twisted at one corner, while her mind heaved a sigh of relief. Not only was he no mindreader, he hadn't picked up on her mistake. She'd implied, over breakfast, her night had been spent with Tarraco—

'Claudia,' he sighed, leaning his weight upon the bent knee, 'we've played mind games long enough. Isn't it about time you came clean with me?'

'But my dear Marcus, I shall. The instant this shell is cracked off.'

The quip fell short of its mark. 'Would it speed our weary progress,' he suggested carefully, 'to know I'm aware of your involvement with Sabbio Tullus?'

Claudia heard something crack, and had a feeling it was her optimism, not the mud coffin.

'What did you take from his strongroom? Uh-uh.' Orbilio held up a hand. 'The truth, please. How much did you steal?'

'The –' gulp '– truth?'

'The truth.'

Claudia's eyes followed the plumes of steam coiling round the ceiling and noticed that lamps had been lit to counteract the twilight. 'Three hundred.'

'What else?'

'All right, three thousand, but you can tell Tullus I intend to pay back every single quadran come the end of the month. I've just had a cash flow problem with that consignment of wine to Armenia – Orbilio, are you listening?'

Never mind Armenia, his mind seemed to have wandered to the Libyan desert. 'Yes. Yes, of course I am.'

The eyes refocused and a sharp light hovered round the edges of his pupils. 'You're saying it was only money you stole?'

'Borrowed,' she corrected sternly. 'You know what it's like, a poor young widow struggling to remain in business when every merchant in Rome is trying to edge her out – what else did you imagine I ran off with?'

Something about the set of his face suggested it wasn't Tullus' jewels or a rare piece of artwork Supersnoop was worried about. Orbilio bridged his fingers. 'Who told you there was a weakness in the wall of Tullus' depository?'

Claudia thought of telling him she'd noticed a looseness round the stonework some time back in the winter, but his face was steeled and unforgiving, and right now he was every inch the Security Police. Whose function, as if she needed any reminding, was to protect both Emperor and Empire! Not a physical bodyguard like the Praetorians, Marcus Cornelius Orbilio belonged to a small and élite corps of men whose job it was to root out fraud, extortion, treason, forgery – in fact any crime which might undermine the foundations of this new and precarious epoch in Roman history. At the moment, Augustus was without legal heir, and whilst this issue was high on the political agenda, nothing concrete had yet been resolved by way of a legitimate (cynics might say acceptable) appointment.

Suddenly Claudia began to feel very, very cold.

'The architect,' she replied, in a voice so croaky she hoped he'd attribute it to the after-effect of her scream. You stupid, stupid cow! You were set up from the outset! 'He . . . owed me a favour.'

'I thought as much.' Marcus stood up and began to

pace around the cubicle, stroking his jaw in thought. 'Are you aware,' he said finally, 'that the day after Tullus reported the break-in, the architect's body was found in a back alley? His throat had been cut, his purse and rings were missing, but frankly I don't buy the robbery theory.'

Claudia concentrated on the lamplight making gold out of the silver plumes of steam, because she was unable to cover her ears.

'I suspect the architect was an unwitting pawn, the same as you were, although I doubt we'll ever know the reason for *his* involvement. Blackmail, probably. How did he seem when he imparted the secret of Tullus' strongroom?'

'Edgy,' she admitted, remembering a few weeks back when the architect had been walking towards her, wrapped round a girl younger than his granddaughter. Please don't tell my wife, he begged. Let's meet and see if I can't repay the favour . . . Suddenly, everything fell into place! His nervousness had nothing to do with his wife finding out, hell, the whole wretched business was a stage set start to finish, the girl no doubt a common streetwalker. And to think Claudia had actually congratulated herself on wheedling out of him the information about that loose brick at the back of the depository! 'Why me?' she asked.

'Nothing personal,' Marcus said, sucking in his cheeks. 'Anyone short of cash and willing to take a risk would have fitted the bill! You see,' he sat down again and crossed his legs, 'a robbery had to take place and it was imperative Tullus caught the thief in the act.'

'Codswallop,' Claudia scoffed. 'I chose the day, the date, the time—'

'Did you?' A smile played around the corner of his

mouth. 'I'm willing to bet that, when you think back over the conversation with the architect, he let slip something along the lines of such-and-such a day is always quiet, especially around dawn – ah.' He nodded smugly. 'I see this is starting to ring a bell with Mistress Seferius.'

'All right, Cleverclogs, so the idea was planted, but I still don't understand. Someone with a beef against Sabbio Tullus set me up to deplete his fortune—'

'Wrong. Tullus is a wealthy man, you'd have to make a hundred trips to empty even half his coffers. No, no, they were after something far more precious than gold or silver, and it didn't belong to Tullus. It was his nephew's property they were after.'

Who happened to be related, however distantly, to the Emperor's wife. Brilliant, Claudia! Absolutely brilliant. Now it's treason good and proper.

'Then why involve a third party?' she asked. 'Surely it would make more sense to sneak in and sneak out, then cement the stone back in place?'

'Because,' Orbilio said, cracking his knuckles in satisfaction, 'it was vital Tullus caught the thief red-handed and drew attention to the robbery. The nephew, you see, had to be made aware of the break-in so that when he checked his casket, he found an empty space inside.'

'Instead of what, exactly?' she asked, and received only a vague gurgling from the back of his throat in reply. 'All right, why not send him a letter, informing him of the theft?'

'Because the theft had to be publicized. It was important that as many people as possible knew that Tullus' strongroom had been turned over.'

Claudia's brain was starting to hurt. 'I don't suppose

you'd care to tell me the reason,' she said wearily, although she already knew what his response would be. Several minutes ticked past, when neither of them spoke, then Claudia said, 'I was supposed to get caught, wasn't I?'

'By the time you'd been arrested, brought to trial, etc, etc, etc, the real scent would have gone cold—'

'Whose scent?'

'But whether you were caught or not, I suspect they'd already taken what they wanted, probably earlier, during the night—'

'Orbilio, you miserable sod, will you please tell me who?'

'Claudia, if I knew that, I wouldn't be here and neither would you—' He broke off suddenly, as his implication became clear.

'And just why wouldn't I be here, Marcus?' Claudia asked sweetly. Not only would she skin him alive and fly his hide as a kite, she'd make a rope of his chitterlings and drag him round the Empire on the end of it!

'Oh.' At least he had the grace to blush. 'Well – I thought that if I took the heat off you in Rome by booking this break in Atlantis, you er—'

No, Marcus Cornelius. *You* erred. 'Yes?' she prompted.

'You might help me on a case,' he finished feebly. 'You see, I'm only on a short leave of absence—' he began, but Claudia cut him short.

'Typical! When the going gets tough, the toffs get going! Well, do I have news for you! Because if you imagined that, in taking the heat off by whisking me away to Atlantis, you'd have me reeling in gratitude, you were way off course, Marcus Cornelius. To then have the gall to expect said gratitude to manifest itself in the form of my doing your dirty work for you is nothing less than an insult.' Why did it rankle, she wondered, that he hadn't just helped her out for its own sake? 'There are many things,' she hissed, 'I stand accused of, but being a copper's nark isn't one of them. Now get out, before I have you thrown out.'

XX

When Marcus Cornelius staggered out of the tavern by the basilica, he'd already lost count of the number of wine shops whose fare he had sampled so far.

Dammit, he thought his plan was foolproof!

Around him, the Agonalia had reached fever pitch. Men covered in fleeces wearing rams' horns on their heads chased bleating young maidens (and some not so young) round the streets, cheap wines flowed from the fountains, the beat of the music was sensual, loud and hypnotic. Some might even say manic. He spiked his fingers through his hair. Goddammit, he'd spent a fortune on Atlantis, none of which he could reclaim in legitimate expenses, in order to advance his bloody career prospects, and what happens? Sod all's what happens!

So much for the Great Pyramid of a case to lay before his boss.

No case.

No excuse for deserting his post outside the Imperial Palace.

Mother of Tarquin, it seemed so straightforward, back in Rome. Because he liked to keep tabs on a certain little firebrand, he'd picked up on the fact that Claudia's name was linked with the Tullus strongroom robbery and he hadn't been taken in for one second with that malarkey about respectable widows not being involved in common smash-and-grabs! This was right up her street, she was as guilty as hell, and he knew it.

On the other hand, he was also aware of darker forces moving in the background. Precisely who was behind it, he couldn't say, but whatever Claudia might stoop to, treason wouldn't enter her equation. And since he had a problem to resolve here . . . The letter purporting to be from an old friend seemed ideal.

Why, though? Why wouldn't she help him for once? Was that too bloody much to ask for, after he'd shelled out a fortune to bring her up to Atlantis? Croesus, he was sleeping in a bloody garret! Had she no heart?

He stumbled into another tavern. Of course she had a heart, he'd heard it beating once. Right under her left breast, and he'd seen that naked once as well. He thumped his fist for a refill. Janus, that woman drove him wild! She had a temper which could set off an earthquake; jousting with her was better than sex.

Marcus felt a stirring in his loins as he fought his way through the crush of the tavern into the screeching multitudes outside. *What the hell would it be like, then, making love to a woman like that?* Heaven. Hell. Torment. Pain. Tumult—

Wasn't there something he was supposed to do this evening?

Orbilio dismissed the niggle in his head and imagined instead what it must be like when the hunter finally won the spoils. He imagined burying his head in that wild tumble of curls, knowing it would smell of spicy, feisty, balsam perfume, and imagined the taste of her skin. Hot and slightly salty from her sweat. In his mind, he pictured himself standing behind her, nuzzling the back of her neck with his lips as his fingers loosed the ribbons which fastened her gown. In his mind, he could hear the soft swish of cotton as it caressed her skin on its way to the floor. In his mind—

'Marcus.'

In his dreams! He turned to find the well-upholstered Phoebe bearing down upon him, her arms open wide to embrace him, stretching the seams across her ample breasts to bursting point, and the part of him that stiffened wasn't the part she would have wished.

'Marcus, where did you sneak off to after breakfast, you naughty boy?'

'I—' His mind was a blank as he tried to extricate himself from this human boa constrictor. Surely there was something he ought to be doing? Something official?

'Such fun, this rustic little festival,' she purred, frogmarching him towards a group of drunken revellers. 'They're playing rams and rustlers,' she trilled. 'Which will you be? A ram?' She nudged his ribs. 'Or would you prefer to rustle me?'

Orbilio forced what he hoped was a laugh, although he had a sneaking suspicion that any neutral bystander would have mistaken it for water swirling down a drain. 'I have a prior engagement—'

'Nonsense,' a female voice rang in his ear. 'Marcus would love to wrestle, sorry rustle you.'

Where the hell did she spring from! 'Claudia—' he pleaded under his breath.

He didn't think she heard, because she beamed a radiant smile upon the lovely Phoebe. 'He finds it so tiresome being a *ram* all the time!' With that, he found himself pushed headlong into the crowd, who yelled 'Hooray!' and clapped him so hard on the back, his knees buckled and Marcus was not surprised that, by the time he'd staggered free, Claudia Seferius had become invisible once more.

'One quick game, then,' he muttered. He wished now he hadn't got pissed so quickly, he knew he ought to be doing something else.

If only he could remember.

In the end, Marcus competed in three more bouts before the prearranged meeting with Dorcan flashed back, and then he couldn't find Tuder's bloody mausoleum.

Shit.

Away from the light of torches, bonfires and upper-storey windows, the cemetery lay engulfed in blackness and twice he stubbed his toe on the jutting steps of the tombs in his effort to locate the banker's memorial.

'Dorcan?' he called softly. 'Are you there?'

Numbed by the city wall, the revelling had been reduced to a vague and distant hum, but it was more noise than the graveyard's occupants were used to. Perhaps he hadn't called loud enough?

'Dorcan? It's me, Orbilio!'

Nothing.

He looked up at the sky, hazy from the sultry heat even at night, and felt a trickle of perspiration run down his neck. Time passed. Once a rat scuttled through the long grass, making a sound like water trickling through a sluice gate, and twice an owl hooted from far down the road, but other than that, Marcus remained alone with just the taste of stale wine for company.

After dark, the old fraud had said. Well, this was certainly after dark!

Settling down with his back against the travertine stone, warm from the rays of the sun, Orbilio sighed and crossed his legs at the ankles, letting his rapidly sobering mind juggle his impressions of this town and its neighbour, Atlantis. Into the air went the roles played by such luminaries as Pylades the Greek; that vinegar-faced Etruscan physician; Tarraco, who had so smoothly usurped the place of the man Marcus now rested against, both on his island and in his bed.

There were other factors, too, to toss in the air and juggle with. Lais, for example. A key player, yet Lais had disappeared without a trace. A man called Pul, a monster of a man in all respects. Not to mention the military, whose representation was so minor as to appear almost imaginary!

So many odd-shaped pieces, Orbilio was reminded of that old Egyptian puzzle consisting of several three-dimensional blocks of wood which, whilst appearing mismatched, when stacked correctly locked together to form a perfect pyramid.

That's what he had here. Separate clues that did not seem as though they'd ever fit together to form a whole, and yet he was sure they did. Somehow or other, he was bloody certain that they did! His problem lay in making sense of the jumble and this is where Dorcan fitted in. The big man always knew how many beans made five. His livelihood depended on it.

So, alas, did Orbilio's. He cracked his knuckles in

impatience. His boss's reply would probably be on its way, though how much leave of absence he would grant him was another matter – and time, Orbilio felt sure, was running out.

'Dorcan?'

He whistled, but no answering whistle returned, although once or twice he thought he saw a figure flitting between the tombs, but the burly giant it was not.

Folding his hands behind his head, Orbilio closed his eyes and felt that same warm glow roll over him as he considered a whole host of reasons why, despite all the obstacles in his way, he was still glad he'd hooked himself to Claudia Seferius' wagon once again. He was definitely making headway in that direction! Another three hundred years and she might, yet, open her heart to him as already she had opened her mind . . .

The scream woke him, and although he didn't think he'd been asleep, the haze had cleared and a thousand stars twinkled up above him, he could clearly make out the Great Bear, the Lyre and the Dragon. But the scream was not human and when the vixen called a second time, he shook his head and instantly regretted it. The wine had begun to take effect, the old bean was pounding like a pestle in a mortar. Groaning, he rubbed the stiffness back into his cramped muscles before shambling to his feet. His left leg had not so much gone to sleep as fallen into a possibly quite fatal coma, and he feared his head might shortly follow suit.

Through the open doors of the triple-arch gateway, fires burned low. No lamps burned in the windows, no torches lit up street corners. Every living soul but he was in bed and that, he concluded ruefully, included the charlatan.

Stepping over a drunkard in the Forum as he made his way back to his roach-ridden rented garret, Orbilio heard the snicker of a horse and exchanged a tight-lipped greeting with the fat man who was heaving himself into the saddle.

The fat man smelled of cardamom.

XXI

As the pitiless rays of dawn burrowed under eyelids rich and poor, groans rippled out like nibbling fish. Some were minnows, some were monsters – few were spared. Coots which yesterday emitted gentle, subdued honks had acquired trumpets in the night and the tree crickets preferred clashing cymbals to rasping their back legs together. In the town, in the villages, in farmsteads all around Lake Plasimene, faces ranging in colour from soapstone yellow to tundra grey squinted in unimagined agony as the light grew remorselessly brighter and spared not one repentant reveller. And boy, were they repentant! Never again, begged their churning stomachs. Never again, promised ermine-covered tongues.

'Morning, Phoebe!' Claudia trilled to the girl struggling into consciousness beneath a marble caryatid in the Athens Canal. By her side an empty goblet lay overturned, and a wine bowl bobbed among the swans in the water.

'Please!' Phoebe groaned. 'Not so loud!' Her hair was dishevelled, the kohl around her eyes smudged and her gown, where it wasn't stretched to bursting point, revealed a plump but shapely thigh. 'Oh lord, that late?' she asked, squinting at the sun. 'I must have passed out.'

'Good night, then?'

The dark-eyed beauty giggled. 'Hope so.' She was

swaying on her feet as she straightened her crumpled robe. 'Unfortunately, I don't remember much after that game of strip chequers in the Forum.'

Quite! Claudia had spent many hours last night wandering round Spesium, analysing the revels of the Agonalia. As the hours progressed, the merrymaking had grown ever more raucous, with behaviour bordering on the manic. Dorcan was wrong, way off course. Last night's debauchery was not born out of fear of the plague. This level of intensity – as though every day must be lived as the last – went far deeper than that.

As Phoebe tottered off, Claudia explored the little domed loggia, whose recent occupants seemed to have left in such a hurry. A plate of still-warm buns wafted their tantalizing aroma across the open veranda, and a jug of what looked like sherbet hadn't been touched. The reason, of course, might be connected with the cat curled up on one of the chairs.

'Well done, Drusilla.' Claudia sank her teeth into a spicy raisin bun. 'I was in need of a quiet place to think.'

And where better? Thanks to huge leaps in technology, domes had become a part of modern architecture, and this dome, being small, required support from just eight stone piers. Each had been exquisitely painted to represent an Olympian deity – Jupiter, symbolized by his famous thunderbolt and acorns from his sacred oak, his consort, Juno, represented by birch and geese and marigolds. Claudia did not think the Queen of Light would object to taking her weight while she polished off a second bun.

Did the sky seem a different colour today, a hint of cloud, perhaps, on the horizon? Or was that purely wishful thinking? According to the archivists, this was the longest heatwave on record, and whilst several historians disputed the claim, citing at least five previous hot Mays, two within a hundred years, on one point everyone agreed. When the rains came, no one would be sorry! Irrigation of crops was proving a constant headache, requiring more and more field hands working longer and longer hours. Live-stock, too, became restless in a heat which spawned worm and intestinal parasites, while for wine producers, like herself—

'Our bailiff's a good man, Drusilla,' Claudia told the dozing cat. 'He manages the vineyard exceptionally well, only—'

'Brrr?'

'The problem is this.' Claudia prised herself off Juno and flung an arm loosely round Venus. 'Despite knowing everything there is to know about a vine,' put simply, the man was a genius, 'and despite having full managerial control over the estate, he never takes a decision without checking first with me.' (As if she'd know!)

'Mrrrrp.'

'Fine for you to say don't worry.' Claudia traced a finger round one of Venus' holy swans. 'Suppose I were to tell you that if we don't get a decent crop of grapes this year, the whole business goes under?' She was hanging on by her fingernails as it was. 'I'm afraid that unless this drought is handled properly, both you and I'll be grovelling for fishheads in the gutter by September.'

'Mrrr. Mrrr-mrrr.'

'You think so?' Claudia examined a painted garland of April flowers, symbolic of the month which came under Venus' custody. 'You really think the bailiff will take these decisions on his own?' She had an idea he was supposed to raise duststorms to shade the roots from the relentless rays of the sun – but suppose he *wasn't* whipping up great clouds of soil? Suppose he was sitting up at the estate, anxiously awaiting authorization from the mistress . . .?

I'm hanging round the wrong damned pillar, Claudia thought. I need Father Vulcan! For a horrid moment it occurred to her that there were twelve Olympian deities and only eight bloody pillars, but praise be to Jupiter, the patron of September, the protector of blacksmiths and the god who also happened to have the vine sacred to his holy personage wasn't one of those who'd been left out! Claudia flung both arms around the fire god and planted a kiss on the pier, right between a bunch of green grapes and a bunch of red.

'You won't let me go bankrupt?' she begged. 'You'll watch over my vineyard?'

But it was not like when, as a child, she flung herself around her father's knees, to be swept in the air and twirled round and round as she nuzzled against his whiskery chin. Slowly, foolishly, Claudia drew away from the pillar. No enlightenment, no whispered words of reassurance, no spiritual comfort ever came from a pile of stupid stonework. Just the filthy taste of paint on your lips. She looked out across Plasimene, where the hills danced in a shimmering blue reflection, and realized it was not just the lake which was hazy today. There was something in her eye, making it water, and she had the sudden urge to travel far beyond those hills and to keep on travelling. Over the Apennines to the turquoise Aegean, where ships sailed for Dalmatia, Egypt, to Cyprus. Or she could take the road north, cross the Alps to Noricum, Raetia, Germanica, see for herself the lands of sparkling rivers and spectacular cascades . . . Oh shit! Whatever was in her eye started aggravating further.

'Mrrrrow?'

Claudia buried her head in Drusilla's soft warm fur, and saw a small child waving her father off to war and never coming home. She saw the child's mother, sliding into an alcoholic spiral until one day it all became too much for her and she left the child an orphan . . .

'You're right, poppet,' noisily, Claudia blew her nose, 'running away won't solve anything.' Heaven knows, she'd tried it enough in the past twelve sodding years . . .

Kissing the cat between the ears, she helped herself to a goblet of sherbet redolent of wild woodland strawberries and found it surprisingly refreshing. Refilling the cup, Claudia carried it and the jug over to the rail, but this time when she looked across the water, no enticing hand of adventure beckoned. The lake was merely a swimming pool for fish, a place for waterbirds and reeds, where men scratched a living fowling and fishing and farming oysters in the shallows. As her gaze moved inwards from the perimeter, it fell on the wooded hump of Tuder's island and more unbidden pictures tumbled through her mind. Peacocks. The villa. A line of tall cypresses with a marble seat which overlooked the lake. The colossus, who sings to his mother, the dawn.

'You see,' a Spanish voice echoed through the halls of her memory.

The hell I will, you conniving, cocky bastard! The hell I'll see the dawn in with you!

As she spun away, her elbow caught the jug of straw-berry sherbet, tipping it over the side. Bugger! Several seconds seemed to pass before Claudia heard the crash, and yet the sound was not as muffled as she expected. Craning her neck, she realized she was overlooking a thicket of willows and alder. Of course! This was where the tunnel disgorged on to the foreshore.

'Great Jupiter in heaven, do you know what that means?'

But Drusilla had drifted into a deep, paw-twitching sleep and Claudia was forced to confine her conclusions to herself. Which was a pity, because she'd like to have told Drusilla how easily she and Cal could have been overheard as they stood at the mouth of the passageway . . .

So what? the cat would have said. You didn't exactly swap state secrets. Cal, Drusilla would have reminded her, had been behaving like any young buck with a pretty girl to impress – it was sex on his mind that afternoon, not mischief-making.

'You're right,' Claudia told the sleeping cat, relieved the theory tied in with that old jealous husband angle. Of a man spurred into frenzy by Cal's seduction of a young widow while the boy still dallied with the man's wife—

On the other hand, thought Claudia, sipping at the remaining glass of sherbet, his voice had been unnaturally loud. Brash, she put it down to at the time. But suppose it had been a veiled threat, deliberately intended for the ears of someone he knew would be up here . . .? Rubbish! She crumbled a bun for a dozen eager sparrows. Claudia had seen for herself how deserted this resort became at siesta time! No, she was barking up the wrong alder trunk by imagining there'd been any significance in the possibility that their conversation might have been overheard.

Tossing down the last corner of the bun, she began to

pace the circular loggia and let her thoughts turn over more pressing matters, because, ghastly as the idea might seem, the prospect of collaborating with Supersnoop needed serious consideration. Until now, she'd assumed it was the theft of some distant imperial relative's money that had rattled the authorities, but now it seemed they were after something else. What? What could be so important that its theft needed to be made public? Why should Sabbio Tullus be set up the same way as Claudia had? The same way, in fact, as the architect who'd had his throat slit down some back alley in an incident which may or may not have been murder!

Claudia admitted it was pure speculation, but suppose someone (let's call him X) had been alerted to the fact that Tullus' nephew had a piece of paper in his possession. Was X being blackmailed on account of this incriminating evidence? Hardly, or he'd want the whole thing hushed up. The very fact that the robbery must come to light suggested the sequence of events was:

1. (Claudia ticked them off on her fingers.) X blackmails the architect into finding a way into the strongroom.
2. A suitable dupe is selected – and no prizes for guessing which silly bitch they chose!
3. X (or X's agent) plants in Tullus' head the need to take his silver with him to Frascati for 'security' purposes.
4. An elaborate scene is staged between the architect and Claudia and some young streetwalker, resulting in Claudia shimmying in through the loosened brickwork a few days later at the very time Tullus 'decides' to make his withdrawal.
5. Meanwhile, X knows Tullus sufficiently well to predict

he'll scream bloody murder at the outrage (or maybe that reaction also has been planted) and, because of the nephew's imperial connections, X also knows the army will become involved.

6. However! This is where Claudia's formative years spent fending for herself in backstreet slums stand her in good stead. Unexpectedly for X, she escapes.

Claudia puffed out her cheeks. *So what?* Had Tullus caught her red-handed, it would very quickly have become apparent that the nephew's property wasn't on her person – and if she didn't have it, where was it? No, on point No. 6 she was wrong. The patsy had been *meant* to escape, leaving the army with a whole score of leads to follow up, possible accomplices to run to ground, absorbing so much time that, as Orbilio said, the real thief's scent would have gone blissfully stale.

What she didn't understand, however, was why. Why make the robbery public? If this document was so damned hot – aha! Suppose that by broadcasting the fact that Tullus had been robbed, it sabotaged the nephew's plans in some way? The seed began to take root. Surely, then, the logical follow-on must be that by making the robbery hot gossip, the nephew was incapacitated, which meant . . . Which meant . . .

Which meant Claudia had absolutely no idea.

Hang on! Yes, she did. It meant X now held the balance of power, the only threat to which lay with the nephew . . . who could do sod all about it, because he wasn't supposed to have it in the first place!

Gotcha!

Claudia gulped down the last of the sherbet. All

Orbilio need do now is work out who X is and life was hunky-dory once again, she could repay that little loan, maybe treat Tullus to a toga, calm him down, and whoopee, life was back on course. Terrific. She clapped her hands. Case closed. And Supersnoop can shove his wretched tit-for-tat!

In celebration, she twirled round and round the pillar until she made herself and Apollo quite dizzy, and it was only when she stopped reeling that she became aware of just how much sound did carry upwards from below.

'Marcus Cornelius Orbilio?' a puzzled voice echoed, setting Claudia's ears aflap. Down on the path, a dispatch rider, his hair plastered down with sweat and his tunic clinging in dark patches to his back and armpits, was holding out a letter to a shrugging lackey. 'Never heard of 'im,' the servant said.

Oh, but I have . . .

'Yoo-hoo!' Claudia waved both arms to catch the rider's attention. 'Up here,' she trilled. 'But don't bother to fetch the letter up, you look like you're in need of a rest. I'll nip down and fetch it.'

'We-ell.' The courier was torn between duty and the prospect of a bath. 'My orders,' he called back, 'are to hand this over personally. Do you know where I can find him?'

'Oh, I'll see he gets it,' Claudia assured him, with a comforting wave of her hand. 'I'm his wife.'

XXII

For a new town rising from a grassy plain beside a lake, Spesium was taking no prisoners, Marcus noticed. Even in this searing heat and with crippling hangovers all round, craftsmen went doggedly about their business, the silver-smiths and cobblers, the carpenters and fullers. But then that's country life, he supposed, sauntering down the main street past the temple. Cows still needed to be milked, that milk needed to be sold, and the same applied to eggs and fruit and meat. Nevertheless, Dorcan's stall was not among those set up in the Forum, neither could Orbilio find the bearded charlatan in any of the taverns or the lodging houses. The big man obviously had more sense than the locals and was taking a long lie-in.

Behind the Temple of Spes, tantalizing aromas from the baker's oven overlaid the smell of dust and dryness, tempting Marcus to part at a corner shop with a brass sesterce in exchange for a pudding of cinnamon and nutmeg deep fried in olive oil and smothered in honey.

He had noticed in the gateway to Atlantis, a poster advertising a foot race in the grounds this afternoon. No doubt Dorcan would be drawn by the hoards willing to hand over silver in exchange for a genuine shell of swan's egg from which Helen of Troy had been hatched. Clearly the giant's information wasn't urgent, or he'd have sent a message suggesting an alternative meeting point. Orbilio would simply have to wait.

With his fingers and chin sticky from the pudding, he was making his way towards the pawnbroker's to wash up when who should come his way? None other than the Spaniard, with his long, dark hair and fancy clothes. Something speared at his gut when he thought about this self-styled stud sucking up to Claudia. Mother of Tarquin, what did she see in him? Yet the professional in Orbilio could not help but admire the professional in Tarraco. Slow, orchestrated movements, designed to show off every well-worked muscle. That well-practised half-glance, expressions veiled by the fall of long hair. On impulse, he stepped in front of the Spaniard and blocked his way.

'Are you down for the foot race?'

'Me?' The Spaniard gave an insolent shrug. 'I never compete.'

Like the half-glance, the half-smile, even his words were spartan. Doled out sparingly, designed to add to the enigma and mystique. Orbilio bunched his fist, but resisted the urge to rearrange the long, straight nose in front of him.

'Then the race is mine,' he said cheerfully. 'To the winner –' he shot a wicked grin over his shoulder, to where Atlantis perched on the promontory '– the spoils.'

Tarraco's eyes narrowed and colour suffused his cheeks. 'You?' he sneered, but the tendons in his neck stood out like bowlines on a merchant ship. 'No chance.' Dark eyes flashed a glance at the rock before travelling with contemptuous slowness over the drips of cinnamon and honey on Orbilio's patrician tunic, his sticky hands and mouth. 'I beat you by a furlong.'

'You're on,' replied Marcus, rubbing his hands together in glee. 'Until this afternoon, then – and be sure to give Lais my love.'

Furrows formed between the Spaniard's eyebrows. 'You know Lais?'

'Never met her in my life,' Marcus said. 'Just wanted to give her my love, seeing as how any old bod round here can,' and leaving Tarraco smouldering in fury, he ambled down Quince Lane and turned left past the grainstore, where the presence of a ginger tomcat washing on the top step of the entrance could not have sent a louder signal to the rats.

Arrogant bastard, he thought. Marries one middle-aged woman, Virginia, who conveniently drowns in the lake and what does he do? Not content with one fortune, he courts Tuder's wife. Such was the isolation of that wretched island, Orbilio had not been able to establish whether Tuder had died before Tarraco came on the scene or afterwards, but it was a curious coincidence that both Tuder and Virginia were dead – and that Lais had subsequently disappeared.

And if there was one thing guaranteed to make an investigator's hackles rise, it was the word coincidence. Like vampires and werewolves, he was an emphatic non-believer!

Further down the street, warehouses gave way to high-rise tenements, where babies bawled through open windows, fathers argued with growing sons and wives scolded errant husbands. Irrespective of the fact that he had not come to Atlantis to investigate a dead banker (or his widow!), Orbilio decided he would not consider his visit wasted if, when he left, a certain Spanish gigolo lay rotting in a jail awaiting trial . . .

Surprisingly, the pawnbroker's shopfront was shuttered and he was forced to make a tortuous detour round the back of the tenement, through the building and out the back, to where the sun rarely penetrated and across a yard criss-crossed with limp wet washing, and not for the first time he thanked Jupiter for his privileged upbringing. For the piped water which flushed his drains. For there being no question of *his* mother fetching water from a standpipe down the street and emptying night soil on the middens! Remus, from the yard it was difficult to tell one apartment from another – which was the pawnbroker's? Which tiny window in the roof marked out his own rented garret? On one of the narrow stone steps, a stout squab of a woman sobbed into the hem of her tunic, revealing calves too meaty to warrant further interest and it was therefore with a ripple of revulsion that Orbilio recognized the pawnbroker's wife.

'Oh, sir, it's you!' She made an effort to pull herself together in the presence of nobility.

'Here.' Orbilio held out a handkerchief, which would have cost more than her coarse woollen tunic and cheap leather sandals put together. 'Is – is there some way I can help?' Her face was swollen and blotchy, her eyes puffy and red, and any fool could see this was not a question of some minor mishap or a squabble with her husband.

'No, sir,' she sniffed. 'No, sir, there ain't.' She scrubbed her eyes with the velvety cotton.

He peered at this allegory of despair. 'Maybe you'd just like to talk?'

'We-ell.' The woman bit her lower lip. 'I don't suppose

you'd have heard about that trouble down the smokery . . .?'

'I gather the couple had an argument resulting in a spot of damage—'

'Is that the word that's been put out? A row? Well, what about the baby, eh? How did they pass *that* one off?' She blew her nose like a conch shell. 'That lad's shed was reduced to firewood, his stock ruined, and you can take it from me, sir, that weren't no row. A gang of thugs ripped that place apart. And the tragedy that resulted, that poor bairn's death, that was nothing short of bloody murder and if you ask me, they should be crucified, those villains, right there on the lakeside for what they put that young couple through and we'll be next, I know we will, if we don't cough up the extra every month!'

A tingle shot through Orbilio's veins. The tingle he always experienced whenever his pick hit a rich stream of gold ore. Kicking aside a cabbage stalk, he squeezed beside the beefcake on the step.

'I think,' he said slowly, 'you'd better tell me the whole story start to finish.'

Across the other side of Spesium, a fat bluebottle buzzed around the rooftops. She'd been attracted by an appetizing smell, and this wasn't just offcuts of offal thrown into the gutter or the remnants of an unwanted pie. Curious, the bluebottle headed for the window on the fourth floor of the apartment block.

The shutters were latched together, but by crawling through the gap by the hinge, the fly could squeeze into the room which so attracted her. She was disappointed to find she wasn't the first. Hundreds of her relatives were already feasting and she was forced to buzz around the room to orientate herself to this unexpected situation.

Through her multi-lenses, she could see an open stove in the corner, clean and neat, the skillets and the ladles hanging tidily on the wall. An open trunk revealed cheap and faded but distinctly feminine attire, of a type worn by girls who plied their trade in brothels. Nothing there for a fly on a mission! She circled the footstool then the table, which had been wiped too thoroughly to be of any interest. Ah, that's better. All those scented pots and potions in a trunk inside the door, and a strange collection of curios to boot, but the jumble of jars and phials only served to confuse the more appetizing aromas in the air. Including something which smelled like cardamom . . .

Now that's more like it! A bed. And beside the bed, in a small flat terracotta dish, a handful of coins. Payment for services rendered. And on the bed, a woman, lying naked. But the gash across her throat was obliterated by gorging flies making it impossible for the bluebottle to settle down and lay her eggs in it. She'd be nudged aside in no time!

Buzzing round the tiny room for inspiration, she realized with a start that the thing was so damned big, she'd missed it first time round! Wow! She circled round and round – so much choice! So much flesh for baby maggots to grow strong in!

Round and round she flew again, taking in the forward sprawl of the man's body, the face twisted in pain, until finally she settled on an area just south of the great bushy beard and, only when she was satisfied her precious eggs would not be disturbed, did the bluebottle move round to feast on the rivulets of dried blood.

Of course she could not get near the wound itself for companions who'd staked an earlier claim, but that didn't really matter. There was more than enough to go round on this giant of a man, and when she'd finished, she perched and cleaned herself quite happily on the metal flesh hook which protruded from his back.

'I've taken your advice,' Pylades said, 'and added in a foot race, plus there's a pageant organized for Thursday afternoon. After all –' his hand slipped under Claudia's elbow '– we don't want our guests to be bored.'

Bored? Surrounded by a rash of mysterious deaths, with the military on my back, a Spaniard after my money and bankruptcy a distinct possibility?

'I trust that's good news?' Pylades indicated the scroll in Claudia's hand and, as he steered her along the path towards the museum, insisting he show her personally his collection of marble busts, either Claudia was getting fatter or the Greek was moving closer.

'Merely a stuffy progress report from my bailiff,' she breezed, covering the distinctive heron seal with her thumb and wondering how the Head of Rome's Security Police might react to the news of his new appointment!

Across the glistening clear waters of the lake, grebe and dabchick dived for snails, and on the stone wall which ran along the path, a snake flicked out its tongue as it tasted the air.

'Whatever brought you to these sweet Etruscan hills, Pylades,' she said, keeping her gaze firmly on the bubbling cloudbank, 'you were very lucky to find a spring on this promontory.'

The hand under her elbow became rigid. 'Luck had nothing to do with it,' he replied.

'I'm sure it didn't.'

There was a moment's hesitation, a stumble in his step, then – 'Mosul tells me you haven't taken the waters yet,' he said smoothly. 'You should, you know. Most beneficial.'

Why should you and that mole-eyed priest be discussing me? 'I have it scheduled for this afternoon,' she lied. 'I meant to tell Leon.'

'Leon?' The Greek seemed sad. 'Leon, I regret, is leaving us today. He has, I'm told, proved entirely unsatisfactory. Clumsy, forgetful. Mosul doesn't feel the boy has the makings of a true vocation with our gentle Carya.'

'As others before him have discovered.' Claudia emphasized the last word. 'Doesn't that strike you as unusual?'

A flicker passed over the Laconian's face. 'It is not my place to comment on the priesthood,' he said coldly, withdrawing his arm and muttering, 'I mustn't keep you from your business,' as he disappeared at great speed through the first available entrance.

On the shore, gangs of workers were busy constructing the grandstand for the foot race and since the sawdust tickled her nose, Claudia sauntered out along the jetty. The planks were warm as she sat down and swinging her legs over the side, she unrolled Orbilio's letter. Around her the lake glistened like broken shards of glass and garganey drakes threw back their heads in vigorous displays of courtship.

'*My dear Marcus—*'

That was odd, the Head of the Security Police addressing his staff with such familiarity. She double-checked the seal but, no, this was no forgery and with a twitch of her brows, she started again.

'*My dear Marcus, You seem to be labouring under a misunderstanding – clearly you did not get my little joke if you thought I meant to sack you. Next time you're in Rome, I'll explain that little pun, but in the meantime, sterling work, old man, sterling work. Take your time about coming back – the Emperor is in good hands, protected by the Praetorian Guard, and as for the case, I have just this day briefed Augustus on our efforts—*'

Our? Claudia would bet her house, her jewels, her vineyards that that weasel's input was nil! She read on.

'*Now, if you could find time to see your way clear to sending me the checklist you mentioned, the "dos" and "don'ts" for Jupiter's priest, my brother might be interested. I believe he mentioned a while back that he had some intention of applying for the post.*'

There was an equally queasy closing line, which Claudia skipped, mainly because she couldn't read it through the tears of laughter which were coursing down her cheeks. Who'd believe it! The Head of the Security Police grovelling to his better-born staff, because he wanted his boneheaded brother in the most important pastoral role in the Empire, the post of Jupiter's Priest!

Clearly Orbilio had acquired a full list of the taboos and regulations governing this role and was using it as a lever to force a leave of absence from his boss, who would, in turn, use this inside knowledge to ensure his brother was at least shortlisted for the post. Frankly, Claudia doubted the brother had so much as considered the application, but that would not prevent an ambitious man from propelling his trusting sibling forward. Orbilio's boss was a creep and a social climber, but credit where it's due, he had suckers like an octopus, that man. Never once had he taken so much as one half-step backwards in the course of his career; his progress was always, always upwards, even though it was invariably at the expense of others.

Still. Claudia let the parchment spring back into a roll and tucked it inside the folds of her gown. There was nothing in that note which incriminated her, and with a bit of jiggery-pokery and Fortune smiling down, she could tamper with the heron seal and make it look like new again. It was a trick she'd picked up in Naples, from a one-armed—

'I don't suppose you are waiting for me?'

Calmly, she studied the reflection which appeared in the water. A man's reflection, dark and swarthy, with a glint of gold in the cloth. 'You suppose right.'

Tarraco crouched down, one knee touching the woodwork, in what she now knew was a familiar pose. 'You must believe,' he whispered, drawing a circle in the dust with his finger, 'the way I feel.' There was a pause long enough for him to draw three more concentric rings. 'The gown was a mistake, I see that, but Lais walked out before you arrived in Atlantis. Why do you not accept the apology?'

Far out on the water, terns dived like arrows for fish and a wagtail trilled and bobbed, sending out alternate flashes of yellow and white. Claudia fixed her gaze on the distant hills and kept her lips tight together, and she heard him sigh, a small, almost insubstantial sound.

'You think that by saying nothing, Tarraco will go

away?' The aroma of pinecones mixed with woodshavings floated under her nostrils. 'What is between us, Claudia, that will not go away.'

Her sole response was a single arched eyebrow.

'Very well,' he said, rising slowly to his feet. 'You attend races, yes?'

Try and keep me away! 'Maybe.'

'Then this afternoon, everything will be decided,' he said, 'one way or another.' He stared out across the water. 'My mother had the second sight and you'll see, Claudia,' he said, turning on his heel, 'my words, also, are prophetic.'

Through narrowed lids, Claudia watched him walk back down the pier. How true, Tarraco. Your words are absolutely pathetic.

Nevertheless, several minutes passed before Claudia's legs felt confident enough to skip up the flight of stone steps to Atlantis, and she'd have preferred some reassurance that the hammering came from the carpenters working on the grandstand, rather than something inside her chest.

'What the . . .?'

A tornado had swept through her bedroom in her absence, tipping over chairs and chests and mattresses. Her tunics lay scattered over the floor, her underclothes, her sandals. Her jewel box had been upended, cosmetics decanted from pots. Globs of creams and lotions and pools of spicy perfume swirled across the dolphin mosaic, along with a less recognizible smell, and feathers from pillows which had been gutted down the middle still floated in the sultry air.

Suddenly a hand lashed out to cover her mouth,

jerking her head back, and from the corner of her eye she saw the glint of a blade.

'Mmmf! Mmmmf!' It was the closest she could get to a scream, but surely someone could hear it? Heaven knows, there were enough servants about!

'Where is it?' he snarled.

'Mmmmmmf!'

'Shut up or I'll slit your throat like I slit that whore's last night.' The cold touch of the steel convinced her. 'Now where is it?' Slowly he released his hand and Claudia could see it was fat. 'Where's that fucking letter?'

'I don't—' What was that smell? Pepper? Coriander?

'Don't mess with me, bitch!' He pulled her head back so hard, she couldn't swallow. 'My client wants his property back.'

Terror snatched Claudia's breath from her body. Other than Marcus, only Dorcan knew she was here in Atlantis – and the amiable charlatan had betrayed her. Involuntarily, Claudia shuddered. She had a very bad feeling about this . . .

The fat man bragged about slitting the throat of a prostitute. It was common knowledge a certain big, black, shaggy bear had a soft spot for whores—

'What . . . happened to Dorcan?'

'What do you think?' the voice in her ear sneered.

Panic fluttered like a trapped bird in Claudia's stomach. What I think is . . . *that without witnesses there can be no repercussions*. The fat man meant business. And his business, she knew now, was murder.

She thought of the charlatan. His booming laugh, which showed off someone else's teeth. His remedies for gout and coughs and impotence, usually the same. His collection of sphinx claws and unicorn horns. Now he was dead. That life – that larger than life – snuffed out. In an instant.

Despite ragged lungs Claudia forced her voice to be calm. 'Very well. I'll give you what you want.' Trembling hands reached into the folds of her gown. She had maybe a countdown of six . . .

'No funny business,' the fat man warned. Down to five . . .

'I swear.' Down to four.

Shaking hands withdrew Orbilio's letter. Three.

A fat hand reached out to take it. *Two*.

In his other hand, the knife primed for action. *One* . . .

Sweet Juno, help me. Help me now! With a flip of her wrist, Claudia tossed the scroll across the floor, ducking back just far enough to evade the flick of the blade designed to slash through her windpipe.

'Bitch!' His free hand connected with her cheekbone and sent her sprawling backwards on to the gutted mattress. The fat man raised the knife to strike.

'HELP!' she yelled at the top of her lungs. '*HELP!*'

Immediately there was a scuffle of response in the corridor outside and the fat man swore. Torn between snuffing out the witness or returning the document to his client, he had little choice and as the running footsteps grew closer, he lunged at the scroll, barging through the squad of servants charging down in answer to Claudia's scream.

'What happened?' they asked, goggling at the mess and at her, sprawled across the floor with a bruise swelling up half her face.

'Lover's tiff,' she explained, dabbing the blood from her lip. 'You know how it is.'

In the tussle with the fat man, survival was all that mattered. Keeping alive. But now he'd gone, Claudia could thread the pieces together. Dorcan, that big, bluff, happy-go-lucky giant, had sold her out. That figured. He'd sell his sister's wedding band for a silver denarius and wouldn't even make a secret of the fact, but Dorcan, for all his mercenary faults, would never intentionally harm anyone. Neither, by reputation, would Sabbio Tullus. *Sending in the fat man smacked of double-cross.*

Dorcan, then, must have sent his information to Tullus' nephew, who in turn sent this thug, his tame assassin, to recover what he believed Claudia had stolen from his strongbox.

With her arms hugged tight to her chest, Claudia thanked her rescuers and watched them file out through the door. Alone in the silent scramble of her overturned room with the smell of cardamom rank in her nostrils, it was little consolation that the double-crosser had been double-crossed.

Sooner or later either the fat man or his master would realize they'd been fobbed off with the wrong document.

Next time, Claudia, like Dorcan, might not be so lucky.

XXIII

The bubbling up of a cloudbank to the west that particular
Sunday was the first of many changes which would impact
upon the lives of every single person throughout the entire
Roman Empire, not simply those cocooned within the
environs of Atlantis. But on that bright, light, sunny afternoon where the sky was as blue as the gentle Aegean and
the clouds as welcome as guests at Saturnalia, there was no
inkling of the momentous times which lay ahead. Simply a
rejoicing, and Pylades' sponsored foot race could not have
been a more fitting tribute to the upturn in the weather.
Suddenly, the same Etruscan hills which had previously
been blurred and distant rushed forward, their oaks and
pines and scrub showing up as clearly as their pebbled
shores, and beyond, more hills hove into sight, rolls and
rolls of them, stretching away to infinity. Islands, too,
jumped closer, became enlarged.

Including Tuder's craggy lump. The whiteness of the
marble on the villa reflected in the new, still clarity of
the lake, yet its more exotic treasures – the ancient
tombs, the colossus on its eastern shore – lay beyond
general view, a testament to the private nature of the
banker who retired here. But no one this afternoon cared
two hoots about the banker. Or his widow. Or the man
who married her.

In the lee of the cliff-like promontory, along the grass on the south-facing shore, the wealthy and the noble milled about, flaunting their hairdos, their jewels, the latest fashions, and round and round they strutted, pomaded and rouged, plucked and pomandered – and that was just the men! Tiers of temporary seating had been set up along both straight stretches of an ellipse marked out in chalk, the two short ends of the oval left clear for the judges, and Pylades strutted amongst the excited babble, a figure of importance despite his stocky, diminutive frame as he passed pleasantries with guests and dignitaries or double-checked the arrangements with the organizers. Kamar, bestowing a wise nod here, a handshake there, was shadowed by his wishy-washy wife, whose desperation to escape was all but tattooed across her cheekbones. Further down, beside the steps and dispensing Carya's cloudy waters to the townspeople, since the gates had been thrown open to one and all this afternoon, Mosul appeared chirpier than at any other time since Claudia's arrival, could that even be a smile hovering on his lips? Thankfully, no such accusation could be levelled at Pul, pug-faced as usual in his tight leather vest and strange kilt, standing watchful at the back.

When he nodded a curt acknowledgement to someone in the crowd, Claudia followed the line of his sights and found, to her surprise, the greeting had been exchanged with Tarraco, dressed to put his peacocks to shame and with the sun reflecting off the sumptuous embroidery on his tunic and the braided torque of gold around his neck, Claudia knew the Spaniard was not unaware of the attention he attracted.

You don't know when to stop, do you? she thought. You just don't know when to stop.

Trumpets blasted out a fanfare, a signal that the show was about to begin. Claudia settled beside Lavinia up in row seven and said, 'Care to give me a swig from that wineskin?'

'What wineskin?' the old woman chortled.

'The one I saw you taking a crafty slug from, before you tucked it back under your wrap.' There was a strange smell in the air, sharp and unpleasant, and it seemed to come from Lavinia. Claudia sniffed again and identified white mandrake. 'No Ruth and Lalo?'

'Tch.' The old woman directed a venomous glance towards the usher. 'Slaves not allowed in the seating area,' she mimicked. 'I'll give him bloody slaves! Because of that, Lavinia's lumbered here with Fab and Sab and I can't take much more of them, I tell you. Mind,' Lavinia let loose a mischievous chuckle, 'I've bet Fabella's silver bracelet the wheelwright son, the blond boy there, wins this afternoon! Oh-oh, here they come.'

The boards vibrated as the heavyweights took their places, oblivious to Lavinia's hand pulling her wrap across a lump on her lap. 'I can't find that bracelet anywhere,' Fabella said.

'She can't,' her sister echoed.

'I'd hate to lose it, it was a present from my hubby and you should see it glisten in the sunshine.'

'She checked under the bed, everywhere.'

'I've asked around, no one's handed the bracelet in, and I just can't think where I could have dropped it. Was I wearing it when we called in to say good night to you, mother? Perhaps you could get Ruth to have a look?'

'Mother-in-law,' Lavinia corrected.

'Mother-in-law, then,' Fabella snapped. 'Just get Ruth to search, all right?'

'She needs to find that bracelet,' Sabella added sadly. 'She's lost without it.'

'Hardly lost, Sabella! My point is—'

To Claudia's relief, their chit-chat was drowned by the arrival of a troupe of dancers in pastel blue and green costumes, gyrating with grace and sensuality and a double-jointed sinuousness to the haunting tunes of the musicians as they invoked the water spirit, Carya, to bless this race. More girls arrived, dressed all in white and carrying in their hands white-painted boards bearing garlands of tumbling flowers – alkanet, anemones, cranesbill – and when they lined up, supporting the boards on their heads, it was a living replica of the colonnade in the Athens Canal! You should hear the clapping and the catcalls, the stamping of the feet, the whistles of appreciation, but if that wasn't enough, a cymbal clashed and a dancer clad from head to foot in silver passed along the human Caryatids to the place where Mosul dispensed his holy waters.

But long before the thunderous applause for this breath-taking incarnation of Carya had died away, a curtain came down on Lavinia. As though in a trance, she sat wooden and motionless, staring out across the lake.

'Lavinia?'

But bright blue eyes fixed on the coracles and the fishing boats and did not blink. As though she'd had a shock of some sort?

'Mother, dear, you don't look well,' Fabella said, and Claudia felt, for once, in agreement with the old porker.

A greasy sheen had appeared on the wrinkled face, a greyness beneath the weather-beaten tan.

'Ooh, no,' Sabella said, peering closer. 'She doesn't, does she?'

'You haven't been taking your medicine, have you?' barked Fabella. 'After all the money we spent to send you here, you throw it back in our faces!'

'She ought to take her medicine,' Sabella echoed. 'Won't get better, otherwise.'

Lavinia's shoulders sagged, her jaw hung slack. 'Could you,' she croaked, 'get Lalo to carry me back to my room?'

Holy Jupiter! Claudia stared at the empty arena, now being swept in preparation for the big race. Could it be . . .? No, of course not, the idea was so monstrous, so preposterous, it couldn't be true. Lavinia couldn't possibly be being poisoned . . .

Stumbling down the wooden steps into the crush of vendors and hawkers, Claudia's brain was on fire. And what of the old woman's stories, the curious deaths which occurred here? Around her, the air exploded with everything from candied fruits to frying fish to spiced apple cakes, still hot and steaming from the oven. Surely there couldn't be a connection . . .? Dazed, she glanced around at the happy throng, guffawing at each other's jokes, drinking wine and effusing on the dancing and the show. Good grief, it was absolutely ludicrous to imagine the guests were being picked off one by one!

Disgusted with her neurotic imagination, Claudia reeled away, to find herself thrust in the thick of the runners warming up for the race. Arms and hands were being shaken, short sprints run, backs kept supple with contortions.

'The very thing I need,' a baritone said. 'A lady's favour to carry.'

'Orbilio?' He was competing in the foot race? Then, goddammit, a scarlet flash whizzed past her eyes. 'Hey, give that back!'

'To the winner,' he grinned, 'the spoils!'

'For heaven's sake, Orbilio,' she hissed. 'What will people think, me wearing just one ribbon in my hair?'

'They'll think you're exactly what you appear to be,' he flashed back, twisting her hairband round and round his wrist and tying a knot with his teeth. 'A single woman!'

'I'll have you know I wear two ribbons in my hair to signal that I'm a respectable married woman, not some flibbertigibbet on the lookout for a—'

'Man like me? What happened to your face?'

'Oh, you know.' With wild mass-murder theories thundering through her brain and still reeling from Dorcan's death, Claudia had actually forgotten her encounter with the fat man! 'Girls will be girls.'

'Thank Jupiter for that,' he grinned. 'Now wish me luck!'

'I wish you a plague of locusts, a burr in your saddle and a really large boil on your bottom!'

'Same thing,' he said, and she watched him trot off, his oiled muscles gleaming in the sunshine.

'I beat him by a furlong and a half!' a thickly accented voice sneered.

Oh, no. Not another one stripped to his loin cloth! With Tarraco, of course, it was not altogether surprising. A tight strip of linen invariably attracts the ladies' eyes.

'I thought you didn't compete in athletics events.'

'Sometimes,' he said darkly, 'one has to make an

exception. Suppose you give me a ribbon? To keep the hair out of my face?'

'Look, being reduced to one band is bad enough, I'll be—'

—damned! The second ribbon was already tying back his long, dark mane to form a mare's tail at his nape. Claudia lunged to snatch it back, but the curls in her eyes obscured her vision and her hand flew wide of the mark.

'Remember,' the Spaniard took her chin between his thumb and forefinger and leaned so close she could smell basil on his breath, 'everything will be decided. Very soon. I can feel in here,' he placed her hand upon his beating heart.

'To the winner the spoils?' she asked, jerking away.

'Of course,' he whispered, running one hand lightly down her arm. 'And I always win what I set out to achieve.'

'Two minutes, boys!' the judge called out, though Claudia could hardly hear for the pounding of her heart. Damn you, Tarraco. Damn you to hell.

Edging her way through the competitors, only a blind man could not be aware of the posturing between them. Glowers. Stances. Muscles pumping up. Then she realized that it was not so much every contestant who was sizing up the opposition, more Supersnoop and Tarraco, and as the runners lined up along the chalk starting line, she wondered what on earth they were getting so riled up about. It was only a silly foot race, for gods' sake!

'GO!'

Standing on the sidelines, she clapped as the thirteen entrants set off over five circuits, and by the time they had completed the first lap, she counted Orbilio fifth, but

Tarraco was ahead in fourth place and forging on to third, though when they swept past a second time, Hotshot had surged forward to run in Tarraco's slipstream as the competitor in second place dropped back to fifth, then sixth, then seventh having shot his bolt too soon. The field began to divide, the race narrowing now to just three runners, Tarraco, Orbilio and the current title holder, the eldest son of the wheelwright, the one whose winning Fabella's bracelet depended on. But come the start of lap five, the favourite was watching his prize money overtake him not once, but twice.

Half a lap to go, the two were neck and neck. Their bodies strained with every movement, sinews stood out, sweat poured down their faces. Faster now, they approached the final bend. Every man, woman and child was on their feet, cheering, clapping, whistling encouragement—

Claudia watched them, side by side, each with a red ribbon fluttering behind them. 'Come on, you wooden clod,' she urged the panting wheelwright. 'Get a bloody move on!'

Something was happening off the field. The tumult was deafening still, but the cheers had changed. Screams predominated. Suddenly spectators down by the lake were pointing, yelling, shouting, and the judge wasn't even pretending to keep an eye on the racetrack.

Frowning, Claudia watched as, with not so much as a change in pace, Orbilio calved away from the racetrack to the lake. What the hell . . .? With no crowded steps to negotiate, no human impediments, Claudia raced behind the grandstand to the shore, where Marcus was wading into the shallows. Pul was there already, up to his kilted thighs, and suddenly Claudia saw the reason behind the hysterical behaviour of the crowd.

Face down bobbed the body of a woman, her long hair streaming, her gown as blue as the balmy waters which supported her.

Together Orbilio and Pul each grabbed an arm and hauled her to the shore. Pylades, Mosul and Tarraco were surging through the crush, but it was Kamar who got there first.

'Somewhat redundant, my services,' he muttered, his mouth souring at the white and swollen flesh, 'but turn her over anyway.'

A collective gasp rang round as Orbilio and the Oriental heaved the corpse on to its back. Retching noises rippled round the circle.

'Mighty Mars!' Mosul made the sign to avert the evil eye.

Pul also opened his mouth to speak, but Pylades pre-empted him. 'Fetch the army,' he ordered a liveried lackey. 'Tell them we have a murder on our hands.'

Full marks for observation. Not only had the poor cow's face been mashed to a pulp, the livid purple bruises round the neck told a story of their own.

Claudia watched as the Oriental pulled back, shaking the drips off his massive hams, leaving Kamar and Orbilio to examine the body. Not a young woman, that much was obvious even to Claudia's amateur eye, nor a pauper, judging by the cut and quality of her gown, *but by the gods, the fish had had a field day* . . .

A shudder ran through her as Orbilio scooped a

handful of green slime from the dyed tresses and Claudia clapped her hands over her mouth.

Pylades was shaking his head. 'This is terrible,' he said. 'Terrible.' And unlike at Cal's funeral, Claudia could see that this time he really meant it. 'What hatred could inspire such an act of savagery?'

'Well.' Undaunted by the condition of the body or the ghoulish curiosity of the crowd, Orbilio peered at the rings on her bloated fingers, the marks on her neck, checking the hair, the wrists, the feet. 'We might be in a position to answer that if we could ascertain her identity,' he said lifting the mangled head. 'Hmm. Only one earring?'

Perhaps it was to avoid looking at the ghastly blob lying on the grass that Claudia noticed the colour had drained from Tarraco's face. How strange. After what he did to the bear, she hadn't imagined him the queasy type. Yet here he was, standing rigid, white, his eyes locked fast on the woman's corpse. Oh, my god . . .

As her lunch curled inside her stomach, another part of Claudia became aware of Kamar answering Orbilio.

'There's no problem with regards to identification,' he was saying, and Pylades and Mosul were nodding sadly with him. 'We knew her well, up here.' He glanced across at Tarraco. 'This poor bitch is Lais.'

XXIV

The army, when it clanked to a halt beside the lake, consisted of one junior tribune flanked by two legionaries, though what it lacked in strength, it more than made up for in enthusiasm. Within seconds of its arrival, spectators had been moved back and out of earshot, grumbling at being short-changed, while the wheelwright's son pestered for a decision on whether two runners dropping out of the race meant he had won.

'Ladies and gentlemen,' the tribune hammered for silence amongst the little group which remained clustered round the corpse, 'I am Cyrus, the Emperor's representative in Spesium. Now we have, as you all know, a new town rising on imperial soil, our reputation stands on our results. This applies to all of us and if we are to play our part in the evolving political climate, an ethic based on peace and on loyalty and trust, if Spesium is to take its rightful place among commercial centres, it is essential we get to the truth of this heinous crime and you have my assurance, ladies and gentlemen, my *word* that I shall not rest until the murderer of this poor woman is brought to justice. It is, of course, and I need not remind you, a capital offence—'

'That man,' Orbilio whispered to Claudia, 'blows more hot air than Vesuvius. Thank you.' The latter words were addressed to the small boy he'd sent to fetch his clothes. He flipped a copper to the child and pulled on his long, patrician tunic, and he had time to buckle it as well before the tribune's speech was finished.

'The victim has not only been strangled,' Kamar was telling Cyrus, 'she has been brutally battered around the head. These lesions here . . .'

Claudia blocked out the grisly anatomical details, leaving them to Cyrus to jot down on a wax tablet. Patrician, like Orbilio, and young, of course – this was a stepping stone in many an aristocrat's career, be it the army or civilian life – but a certain podginess was beginning to show, a puffiness around the cheekbones suggestive of indulgences on quite a grand scale.

'When,' he asked the Spaniard, 'did you last see your wife?'

Tarraco buffed his fingernails against the palm of his hand. 'Why?'

Claudia rolled her eyes to heaven. You idiot, Tarraco. Won't you ever learn?

'Remorse is not your strong point, is it?' Cyrus sneered. 'Well, let's see what other little weaknesses you have.' After each question that he fired off, he scratched another annotation on his hinged tablet. 'Right,' he said eventually. 'Let's see if I have this straight.' He read back over his notes. 'The last time you saw Lais was Wednesday, correct?'

Tarraco made no response and the chubby tribune's hackles began to rise in earnest.

'Moreover, you say she walked out on you after a row?'

This time he received an imperceptible shrug and,

stung, the tribune jerked his thumb at his legionaries. 'Row out to the island. See whether anyone can corroborate that story.'

For the first time, Tarraco looked Cyrus in the eye. 'No need for the army to start straining itself at this late stage,' he said. 'My staff come today to watch the race. You *may* interrogate them here, *if you wish*.'

'Don't get cocky with me, you money-grubbing dago,' Cyrus snarled, jabbing a finger into Tarraco's muscled chest. 'I know your game. First it was Virginia, now Lais. What happened, eh? Laughed in your face, did she, gigolo? Told you she was cutting you out of her will?'

A dark flash of anger sparked Tarraco's brooding eyes, and Claudia realized that Cyrus had hit a raw nerve. The Spaniard's mouth clamped tighter and the knuckles of his bunched fists turned whiter.

'In a fit of rage, you strangled her – but that wasn't enough for you, was it? Consumed at what you considered her betrayal, you rained blow after blow—'

Claudia could not listen. She stared up at a pair of hawks, wheeling overhead, and remembered Tarraco as she had seen him this morning, strutting like a peacock with his gold torque and fancy embroidery. *Dressed to kill.*

'Admit it, you snapped and you killed her. You put your dirty hands round her throat and you squeezed—'

Dammit, Cyrus, that's no way to elicit a confession from a man like Tarraco. And without one, there can be no true justice.

Claudia cleared her throat. 'Tarraco did not murder Lais,' she said. 'He was with me.'

From the corner of her eye, she saw Orbilio's head shoot up

The Spaniard, too, was taken by surprise, except in his case you'd have to know him well to recognize that sideways tilt of the head.

'And you are?' With slow deliberation Cyrus crossed to where Claudia was standing, and her scowl defied him to comment on the mass of tumbling curls which no self-respecting Roman lady would be seen dead with out of doors in daylight hours, let alone with a flaming swelling on her cheek.

'Claudia, widow of Gaius Seferius, wine merchant in Rome.'

'Widow? I see.'

No, you do not, you dirty-minded bastard, she wanted to shout, and bit her lip instead.

'And you were with Tarraco – er, when exactly would that be?'

'Claudia,' Orbilio growled under his breath.

She tasted blood in her mouth. 'Last night,' she said, adding a forceful toss of her head.

'Ah.' Purposefully, the tribune walked back to stand over the corpse, nodding to himself and flipping open his hinged notebook.

Claudia stole a glance at the grotesque creature at his feet. Once a tall and slender socialite, wealthy – ah, but lonely with it – she had married a man for his prowess in bed and . . . And what?

'Would that be *all* night?'

The bastard was relishing her public humiliation. 'Yes, Cyrus, all bloody night, if you must know.'

Tarraco had looped his thumbs into the waistband of

his loincloth and was staring out across the lake as though it was a picnic he was attending. From the side, Claudia felt angry patrician eyes burn into her head.

'Much depends,' Cyrus said, 'upon the testimony of the slaves, but then again,' he gave a brittle laugh, 'much doesn't.' He walked back and forth across the grass, finally stopping in front of Claudia. By now the little group had fallen silent, and you could have cut the atmosphere with a carving knife and served it up with mustard sauce. 'Nevertheless you are giving Tarraco an alibi, is that correct?'

'The message appears to be getting through at last.'

'Then as I see it, *Mistress* Seferius, this makes you an accomplice to the crime.'

'*What?*'

'You imbecile.' Tarraco sprang forward like a lion on a chain. 'She is no accomplice, because I am no killer!'

'It doesn't really matter,' Orbilio said, stepping forward, 'where this lady spent the night.' He shot a fiery glance at Tarraco. 'Lais has been dead for several days, is that not correct, Kamar?'

Goddammit, why didn't someone say so before!

'Undoubtedly.' The bald Etruscan nodded. 'It's hard to be precise, considering the damage done to tissue by the fish, but my professional opinion is that she's been dead four days and that, I'm afraid, is the minimum.'

The tribune's nose wrinkled at the mangled corpse. 'It's the lovely widow who is labouring under the impression that Lais died last night,' he said, 'not I. I merely make the point that she has, by her own admission, admitted aiding and abetting in a murder.'

Not so much blood and thunder, you silly bitch, as thud and blunder. What *were* you thinking of!

'Speaking from experience.' Smoothly Orbilio took hold of Cyrus' arm and murmured in his ear. 'We're invariably inundated with oddballs either confessing to the crime or else providing cast iron alibis for suspects. I wouldn't be at all surprised if it turns out the little lady,' he flashed a patronizing smile, 'also suffers from some type of attention-seeking disorder. Ouch!' He leaned down to rub the place where the little lady's sandal had connected to an attention-seeking shin.

The tribune was not won over. 'And you, sir? Who might you be?' He was even less impressed with the answer. 'Do you have official jurisdiction to interfere in this investigation?'

'None whatsoever,' Marcus said cheerfully.

'Oh, yes, he does!' Claudia piped up. 'I intercepted a letter from his boss, empowering him—'

Cyrus smiled a tight smile. 'And where is this official authorization?'

'Stolen by the man who gave me this, of course.' She pointed to her bruise. 'He's an assassin sent to retrieve a certain document, except I palmed him with . . .' Her voice trailed off, as it became clear that everyone, not just the tribune, felt that the heat had finally got to her.

'Quite.' Cyrus turned to address the group as a whole. 'I suppose I have to follow through with this charade,' he sighed. 'So can we please clear up the question as to whether or not an intimate relationship exists between these two which might implicate her in the crime?'

'I fear Marcus Cornelius may be right,' Pylades said,

flashing a sad smile at Claudia. 'You see, she did not arrive in Atlantis until Thursday, I can vouch for that personally.'

'As can I,' put in the constipated tortoise.

'I've a good mind to throw you in jail for wasting time and perverting the course of justice,' Cyrus snarled in Claudia's ear, 'but I need to get this enquiry moving. Ah, the servants.' With a smile of encouragement, Cyrus beckoned the contingent from Tuder's island forward. 'I presume you've heard about the tragedy?'

Dumbly they nodded.

'Good, because I have a few questions to ask concerning your late mistress.'

Shuffling from foot to foot, the servants stared at the ground, at their hands, at anything except Tarraco or the tribune, but the answer from each slave was the same.

Yes, they recalled the row on Wednesday.

No, they had not seen Lais leave the island.

'You are certain of these facts?' Cyrus pressed. 'None of you rowed Lais ashore that night, or perhaps the following morning? Think very carefully about this.'

Weights shifted from foot to foot, hands were wrung, noses sniffed, but the reply remained in the negative.

'None of the rowing boats was missing? You're positive?'

They nodded in glum unison.

'It couldn't be possible, perhaps, that Lais took a boat, rowed over to Atlantis—'

'Lais could not row,' one voice put in. 'She was not strong enough, not for that distance.' Incredibly, the voice was Tarraco's. 'Someone must have come for her.'

'Is that a fact?' Cyrus said patiently. 'Well, then, did

any of you see a boat come ashore on the island either that night or during the following day?'

Downcast heads shook as one.

'No one saw Lais leave?' He gestured to his legionaries, who each took one step closer to the Spaniard. 'So what do we conclude from this?' Cyrus pretended to consult his notes. 'Lais was alive on Wednesday. She had a flaming row with her husband—'

'I did not kill her,' Tarraco said. 'You get that through your thick skull.'

'—has not been sighted for three days until, on the fourth day, she turns up, floating in the lake, having been strangled and battered in a brutal and vicious attack which, funnily enough, also took place three to four days ago and where robbery, clearly, was not the motive. Look at her rings, the amber pendant.'

Cyrus clapped shut his wax tablet and snapped his fingers.

'Arrest the bastard,' he said. 'But don't harm him more than necessary.' He smiled a lizard smile at Tarraco. 'I want this specimen in prime condition for our first public execution.'

XXV

'Feeling better, master?'

The dwarf's face was twisted in concern as the nephew of Sabbio Tullus staggered out of the latrines.

'Much,' he croaked, rubbing his belly. And better still, when this fucking mess was sorted out, it was making him ill. That, and the rasping dry air from the marble merchant's warehouse next door.

'While you were . . . indisposed,' the servant spoke with a faint lisp, 'your well-built friend dropped by, the one who seems so attached to cardamom pods.' They could be used medicinally, as a stimulant, or to ease flatulence, or maybe he just liked the smell. 'He said to tell you the situation in Atlantis is under control and—'

The weasel nose twitched visibly. '*Under control?* Either he's carried out my instructions or he hasn't, what the hell does he mean, under control?'

The dwarf spread his hands in helplessness. 'Alas, he did not confide in me, sir, merely asked me to pass on the information that he is embarking upon the next phase of his mission and will report back when it's complete.'

'And the—' the nephew stopped short. 'My . . . property,' he said carefully. 'Did the fat man mention my missing property?'

'No, sir.'

'Fuck.'

Sabbio Tullus followed his silhouette through the hucksters in the Forum where, despite the ferocious heat, a man could still purchase anything from buskins to buckles, oysters to ointments. The moneylenders' stalls outside the Aemilian Basilica were doing brisk trade, their balances glinting in the sunshine, and the red roofs of the temples and the public buildings shimmered like wine in a palsied hand.

Tempted to loiter by a dazzling display of Parthian skill, warriors leaping high in knee-length tunics with great swirling moustaches and even greater broadswords, in order to advertise a fuller display later this evening, Tullus decided better of it. He'd already booked his seat, there'd be time enough to appreciate their talents then. Right now his secretary was waiting with quill and ink at the ready, because Tullus had something to tell his wife . . . what was it? Oh, yes. That he'd not be in Frascati by Tuesday after all.

Clad in that epitome of rank, the mighty toga, Tullus feared he might poach to death in his own perspiration, but that, he supposed, was the price a man paid for success. He squinted up at the merciless sky and thought, by Croesus, if he'd only left his mucking silver in the repository, he'd already *be* in the country by now! Amongst the green and rolling hills, dining with his neighbours, making babies with his wife. Instead he was up to his armpits in shit, and still wasn't making any bloody headway!

Tullus felt a vice-like crush within his chest. He couldn't breathe. Jupiter, he couldn't bloody breathe—

'Drink this,' a soothing voice said. 'You'll feel better soon.'

Accepting the proffered cup of water from the warden who attended Juturna's holy spring, he slumped over the rail. Calm down, old man, calm down. Take it easy, take it easy . . . That's better. In, out, in, out, deep breaths. De-ee-ep breaths. He saw his pale reflection in the pool. Chubbykins, his wife nicknamed him and suggested he lose a bit of weight. Well, maybe he just might – why not – when this mess was over. Gradually the claw around his heart released its grip, and with a grateful nod to the warden and a coin flipped into the pool, Tullus set off once more across the Forum.

Originally a boggy valley full of bulrushes and reeds and surrounded by a straggle of thatched huts on each of the famous seven hills, Rome had been transformed into the seat of an empire stretching thousands of miles in every direction. With a swelling sense of pride, Tullus' eyes flickered down the streets which led from this small and bustling oblong and thought, incredible! From these few roads are linked even the darkest of our outposts. Every single navigational passage in the world ends up here in Rome!

Now that bastard of a nephew plans to undermine it . . .

Janus, what a mess, what a stupid, mucking mess he'd got sucked into, but it was unavoidable. Family was family, and it never occurred to Tullus to refuse a request to deposit a small casket in his newly constructed strong-room. Why should it?

Why? You sad, moronic oaf, I'll tell you why! When have you ever taken anybody's word at face value, tell me that. Especially where business is involved! What imbecilic madness inspired you not to check? Not to demand a look at the contents? The boy would have refused your request – and this whole ghastly situation would have been averted. *Or would it?*

The puff of self-castigation burst. No man who entrusts safe keeping of his records expects them to be read over by the trustee!

Muck!

Still, no use moping; the theft had taken place, the question was how to limit the damage. Or more accurately, how to reunite his nephew with that bloody piece of parch-ment and after that, the problem was no longer Tullus', it was his nephew's headache and best of bloody luck, the little prick would get no further help from him!

Tullus turned right past the Senate House and sighed. That's another thing. Rumour had it, Augustus was about to propose his stepson, Tiberius, as his heir. Well, the lad had proved himself on campaign, heaven knows he'd be a popular enough choice. Intelligent, courageous, happily married to a wife swelling with child, the people would be right behind him . . . were it not for the problem that Tiberius was unconnected to Augustus by blood! As a result, much debating would be required in the Senate House, which, goddammit, was in unofficial recess until the end of the month!

Tullus resolved to make a sacrifice to Apollo, because the gods must be against him. If only the Senate had been sitting, there'd have been no problem over that bloody scrap of paper . . .

Away from the hawklike eyes of his peers, Tullus slipped off his toga and instantly felt half a ton lighter and five years younger. Mopping the sweat from his forehead, he turned right again, through the crush of armour makers and glassblowers, pitchsellers and potters. He rolled the toga into a ball and bundled it under his arm. Funny thing about that stolen document. Because of his widespread business connections, Tullus had agents in virtually every commercial centre for two hundred miles and yet no word had come back regarding the whereabouts of Claudia Seferius. Very odd, that, very odd indeed. Especially considering she was such a hot-headed creature. A filly born from Impulse out of Recklessness, Tullus would never have imagined her hanging on to such a thing. Surely she'd be asking a four-figure sum for its safe return by now? Tullus stuffed the woollen ball under the other arm as he turned left and away from the main thoroughfare. Jupiter alone knew how deeply he'd delved into that girl's affairs, and whilst much of her private life remained a mystery, it hadn't been too difficult for a rich man with contacts to see how the land lay with the business she was trying so desperately to run. With a full appraisal of her financial status, Tullus could understand the theft – hell, given the girl's audacity, he might even have had a few words of advice to offer her about how to handle the merchants she was up against! But as to that scroll . . . Something of a conundrum, what?

He chewed his lower lip in thought. There's no way, reading it, she could have failed to comprehend its sensational impact, unless – *of course!* Tullus slapped his forehead with the palm of his hand. Silly arse! She'd been *paid* to steal the bloody thing, it was obvious! He saw it now. Someone had paid Claudia Seferius to break in and steal his nephew's letter – taking Tullus' money had been no more than a diversion tactic! *No wonder* she couldn't be found! Whoever was masterminding the theft was hiding her as well – ha!

His step lightened considerably, despite the steep incline.

Wasn't that a weight off his mind! Surprising, really, his nephew hadn't seen it all along! Well, well, well. What a pleasant prospect, putting one over on that cold little reptile, telling him that, furthermore, family or not, he'd have no further involvement in the matter, it was up to the boy from now on to find out who had known the incriminating document was in his possession. Let the little sod work backwards from there.

Wonderful. Tullus was off the hook, the problem was back where it belonged. His loins stirred. How long had it been since he'd pleasured his wife? Well, there was no reason now why he couldn't set off for Frascati first thing in the morning!

Down a quiet backstreet lined with six-storey tenement blocks, Tullus felt a chill run down his spine. Ridiculous. This is a respectable neighbourhood. But all the same he turned around to check. It was the height of the buildings, of course, casting the narrow street into shadow and blocking out the clamour of the workmen and builders back down the hill. Everything was normal. A group of small children, one rolling a hoop, two playing piggy-back, scampered down the street. An old man with badly bowed legs led a donkey towards a stable, and a foreigner, a fat Edessan from Mesopotamia judging by the turban, peered at windows and doorways as he sought a particular address. Tullus was ashamed of his imaginings. All because someone mentioned that the man who designed his strong-room had been found dead in some back alley with his throat cut! Hell, with the army stretched to breaking point as it sorted out clogged roads, choked drains and arranged mass burials out of town, crime – especially robbery – was rife at the moment. Tullus was not unduly worried. He had his dagger at the ready. No thieving scumbag would take his purse off him!

Before turning the corner, he still felt it prudent to glance back down the hill. No cut-throats lurking in doorways. No shaven-headed gangs. No sneak thieves darting from balcony to balcony with bulging sacks. Much to the delight of the mimicking children, the Edessan's turban wobbled from side to side as he sought directions from an uncomprehending Celt in pantaloons. From the top storey of the adjacent building, a young woman's voice rang out in pure soprano. A yellow mongrel cocked its leg against a doorway, and lunchtime cooking smells of pork and sausages and fresh-baked bread filtered through the torrid heat. Tullus smiled as the Celt shrugged off down the street leaving the exasperated Edessan to adjust his blue hat, and up on the roof, two cats howled at stand-off.

Even the plague, thought Tullus, trudging up the winding alleyway, cannot dim the spirit of humankind. When the contagion first hit the city we couldn't eat, we couldn't sleep, we lay in our beds at night, wondering who'd be next, would it be me? We watched our neighbours die, we lost a friend, perhaps a relative, yet we ourselves were spared. And as time passed, we learned to cope with this cloud of uncertainty until one day, before we know it, we find ourselves singing again! Humming marching tunes instead of dirges, and when we gaze upwards at the unforgiving sky we no longer pray 'spare me, mighty Jupiter, spare me from the plague'. We find ourselves listening to songbirds – the finches, nightingales and warblers – and realize it is not death itself we fear, but an erosion of our spirit. Man is born to survive, and fear of fear is more crushing than any—

'Excuse me?'

Instinctively Tullus' hand flew to his dagger, but when he turned it was to look into the baffled face of the flabby Edessan.

'I am looking for a coppersmith who goes by name of Mita. He is kinsman of me, and I am wondering whether you are knowing where he lives?'

'Of course.' Tullus had had many dealings with the wily Mesopotamian. 'You'll find his premises in the next street, just –' he turned and pointed '– down there.'

The punch to his chest knocked the breath from his lungs. He wanted to yell, 'stop, thief,' but he couldn't catch his breath, and in any case the Edessan was still standing in front of him, his face frowning with deep concern.

'Help . . . me,' he rasped. 'Help . . .'

Mighty Mars, his heart was giving out! His arms were wood. He couldn't lift them. Then he looked down.

And saw the knife embedded to the hilt.

'What . . .'

The turban was gone. The smile was gone. The stranger pushed still harder on his dagger, grunting with the exertion. Tullus was confused. This was a joke, right? A practical joke. It had to be, because there was no pain—

Janus, Croesus, yes there was!

As the blade came out, the pain hit him like a thunderbolt, screaming through his bowels, shooting white-hot sparks of agony into every bone and muscle. His head caught fire, there was a drumming in his ears, as though several wagons passed across a wooden bridge at once, and for a moment he thought someone whispered 'No witnesses,' but that made no sense. No sense at all.

As he dropped to his knees, his bronze purse clattered to the cobbles, spilling copper, bronze and silver everywhere. No hand picked them up.

'Why . . .?' he gasped, but when he looked round, Tullus was alone in the alley with only a faint smell of cardamoms and a blue turban, which rolled like a drunk in the gutter.

Doubling up, Tullus clawed at his chest.

His breath wouldn't come, and as he keeled over on to the cobbles, he saw the sky go dark. Rain, he thought. Rain at long last. And he knew it was true, because liquid trickled over the hands clasped to his chest.

As the sky closed in, black as night, Tullus remembered his secretary was waiting for him at home. With quill and ink at the ready, to write a letter to send to his wife.

What the hell was it he wanted to say? He had to tell her . . . Tell her what? Oh yes.

That he'd not be in Frascati by Tuesday after all.

XXVI

'What's in the sack?'

The soldier leaned across and was about to swoop the package from Claudia's hands when Cyrus intervened.

'That's all right, lad,' he jerked his head in dismissal, 'you can leave this to me.' He waited until the legionary had closed the door behind him, then said, 'This is highly irregular, I'll have you know.'

'And don't think I don't appreciate the fact,' Claudia replied, removing a large, stoppered jug from her bag. 'Absinthe,' she whispered. 'Purloined from Pylades' supply!'

The tribune chuckled. 'I'm not sure whether that's another crime or not,' he laughed, removing the cork and sniffing, 'to add to your tally, but I'm partial to a drop of absinthe.'

Oh, I know your little weakness, Claudia said silently. Pylades told me all about it when we visited the barracks earlier.

It had been shortly after Tarraco had been led away in irons, his obscenities and expletives showing a wider range to his Latin vocabulary than might have been expected, when Claudia had approached Atlantis' architect and founder as the group was breaking up.

'I'm sorry about that incident back there,' she said. 'It was good of you to bail me out.'

'Nonsense,' the stocky Laconian beamed, 'I was happy to put the situation right – though just between you and me, you're not the only girl to have fallen for his smarm.' He glanced across to where Lais was being heaved on to a stretcher.

'I thought I understood him,' Claudia said, with a sad shake of her head. 'That's why I . . . you know, made a fool of myself. Now the tribune has me pinned as a mad-woman.' She gave a self-conscious laugh. 'I hardly know which is worse. Being thought a strumpet or a lunatic!'

Pylades patted Claudia's hand. 'No one here believes that you're either!' He laughed. 'Now, let's put the horror of the day behind us with you accompanying me to my personal quarters, where we can take a little refreshment, listen to a spot of music—'

'Pylades –' Claudia coiled a ringlet around her little finger and smiled a cute little-girl smile '– Pylades, would you put in a good word about me to the tribune? Explain that bit of nonsense just now . . .?'

'My dear.' He offered her his elbow and turned towards the flight of steps, 'nothing would please me more—'

'Excellent!' Claudia took the proffered arm and spun him round. 'We shouldn't be too far behind him.'

'What . . . you mean, *now*?'

'I knew you'd understand,' she said, tossing back the mop of curls. 'The sooner we get this clarified, the better! Just bear with me while I slip some ribbons in my hair, and on the way you can tell me all about your plans for extending Atlantis.'

Plus everything you know about Lais, the tribune's peccadilloes, how far Pul's influence extends, plus . . . plus . . . plus . . .!

If Cyrus had been surprised to see them turn up at the garrison, he masked it well, and with Pylades patting Claudia's lovely hand as he glossed over the misunderstanding, the tribune even seemed to find it rather funny. In fact, he barely minded when, in a fit of clumsiness, the lovely widow accidentally overturned his desk. The shame of being here, she mumbled. Of having to explain oneself after such public humiliation—

Finally, with all sides parting company in good humour (he even went so far as to kiss her hand himself), how could Cyrus not mind bestowing one more favour?

It concerned a harebell gown, she said, fluttering her lashes as, in a hushed whisper, she confessed at being duped by Tarraco's slick charm. The gown had actually been Lais', she added. Imagine that! Well, now she'd like her revenge . . .

And an hour later, she was back.

This time without Pylades, just absinthe from his personal supply.

'Hooo,' Cyrus said, making a fanning motion with his podgy hand. 'Powerful stuff!' Carefully he replaced the stopper. 'Now I apologize if what follows implies a lack of trust, but you must appreciate the prisoner is facing a capital offence, I cannot afford to take chances.'

'You're asking if you can search the sack and the answer is I should jolly well hope you would,' Claudia began, but the tribune held up an embarrassed hand.

'The bag, yes, but I, um, well, it's like this.' He didn't need to elaborate. An amazon with a face like a boot appeared in the doorway, and for five minutes Claudia was subjected to a punishing search before Granitepuss finally called out to Cyrus that the visitor had no keys or weapons on her person, indeed nothing that could endanger the safe custody of the prisoner. By the way, she'd searched the sack as well, but, she shouted, there was only one silver bell inside (no clapper) plus one dead rabbit.

'Hare,' Claudia corrected. 'The animal is a hare, and it is revenge for a dress.'

'I don't care what it is, it stinks,' Bootface said, wiping her hands down the side of her tunic. 'The jailhouse is over there.'

The legionary assigned to escort her seemed more concerned with the probability of rain by morning than an impending murder trial, and as he chuntered on, again Claudia was struck by how quiet the garrison was for such an up-and-coming town. Typical of barracks anywhere, the buildings consisted of four blocks built around a central rectangular yard, yet they seemed eerily empty. No soldiers drilling. No barked orders. No hobnail boots clattering over the cobbles. Merely a coil of black smoke from the smithy and the thwack of meat being chopped on a block.

'What? Oh, Cyrus keeps us out on foot patrol, mostly. Making the roads safe to travel, and all that. After all –' the soldier pulled a face '– there's sod all else to do around here, pardon my Phrygian.'

Behind the stable yard, a small stone-built structure with iron bars at the small and solitary window sat forlornly on its own, allowing every angle to be covered, because whilst cells acted as storage space, rather than as places of punishment, it wasn't to say the occupants were content to remain incarcerated and bandits tend to have friends. Still, it was a hell of a sight better than Rome's dank, dingy holes which adjoined the Great Sewer!

'I'll have to lock you in,' the legionary mumbled apologetically. 'But if there's any trouble, Miss, just holler – I'll be right outside this door.'

'Thank you, officer, I'll bear that in mind,' she said, as the heavy wooden door swung open on hinges so well oiled, it showed even the maintenance men were desperate for tasks.

Tarraco was leaning against the far wall, supporting his weight on his forearm and despite the burst of light which invaded the isolated, darkened cell, he continued to stare at the low stone ceiling, his jaw tilted upwards in either arrogance or defiance, or both.

'You have a visitor, my son!' the soldier boomed. 'Make the most of it, 'cos you won't be having many more!'

Long after the key clanked hollow in the lock, long after Claudia had acclimatized to the gloom, the rough wooden pallet, the hole in the floor which served as a latrine, Tarraco moved not a single muscle and it was left to Claudia to break the silence.

'Nice duds,' she said, indicating the coarse peasant tunic he'd been given. 'But I see it didn't match my scarlet ribbon, you've thrown that away.'

'Confiscated,' he growled. 'In case I use it to tie round iron bar and strangle myself. Me! Tarraco! They think I take coward's way out!' There was a pause, before he gave a gruff laugh. 'Did I not tell you everything would be decided between us?'

'I shouldn't boast about second sight, if I were you,'

Claudia replied, prodding the lumpy mattress. 'Had I been in your shoes and seen into the future, I'd have been in Ancona by now, heading for Dalmatia.'

'Second sight is not seeing the future, it is feeling. Understanding.' He half turned towards her, but his eyes remained on the ceiling. 'I did not expect this.'

I'm sure.

'You know, is strange,' he said quietly. 'When you think me single and rich, when I save you from being killed by a bear, you do not wish to know. Instead, when I butcher two wives to get my hands on their fortunes—'

'There's nothing quite like a confession of brutality to lift the heart.'

'You expect me to plead? On my knees, swear I did not murder Lais? Whatever I say, Claudia, I will die and what's more, that fat slug of a tribune will devise some slow and painful execution, he hates my guts.'

'Don't you rather think you might have under-estimated us Romans, Tarraco? Silly things, we will insist on fripperies. Like a trial, for instance.'

'Where you find judges, lawyers, jurists here, eh? This afternoon the tribune and your tall friend, Marcus, they go out to my island – they say, to look for evidence.' He hissed in his breath. '*I say to plant it.*'

'So what's your defence?' Claudia asked, tipping out the dead hare and the bell. 'Still sticking to the theory that someone rowed out purposely to strangle Lais, are we?'

'That's not what I said!' Tarraco slammed his fist into the stonework. 'Why do you always belittle me?'

Blood oozed down his knuckles to drip-drip-drip on the tamped earth floor, and outside a flycatcher trilled from its perch.

Claudia wrapped her fingers around the iron bars of the slot which called itself a window and heard the blood hammer in her ears. With his back against the stable block and his arms folded over his chest, the soldier drew pictures in the dust with his toe and smells from an unappetizing stew filtered across from the kitchens. The clouds from the west had moved over to cover the sky, and they were low and grey and trapped the stifling heat.

Which surely explained why she could not breathe?

'Even you, you cannot resist coming to gloat.' She heard him swear under his breath. 'You bring me a smelly bunny and think, ha, ha, that is so funny.'

Claudia counted silently to ten. 'I do not think murder is funny, Tarraco. In fact, I'm not amused at all.'

From the stables, a horse whinnied softly, and raucous laughter drifted down from the lookout tower as the shift changed over.

Tuder's dead, Virginia's dead, Lais is dead but most of all, my arrogant young stud, Cal, is dead. Deep in the pit of her stomach, something primeval slithered.

Holy Venus, it's not too late to stop! Pick up the hare and bell, walk away. Justice is for others to administer, not you. Call the guard. *Walk away.* Then she heard an echo of a young man's laugh. Saw again his beech-leaf eyes, caught a whiff of mint and alecost. And Claudia knew then that she could not – would not – walk away.

'So then.' Taking one last, lingering glance at the bored legionary, she composed herself and turned to Tarraco. You really have no option –' with her toe, she indicated the items that she'd brought '– other than to be a good boy for Mummy and play with your toys.'

XXVII

'A *key*?' Even Tarraco could not disguise the amazement on his face. 'How did you get hold of a key?'

'Sssh.' The soldier's head had jerked up at the change in voice tone. Claudia waited for his interest to dwindle, and while she did so, patted herself on the back. She'd fooled the tribune, she'd fooled the amazon, she almost fooled the Spaniard . . . for who would suspect this mad March boxer, glassy-eyed, with drips of blackened blood around the nostrils, had previously been gutted, filled and sewn back up again?

'Won't Cyrus be looking for this?' Tarraco said, fondling the heavy iron key.

Claudia dismissed his worries with an airy wave of her hand. Before she frogmarched Pylades to the garrison, she had excused herself, ostensibly to replace the ribbons in her hair, but in practice to slip a wax tablet into the voluminous folds of her robe. Having engineered the overturning of the tribune's desk, taking an impression of the jailhouse key was child's play and all that was required from there was a visit to the locksmith in the town. There was nothing for Cyrus to look for, because nothing was actually missing.

'Why do you do this for me?' Tarraco asked, his head tilting on one side.

Outside the sun was sinking fast, turning the sky an ominous storm-coloured yellow.

'There's sufficient money inside that hare to buy you basic provisions for five or six days,' she said, taking care to watch a cloud of midges dancing in the courtyard, 'providing you sleep rough, I'm afraid. Too many coins, you see, and the hare would be suspiciously weighty.'

'Why, Claudia?'

'The silver bell you can sell. It might, if you're lucky, buy you a passage back to Iberia.'

'Hey.' His voice was a whisper. 'I ask you a question.'

A fluttering of wings beat inside her chest. 'Because I don't believe you killed Lais.'

'You are in a minority,' he rasped, and her nostrils tingled with pine and woodshavings even above the smell of his coarse woollen tunic. 'The evidence is over-whelming, is it not?'

'I don't believe you killed Virginia either.'

'Of course not,' he said. 'Damned pig-headed woman! She would take that boat out in the storm – she was like you.' In the darkness of the cell, a flash of white showed clear. 'Knows it all!'

'Where—?' She could barely speak for the lump in her throat. Tarraco was right. There would be no fair trial in Spesium. Cyrus would nail his hide to the wall. 'Where will you go?'

As the setting sun snuffed out the last trace of twilight in the jail, Tarraco shrugged. 'I don't know,' he said simply.

Claudia swallowed hard. 'I have to go,' she said, and strangely her eyes appeared to be allergic to something in the cell, they'd begun to sting.

'Claudia—'

'Don't say it, Tarraco,' she whispered. Don't say anything at all.

Outside, night had darkened the waters of Lake Plasimene and in the hills which cradled this idyllic paradise, foxes yawned and stretched and set off to hunt, leaving their newborn cubs curled up cosy in their dens. In ravines and woods and gullies, porcupine and badgers would be rooting in the undergrowth and in the reedbeds, melancholy frogs called and answered one another. Ribbit-ribbit. Bedeep. Ribbit-ribbit. Bedeep. The scents of flag irises and valerian, marsh mallows and wild allium mingled in the dense, trapped heat and a deer ventured down to drink.

Now what? Claudia asked herself. She had no stomach for food, but as she sat, chin in hands, on a fallen birch, she realized dinner would have long since been cleared away, the roast meats and fricassees served by liveried waiters while rose petals showered from the ceiling and flautists piped sing-a-long tunes. Even the kitchens would be quiet, the pots scrubbed out and turned upside down to drain, the oven fires raked.

Far in the distance, a jagged flash of white lightning flickered and then died.

Death.

Like Plasimene, death was all around her – Tuder, Lais, Virginia and Cal – and it was water, this water, which connected them. Tuder, out on his island. Virginia, found drowned in the lake. Lais, floating face down in the reeds. And, of course, Cal. Somersaulting, backflipping, cartwheeling Cal, found sprawled on the shingle beneath the sacred spring of Carya.

Gone. Each and every one of them. And soon Tarraco, too, would be gone.

Why, he had asked. Why set me free when the evidence against me is overwhelming?

Well, that was the problem, wasn't it? It was too overwhelming, too contrived. Like Cal, it just didn't feel right, and besides . . . That the Spaniard was capable of killing Claudia had no doubt. (Oh yes, this man could kill – passion ran through every bone, every artery, every single sinew!) But to take a life in anger is not the same as battering a woman over and over again, and most troubling of all was the way the corpse had been discovered. Tarraco, had he killed his wife, would have either left the body where it lay and to hell with the consequences – or else he'd have weighted it down in the lake where it would have remained undiscovered for ever. It was almost as though Lais had been delivered to the foot race this afternoon . . .

An owl hooted in the sultry night and Claudia didn't hear it.

I ought to go, she thought. I ought to warn Lavinia of my suspicions that she's being poisoned, but even with that there was a problem. Who was the person who had fed Claudia the information about the rash of mysterious deaths in the first place? Who, with abominable cunning, made sure she linked up the string of innuendoes? That's right, the old olive grower – and why should she do that? Why choose a fellow guest to load her suspicions on to, instead of Cyrus or Pylades? By her own admission, Lavinia lapped up every juicy story, embroidering them, as Ruth had pointed out, with details of her own. The old girl enjoyed gossip, she enjoyed mischief, she enjoyed being pampered – and from the way she acted after the death of her husband, it was also obvious Lavinia was a consummate actress. Add these together, and the foundations are laid for the fiction that her own life is in peril – could an old peasant woman ask for more? The wealth of attention, doctors and bureaucrats, the army – suddenly all solicitous; Fab and Sab running after her for once; think of the commotion!

No, there was only one thing to do with the rest of the night, Claudia decided. Go get steaming drunk.

XXVIII

In his office on the Aventine, in the shadow of the Temple of Minerva, Sabbio Tullus' nephew rinsed the vomit from his mouth.

It was the dust, it had to be. Desiccating marble dust from the warehouse next door. You could see it in the air, making the whole room white and hazy like cobwebs spun across the walls. Day after day, this distorted, fuzzy view was enough to make anyone throw up, never mind the torrid heat. There was nothing to worry about.

In the street below, the timekeeper called out the hour. Midnight. Mopping the perspiration from his face, the young man was surprised how damp his handkerchief was when he went to fold it up. Caused by the vomiting, that. Makes one sweat like a racehorse. That, and the diarrhoea, of course.

When he tried to stand up, his knees refused the rest of him permission and he sank back against the hard maplewood chair and rested his head on the desk. Not surprising, this bout of the squits. It was all that bloody fruit juice he'd been knocking back, because any kind of wine had made him hoarse. Come to that, so had the fruit juice, be it apple, peach or cherry, but what was the alternative? Milk, curdled before it left the cow? Water, warm and brackish? Or that foul beer the Egyptians drank, which made his stomach heave?

Lifting his head, he checked his appearance in the mirror. In the cobweb haze of this marble-dusty room, his skin appeared yellow, but he knew that couldn't be the case. Picking up a gavel on his desk, he hammered on a metal plate. The dwarf came running.

'You can take this bucket away,' he instructed. 'But bring a fresh one, in case.' Several times before, he thought he'd finished being sick . . .

'Very good, sir.'

The dwarf withdrew, leaving the nephew toying with the mirror. Praise be to Mars, he didn't have the bloody plague, that's all he was grateful for. At least there were no livid rashes breaking out on his stomach! Nevertheless, he peered down his tunic, double-checking with the mirror. Told you. You've got the squits because of all that fruit. You're throwing up because you're weak from diarrhoea and from being stuck inside this hot, dry, dusty room. That, coupled with the strain of waiting!

He sighed. He was *this close* to changing the course of the Empire, *this close*, and when he got his papers back, then he'd see a difference in his health. A very rapid upturn!

'You must drink, master,' the dwarf cajoled, setting down another bucket. 'Drink to keep your strength up.'

The nephew felt a glass of pressed bilberries against his lips and he tried to swallow, to wash away the sour taste of bile, but half the liquid dribbled down his chin. That's all he was bringing up, of course. Bile. Black and stinking, it made his head pound like bloody thunder and he could barely stand of late, but that would pass. Like those ridiculous hallucinations his manservant assured him were simply the product of a stomach empty for too long. Hell, he was even getting used to seeing multi-coloured haloes round the lights and double, sometimes treble, vision when people moved about, like the dwarf just now, helping him out of his stained shirt, and sometimes it seemed normal, viewing things as though he was peering down a rabbit hole. But the dwarf was right. He really ought to start keeping something down, because a couple of times of late he'd been haunted by strange, disturbing visions. The faces of demons springing out of the walls, with teeth like a rabid jackal's, snarling, foaming . . .

Delusions come with fever. Fever comes with vomiting. Vomiting comes from diarrhoea – a side effect of fruit juice which is the only thing I can take because of nerves.

Which will settle when I get that fucking paper back!

He slumped forward and closed his eyes, imagining how his fortunes would change. He had just nine more days before the Senate reopened after its unofficial recess, before Augustus made his pronouncement about the future of the Empire. Nine days.

'*Janus!*'

Slavering wolves began rising out of the desk, snapping at him with their sharp incisors, baying for his blood.

'Go away,' he screeched. 'Get away from me!'

Diving off his chair, he flung himself under the desk, coiling into a ball, his eyes screwed shut, and after a while, a very long while, the howling died off and the desk was a desk once again.

'Master, what's wrong?'

'What?' For an instant he feared the delusions were

back, but no. It was the face of his servant, made uglier with the pucker of concern. 'Oh. I . . . dropped my pen—'

Sweat poured down his face, soaking his tunic as the dwarf helped him back to his chair. Fucking hallucinations! The quicker he got this sorted out, the better.

Nine days, didn't he say? Retching another stream of black bile into the bucket, he considered the timescale was ample, providing he recovered what that Seferius bitch had stolen.

'No delivery from the fat man?' he rasped.

'N-no,' the dwarf replied, and the nephew wondered, was that also a figment of his imagination, that hesitation? He thought he heard, a few moments ago, an interchange between his servant and the man who smelled of cardamom. And through the fuzzy lamplight, he also thought he saw a piece of parchment, lying on a silver plate on the table in the hall. His mistake, surely. The dwarf was a model of efficiency and no doubt the fat assassin was already back in Atlantis, taking care of unfinished business. It was more than either of their lives were worth, to try and double-cross him.

'Master. Please. You must replenish lost fluids.'

'I can't,' he gasped, 'keep anything down.'

'Try, master. This is good chicken broth.'

'It tastes bitter.'

The dwarf tutted and pressed the bowl to his lips. 'Your tastebuds are out of sorts, sir. Come now,' there was a distinct edge to his voice, 'drink up.'

Swallowing the filthy brew, the nephew wondered what drove a woman, teetering on the brink of bankruptcy, to steal his letter then just sit on it. What the hell game was this tart playing? Was she holding out for him to divorce his wife and marry her, to share in the power and the glory of the next phase of the Empire?

Think again, he told her a few minutes later as he spewed noisily into the leather bucket. If you could see me now, you'd see I'm wearing black, in mourning for my dearest Uncle Tullus. What path I take, after wreaking my cataclysmic change, is up to me, and so is who I walk with on that path, but one thing is quite certain.

There will be no witnesses left behind to testify to this fiasco. Ask Uncle Tullus, if you don't believe me.

Behind him, the dwarf smiled.

XXIX

'All rise for the Emperor!'

Claudia squinted open half an eye, grunted, then rolled over. The man was insane. It was still morning. Also . . .

'What the hell are you doing in my bedroom?'

'Opening the shutters.' Orbilio seemed oblivious that the brightness might cause permanent damage to her retina. 'It smells like a winery in here!' She heard a brisk rubbing of hands . . . 'Right, then! Five minutes, and I'll meet you at the jetty.'

'Bog off.'

. . . followed by an ominous chuckle. 'How much did you knock back last night?'

Claudia burrowed deeper under the sheet. 'One.' Which happened to be followed by another after another after another . . .

'So why am I counting two, correction three empty wine jugs?'

You've missed one, try under the bed. 'I'm a vintner, remember? We take a sip of wine, swill it round our mouths, then,' she pulled the pillow over her head, 'we spit it out.'

'And I'm Mars, the god of war. Never mind, for a hangover on this scale, I'm prepared to extend the time limit to six minutes,' he said. 'The countdown starts from now.'

'You're unnatural.'

'You're out of bed.'

And with that, Claudia found herself in an ignominious heap on the floor and by the time she'd disentangled herself from the sheet, it was against a closed door that the missing wine jug smashed into a hundred smithereens. Damn. Bleary eyes consulted the reflection in the mirror and instantly regretted it. Was that a dead vole protruding from her mouth, or just her tongue?

'I need to talk to someone,' she yelled down to Orbilio, striding out along the path below her window.

'Later,' he called back, indicating the jetty. 'This is urgent.'

What is? Claudia withdrew her head and stuck it in a washbasin full of cool, clear water, watching the bubbles bloop to the surface. What could be so important that Supersnoop had to prise her out of a perfectly good sleep . . . *holy shit!* Claudia surfaced and shook her head like a dog. Tarraco must have left the hare behind, its slashed underbelly pointing loud and clear that a key had been smuggled into jail . . . how else could he have escaped?

Hell, Cyrus would go absolutely rabid!

Like a cat with mustard on its tail, Claudia hauled on a fresh tunic and raced to the jetty. What was the penalty for jailbreak? She had a sneaking suspicion it made exile from robbing Sabbio Tullus' strongroom look tame . . .

With her heart thumping like a kettledrum, Claudia shot a glance back down the path which ran around the promontory. No clunk of soldiers' boots, no snickering horse bearing a tribune's weight. Not yet. She practically jumped in the boat. Thank heavens for Marcus Cornelius, having a boat at the ready, how could she ever thank him for saving her bacon?

He had stripped off his tunic and began to take the boat across the lake, and it may only have taken half an hour, but for Claudia it seemed half a lifetime. Every slurp of the oars made her jump, every grunt of exertion from Marcus made her swivel over her shoulder to check Cyrus wasn't rowing behind. Getting closer . . .

'Do you have any paper on you?'

'Oars are made of wood, as a rule,' he said.

'But I need to send a letter,' she protested. To warn an old woman. Just in case.

'You need to sober up.' He grinned, and she didn't see what was so funny. Croesus, what time was it she stumbled into bed? Dawn was breaking in the east, she remembered that, and the something hot and horrid which had twisted inside her as she recalled the fifty-foot colossus, Memnon, who sings to his mother, the dawn. For an instant, Claudia could almost hear the peacocks 'rrrow, rrrow', could almost smell his valerian and roses wafting on the sultry air. This morning Tarraco would not be around to hear Memnon sing. No longer could he spin his magic on a dead man's island, or suck up to wealthy women in Atlantis . . .

Unexpectedly her vision blurred, and a lump formed in her throat. Dammit, she should be glad she'd never feel the charge which shot through her veins when his hands latched over her wrists or watch his long mane shining in the sunlight. The same damned mane he used like a tool, one moment to veil his expression, another to tie back with a long, scarlet fillet—

'It must be one lulu of a hangover,' Orbilio remarked cheerfully, hauling on the oars. 'You look as though you're chewing a wasps' nest.'

'Then bee quiet and let me get on with it.'

They rounded a sharp jutting point and suddenly green eyes loomed up, not black, bringing back memories of a cave, a tunnel, a hundred whispered secrets . . .

Hurry, Marcus, hurry! Get me away from this place!

So jumbled were her thoughts, her fears, her vivid recollections that Claudia was taken aback when Orbilio pulled up at a small rocky beach beside a stream which danced down a gully to disgorge into the lake. She looked upwards, where the hill rose sharply, pines and birch and juniper and hawthorn, dense and seemingly impenetrable.

Claudia frowned. 'Where's the horse?'

'Try to exercise a modicum of restraint.' Orbilio laughed. 'Your humble servant has not yet secured the painter and you're asking—'

She was immediately contrite. Heavens above, he'd risked his reputation to do this thing for her, the least she could do was let him get his breath back. Helping him heave the boat ashore, she watched him lug a heavy basket out from under the seat. Drusilla! Good grief, in her panic she'd forgotten all about her cat or the packing! Idly wondering what tactics this intrepid investigator had used to lure Drusilla into a strange basket, Claudia scrutinized the sky. Clouds hung low, like a grey canvas awning, trapping heat which grew stickier by the minute. There was a rumble, grumble growl in the distance. The Titan rattling his chains.

'Great spot for a picnic,' Marcus said, chasing the sweat from his brow with the back of his hand.

'Excuse me?'

'It was you who said you could eat a horse, remember?'

'What I said was . . .' Claudia's voice trailed off. *That's not Drusilla in the basket?* 'W-what about the tribune?'

Marcus shot her an amused sideways glance. 'You wanted him along as well?'

'Not exactly.' Claudia scratched her head. Well, this rather changes matters! Maybe she wasn't wanted by the army, after all? At least, not yet! Of course, had it not been for this dire hangover, she'd have realized long ago that Tarraco would leave no trace of *anything* behind him. 'Why the sudden urgency?'

'This, of course!' He tapped the wicker basket. 'I'm starving, aren't you?'

Actually, now you come to mention it . . .

'Besides,' he said, spreading out a selection of cold cuts, wine cakes, cheeses, fruit and some fresh-baked steaming pies, 'this is one place where we can talk openly without risk of being overheard.'

'Funny you should say that.' Claudia sank her teeth into the crumbly pastry of a venison pie and decided now was as good an opportunity as any to re-evaluate the situation. Win him over. Make him understand. (Perhaps.) Far out on the waters, fishermen were casting their nets. 'Because,' a trickle of sweat ran down her neck, 'I have a tiny confession to make.'

'You know, that place,' Orbilio said, perching on a square, flat chunk of rock and nodding backwards to Atlantis, 'reminds me of a snowscene. Snow is nothing but pretty frozen water until you scoop it up and make a snowman. Then it becomes something altogether different.'

Excitement stirred in Claudia's blood. *But at base it's still snow*, she thought, consigning her confession down a mental shute. 'What if I tell you,' she said, licking the last vestige of gravy from her fingers, 'there might be a connection between certain seemingly isolated incidents? Deaths, for instance, which have been dismissed as accidental, but which might have had a more sinister motivation?'

And before his eyebrows raised themselves up off their elbows, she launched into the rumour surrounding the woman who wore red, the silversmith, the lady in the mud room and expected him to laugh, pass it off as idle speculation, and say the same could be true of oysters, and there was a vast difference between a grain of grit and an iridescent pearl. Except he didn't. He merely scooped up a handful of pebbles and began skimming stones across the water.

'Why don't you just marry me and have done with,' he said mildly. 'It would cut out so much duplication, minimize the workload—'

'It's your brain which has been minimized,' she snapped, reaching for a wine cake. 'Goddammit, Orbilio, I've just told you Atlantis is nothing short of a bloody murder factory and all you're concerned about is getting your leg over!'

'So was that a yes, then?' Orbilio skipped another half a dozen stones before swivelling round to face her. She mashed the wine cake underneath her heel and wished it was his nose. 'I notice,' he added, crossing his feet under his thighs, 'you made no mention of a young man in his prime who falls fifty feet in the middle of the afternoon and no one sees it happen.'

As though an unseen hand had added a pile of logs to some celestial fire, the temperature on the lakeshore seemed to soar. Plucking a white arabis, Claudia began to strip the petals off. She wished they were his ears.

'You have to admit,' he grinned, 'we make a damned good team.'

'Whatever I do, you're always against me.'

'Oh, Claudia. If only that were true.' Marcus unfurled his legs and stretched full length on the rock, supporting his weight on one elbow. 'Anyway, let's go back a bit, to the part where I – rather foolishly with hindsight – thought that by bringing you to Atlantis, it would keep you out of trouble. I was rather hoping that with your, shall we say, natural curiosity—'

'Insight.'

'—you might be able to pinpoint some of the anomalies and clearly I was not disappointed. Now then,' he rolled on to his back and folded his hands beneath his head, 'suppose I tell you that the case I was working on in Rome involved the curious death of a woman who kept cats. Twelve of them, I recall.'

Claudia reached for a terracotta pot and lifted the lid. 'Her bastard of a husband,' she said, fishing out a peach preserved in honey, 'strangled them.'

'Which in itself is curious,' he said. 'Did you know he strung them up the day after she left home?'

The day after she left home. Claudia lobbed the peach stone into the trickling stream. Not the day he received news of her death . . .

'His reply, when I tackled him, was not so much that he wasn't anticipating her return as he didn't give a damn about the consequences.' Marcus sighed, and a wasp probed the lid of the terracotta pot. 'Nothing could be proved, of course, I doubt it ever will, but once I began to delve, I saw a pattern forming. A whole series of untimely deaths surrounding this luxurious establishment, and out of the eleven deaths which have occurred in Atlantis over the past few months, on at least five occasions the victim's death was premature and—'

'They all had relatives who benefited financially.'

'How did you know that?'

Claudia shooed the wasp away, then wiped her sticky hands on the grass. 'Everyone who comes here is, for the main part, inordinately wealthy. It stands to reason, but there's a problem.' Her fingers prodded around in the honeypot until she found an apricot. 'No one benefits from Cal's death, his heirs are richer than he was. I've checked.'

Orbilio chewed on a blade of couchgrass and stared up at the darkening clouds. 'Which means Cal was killed for an altogether different reason,' he said slowly. 'Let me tell you what's happening in Spesium.'

'Has this any connection with the crimes in Atlantis?'

'Crimes?' he mocked. 'With an "s"? Oh no, we're dealing with one crime, just one, but it's so big, you can't see it close up.' Marcus spat out the stalk and sat up. 'Thanks to Pylades building this resort,' he said, 'all manner of shops and businesses were attracted to the area. First a few lodging houses appeared for those unable to afford Atlantis prices, then bootmakers, glassblowers, goldsmiths and so on trickled in, tempting the clientele to take home reminders of their holiday. Then one day, someone looks around and notices a whole new town's sprung up. Brickworks, granaries, tile-makers, you name it, it's here. In fact, everything and everyone is represented over there in Spesium except, funnily enough, law and order. Because it has all happened so fast.'

'Hardly,' Claudia reminded him. 'There isn't a single part of the Empire which isn't under someone's governorship.'

'Correct. But the Prefect whose patch this includes has a massive area to cover – don't forget, until Pylades moved in, Plasimene had been left to the fishermen for two hundred years. Indeed, just across the stream, on the far side of that gully there, lies the expanse of marshy wasteland known as The Place of Bones.'

Claudia kicked off her sandals and dangled the tips of her toes in the brook. In contrast to the sweltering steambath formed by the clouds, the water was a delicious icy cool. Upstream a dipper negotiated the current.

'So then,' Marcus turned over to lie on his stomach, running his finger round and round the rim of the honeypot, 'we've established that the Prefect more than has his hands full policing the Etruscan countryside while Spesium continues to expand at breakneck speed – and even when he does put in the odd appearance, what does he see? A gentle, law-abiding community too busy building houses and laying out its temples to allow something as ugly as crime to intrude.' Orbilio tossed her a pie and reached for one himself. 'The Prefect files his report accordingly, a garrison is built – small, but effective – and Cyrus is appointed on the first leg of his career. But what the Prefect doesn't see (in fact no one does), is the spectre of greed moving about in the background. One who covets Spesium's flourishing new trade.'

He paused to munch on the pie.

'One by one, shopkeepers, landlords, property owners are approached and it's pointed out to them that, without military protection, all manner of things might occur, and a hint is dropped that for a few sesterces per month . . .'

A sudden shudder ran through Claudia, colder than the mountain stream in which her toes splashed. Coming from the slums herself – lawless, dangerous places – she knew all about rackets like those. Traders who took a stand against protection would find their shopfront smashed in, their stock tainted and unfit for sale, and since the insurance was low, it would be stupid not to give in. Gradually, though, the premiums would be stepped up and those who refused to pay would wake to find fire raging through their premises or find their wives and children beaten up, and once again they would be terrorized into submission until finally, destitute and broken, they had nothing left to give. Either the business was sold for a pittance or else the craftsman/shopkeeper/landlord was retained as a poorly paid manager. But whichever way it went, it ended in tragedy.

No wonder they needed to trade through a funeral. No wonder that when they had the chance to unwind, they went overboard!

Claudia made a pastry raft and floated it on the bubbling waters. It had eddied round two rocks and was heading for the lake before she said, 'Naturally, this mastermind would want a henchman to oversee the day-to-day running of his investments – a chap of particular distinction, charm and grace, you'd think. Such as Pul?'

Strange how a man she'd never met, had never spoken to, had instinctively stirred up such deep-rooted misgivings. And it went deeper than that sinister walrus moustache, the curved blade at his hip, his menacing attire. It was more than curiosity which made her question where Pylades (who else?) would have met such a man . . .

Marcus hauled himself to his feet and watched an otter swim towards the marshes round the headland. 'This whole sordid business – call it murder, extortion, whatever – it all boils down to money. Just the cold, hard jangle of coins.'

Sweet Jupiter! Claudia was suddenly transported back to Thursday afternoon, when Cal had shown her the secret of the concealed door, the hidden cave, the tunnel leading to the foreshore. '*Remember the golden rule,*' *he had said.* That whoever possesses the gold rules . . .

Now she understood why Cal had been killed. How easy for Pylades, standing in the loggia, to overhear the conversation below, and hadn't Cal deliberately raised his voice? Knowing full well, Pul's paymaster was listening, to let him know that he could, if he wished, spill the beans and destroy the Greek's evil business in one swipe?

'Why don't you have Pylades and his succubus arrested?' she asked.

'Well, for one thing it's pretty obvious Cyrus is also on the payroll. He deliberately keeps the few troops he has well clear of town. Which means that if I start rocking the boat by bringing Pul in for questioning, it's going to alert everyone involved in this racket.'

Claudia remembered Lalo with his split knuckles, disappearing for hours on end . . . 'But that's not the reason, is it?'

'Nope.' Marcus punched his fist into the palm of his hand. 'Dammit, Claudia, Pylades is the obvious suspect, but I tell you, I've searched his office top to bottom, rummaged through his records, sat up all night last night going over his accounts and I can find nothing, *nothing* to indicate the incredible wealth which would have been generated from squeezing Spesium dry. He's rich, yes, but so obsessed is our friend the Greek, he ploughs everything back into Atlantis. A library here, a loggia there, but nothing on the scale you'd expect from mass extortion.'

'Well, if Pylades isn't masterminding it –' Claudia watched coracles reel in their lines, and realized it must be late afternoon by now '– you don't have many options. That only leaves Mosul or Kamar.'

'I've investigated them, as well.' Orbilio shrugged. 'Mosul is a wealthy man, which you would expect of a priest of his stature, although there's nothing to suggest he's anything other than a conscientious pawn in a very successful enterprise.'

'I'll say Atlantis is successful!' Claudia retorted. Miracle or *mirage*? 'From the moment I arrived and Cal revealed the secrets of the spa, I wondered . . . why? Why hide a door in a niche behind a statue? Why hide the entrance to the cave? Come to that, why hide the cave at all? Why not encourage pilgrims to visit the spring, rather than dispense water from outside the shrine? But most of all, why have the tunnel's entrance at the rear of the grotto and its mouth concealed by a thicket? Why disguise a masterstroke of civil engineering?'

There was a light dancing in Orbilio's eyes. 'I'm assuming you found the answer?'

Damn right. And I stumbled across it the day poor Leon took a beating.

'It all hinges on whether Mosul is a conscientious priest – or a man with something to hide.' Cal had virtually told her, hadn't he? In his own way, he'd shown Claudia the answer. 'You said it yourself, Lake Plasimene had been left to its own devices for two centuries,' she said, 'and suddenly a Greek architect appears on the scene and stumbles across an underground spring – hey presto, it's a miracle. But what if that Greek architect had done no such thing? What if that Greek architect saw a vision for a splendid place of luxury? The only thing missing was the reason for its generation, but what the hell, there's water all around, let's invent a reason.'

'So he gouges out a tunnel by which lake water is ferried up in secret and stored in a cistern in the cave? No,' Orbilio scratched his head, 'it can't work. Carya's waters are a cloudy white.'

'Only because Mosul makes regular additions. Chalk, I think.' While she was hiding in the cavern, she'd watched the mole-eyed priest stir the waters with his hand and when she'd tried to drink it, the water was bitter where he'd overdone it. 'That's the real reason he won't tolerate acolytes. He makes excuses to get rid of them before they can discover the scam.'

'Which suggests Mosul and Pylades are both in on the secret of Atlantis, but not rich enough to be associated with the extortion racket. Hmm.'

'Unless they're salting it away. What about Kamar?' Sweet Juno, please let it be Tortoiseface sent to a slow and painful death, if only on account of that poor infant he all but murdered the night before the Agonalia!

'Whilst our physician friend has plenty in his coffers, it's not sufficient to arouse suspicions, and since they'd have no call to imagine they'd be under surveillance, there's no reason for any of them to stash their money away.' Orbilio combed his hands through his hair. 'Which brings us right back to where we started,' he said sadly. 'Who's behind all this? Who is pulling these unseen strings?'

Claudia sat down on a tuft of grass and drew her knees up to her chin. Marcus tossed more stones into the water. Two swans skimmed the surface of the lake and disappeared around the headland. The only sounds were the gabbling of the stream, the gentle drone of bumblebees and a cuckoo in the distance. The little pastry boat had disappeared, dinner for a pike.

'Don't you think it odd,' Claudia said eventually, 'that no one has approached Pylades for protection money?'

'We don't know they haven't,' Orbilio said, settling beside her, one knee straight, the other bent. 'But if I was masterminding this operation, I'd wait until I had the whole of Spesium in my hand before making my move. By then, Atlantis will be an island in a sea of corruption – *Croesus, that's it!* That's bloody it. The island!'

He jumped to his feet. A thousand cockroaches began to abseil down Claudia's spine.

'That little lump of rock,' he said, 'is in danger of sinking into the lake with the weight of gold and marble and its treasures of antiquity.'

Claudia's teeth began chattering. He could be wrong, of course . . .

'Who else,' Marcus said, 'could *afford* to finance that racket?'

He had to be wrong. It was Pylades behind it. Pure coincidence that Tuder's villa was bursting its seams with rich treasures. Clever investments, that's all. Nothing to do with the fruits of extortion . . .

'Perhaps Lais rumbled him, maybe she'd simply outlived her usefulness, but Cyrus is so deep in Tarraco's pocket that between them they decide to stage that fiasco on the lakeshore yesterday.'

Claudia wondered whether she might be physically sick. 'Fiasco?'

'Don't you think that "dirty dago" routine was just a smidgen over the top? Can't you see, the whole damned thing was a put-up start to finish! You know, it struck me as odd at the time that Lais just happened to turn up like that – and wouldn't you know it was Pul, of all people, who suddenly plays helpful citizen and lends his hand to pulling Lais from the water! Even then, it smacked of a stage set.'

Tell me about it!

'But Cyrus arrested him,' she said feebly. 'Had him thrown into jail.'

'Sure, the tribune goes through the motions, but you wait! Tarraco will be set free on a legal technicality or else a fake suicide note will turn up beside some poor vagrant's body, confessing to the murder.'

'Why . . . go to those lengths?'

'Because not only will the outcome be made public, thus clearing Tarraco of any suspicion, it will give the two of them the perfect excuse to be seen together afterwards. No hard feelings, eh, old chap? No, no, none at all – a man has to do his duty, what! Then guess who's the best of friends? No skulking around, it's all open and seemingly above board, what more perfect cover? That's when I suspect the squeeze will be made on Atlantis. Once their armour plating is in place.' Orbilio kicked over the remains of the picnic, now crawling with reddish-brown ants. 'Well, he's clever enough, and greedy enough, to get away with anything, including premeditated murder – except this time our friend Tarraco has overstretched himself.' He sprinted over to the boat and untied the rope. 'Come on.'

'What are you going to do?' Claudia asked, and wished with all her heart that she could make time stand still so she wouldn't hear his answer.

'Bring the curtain up on this vile trade, of course, and even if it means pulling his toenails out to obtain a list of his confederates, you can be sure that by the time I'm finished, not only Pul and Cyrus, but every rotten apple in the pile will have been rooted out and pulped. Hop in.'

Claudia's legs could not have moved if they'd wanted to. 'Orbilio . . .'

'That's me.' Only the top of his head was visible as he stashed the basket underneath the seat.

'What would be the consequences of not compiling that list?'

'Hmm.' He puffed out his cheeks as he considered the prospects. 'I suppose the extortion would ease up for a while, but with so many mechanisms still in place and built on such solid foundations, even with the army being vigilant, I don't see how you could stop it opening again two or three months down the line.'

As the light began to fade, pictures appeared before her in the water. The tear-stained faces of women forced into prostitution. Children, made old before their time, stripped of their innocence as they slaved in sweatshops to pay off the thugs.

A sudden flash of white lightning shot down the valley.

'Nothing to worry about,' Marcus breezed. 'We're quite safe on the water.'

Like Virginia was safe? Claudia leaned over the stream and brought up the pies and the apricots and quite possibly yesterday's breakfast. When she held out her arms, they were quivering. Holy Jupiter, what had she done? Not only had Spes, the goddess of hope on whose virtues this town had been modelled, abandoned her people, Claudia had contrived to kick them while they were down. Her stomach turned somersaults.

The evidence had been there all along and she had chosen, yes chosen, to disregard it and for what reason? Simply because she hadn't believed Tarraco capable of cold-blooded murder! Well, at least there was a core of truth in that. The bastard employed minions to do his dirty work!

She leaned over and was sick a second time. From the outset, Tarraco had manipulated her to lure her in and win his trust. *His trust!*

Barbed lightning flickered, reflecting double in the oily waters of the lake and thunder echoed, low and distant, round the wooded crucible. Her tunic was sticking to her body like a second skin, but despite the heat from the celestial inferno, she found herself shivering. Sometimes, Claudia Seferius, you can be a very silly cow.

Her memory clock flipped back to that first night on the sun porch to where, out on the island, shortly before dawn, a light had sprung up. Instinct told her at the time it was a signal and sure enough, shortly afterwards wasn't

Tarraco hauling on the oars of his little grey rowboat, heading home? Right back then, Claudia had sensed he'd been visiting some kitchen wench with dimpled cheeks and a heaving, ample bosom, the pair of them rolling like puppies in the hay, and now it made sense more than ever. To counteract the shrill and desiccated Lais, Tarraco would tumble with girls who asked for nothing in return and left behind only a smile, to restore the masculinity and pride sucked out by women such as Lais and Virginia. But suppose his wife had got wind of the affair? How would that make her feel?

To try and comprehend what made him flip and snuff out her life with such brutality, Claudia put herself in the other woman's shoes. Tuder had brought her out to Plasimene, and in an instant Lais had been upheaved from a bustling, lively environment in Rome to an island on which she was virtually marooned. With Spesium not yet in existence and Atlantis in its mere infancy, what desolation must Lais have felt? Then, when Tuder dies, she sees in the mirror a middle-aged woman with twenty long and lonely years ahead. Desperation sets in. She tries to turn back the years with dyes and cosmetics and girlish attire – and then, whoosh, Tarraco drops from the sky. Brooding good looks apart, Lais is charmed by his attentions, flattered by the court he pays her. He's rich. He can't be after her money. Which leaves only one scenario: Tarraco must love her for herself!

She doesn't question his comings and his goings, she adores him. He heaps wealth upon her, upon the island. Peacocks appear on the scene, bronzes, splendid works of art – demonstrations, surely, of his fidelity. His love. Until one day she finds out about the kitchen wench. Tormented, she follows him and sees the laughter, the romping, all the things she never shared with him . . .

Desperate and betrayed, she confronts him. Mocks his lack of education, his lowly birth, perhaps even his lovemaking skills. Years of low self-esteem burst their banks. Tarraco flips. And too late Lais discovers the true meaning of the phrase drop-dead sexy—

'We need to get going,' Marcus said. 'It's not safe to be under trees with lightning about.'

His warning passed over her head. Like Lais, like Virginia, she'd been conned by cheap tricks, though it was easy to see why women fell for him. Not his muscled good looks, not even his arrogance. It was the irresistible aura of danger. They would have sensed it, as Claudia had sensed it, but men and women reacted so differently. Marcus, she recalled, had shown instinctive hostility! However, this was no time for self-flagellation. To acknowledge that, due to her stupidity, he'd go to ground until it became safe to strike up again. When it would be innocents, not Claudia, who'd pay . . .

'Suppose Tarraco *couldn't* talk?' she asked.

'Ha!'

'No, really. Suppose, for some reason, he wasn't able to? Pul or Cyrus could still provide the list of confederates, right?'

Marcus laughed. 'Pul is not the type to buckle under interrogation, not even torture, it would be a matter of honour with him, and Cyrus, I can tell you now, will fall on his sword the second he sees us coming to arrest him, it's patrician creed. But have no fear, my pretty damsel, I know human nature. Our little Spanish captive will sing like a linnet!'

'Actually,' Claudia smiled a sickly smile, 'there might be a bit of a problem with that.'

'Trust me, he'll sing! Now what are you hanging about for, we need to get back to the jailhouse.'

'I tried to tell you when we arrived . . .'

Preoccupied with shipping his oars, Orbilio merely grunted a 'huh?'

'The thing is,' she drew a deep breath, 'I paid a visit to Tarraco yesterday.'

'And?'

'And . . .' She swallowed hard. 'I let him out.'

XXX

As Jupiter shook his great cloak of storm clouds, Livia, wife of the Emperor, Augustus, beckoned her servant across. The window of her private, upstairs chamber was shuttered. A single flame burned from the lampstand, casting two shadows across the polished cedarwood boards, one tall and slender, the other stumpy and mis-shapen.

'You have done well, Spaco,' Livia said. 'But then,' she added with a smile, 'you usually do. What enticing cocktail did you serve up this time?'

'Aconite, baneberry.' The dwarf smiled in return. 'The odd dash of hemlock, our old friend rock cedar . . .'

'He suspected nothing?' she marvelled. 'Nothing at all?'

'Right up to his last living breath, he believed it to be an illness brought on by the tension. Even the hallucinations I managed to convince him were the product of too little food for his system to work on.'

'Surely the doctor . . .?'

The assassin spread his hands in a simplistic gesture, and Livia nodded in mutual understanding. The plague may have peaked, but bodies were still piling up. What careworn physician would think twice about the nephew of Sabbio Tullus succumbing to dysentery in this heat?

Despite the lateness of the hour, the crisis which ravaged the Empire meant that the clamour of a hundred bawling scribes, petitioners, justices and heralds still drifted up from below. Livia heard all of them and listened to none. Around her, on the walls, Dido and Aeneas played out their bitter tragedy in paint and on an inlaid tortoise-shell table a crystal bowl shaped like a duck perfumed the chamber with its candied contents.

'Your loyalty, Spaco, will not be forgotten.' The chamois drawstring purse chinked when it changed hands. 'And you say there is more?'

'Oh, yes. Just as your majesty predicted, there was no question of him not falling for that ploy of a burglar breaking in expressly to steal his papers and, as my lady also predicted, he set his own assassin on the trail to kick over the traces. First, his uncle; then his uncle's agent—'

'The chit who broke into the depository?'

'According to the fat man,' Spaco replied, 'the situation in Atlantis was – and I quote – under control. I think we can safely agree on what that means, the man was no slouch. In fact,' he sniggered, 'so desperate was he to retrieve his client's property, he returned with this.'

With his tongue pressing out a lump in his cheek, he handed over the letter sent to Orbilio from the Head of the Security Police, mistaken by the fat man for the genuine article, and watched the face of the Emperor's wife crease up with laughter. 'Fools, the pair of them,' she said, wiping her eyes. 'Nothing, but fools.' She popped a candied cherry in her mouth and turned her considerations to the deeper implications of her servant's report. 'What plans have you for this fat man?' she asked eventually.

'Already disposed of,' the dwarf replied airily. Popped his very last cardamom. 'No loose ends remain, trust me.'

'I do, Spaco,' she said softly. 'I do.'

With his ugly face suffused with pleasure, the diminutive assassin hammered his fist against his heart in salute as he retreated towards the trapdoor at the far end of the chamber, but her imperial majesty had already seated herself and was occupied with distaff and spindle when her husband popped his head round the door.

'Spinning again?' he mocked gently.

She simply smiled and said, 'You know how it relaxes me, dear.'

It was unlikely, she decided, preoccupied as he was with the business of reining in the Empire, that Augustus would have heard the dwarf's footsteps on the secret, wooden staircase.

Come to that, it was doubtful a mouse could have heard them.

Out along the Athens Canal, the heat throbbed like a brickworks kiln as Claudia leaned her arms on the balustrade and watched forked lightning dance across a sky the colour of driftwood. Why don't you rain? Get it over with! But she knew in her heart, as another thunderclap drowned out the gurgling from the marble nymphs' jugs, that this was yet another twist of Fate's knife. Another spoke in her personal wheel of fortune.

'You let him go?' Orbilio had said slowly. 'You set Tarraco free?'

They had been rowing back to shore and Claudia deliberately trailed her fingers in the water to avoid catching his hang-dog expression and explained that she didn't, at the time, think he'd killed Lais.

'Half of that I can't quibble with,' Marcus had replied so quietly she had to strain for the words. 'The part where you didn't think.' She heard him sigh as he pulled on the oars, and wished to hell he'd shout at her, or swear or throw a tantrum. Instead he shook his head sadly from side to side. 'Oh, Claudia. Why must you always rush in feet first to follow your heart?'

'Wouldn't one have to be curled in a ball to go feet first and still follow one's heart?' That ought to do the trick. Spur him into anger. But Marcus Cornelius did not rise to the bait.

'Why not hang on for a while? Even – dare I suggest it – talk it over with me first?'

What could Claudia say? That if she'd waited, Cyrus would not have granted her permission to visit the prisoner? That, if she lived to be five hundred like the ancient Sibyl of Cumae, she could never justify to this high-born policeman her faith in a low-born Spanish gigolo?

Now, as the storm lowered itself on its hunkers over Plasimene, smells of roasted duck and game from the banqueting hall became entwined with the colonnade's scents of marigolds and bay, and the clatter of knives on silver platters made music with the thunder along the Athens Canal. The combination of pleasure and oppression made her feel faint.

That she *had* believed in Tarraco was what made it so bloody hard to swallow! Eight years of acting the role of, what did he call it, 'pleasure boy' had honed his acting skills and with hindsight, Claudia saw that, after killing the bear, he was not just reading her character. The professional had been sizing her up!

With a violent shove, a terracotta pot filled with white, scented lilies went flying off the balustrade, to smash into a thousand smithereens. By admitting his crimes, actually even stressing his guilt ('The evidence is overwhelming, is it not?'), Tarraco had manipulated her into believing him innocent, and now, thanks to her, he was free. Free. To keep his head down until the dust had settled. To slither back when the furore died down and step up his filthy campaign.

Croesus, he was going to get away with it, as well!

Claudia's hands raked her hair. With any number of caves and hidey-holes dotted round these wild, Etruscan hills, he could be anywhere! Him and his cronies, biding their time – and how long before the authorities stopped searching? *If, indeed, they began.* Claudia sent another pot crashing to its doom. As long as the gang remained at large, the townspeople would be too terrified to testify against them for fear of retribution, which begged the question, on what evidence did this conspiracy exist? The hunch of a young investigator whose ambitions were widely recognized? Backed up by a woman whose double-bedded accommodation he was paying for? A woman, moreover, connected to a potential treasonable theft?

Goddammit, were Tarraco to spend a week holed up in those hills, he'd be lucky!

Well. Claudia swiped the hair out of her eyes with the back of her hand. All the fragrant lilies in the world lying shattered on that path won't solve the problem, but maybe – just maybe – there was another way to fell this mighty oak. It all hung on the courage of one old olive grower, who might or might not be being poisoned . . .

In the Great Hall, where the air was artificially cool, the hard-eyed, ravaged harpy for whom Claudia's nickname of Stonyface seemed never more appropriate came bearing down on her. But not in greeting, the way she had the night she'd been conferring with Kamar behind the statue. Lips pinched, eyes narrowed, Stonyface thundered down the stepped marble floor, her snub nose set to the ground and seemingly oblivious to the sparkling watercourse, the guffaws of laughter from the dining hall, and also, it seemed, to pedestrians.

'Out of my way, you stupid –' preoccupied features suddenly leaped back into focus '– Oh.' The hand which was about to barge Claudia aside froze in mid-air and the concrete jaw forced itself into some semblance of a smile. 'I thought you were a slave girl.'

Claudia's reciprocal smile told Granitepuss how she felt about that!

'Only I imagined everyone was at dinner,' the woman snapped in what presumably passed for an apology, before brushing past and slamming the door in her wake. But not before Claudia had caught the full force of the stewed walnut liquor which had freshly dyed out her grey.

Dear me, can't she see, at her age, that less is more? If she fell into that watercourse right now, all you'd see would be her feet, the sheer weight of cosmetics would keep her under! No, no; subtlety's the key in middle age. The hand that paints on those eyebrows should be light, and playing down her snub nose would make her infinitely more winsome than the girlishness she insisted on trying to achieve. Yet such was the haughtiness surrounding this old bag, it suggested not so much a blindspot as hardline inflexibility. In fact, so preoccupied was Claudia with wondering what turned perfectly attractive women into dogs that she almost failed to note the significance of what Lavinia was doing as she flung wide the door—

'NO!' she cried. 'For gods' sake, Lavinia, no!'

The little sparrow of a woman lay propped up on her daybed, her fleece of white hair cascading over the strawberry damask bolster, her wig sitting in her lap like a docile, curly lapdog. One wrinkled hand held a red medicinal phial, the other held the bottle's clear glass stopper.

Claudia flew across the room. 'Don't drink that!'

'Tch!' The old woman raised the phial to her lips. 'You can't win in this place,' she said, although there was no punch in her voice and those mischievous eyes twinkled like sapphires in the sun. 'One minute they tell you to finish off your medicine, the next they try and stop you. Well –' half a second before Claudia reached the wheeled couch, she tipped the contents down her throat '– Lavinia has a mind of her own!'

Now what? Oil of lavender burned in a brazier and beside a board set out for Twelve Lines, a silver bowl sat heaped with candied fruits. Much to the delight of a shiny black beetle. A roll of thunder crashed overhead, rattling the counters.

'I need to talk to you,' Claudia said.

Lavinia peered down the end of her nose. 'You didn't come just to intervene, then?' If anything, the eyes were brighter than ever.

With slow deliberation, Claudia moved one of the

onyx soldiers to a different square on the chequerboard. 'In a manner of speaking,' she said, 'yes.'

As the storm rumbled round the cupola that was Plasimene, she perched on the edge of Lavinia's couch and gave the old woman a summary of Tarraco and the racket he was working. The figure on the couch didn't stir, except to fold her arms across her narrow chest. It won't take long, Claudia calculated. It won't take long for the medicine to kick in, and then I've lost Lavinia until tomorrow. We must move fast.

But for two long minutes after she'd finished speaking, Lavinia remained in silence, and Claudia wriggled as a rivulet of sweat drizzled down her backbone. Two more trickles followed it before the sparrow finally spoke.

'That's all very interesting,' Lavinia said. 'But I don't see where I fit in.'

'Through *this*.' Claudia picked up the red glass phial and thought, here goes. We arrive at the moment of truth. 'With your testimony and the contents of this little bottle as evidence, we can build a case against Kamar and—' she drew a deep breath '—your son.'

'*My son?*'

'All we need is one stepping stone, just one, and from there the investigation will avalanche.' Tarraco's associates would squeal like rats in a trap, he'd be back in that cell before the end of the month!

'I'm sure it would,' Lavinia said dryly, and a wizened claw lashed out to move an onyx soldier from the sidelines on the chequerboard. Instantly the draw was transformed to an out-and-out rout. 'But I repeat. I don't see what this has to do with me.'

'Don't you.' It was not a question – the old woman

knew full well. One glance at the chequerboard showed that. Claudia thought of the medicine Lavinia had just swallowed, and knew time was running out. Especially for playing convoluted mind games. Nevertheless – 'So there was no ulterior motive behind your repeating all that gossip?' And in such technicolour detail, too!

'Motive?'

All right. Let's play this little charade, if that's what makes you happy. 'So much scandal.' Claudia shifted position on the couch and crossed one leg over the other. 'Adultery, crooked business deals, character assassinations – Atlantis is dripping from the gutterspouts with social sabotage and political intrigue, yet you choose to tell me stories about people who have died in seemingly natural circumstances.'

Wrinkled eyelids closed, and for one heart-stopping second, Claudia thought the draught had kicked in, but no. Lavinia let out a loud sigh and laced her fingers together. 'You're right,' she said. 'I did set you off on a paperchase, and I'm jolly glad I did. What else could an old cripple do?'

Of course, Claudia told herself, she hadn't *really* doubted the paralysis. Or suspected the old bird of fabricating an attempt on her life in order to gain a bit of attention. Had she?

'Until you showed up,' Lavinia was saying, 'there was no one in whom I dared confide my suspicions – especially not that sourpuss physician. Half of them were his patients!' Tears welled up in her eyes. 'It was the boy, you see,' she said quietly, 'the orphan who died in the hunting accident, and whose cousin so fortuitously inherited. Things like that must not happen again.' Then she cleared her throat, and when she spoke, there was a distinct edge to her tone. 'However, I didn't expect you to drag my son into this. Anyone would think you're suggesting he was part of the conspiracy, trying to bump off his old mother to get his hands on her olive grove.'

For Claudia, patience was more a sideline than a strong point, but she was prepared to invest it in this and since Lavinia's wits hadn't dimmed with the medicine, Claudia knew that to rush it would not be the answer. She would need to be reeled in carefully, especially when the foundations of her whole life were about to wobble. Were Ruth or Lalo in on it, too? Or the ugly sisters? Claudia sniffed at the phial and was about to launch into a complicated dissertation on herbal poisons, when she realized the contents were far from medicinal! No wonder Lavinia hadn't fallen asleep!

Dammit, the harpy was cackling. 'Don't tell Fab and Sab,' she said. 'It's the only way I can sneak wine past them these days!'

So much for hard evidence! Shit!

'You're wrong, you know,' Lavinia said, pulling on her wig, 'about my son. He means his old mother no harm.'

'You're biased—'

'Oh, Lavinia can prove it.' Carefully she tucked her white frizz under the pile of immaculate curls. 'Open that box, the one with the elephant carved on the top. That's the one. Now take out the blue phial and sniff it. You can even,' she let out an evil chuckle, 'drink it, if you like.'

Medicinal smells exploded into Claudia's airways, but one stood out clear above the rest. She sniffed again to make sure – but yes. Loud and clear came out balsam, gentian, peppermint and – goddammit . . .

'Hemlock!' In the distant recess of her mind she heard two fat women chanting. '*She wouldn't take her medicine, you know.*' '*Wouldn't. Not a drop.*' Holy Mother of Mars, had Lavinia drunk it, she'd be dead already!

'I'm fully aware of what it is,' Lavinia said slowly. 'Kamar brings me a gallon of the frightful mixture every single morning, but,' she pierced Claudia with her scimitar blue eyes, 'even if I downed the lot, it wouldn't kill me. Just make me very woozy.' The wizened claw now wrapped itself round Claudia's wrist and gave it a motherly shake. 'You're young,' she said, 'and Lavinia's not just old, she's a country woman, who happens to know more than a thing or two about hemlock. Have you, for instance, ever seen me retching? Vomiting? Complaining of stomach cramps?'

'No-o,' Claudia said, trying to hide the gloat in her voice. 'But I've witnessed first hand some of the other side effects. Take those occasions when you've been rendered unable to speak, for instance. How do you account for those, eh?'

That first night on the sun porch, when Lavinia had gone all stiff, eyes bulging, throat too tight to speak . . . if that wasn't classic hemlock poisoning, what was? Looking back, Claudia realized Lavinia hadn't been concerned with someone moving in the shadows; she'd been in the early throes of an attack! Dammit, the same thing happened on the grandstand during the run-up to the foot race. No more, though! Lavinia was safe from now on. No more hemlock, no more poison, goodbye Fab and Sab. They had to be in on it, Claudia thought. But then again, those two were so bound up with themselves, maybe not. Lavinia's son probably used them as cover!

'And,' she pressed relentlessly, 'have you ever asked yourself why Kamar should prescribe hemlock in the first place?'

'Mercy, child, I can see you're not going to let me go without a fight.' The old woman laughed. 'Lavinia's going to have to own up.'

'Own up?' Claudia's speculations reeled themselves back with a jolt.

'Claudia, the reason Kamar brings me hemlock every day is because I'm dying.'

A burning pain shot through Claudia's gut.

'Tch, stop that!' The old woman sliced the air with her hand to brook any sympathy and clucked her tongue again. 'In very small doses, hemlock can actually relieve pain, you know. Acts as a kind of anaesthetic. But time is precious to me, you can understand that, I know you can, the same as you can appreciate that Lavinia doesn't want to spend her last days – yes, child, we're talking days – I don't want to lose these precious moments in a woozy haze. I want to see and taste and touch everything around me to the very end – that's why my son mortgaged the grove to the hilt to send me here for a holiday. That ship sinking off Alexandria really fetched him to his senses and for the first time in her life, Lavinia's confident he'll settle with our little patch of olives and find contentment there.'

Claudia could not speak. There was a trapdoor across her throat and a mountain in her lungs. No, not a mountain. A volcano. Desperate to erupt.

'Lavinia—'

'That,' Lavinia said purposefully, 'is why I won't drink that wretched medicine. Since they found that tumour inside me, large as a fist and hard as lead, well . . . since

277

then, I put myself into a trance whenever I feel the pain coming on. It's a trick I picked up nearly fifty years ago, and it's served me well ever since. Now, stop that grizzling, girl, I'm not dead yet. There'll be time enough for sorrow, then, if that's what takes your fancy.'

Claudia gulped back her sobs. Lavinia was right. If her estimation of the timescale was correct, better she lapped up every moment.

'H-how long have you known?' she asked. A quernstone seemed to have settled in her stomach.

'Long enough for the pain to have aged me ten years,' Lavinia replied. 'But if I don't make my sixty-fifth birthday, so what? Can you think of a more idyllic way to end my days, and if I have no regrets,' she reached for another wine-filled phial, 'neither should you!' She gulped the contents down in one go. 'But as I said, Lavinia's not dead yet, in fact, she's thoroughly enjoying her role in rooting out these murders. So then.' She smacked her wrinkled lips. 'Without any hard evidence from me, where does that leave the investigation?'

'Grounded,' Claudia snapped. Completely and utterly grounded.

Tarraco, goddammit, was going to get away with it!

XXXI

The electric storm trapped by the Etruscan hills which surrounded Lake Plasimene had little impact down in Rome other than to compress the clouds low on to the rooftops and tickle the tiles of the Imperial Palace. As more lamps were lit to counteract the blackening sky, the wife of the Emperor picked up a silver hand mirror and patted her hair in place. Greying only at the temples, she was still a handsome woman and she knew it. Straight of back, sharp of eye . . . and sharper still of mind. For a quarter of a century she had been married to Augustus and for a quarter of a century she had striven to bear him a child. She ran her tongue over her teeth. Neither of them was at fault – both had been parents in previous marriages, he with Julia, she with two sons, Tiberius and Drusus – therefore, by definition, this barren marriage must be the will of the gods. Livia breathed on the mirror, then cleared the mist with the heel of her hand. Surely, then, it followed that the gods were pushing Julia and Tiberius together?

Downstairs, the clop-clop-clop of legionaries' boots on stairs and mosaic and marble was finally beginning to fade and in the flickering half-light, Livia allowed herself a hint of a smile. With the two most influential houses in the Empire joined in matrimony, Rome would soar to even greater heights, rise to grander challenges, take on the

Dacian kings for control of the goldmines, annexe Arabia, Germany, why, then even the Orient would be ripe for the taking . . .

True, Julia was heavy with the dead Regent's fourth child, but their firstborn, Gaius, was only eight, for gods' sake, and the instant she'd received news of Agrippa's death, Livia swung her considerable intellect into action, selling her son's virtues to the pregnant widow in such a way that the silly cow was virtually begging Tiberius to divorce that bookish wife of his and marry her instead. Knowing her son would do anything to secure the future of the Empire, Livia had brusquely dismissed his protestations of love for his wife. Tiberius would come around eventually!

So then. That was settled. All it needed now was a quick stamp of approval from the Senate and the question of Regent (and heir!) was assured.

Smoothing the rug which covered the trapdoor over the secret staircase in her spinning room, her imperial majesty's wrath turned to the fool who imagined that, with that one scrap of paper, he could wield power over a man as mighty as Augustus. Did Tullus' weasel-faced nephew seriously imagine that she, wife of said Emperor, would stand by and watch twenty years of peace and stability washed into the Tiber simply for that little shit's personal profit?

Imbecile! Livia spat in disgust at his memory.

His mistake, of course, came in his claim to a blood link. Snobby little turd thought it gave him protection! *As if*! Still, all things considered, it was as well the nephew's approach had come through her. The Emperor was a clever, often devious opponent, but his wife was downright ruthless and unlike Augustus, she had not softened with time. Like a cat at a mousehole, she watched and she waited and she waited and she watched and it hadn't taken long before she'd discovered where the nephew had stashed his precious piece of paper. From then on, it was simple. Twist the architect's arm into co-operating with the plan. Steal the incriminating letter. Find a patsy to raid the depository at the same time Sabbio Tullus collected his silver. Then sit back and let Spaco the dwarf work his charms . . .

Neat, or what?

Livia opened a casket and delved beneath the ropes of pearls and necklaces dripping with emeralds and agates. She had hoped, naturally, the day would never dawn when this paper surfaced, or that by the time it did, it would be powerless to cause damage.

Which is not to say she hadn't been prepared!

From the early days of her marriage, she had been aware of its existence – there were no secrets between herself and Augustus in those days – but as long as Marcus Vispanius Agrippa remained married to the emperor's daughter, there was no problem. Until Agrippa died both unexpectedly and prematurely, throwing the Empire into confusion. With Augustus away in Greece at the time, there was no official inquest and a whole range of question marks flew up. Most of those the Emperor had calmed down, but the biggest question remained – who was eligible to take over?

To Livia, the answer was simple, and having ensured the circumstances were ripe for a union of the Emperor's child with his well-respected stepson, and with the immortals smiling upon them, what could stand in their way?

Apart from one small piece of paper, yellowed and softened with age?

An order, issued over thirty years before, penned by Augustus himself?

How it had come into that weasel's possession, Livia would never know and moreover she did not remotely care. Suffice that it was back where it belonged (not that Augustus was aware of it, of course!) and with the mouth of every witness sealed, that little scrap of handwriting could inflict no further damage.

Livia's hand faltered over the flame. For one brief second, she felt the weight of the parchment's responsibility and her mind drifted back through the years.

Julius Caesar lay dead, slain by men he called his friends. In his will he appointed his adopted nephew, Augustus, as his heir, who quickly won the people over with his charm and generosity, paying out of his own funds the legacies the Divine Julius had bequeathed the city but which Mark Anthony, hard-nosed as ever, refused to release from the treasury. Most of all, however, the young Augustus won them over with the sheer power of his personality and his dynamic leadership, bringing them unimagined peace after three generations of civil war.

Deep inside, Livia felt a warm glow envelop her. Twenty years on and thirty-two years after the death of Julius Caesar, the people still adored him, the Senate backed him to the hilt, Augustus was a hero to one and all.

But Augustus was a man. And one day the man would die.

Born of patrician rather than imperial blood, Livia was the first to admit that her own son, however magnificently he had proved himself in the field, would not be the Senate's first choice! And supposing a small piece of paper was handed in at the next session?

The original order, penned by the nineteen-year-old Augustus, issuing the death warrant of Caesar's natural-born son.

It was murder, pure and simple, but civil war had been raging, tearing the country apart, and whilst no one at the time doubted the event occurred, fewer still had cared. Most simply accepted that Augustus had acted in the Empire's interests, as much as his own.

However, times had changed. And at such a critical juncture in Rome's future, that damning piece of evidence would be sufficient to discredit Augustus and for questions to be asked.

Questions such as . . . *who is Caesar's closest living relative?*

Suddenly, instead of facing an academic debate in the Senate House, the field would be wide open, contenders trampled underfoot as they jockeyed for position, and this was the purpose towards which Tullus' nephew had been working. He had his own candidate to propose. A weak man, a puppet to be manipulated, but a threat nonetheless.

Augustus would be safe – but only during the length of his lifetime. *How long before the assassins' knives flashed in the dark?*

The nephew's downfall, she reflected, came from his need to brag about the power that he held. The need to taunt her with the evidence, to make her fearful for the future. Imbecile!

With a slow spreading smile, Livia lowered the yellow paper to the flame and watched an ancient secret turn to smoke.

XXXII

The sky had turned to obsidian as Claudia sat with her knees drawn up to her chin, staring out across the lake to Tuder's island.

Defeat stared defiantly back.

She was sitting with her back to the wall at the mouth of the tunnel, and high above, the babble of post-dinner conversation filtered down from the little domed loggia, broken by the occasional lewd chuckle or high-pitched fluting laughter. She could picture them. Halfway to rolling drunk and with slaves on hand to top up their goblets, senators making the most of this unofficial recess with casual affairs which would be frowned upon (nay, condemned) in normal times.

But these were far from normal times. In Rome, Plague marched in triumph through a city hammered to its knees with the death of the Regent, and with its Emperor driven ragged over these twin crises. Who exercised restraint over absent senators and magistrates, legates and commissioners? Goosepimples raised themselves up on Claudia's skin at this foretaste of what the Empire would be like without Augustus at the helm. Decadent, debased. Devalued. A thousand Tarracos would spring up across the provinces, flourishing in the void created by general locking horns with general, of senators vying for ascendancy. In their struggle for personal glory, the common man would be forgotten – except by pimps, racketeers and loansharks.

With the spectre of anarchy chilling her veins, Claudia glanced up the tunnel, towards the cistern which Mosul filled from the lake then doctored with chalk to palm off as holy water. It was from one of the apertures in this rock that Claudia had seen Cal's body, red and twisted, lying on the shingle and it was here, at this very spot, that his blood still stained the stone. Even in the darkness, she could see it. Feel it. Hear it calling out to her . . .

Shit!

Knowing Atlantis held a sackful of secrets to its bosom, and buckling under the weight of her determination to unveil Cal's killer, Claudia had sought refuge with the one man she imagined outside this wretched tangle – only to find he had been at its very core. And even then, the situation might not have been exacerbated, had Claudia not been hooked by Lavinia's tales of mysterious deaths, recounted in such a clever and roundabout way as to first deny there was anything odd about the stories, yet stringing enough of them together to suggest the very opposite was true. Claudia buried her head in her hands. What was that old proverb about cats and curiosity!

If only she could find a way to snare the Spaniard. Bring him to justice . . .

'Ruth!' a husky voice commanded. 'Ruth, we have to leave.'

Claudia's head jerked up. Down by the jetty, two outlines shot into stark relief by a vivid streak of lightning, showing bright the yellow bodice and fringed skirt of

Lavinia's young Jewish servant. Her midriff glistened in the cloying humidity of the electric storm, as the tears ran down her cheeks. Claudia rose to her feet and, fully aware of the irony about cats and curiosity, moved closer to the couple, her presence concealed by an alder trunk.

'I can't.' Ruth's head shook violently from side to side. 'She's sick. She needs me.'

'But there's nothing we can do.' In his hand, Lalo held a large canvas sack and there was an edge of exasperation in his voice. 'You heard what she said. Get out, get away while you can. Come on, love. In the boat.'

He tried to drag her by the arm, but the girl began to whimper like a wounded animal and fell, prostrate, to the ground, great gulping sobs racking her body. 'She's only got a few more days left,' she wailed. 'A week at the most. Who'll be there to dose her with mandrake when the pain becomes too great for her to bear?'

'Ruth, we're slaves,' Lalo hissed. 'Which is worse? To be separated – or to get away while we can and be happy for the rest of our lives?'

Separated? Then Claudia realized why Lavinia was urging the two people she loved so dearly to abscond and risk the penalties which went with running away. She knew Fabella well enough to know she'd sell this big, broad, handsome field hand the instant Lavinia breathed her last, and there's no way Fab would have Ruth around, with her Hebrew dress and familiar manner.

'I've made enough these past weeks to buy us a fresh start.'

Claudia's heart cartwheeled as she recalled his constant succession of raw and swollen knuckles. Was Lalo, heaven forbid, a cog in the wheel of extortion, moonlighting as one of Pul's heavies? Horrified, she watched as he opened the top of his bag to run a river of coins through his fingers.

'All that boxing, all those wrestling matches after hours – please, Ruth.' His voice had thickened with grief, but Claudia's knees nearly gave way with relief. 'We've come so far,' Lalo begged. 'Don't throw our last chance away.'

'I will never leave her, and that's final.' The determination in Ruth's voice carried over the rumbles of thunder. 'Anyway,' a note of stubbornness crept in, 'I don't believe Fabella would be so cruel as to separate us. You go if you like,' she said, turning away, 'but I'm staying here with Lavinia.'

Lalo's massive, gleaming shoulders sagged and behind the alder tree, Claudia's mouth set in a line. To pass themselves off as Roman citizens, the risk was execution for the pair of them. Maybe Ruth had a point? But then again, from what Claudia had seen of Fabella, that old heifer would baulk at shelling out money for a tracker! And Lavinia was not some half-baked nitwit making suggestions she didn't really mean. If that old peasant woman said go, she meant go. She avoided as much medication as was possible because she wished to die with dignity, her faculties intact – and those, as Claudia knew only too well, were sharper than splinters. Lavinia, she felt certain, was more than capable of putting herself into trances to shut herself off from the pain, and if she was capable of that, then she was equally capable of guzzling down a painkiller when it all became too much.

A stinging sensation welled up in Claudia's eyes as she considered the proud old bird that was Lavinia. But

Lavinia wasn't dead yet . . . and she'd be mortified to know the two people she loved most would be torn apart over her. Purposefully Claudia stepped out of the shadows.

'Lovely evening,' she remarked, taking care to look at neither of them. A boat was moored to the jetty, in which a small battered trunk had been laid in the middle. Smart move. Row to the far side of the lake, take the quickest route to the Adriatic, and from there it's only four days to Greece, five if they were heading for Egypt.

'Oh, Ruth,' she said, 'there was something I wanted to ask you about the strength of white mandrake.' Not one, but two ideas had begun to germinate in the fertile furrows of her mind.

'Huh?' Ruth didn't seem predisposed towards convivial conversation, but there you are. Such is life.

'I'm right, aren't I, that about this much –' Claudia indicated the amount between thumb and forefinger '– of the neat decoction can lay a man out cold for up to three hours?'

'Um. Yes.' Ruth wrestled to bring herself to be polite. 'Yes, I suppose it will.'

'Thank you.' Claudia winked at Lalo. 'Oh and Ruth?'

'Mmmm?' Through brimming tears, the girl turned round. And too late saw the blow which laid her out.

'Lalo,' Claudia grinned, sucking at her knuckles, 'I do believe Ruth is ready to accompany you on your travels.'

XXXIII

Kamar didn't stand a chance.

He had been boiling balsam resin in his tripod to mix into a salve with rue and myrrh to reduce an imaginary inflammation round the stone merchant's eye when he heard the rap at his door. Cursing at having to leave his brazier at so critical a juncture, he bumbled over to admit the next hypo-bloody-chondriac who needed his services – and failed to see the wad of white cotton before it was under his nose. By then, of course, it was too late. Gasping, gagging, sagging backwards to the floor, he also missed hearing the door kicked shut and it was only when he tried to move his arms that he realized they'd been shackled behind his back.

'*What the . . .?*'

'How much were you paid to kill them?'

'What?'

'Answer me, you bastard!' Claudia crunched home the lock. 'How much?'

'I'm a physician,' he spluttered, shuffling backwards on his bottom. 'My job is to save lives.'

Dropping the wad which had been drenched with white mandrake, Claudia flexed the birch cane she'd found nestling beside the manacles in the adult play chest in the bath house. 'Tell that to the families of those poor unfortunates ferried across the Styx before their time.'

'I don't know what you're talking about!' But his leathery face bore none of the purple bluff of indignation. His complexion had drained to ghostly white.

'Then allow me to assist your lapse of memory.' With a whine, the switch cut through the air. 'There was a silversmith, I believe.'

Kamar yelped when the cane made contact with his calf.

'A woman who kept cats. Ooh, did that hurt? The middle-aged bride who died on her honeymoon. Gosh, that one made your eyes water, didn't it? Where was I? Oh, yes, the woman whose heart gave out in the mud room—'

'Y-you're mad!' His tortoise eyes bulging from their sockets, Kamar slithered backwards across the floor.

Madder than a rabid wolf sucking on a red-hot cinder, you haven't seen the half of it. 'And let's not forget that poor orphan boy.' For him, Claudia brought the cane down hard across the physician's cheek, knowing it would leave a permanent red scar.

'For heaven's sake!' he wailed. 'You're not suggesting . . . not seriously . . . Oh, come on!'

Claudia paused by his instrument rack and selected a bronze probe, fine and flexible. 'This should flex nicely up your left nostril,' she said cheerfully.

'All right, all right.' There was a rising note of panic in his voice. 'From time to time, I may have . . . eased . . . a patient out of their distress. I believe I do recollect the silversmith, now you come to mention it—'

'And the woman who kept cats?'

'She was ill,' Kamar bleated, 'very ill.' He edged backwards from the bronze probe, jarring the leg of a table and sending clouds of white powder into the air. 'I was only easing her passage—'

Pastilles from a limewood box cascaded on to the floor. 'The same way you helped Cal?'

The Etruscan's tongue darted round his lips. 'I didn't kill Calvus!' His voice was shrill in protest and Claudia knew she had him on the run. In fact, one quick flex of the bronze probe was sufficient. 'All right, all right – I admit, I knew the body had been placed to make it look like an accident, but . . .' His eyelids were beating faster than a bumblebee's wings. 'I – I – don't know why I covered it up. I just panicked. Then when everything went quiet . . .' His voice trailed off and he offered up a look of utter helplessness.

Claudia waited. And the silence was more effective than either the probe or the cane.

Kamar groaned. 'Look. Now and again, Pul tips me the wink about clients with terminal illnesses and for their sakes well, yes, I do occasionally help them out of their suffering.'

'For which the relatives are no doubt very grateful.'

His voice turned to a whine. 'Why shouldn't they show their gratitude in tangible form? I'm only doing my duty . . .'

Goodness gracious, he genuinely expected her to swallow that, too! Heavens, if this man was any dimmer, he'd need watering three times a week!

'Wh-what are you doing?'

'Trussing you up like a peahen for the table.'

When Claudia tied his ankles to the table leg with a

sturdy linen bandage, his circulatory system was the last thing on her mind. She didn't even hear him wince. Behind her, his balsam resin spluttered in the brazier and on the shelf above his balances an array of tins and flasks and copper vessels glinted in the lamplight.

'Now, Kamar, you have a choice. Either I holler and bring Pylades running with a whole host of witnesses to hear what you've just told me, or you can whisper in my dainty shell-like ear where I can find him and we can negotiate your departure from Atlantis with some degree of dignity.'

'Who's "him"?' Kamar blinked slowly several times.

Still playing games, eh? Claudia leaned forward and placed the tip of her nose to the tip of his. 'He sold you out, you know.'

'Who did?' A flicker of puzzlement danced across the turtle face. 'Pul?'

'I'm after the miller, not the donkey grinding the corn. Where is Tarraco holing up?'

'How should I know where he is,' he said testily. 'He escaped from bloody jail, he could be any . . .' His voice trailed off, and a strange expression came over his face. 'Wait—' It had to be fear. Yet he looked suspiciously smug. 'You said Tarraco sold me out, right?'

Claudia nodded.

'Then why do you need me to tell you where he is?'

Shit. 'Because.' Claudia straightened up and to buy time pretended to read the papyrus label gummed to a small horn container. Think, girl. Think! Make it plausible. 'Because Orbilio –' (yes!) '– believed his story that you were the mastermind behind the racket and he was the innocent dupe, and so he . . . let him out of jail. Now, of course, we know otherwise, and while Marcus is chasing his tail with the er, paperwork, I've been authorized to make a deal with you.'

Kamar's low brows knitted together. 'You wouldn't be lying to me?'

'Now why should I do a thing like that?' she smiled back. 'You've seen me talking to Orbilio, you know he's paid for the room. I'm his top undercover agent.' Oh, lord. Had she pushed it too far?

'A deal, eh?'

'You have my word.'

'And you promise that, if I give you what you want, you'll let me walk away? No repercussions?'

'My solemn oath.'

'Very well,' Kamar said, with what could almost pass as a twinkle in his eye. 'In that case, I'll tell you exactly where you can find your Tarraco!'

XXXIV

You could cut the heat with a wood saw as Claudia's oars slurped through the oily, black water. She shivered. Clouds had long since swallowed the hills and behind her, dark and silent, Tuder's island rose austere and jagged in the spears of white which flashed and flickered as the thunder rolled and rumbled. She swallowed the lump in her throat.

The Titan was breaking free of his chains . . .

With a boulder in her stomach and a stranglehold round her throat, she hauled the boat ashore, the crunch of gravel a pinprick in the wild night, and to the croak of a million frogs and with crickets buzzing in the grass, she zigzagged her way towards the villa. Along the colonnade, torches hissed and spat in the torrid night air, their pitch and their sulphur sour in her throat. Keeping close to the shadows, she worked her way round to the dining terrace. The purple unholstered couches had been taken indoors, but the pots of spiky palms pointed accusingly and the scent of the garlands was overpowering. Slipping off her sandals, Claudia padded up the steps, alert for the least sound or sensation. The last time she had seen the atrium, inhaled its myrrh, marvelled at its gilded rafters, had been the night Tarraco tried to seduce her . . . The night he presented her with his wife's harebell-blue gown . . . She shuddered again, and mastered the brief spell of nausea.

Tonight, as before, the hall was deserted, and flitting between the soaring columns and cold-eyed statuettes, Claudia paused to take stock. It was the old, old riddle, wasn't it? Where's the best place to hide a pebble? Answer: on the beach. With hindsight, it was obvious Tarraco would not hole up in the hills, but would scuttle back to home – he had his slaves to cover for him, they would be his eyes and ears until the furore subsided. Meanwhile, any number of legionaries could search Tuder's island and not find his hiding place – unless someone confessed.

An explosion of thunder overhead sent Claudia's heart hurdling into her mouth and when a second roll joggled the ceramic votive dishes in the family shrine, her jittery wrist almost sent a vase of deep blue delphiniums crashing to the floor. Calm down, she told herself, steadying the jar. Relax. You *can* do this on your own!

Typical bloody aristocrat, bunking off. She rolled her eyes to the ceiling. The one time you need help, and where is he? Probably finishing off his game of rams and rustlers with the luscious Phoebe, her of the straining seams, kohl eyes and generous bosom. (Generous in the sense that she gave it to anyone who wanted it, that is.) Well, wherever he'd slunk off to, Claudia had no time to lose. Sooner or later Kamar would come round and although she'd left him trussed up like a waterfowl and dosed with enough of his own anodyne to lay him out flat for three hours (thanks, Ruth!), at some stage his wife would wonder where old Turtleface had gone . . . and next time Tarraco would take care *not* to choose a hiding place which could be blabbed about.

It was now. Or it was never.

The atrium fountain splashed and sputtered as another

silver shaft splintered the heavens, lighting up the potted ferns and herbs and animating the paintings on the wall. From a distant wing came the clatter of pans and skillets as supper pots were washed and cleared away, and the faint smell of leather permeated the air. Suddenly masculine voices drifted across. Tarraco? Claudia flattened herself against the stonework just as two swarthy slaves appeared in the doorway, rolling an amphora of olive oil across the floor to the storeroom. She dared not breathe. Please, Jupiter. Go easy on the thunderbolts! Her prayer was answered. The men trundled their cargo right past her, chatting, laughing, not thinking to peer in the shadows . . .

Her knees needed several minutes after the slaves had locked up before they were capable of darting across the open hall to the courtyard. First on the right, Kamar said. Looks like a bedchamber, but behind the tapestry depicting Jason's search for the Golden Fleece lies a door which leads to a hidden chamber. Tarraco, he grinned, will be in there.

'How can you be sure?' Claudia had demanded.

'I've been there many times,' Kamar said smugly, and was so confident of his trade-in value that Claudia observed a distinct glint of victory in his eye as she stuffed the saturated wad of mandrake up his nose.

Now, as the heavens bellowed like a wounded bull, Claudia glanced along the courtyard to the two oak doors which faced a long line of clipped box trees and found her hands were trembling. With Orbilio nowhere to be found, who else could she enlist? As ever, Claudia Seferius was on her own . . .

Drawing one long resigned breath, she slipped through the door on the right. So far, so good. Kamar's information was correct, the room did look like a bedchamber. In fact, it looked like the very same bedchamber in which Tarraco had intended to serve his fresh honeycombs! Pulling aside the very same tapestry he'd pulled aside, Claudia peered into the antechamber which led to the atrium. The same high-backed chair with its headrest of bronze and legs shaped like lion's paws. The same desk, with its reed pens, pells of parchment and inkwells.

Claudia let the curtain fall back into place and tiptoed across the room, grateful for the jagged flashes of brilliance which lit her way through the blackness. She paused by the tapestry and waited for the next white flare to identify the marine adventures of a band of heroes in search of a golden ram's fleece. Tugging on the embroidered dragon which guarded the fleece, the curtain slid aside on its pole to reveal a door so plain-faced it was clear it had never been intended for show. Claudia put her ear to the woodwork and listened.

Nothing.

Her heart was pounding faster than a threshing machine. She could delay. Go back and wait for Supersnoop to return. Jokes about Phoebe aside, she presumed he was out, rounding up loyal troops with which to confront Cyrus, but suppose, when they returned, Tarraco wasn't here? He'd slip through their fingers once and for all! She pressed her ear harder, and heard only silence between the relentless rumbles of thunder.

Claudia's forehead collapsed on to the wall as the weight of Spesium descended on her shoulders. This whole sordid mess was down to her – any future killings, any future beatings, any future misery, they were down to her. *She* had set him free. *She* must redress the balance.

From the kitchens a ripple of laughter broke out, and behind her, in the bedroom, the floater on the water clock pinged the hour. She had no idea which.

Her mouth was dry as she lifted the latch. Thank heavens she'd had the good sense to bring with her a small, thin-bladed knife—

A faint chink of yellow appeared as she pulled the door towards her, but it was only a minuscule crack. Another tapestry hung on the inside. Damn! Claudia forced herself to stand still and absorb as much data as she could. Information was ammunition, she had to cling to that. Her mouth was dry, her palms sweating as she reassured herself with the touch of cold steel. *You have to get this right. There will be no second chance.* A musky scent (ajuga?) filtered through the cloth, and a few seconds later, she was rewarded with the haunting strum of a lyre. Juno be praised, Tarraco was trapped in his den!

Dammit, there was no time for sentiment. No time to recall aching melodies, conjuring up sun-drenched Iberian hills and unrequited love; no time to consider scarlet fillets tying back his hair . . . With a toss of her head, Claudia jerked open the screen.

'Freedom,' she declared, sweeping into the windowless chamber, 'invariably comes with a price round its neck. Don't you agree?'

The lyre stopped in mid-pluck, at the same time the colour drained from Claudia's face.

'I most certainly do.' The mastermind behind the reign of murder and extortion turned in the chair and lowered the instrument to the floor.

Claudia's eyes darted round the room as her brain made rapid calculations. Those two doors facing the courtyard were obviously false fronts. This was the only one entrance. Therefore the only exit . . . Run! But her feet had welded to the floor. Behind her, a huge shadow loomed up. The smell of leather was strong in her nostrils.

The lyre player smiled a smile which did not extend to the eyes and slowly rose from the chair.

You silly cow! To come here alone, how could you be so utterly stupid!

The occupant of the hidden room took a step forward.

Claudia took a step back.

And collided with a mountain with a walrus moustache.

With panic rising in her throat, Claudia knew her thin-bladed knife would be useless against the awesome force that was Pul. A hand clamped round her throat and propelled her forward into the room.

'My mistake. I-I was looking for . . .'

'I know what you were looking for.' The laugh of the Oriental's paymaster was deep and throaty. 'Bring her closer, Pul.'

Kicking, squirming, grappling was useless against the massive henchman, and Claudia found herself dragged across the floor like flotsam on a rip tide. Yet even through her terror, she was absorbing the opulence of the furnishings. The imaginative frescoes. The brilliance of the golden lampstands which lit this hidden chamber. A cry caught in her throat. The chamber where the campaign of terror was mapped out. Where orders were given for lives to be bought and sold, for human misery to be traded for treasure – and what treasure! Against every wall stood chests of maplewood, chests of cedar, chests inlaid with mother-of-pearl, each lid flung wide to reveal heaps of gold and silver plate, ivories, crystals and jewels. This, then, was what profit looked like from a trade in human souls . . .

'Closer.'

Like a knitted doll, Claudia was hurled across the floor, where lampglow cast a long, slim shadow across the fine mosaic. From her sprawling position, Claudia's eyes ranged upwards from the hem of the pleated linen tunic, whose gold thread rippled like a mountain stream. They paused at the emerald-studded pin clipped to the shoulder, then moved on to the chin jutting out defiantly.

Of course, it was not the chin she had expected to challenge in its lair.

She had expected a chin with a hint or two of stubble, a jawline firm and muscled. Instead the chin required no razor, and the jawline, as she remembered only too well, was truly a borderline case.

Upwards her gaze continued to amble. To the snub nose. To the eyes, glittering and hard, and skin plastered with too much cosmetics . . .

'Now then,' Lais said, sinking regally into her high-backed chair, 'what put you on to me?'

XXXV

Like a meteor crashing to earth, a thousand fragments exploded in Claudia's mind. So much for her and Orbilio's arithmetic! By a process of elimination, they had arrived at a figure of one – when in fact, there had been two contenders in the frame. Tarraco, of course – and Lais. But then again, who could have imagined she'd fake her own murder? Hell, even Tarraco had been fooled when the body was dragged out of the lake!

So close, and yet so wide of the bull's-eye! True, they'd pinpointed the nerve centre as being here, on Tuder's island, and their conclusions that only riches on the banker's scale could finance such bold ventures and buy silence were correct. But never in a million years could either of them have envisaged old Stonyface as the mastermind.

And with hindsight it made sense . . .

'Don't be shy,' Lais sneered, pouring herself a glass of wine. 'I've known all along you were a spy. Who are you working for? My late husband's brother? Or that brittle bitch of his sister?' In the harsh artificial light, the roots of her hair showed grey and the moleskin patches merely highlighted the multitude of blemishes on her ageing skin.

Claudia made to stand up, but a huge hand sent her crashing back down and a boot on her back kept her there.

There was a look on Lais' face which suggested this wasn't her first experience of violence – or that she did not enjoy what she watched. Bitch. Claudia licked away the dribble of blood which trickled from the side of her mouth and tried to ignore the swelling coming up on her cheek.

'I'm in Atlantis on holiday—' she began, before Pul's boot slammed her forehead against the tessellated floor.

'Nice try,' Lais said, sipping at her wine. Claudia could smell the strength of the vintage even through the taste of her own blood. 'But Pul watched you when you arrived, observed you taking note of your surroundings like a true professional, even to weighing *him* up. Oh, don't be fooled. His expression is impassive enough, but he doesn't miss much, do you, Pul?'

Claudia could not see, of course, but she knew that the walrus moustache had lifted in a blood-curdling grin. But with his foot on her neck, she was powerless to move. There was no way she could reach for the blade—

'He watched you make a beeline for Cal,' Lais was saying, 'and I overheard you myself from the loggia, pumping him for information while he bragged about how much he knew. Why, you practically signed his death warrant yourself!'

Don't you dare pin this on me, you bitch! 'Taking a risk, weren't you, Lais?' Claudia tossed back. This was not the time to let them see she was scared. 'Out and about in broad daylight, when you were supposed to be dead?'

Hooded eyes glinted in unashamed triumph, rings glistening off every finger joint, and despite the jab of revulsion at her crimes, a part of Claudia could still acknowledge the woman's cunning and admire her daring.

'Who's to see me?' laughed Lais. 'The slaves in Atlantis? Those overworked, obsequious morons don't differentiate between one paying guest and another, and as for Pylades, please don't insult my intelligence. I conduct my business only when it's essential and only when everyone's asleep, either at night or during siesta or even, like today, during mealtimes, if needs must.' Her tongue flickered in and out like a snake's. 'Not that I need explain this to you. Since you've been tracking me, you must be familiar with all my movements.'

Pul's boot was heavy on Claudia's neck, pushing her chin hard on the floor. 'Now why should I be interested in you, Lais, my peach?'

'Oh, cut the crap,' Lais snapped. 'You've been hanging round me like a bad smell ever since you arrived, or are you going to pretend it was coincidence that night I met Kamar in the hall?'

Claudia felt the room spin. How could she explain that it suited her own purposes to be out and about during those same antisocial hours? Her only chance for survival lay with pretending she was employed by Tuder's relatives . . .

Croesus, she needed to buy time. Somehow she had to win Lais' confidence!

'Whose was the body they fished out of the water?' she asked. No wonder the victim's face was mashed to a pulp, it was to render the poor cow unrecognizable. And now it made sense, Pul playing the model citizen role by 'helping' to retrieve the corpse. It would have been him who had choreographed the event.

Lais waved an airy hand. 'Who knows?' she said. 'Who cares? Right height, right size, right bone structure

– dressed in my clothes with a few of my jewels, let the fish take care of the rest.'

Claudia suppressed a shudder of revulsion at this foul and premeditated crime. 'How long had you been planning your own murder?'

'A couple of months,' Lais shrugged, 'maybe three had passed, since I set Pul to search for a suitable double.'

Claudia goggled. 'You held her prisoner all that time?' Did she know? Did the poor bitch have any idea what they planned?

'We could hardly have the body decomposing, now could we? The timing was crucial, you see; a public occasion, a crowd – and my little bit of Spanish rough fell right into the trap. But then I knew that he would.' Lais slipped out of her chair and lifted Claudia's chin with her exquisitely crafted sandal. 'Tarraco is so predictable, don't you agree?'

Meaning that under attack, he would throw back his head rather than cringe. Would defy, rather than defend. 'I don't know him as intimately as you,' Claudia purred back.

'The bastard gave you my harebell gown for nothing? He's slipping!' When Lais laughed, deep furrows appeared in her cheeks. 'You don't know what you missed! In that department he is truly exceptional. However, one expects loyalty from one's subordinates.'

She clicked her fingers and Pul released his boot. Claudia wondered whether she might be reduced to looking right for eternity.

'Also –' incredibly, Lais appeared to be offering her a glass of wine. Girl to girl, and all that! '– my husband,' she sneered over the word, 'had ideas way above his station.' She indicated Claudia take a seat. 'You know, that little toe-rag began to imagine he *owned* me. Me! Can you believe it? After all I'd done for him, as well!'

As though her face was not bleeding, grazed and swollen, Claudia accepted the chair. 'Such as?' she murmured.

'Disposing of that awful Virginia, for a start.' Lais rolled her ridiculously painted eyes. 'Dreadful woman! Brayed like a donkey, stank of cheap scent, Virginia had absolutely no conversation whatsoever. Tarraco was far better off with me.'

'You drowned her in the lake?'

'So gullible, that woman. And you'd think Tarraco would have shown a pinch of gratitude – hell, were it not for my intervention, Virginia would have willed everything to some silly daughter in Gaul instead of him!'

Except, mused Claudia, at that stage Tarraco believed he had done Lais a favour! There was a subtle irony in the two of them playing off against each other.

'Unfortunately,' Stonypuss said, 'despite the clothes I bought him, the trinkets I lavished on him, indeed the decent manners that I taught him, that little dago bastard had the temerity to shag some kitchen slut from Atlantis and expect to get away with it.' She flashed her flint-hard eyes at Claudia. 'No one crosses me,' she snapped. '*No one.*'

As though in a theatre, the play ran before Claudia's eyes. The staged argument. A weeping prisoner secretly throttled and beaten. Innuendoes whispered concerning Lais' disappearance. The athletics display. The body, weighted underwater in the oyster beds for the requisite length of time, now cut loose to be 'discovered'. Cyrus enters the stage. So, too, Tarraco, strutting, arrogant, haughty, defiant. A dramatic arrest. Execution follows . . .

Revenge was clearly a dish Lais served icy cold.

'After a couple of months,' Claudia supposed aloud, 'no doubt the grieving widow would make her reappearance, admitting the row, to storming off, saying – what? you'd sought solace with a friend in Ancona? – and my, my, how horrified you'd be to hear of your poor husband's fate.'

'Another superlative performance,' Lais agreed, 'with not a single flaw.'

Except that Tarraco didn't care you'd done a bunk.

'Except that Tarraco is free.' Unwise, Claudia felt, to declare her role in that particular interlude!

'Pity,' Lais said sadly. 'I'd set my heart on seeing him pay, but I know that boy. He'll be in Cadiz by now, out of my grasp.'

For once, Lais, I am in total agreement with you. He'll bluff, he'll bluster, yet deep down Tarraco is insecure. Cyrus had played on that aspect beside the running track, when Lais' double was fished out of the water, and Claudia had added to it, when she provided him with the means to escape. A bittersweet chord tugged inside her. At least she was right on one count. Tarraco was not capable of killing Lais in a murderous frenzy.

'Do have another glass of wine – you have no idea how I've longed for an appreciative audience,' Lais was saying.

Claudia glanced at the door, guarded by the massive Oriental in his leather vest and kilt, feet solidly apart, hands across his chest. She did not like the gleam in his eye.

'Efficient, isn't he?' Lais gloated.

Efficient. The word sent shivers down Claudia's skin. Like a well-greased machine, Pul arranges for families to be evicted, men beaten up, property destroyed, he calmly tells Kamar who should die. Did Pul, she wondered, experience no flutterings of remorse when he brought food to the woman scheduled to die in Lais' place? Was there the slightest nip of conscience when he put his hands around her throat and squeezed? And what skipped through his mind when he crept up behind Cal and snapped his neck like a dry twig?

Cold-blooded, cold-hearted, but Claudia felt a faint glimpse of comprehension. All men have a living to earn, even Pul. *But Lais?* Claudia swallowed her revulsion along with the wine. 'Why?' she asked simply.

With a short laugh, the hard-eyed, ravaged harpy indicated the rows of chests, embellished by glorious lamp-light. Gold plate, gem-studded salvers, goblets, vases, silver pitchers twinkled back.

'Tuder was a banker, a successful one at that, but he also was a miser.' She let out her deep, throaty chuckle. 'And in that he was most successful, too. Which is why he purchased an island isolated from virtually every living soul and built himself this hidden chamber. Day after day he spent closeted in here, feasting his eyes on the proceeds of his business, running his fat hands over their contours, yet what of his wife of thirty-six years? What of the wife who had buried three sons all aged under five? The first good old Lais knew of our move to this hellhole was when the wagons arrived to transport us from Rome!'

For one brief second, Claudia was almost tempted to feel sorry for her.

'Faced with a choice, twenty years of obscurity against the chance of fulfilling a vocation, what would you do?'

A ball of lead settled in Claudia's stomach. 'I'd get rid of my husband,' she said quietly, 'with the aid of a greedy physician.'

'Exactly!' When Lais clapped her hands, Claudia counted seven liver spots. 'After that he kept on doing my bidding, for which he received ample rewards, with the choice of keeping quiet – or me screaming to the world that he murdered my dear, departed husband. And who would be believed in this scenario? A sexual pervert or the faithful wife?'

'A . . . what?'

'You didn't know about his predilection for little boys? He likes them tender, does our Kamar. Nine's too old for him.'

Fire shot through Claudia's veins. Janus, Croesus, she had him in her power, there was ample hemlock in his dispensary! Instead, she didn't just fall into his honeyed trap, she pinched her nose and jumped! *Small surprise he led her here!* When she'd given the game away by saying it was Tarraco she was looking for, he'd leapt at the chance to hand her over to Lais.

Idly, she wondered what expression would be on his face when he was chained in the arena with a pack of snarling, starving dogs and a warm glow spread over her.

Then Claudia recalled what Lais had said earlier and snapped out of her reverie. '*What* vocation?' she asked. Pretending to smooth her skirt as she crossed her legs, she felt for the thin-bladed knife. Juno be praised, it was still there!

'Have you ever been in the position where you know

there is something missing in your life, but have never known what that gap might represent?' Lais moved across the room to drape herself across a blue upholstered couch and began to toy with the arm carved in a lion's head. 'When I was younger, I suspected it was children, my lost boys, but then we arrived here –' she waved her hand around to indicate not just the villa, but the island '– and I knew. Just –' she snapped her fingers '– like that, I understood my destiny was to be Queen of the Lake.'

'Ex-cuse me?'

Lais smiled a patronizing smile. 'Let me simplify it for you. You see, for so long, Plasimene, like myself, had been spiritually abandoned, and suddenly here was my chance to redress the balance. Using Tuder's precious fortune, I was able to start building up my empire – indeed, Pul reports that in another three months, maybe four, the entire town and its environs will belong to me.'

'Apart from Atlantis.'

Lais shrugged. 'That shouldn't take longer than another six or seven weeks to acquire once I have the rest, I'm practically there – and I can see from your face, you're impressed.'

Your majesty! But maybe this was her chance? 'Who couldn't be overwhelmed?' Claudia gushed. 'And your . . .' she forced herself to say it. 'Your people?'

'Will revere and respect me,' Lais replied, stretching out along the couch. 'Until Atlantis is under my control, I shall naturally refrain from announcing myself, but you'll find I shall rule my subjects fairly, I shall be just in quarrels, generous in famine, they will have no cause for complaint.'

Lucky them!

'And what of the killings which take place under

Kamar's medicinal aegis? It's tantamount to a murder factory up there!'

'Don't be so suburban!' Lais snorted. 'No one dies who doesn't deserve it.' Her face softened. 'Look upon them as dead wood, and you'll understand. In life these people serve no useful purpose, whereas in death, whether into money, business or marriage, so many others are made free. I am merely performing a service.'

Claudia thought of a woman she'd never even met. The woman who kept cats. Twelve of them, strangled before their mistress had had her first luxurious massage in Atlantis . . .

She thought of a silversmith, the woman in the mudbath, the orphan killed in the hills.

She thought of Cal. Vibrant, laughing, walking the tightrope between danger and fun. She didn't know which way he'd end up living his life . . . but the choice should have been his to make, not Lais'. *Whoever possesses the gold rules.* Not any more, they don't. Not any bloody more! People have families, they have feelings, you can't prune them like old trees!

'What did you expect to achieve, coming here?' Lais asked, arching one thickly painted eyebrow. 'Me to row back with you and confess everything to – who is it pays you? Tuder's buttoned-up brother?'

Claudia nodded. 'You shouldn't have cut him out of the will.' She was taking a chance, but—

'Why not?' *It worked!* 'I needed the money to finance my operation, and you don't seriously expect me to give up everything I've worked for?'

Claudia's heart raced like snowmelt down a mountain. This was the moment she had been building up to . . .

With a studied languidity, she leaned back in the chair and stretched out her hands to examine the half-moons on her fingernails.

'Hardly.' She kept her eyes on her hands. 'You see, it occurred to me that once you knew I was clever enough to trace you and confront you with my findings, you might be inclined to cut me in.'

Lais chewed her lip. 'You have guts, I'll give you that. The fact you came out here alone inclines me towards you, but it's a firm rule of mine. Never deal with blackmail.'

Claudia breathed on her thumbnail and buffed it against the lap of her gown. 'I had you pegged as a smarter businesswoman than that,' she replied, and without even looking up, she knew she had Lais' full attention.

'You don't want a pay-off?' Old Stonyface couldn't hide the intrigue from her voice.

'Oh, no.' Still Claudia refused to meet her eye. 'I want you to add my name to the payroll.'

'Hire you?' Lais nearly fell off the couch.

'My financial situation is somewhat rocky,' Claudia smiled. 'My wine business is faltering, I need funds to shore it up – and let's face it, Kamar and Pul can only do so much without attracting attention. Imagine what another *woman* can get away with.'

Was she hooked? Claudia pressed on.

'Don't you think that if I meant you harm I'd have approached the authorities? Had you and Kamar and Cyrus arrested? Pul, too?'

'I'd considered that,' Lais said slowly. 'You are either very arrogant or very stupid.'

'Or very skint.' Oh dear. It wasn't working. 'Test me,

then,' she blurted out. 'Tell me who's next on your list and I'll kill that person for you. Tonight.'

There was a moment's hesitation, almost a smile played on Lais' lip, and Claudia capitalized on her moment's good fortune.

'What's there to lose?' she asked eagerly. 'I go back to Atlantis and shout my head off and what happens? Either Kamar dopes me or your creature Cyrus declares me insane and whoosh, Claudia Seferius disappears for ever. On the other hand, you might just have one very valuable asset on your side. Can you lose?'

Long seconds ticked past on the water clock, then eventually Lais smiled. 'Very well,' she said, 'I'm prepared to take a risk. The woman's name is Phoebe, her husband is sick of her philandering, she has become an embarrassment. Kill Phoebe and you will never want for funds again, I promise you.'

Claudia's face betrayed none of the emotions which tumbled within. Fear. Satisfaction. Anticipation. Relief. Soon, she thought, very soon, Lais and her cronies will be in irons, on their way to be tried for their crimes, and let's see the faces of the families involved. Some guilty, standing alongside. Some innocent, horrified at what had befallen their relatives. The townsfolk of Spesium would find the trip to Rome well worth their while, jeering and spitting as they were hauled through the streets.

With commendable calm, Claudia uncrossed her legs and stood up. 'By morning,' she assured Lais, 'Phoebe will be history.'

Not too fast, not too fast. Casually she walked towards the door. 'Thanks for the wine,' she said.

'My pleasure.' Lais held up her goblet. 'To a successful union.' She laughed.

As Claudia turned, the laughter changed to an echo. Shadows closed in. Her ankles could not bear her weight and suddenly she was falling . . . falling . . . and the room was growing darker. *Dammit, the wine had been drugged!* As though down a long tunnel, she heard a woman's autocratic instructions weave in and out of her consciousness.

'Dump her in the . . . (mumble, mumble) . . . should not pose a problem . . . (mumble, mumble) . . . natural causes . . .'

Bitch! Claudia flung out an arm. She'd kill her. She'd kill that bitch Lais for this! The room was swimming, but she had time. The wine was just making her dizzy. Disorientated. She could fight it. Win. Old Stonyface would regret doing this—

But before Claudia's hand had a chance to close round her knife, a great rush of blackness had swallowed her up.

XXXVI

She was dead. Lais' doped wine had killed her. Claudia had crossed the Styx and here were the caves of the Underworld, the ghosts of her long-dead ancestors writhing in some grisly welcome ritual. Drums were throbbing. Claudia prised open her second eyelid and winced from the swelling which surrounded it, a sweet memento from Pul. Once more, she was lying face down, although here was no fancy mosaic, no opulent marble. It was dust, she could smell it. Taste it. Sour at the back of her throat. Great! Charon the Ferryman had dumped her without so much as a guide or a hint to direction!

Lifting her head was like lifting a hippo. All around, the ghosts – red ghosts, if you please – danced to the pulsating drumbeats with rigid, flickering movements. Wooden puppets jerking on strings. Oddly repellent. Far from comforting. Someone groaned when she tried to sit up. Claudia had a feeling it was her. No one put out a hand to assist.

The dancers reeled towards her, then receded. Forward and back, jerk and jolt. Forward and back, jerk . . . Slowly her vision cleared, and Claudia saw they were not phantoms – hell, they were not even real people! These were painted figures, lit by a flickering flame. Red? Yes, they were red. Etruscan red. Their bodies, their faces, their hands. And they danced round a wall to a drum which pounded inside her head.

Using a stone tabletop for support, Claudia hauled herself to her knees as a wisp of fear tugged at her gut. *Why should these painted Etruscans dance around a stone slab?* She brushed the wisp away and rose groggily to her feet. A cheetah came into view, its painted spots brilliantly preserved. *Preserved where?*

Rats with razor-sharp teeth began to gnaw at her insides. She was cold. Icy cold.

There was a dark patch on the floor. And something glinting in the flickering, stinking tallow light. An emerald. *Don't look*. Block it out, block it out, for as long as you can . . .

'The dark patch on the floor there, that's blood,' she tried to tell the yawning cheetah, except there was a pebble bunging up her voice box. Human blood, stale and dry, and the emerald clinched any doubt. It was set in an earring. The one which was absent from the body fished out of the lake . . . 'I suppose you got to know Lais' double quite well, while she was kept prisoner here.' But the cheetah was bored, it kept yawning.

While a giant's hand crushed her heart in his fist, Claudia forced herself to pick up the candle and hold it up to walls covered with these Etruscan paintings. *Tomb paintings*. The stone tabletops were sarcophagi. The giant squeezed tighter. All Etruscan burial sites were the same. Gouged underground out of the rock. Leading off from this central chamber would be other, narrower resting places. But one thing was certain.

There was only one entrance.

Sealed with a huge block of granite.

'It's all right,' she added, trying for a smile – not that the Etruscans cared whether she was grinning or not, 'Tarraco said the graves had been robbed generations ago, probably during the time of the Great Battle up on the lakeshore.'

Claudia felt hysteria rise in her breast.

One woman had been imprisoned in this ancient tomb of the kings and then killed on this spot. Was it Lais' intention to make it a double? Would Pul heave back that granite door any minute, and place his large hands round her own neck? As though in a dream, two words barrelled through this ancient tomb. *Natural causes.* Lais had it all planned! She'd been humouring Claudia from the start, knowing how long the drug would take to work in the wine. With an aching wrench of self-pity, Claudia realized too late that to keep up the pretence of being a spy was the last thing she should have done. She should have tried to run, go down fighting. Instead she set herself up as a swooning, love-sick girl coming in search of the man she'd set free from the cells who seeks refuge from the storm, and where better than the old Etruscan tombs? But, oops, there's an accident, look. Lightning fells a tree, traps her inside . . . In a couple of months, when Lais makes her miraculous reappearance, she discovers this fallen tree trunk. How tragic!

Natural bloody causes, all right.

Claudia was destined to die of thirst and starvation.

XXXVII

'Sit down, Kamar, you're making me dizzy.'

'Sit down?' The physician's voice was shrill with panic. 'After what that bitch did to me? This, this, this –' he pointed to the weals on his legs '– and what about this, eh?' A bony finger indicated his cheek. 'The fucking bitch has scarred me for life. How am I supposed to explain that to my patients? To Pylades? Croesus, he'll sack me the second he claps eyes on me!'

'I'm sure you'll think of something,' Lais soothed. Inside her hidden room, lamplight shone brighter than a midsummer noon, bouncing off the gilded statues and solid silver figurines, although she had taken care to close the lids of the treasure chests when Kamar was announced. Pul she could trust. But Kamar? Too self-centred for unconditional allegiance.

To counteract the stench of white mandrake which still clung to the lanky physician, Lais dabbed her musky scent behind her ears, on all her pulse points, wrists and throat and ankles, and trickled a few drops down her cleavage. Ah, there were times when she missed Tarraco! Those expert hands, tender lips ... She shivered at the delicious memory. There would be others, of course. Just as young and equally devoted, but she would take care never to marry again. She had been burned by the Spaniard's betrayal. It would not happen again.

Shit! She hurled her glass against the wall, watched it shatter into a thousand shimmering pieces. What made him shag that kitchen wench? Wasn't one woman enough for his overpowering ego? Lais recalled the twinge of remorse when, a few days after staging her dramatic disappearance, she'd sneaked out of this hidden chamber one night and found he'd left honeycombs on her bed. A tender thought, but one which unfortunately came too late. The damage had been done.

Her toe tapped furiously against the tessellated floor. Bastard! Sneaking off to liaise with some common slave, and expecting to get away with his little indiscretion. Got a bit above your station, didn't you? Thought you owned this bloody place, strutting round like one of your peacocks, when it was me, *me*, who put the gold thread in your robes and introduced you to the subtle pleasures of antiques and art. Lais grabbed a mirror. By the gods, she was still a fine-looking woman, what did he need that little scrubber for? Sex? Wasn't he getting enough here, with his wife? Lais hurled the mirror across the floor, oblivious to Kamar jumping out of its path. *Bastard!* She had chosen him, for gods' sake, not the other way around. She had been the one to dispose of that stupid, braying donkey Virginia, and how had he repaid her?

'He loved me once, you know.'

'Huh?' Kamar had been preoccupied with matters of his own.

'Nothing.' But it was true. She might have made the initial overtures, but from that one spark, Tarraco had fallen for her, courting her, fetching gifts, playing on his magic lyre. She remembered the night he first seduced her, softly, tenderly, arousing every passion, and Lais knew it could not be for her fortune. Virginia had (thanks to her!) left everything to him. No, no. Tarraco had loved her for herself, and whilst Lais had not loved him in return, she had felt a certain tenderness for her little bit of Spanish rough.

Not enough to let him live with her, of course – he was a consort, not a partner. His quarters were on the far wing, over there, far from her hidden chamber and her secrets, but all the same – there were times of late when she missed his whispered words of love and the way his lips nibbled the back of her neck. The kitchen wench had been disposed of, naturally. A bauble stolen from a guest and planted in her room. Instant dismissal. But that was only half the story.

The other half was on his way to bloody Spain, when by rights he should be facing down a half-starved tiger in public execution for that monstrous act of betrayal!

Still. A queen does not necessarily need a consort. Her strength to stand alone would be inspiration to her people, another cause for them to revere her. How long, Lais wondered idly, before Pylades would bow to the pressure . . .?

'I don't like it.' Kamar's thin lips had all but disappeared. 'I don't like it at all. Suppose someone raises the alarm?'

'What are you gabbling on about now?'

'That Seferius bitch,' Kamar said. 'Suppose someone goes looking for her?'

'Who?' Lais sneered. 'She's a wild one, that girl. Unpredictable. Some skivvy will quietly pack up her things, people will assume she went back to Rome.' And if anyone down there asks questions, then they won't find many answers!

'No,' Kamar said, wringing his hands. 'I mean, suppose someone comes looking for her *out here?*'

'Then they'll go back empty-handed, won't they? She's a hundred yards under the ground, sealed in by a great slab of rock. No one heard that other poor cow screaming her head off, now did they? Well, they won't hear our Claudia yell, either.'

'She's in cahoots with some Security chap. I don't think he'll take no for an answer.'

'Marcus Cornelius?' Lais licked her finger and ran it lightly over her eyebrow. 'I shouldn't worry about him.'

'None of the soldiers other than Cyrus is in on the scam.' If anything, Kamar seemed even more agitated. 'Suppose he brings the rest of the legion out to the island and turns this place over?'

'I imagine that highly unlikely.'

'Why not? This is the obvious start point.'

'Too true,' Lais said, rubbing in wine lees to redden her cheeks. 'But power is nothing without responsibility, Kamar. I suggest you remember that. You see, I haven't reached this exalted position without covering every single angle and making plans accordingly. It was to be expected, Orbilio coming here. I simply took counter measures.'

'Which were?' In spite of his predicament, Kamar was impressed.

'Isn't it obvious?' Lais reached for the kohl to highlight her eyes. 'I disposed of him, too.' A vision flashed through her mind of the blood, pumping out of his body to soak into his white linen tunic. The same warm blood dripping off the end of her knife. 'I slit clean through his tanned patrician throat.'

Because dead men can't cause trouble.

XXXVIII

There is no such thing as total silence. Indeed, a hundred paces deep in the rock face, where even the wrath of Jupiter's storm failed to penetrate, certain sounds still crept in to fill the void.

The throbbing heat of the night.

The blood, thundering past Claudia's ears.

The frantic flaps of her heart, as it tried to burst free of her breast.

But they were flimsy, whimsy, personal sounds and, like snowflakes gliding down in midwinter, they did not ruffle the dreams of the dead. Secure in their solid sarcophagi, the Etruscan nobility reposed for eternity, surrounded by their painted friends and relatives, their servants, their pets, their boats, their painted jewels and banquets.

Claudia was not prepared to wait for eternity.

Alabaster images of these ancient peoples, which once reclined upon the coffin tops, now lay smashed and scattered far across the tamped earth floor, swept aside in the grave robbers' impatience, and whilst the sarcophagi had been ransacked – every gold torque, every ring, every last ivory ornament gone, even the bones tossed aside – it was the thieves' very haste which gave Claudia inspiration as she scratched among the shattered shards for some means of escape.

In a corner of a chamber where the walls were covered with twirling dancers and musicians blowing on traditional double flutes, underneath the piles of debris, she had found a scrap of azure fabric. The colour was so vivid, so dazzling in the flickering candlelight, that it had given her an idea . . .

From the outset, Claudia knew she'd need a lever to dislodge that rock across the entrance, and not only was nothing remotely suitable inside this maze of chambers, with the tunnel heading downhill at such a sharp angle, how would she ever get leverage? That, therefore, was out of the question.

But suppose she inched the slab up? Just a fraction? And wedged a strip of her tunic in the slot?

Such was human nature that it would be unnatural for Pul not to be curious. Along he'd come, down this twisting stone path towards the tomb. He'd cast a professional glance at this circular, earth-covered mushroom, would check the granite slab as a matter of course. Then his slanted, almond eye would alight on the scrap of torn cotton. He would recognize the startling shade of yellow. Know it was Claudia's gown and that it was not there, definitely not there, when he rolled the rock into place. Her? Escape? No way. Not possible. Of course not. But the professional in him would force him to check—

As the bobbing flame of the tallow moved inexorably south, Claudia swung herself up on to the lintel of the principal chamber. There was a niche here, large enough, if she curled into a ball.

All she had to do was to wait.

To one side of her, wine was poured at a banquet. On the other, painted cheeses, grapes, sardines and pears were being guzzled at this family feast. Her skin was grazed and bleeding from shouldering the massive lump of rock, and it had been the tenth exhausting uphill push before she'd finally succeeded in holding that quarter-inch of space open long enough to push her skirt through the gap with the blade of her knife. Miraculously, the knife hadn't snapped. Claudia's lips were dry, her back raw as she contemplated Pul heaving aside the granite slab. So narrow, so low was the passageway in this subterranean world, he would be forced to hunch over as he made his way down, ducking further to avoid this low-hanging lintel.

One fist would clutch his wicked, curved blade, the other a torch to see by. His back would be bowed as he passed beneath the lintel, his movements slow. Suspicious. While his eyes searched forward, Claudia would spring. Land on his back. Her knife would slice through the top of his spine.

He'd be dead. She'd be free. Cal would be avenged, as she'd promised.

But! Her pulse raced with the tension. How long before Pul became curious? How long before he decided to check?

With a splutter, the candle in the tomb flickered and died.

XXXIX

Dizzy from exhaustion, the drug and the heat, Claudia twisted uncomfortably on her roost above the doorway. Funny how you lose track of time in the dark. Hours could have passed. Or just minutes. She wondered whether the lightning would have burned itself out yet. Had Drusilla had enough supper? Would her vineyards be scorched by the time she inspected them, leaving her bankrupt, the business in tatters?

She shifted position again, conscious of stone gouging out more of her flesh and damning to hell the tomb builders who could have made a bit more effort on the lintels! The shreds of her tunic had been welded to her wounds with blood and dried stiff. Claudia wriggled numb toes and flexed aching arms. Come on, Pul. Surely you've noticed by now?

More time passed, yet not once did she regret being poised up here for attack. Sure it was unpleasant, but this happened to be the only place in this wretched subterranean prison where she would have the advantage.

Legs which were bare from the thighs down began to feel every pitting of stone. Come on, Pul. Earn your keep! Go out on patrol.

Nothing happened.

Claudia's throat was swollen and throbbing from

thirst. What the hell had Lais slipped her? Colchicum? No, she'd be retching by now, feeling cold. Probably pheasant's eye, the Adonis plant. Mixed with the juice of the prickly lettuce. The bitch. But she wouldn't get away with it. Sooner or later, Pul would *have* to check on his captive—

What was that? Yes, that scratching sound? There it was again. A scraping. Grating. Like stone, yee-ha, wrenching on stone . . .

All right, you bastard. Come and get it!

For what seemed an eternity, Claudia waited as the mighty slab was rolled aside. The whole tomb seemed to shake when it landed. She held her breath as tightly as the thin-bladed knife . . .

Cautious footsteps padded down the steep incline of the tunnel. A voice whispered her name, calling . . . To fool her. To lull her into trusting him. Dear Diana, did he think she was stupid? A rumble of thunder echoed through the underground chambers like the roar of the Minotaur. Claudia stiffened. The pain in her lungs was intense. The Oriental paused before ducking under the doorway. Claudia was poised. She'd been over this moment a hundred times in her head. The second he passed through, she'd dive on his back, knocking him flat to the ground. She'd lunge for his topknot with one hand. With the other, she'd bring down her blade—

'Claudia,' came a sibilant hiss.

It was the first time she'd actually heard the sound of his voice. The accent was guttural. It reminded her of—

'Are you there?'

Damn right I am, buster! As Pul ducked beneath the lintel, she sprang. Down he went. Flat. She grabbed the topknot. There was more of it than she thought. Her right hand went up. Lightning flashed. The blade came down. Hard. And bounced right off the stone floor . . .

'Tarraco?' The guttural accent. The mane of hair. 'What the hell are you doing here?'

'Hey.' The Spaniard spat out the dust from his mouth. 'You complaining?'

'I damn near killed you, you oaf.' She rolled off his back and stood up. 'Had the storm petered out, you'd be dead.' But for that one spear of light . . .

'Maybe.' He shrugged, and she could have killed him then and there for pure insolence! 'Now I suggest we get out of here, yes?'

Good idea. Spinning on her heel, Claudia raced behind him up the passageway. He was no longer wearing the coarse workman's tunic he'd been given in jail. He was back in hunter attire, short to the knee, one shoulder bare. This time, Tarraco was dressed to kill. At the entrance, he jerked his thumb towards the granite slab.

'How did you shift it?' he asked.

'How come you're back on this island?' she countered. For a second, she feared she could smell double-cross as strong as the scent of woodshavings and pine and the storm which whipped up the water.

A flash of white teeth shone through the black of the night. 'I am ten miles up the road, and I think, why? *Why* should I leave all this money behind?' Tarraco picked up a quiver of arrows and slung it over his back. 'Lais is dead, I did not kill her, why should I not take what is mine?' He shouldered a bow and picked up the spear which leaned against the jamb of the entrance. 'So I row back out here, to the north side, where I know no soldier will keep watch, and I creep round to the villa. But what do I see? Not guards, but Cyrus. The tribune himself. He's with Pul and they're laughing and drinking my wine on my terrace. I wait – and then who else comes along? My dear, sweet wife, Lais! Is clear then I am set up and sure enough, they start boasting about it. Laughing at me.' He spread his hands expressively. 'Now I must kill them.'

'How did you find me?' Claudia asked.

'I come down to fill the boats with holes, but of course I cannot take the main road, so to speak, and that is how I see your flag sticking out of the entrance. Did anyone ever tell you what pretty knees you have, by the way?'

In the darkness, Claudia flushed. It was like the very first time, with the bear . . .

'I must go,' Tarraco said. 'Soon dawn will break, the advantage of night will be lost.'

'For gods' sake,' Claudia hissed, 'you can't tackle them all by yourself! Half the slaves are in on the payroll, we have to fetch help.'

I can't wait to see Supersnoop's face when I tell him about this! He'll be eating humble pie for a month!

'There is no help,' Tarraco said soberly. 'I'm on my own here.'

'Nonsense! Cyrus might be corrupt, but the others aren't, and I'll bet you a copper quadran to a denarius that Marcus Cornelius is rounding up the soldiers, the entire garrison will be landing any minute.'

'I don't think so.' Claudia had to strain to catch his words in the storm.

'You don't know Supersnoop.' She laughed. 'Him, miss the kudos of this?'

'Claudia.' There was a sound in his throat which she could not interpret. 'Claudia, I have bad news, I'm afraid.'

An earthquake shook Tuder's island and her knees fell away. Everything swam. Became viscous. Obscure. 'How bad?' she asked.

'The worst.' She heard him gulp. 'Claudia, Marcus is dead.'

'D-don't be s-silly.' He can't be. Not Loverboy.

Tarraco's face was twisted in pain. 'I'm sorry,' he said, and strangely she believed that he meant it. 'Come.' A strong hand latched round her wrist and hauled Claudia to her feet. 'Perhaps you believe, if you see for yourself.'

He lay there, on his back, under a willow.

Wide-spreading branches hung over him. Concealing. Protecting. Discreet.

For a moment, Claudia simply stood there, admiring the tree, its elegant lines, its silky green leaves, the way it forked out from the base. Such a *pretty* tree. Spoiled by the puddle of red which leached into its roots. By the sprawl of the man who lay under it.

His face was so white. White as his bleached linen tunic. Except for the breast, where the blood had soaked through. She brushed the branches aside, and saw skid marks where he'd been dragged. Tarraco? More likely Pul. Blood matted the curls in his hair and ran down his face, to mingle with the blood round his neck. The blood ran in a perfect semi-circle . . .

Somehow her fingers were twisting themselves in his curls and she heard someone yelling. It was a woman's voice, berating Apollo, for whom the willow was sacred.

'You're supposed to be the god of healing,' she bawled. '*Why can't you heal this?*'

Vaguely Claudia thought the voice might be hers.

The rains had begun. She could hear the droplets drumming on the leather leaves, bouncing off the hard-baked soil. They were running down her cheeks. They were salty.

'Orbilio, you idiot,' she said softly. 'What did you have to do this for?'

Anger began to well in her breast. The fool! How could he have been so reckless, so stupid, as to come here alone! Her fingers were digging into his shoulders as she shook his lifeless body. So bloody arrogant, you thought you could take on the world single-handed! Bright red drops of rain spurted into her face, her lap, her eyes. Selfish pig. Never a thought for anyone else – *Wait a sec!* Do dead bodies bleed . . .?

'He's alive!' she yelled at the top of her voice. 'Marcus is bloody alive!'

'Not for much longer,' a baritone said dryly, 'if you continue to shake him like that.'

Through the tears which coursed down her face, Claudia watched his long, curling eyelashes flutter and part and saw the smile which tweaked at one side of his bloodless, pale lips.

For once in her life, she had no rejoinder.

XL

Rain was belting down in earnest, stippling the lake and bouncing off the octagonal slabs of the path as it filled the air with the smell of freshly turned soil and the perfume of a million and one flowers. Hands on hips, Claudia stood in the cleansing torrent, her hair and her bodice plastered to her skin, and jotted down a mental note to sacrifice a bull, when she returned to Rome, to flame-haired Apollo. Who might (just might) have been listening . . .

Orbilio's story was simple. Suspecting Tarraco would go to ground on his own territory, he had come out here to confront him and instead had seen, walking along the colonnade, the ghost of the woman he'd fished out of the lake. Moreover, she was conferring with the very man who'd lent his strong arm to assist! While Orbilio's mind was absorbing this new arrangement, the woman clicked her fingers to dismiss her moustachioed henchman and the scales had fallen from Marcus' eyes. This was Lais, not a ghost, but in the flesh, who had obviously murdered her double! Which turned the whole issue on its head and it was Lais, he realized, not Tarraco, behind the racket. Behind the rash of premature deaths in Atlantis.

Arresting her was easy, he said, although Orbilio's voice dropped to a muted mumble at the part where he was forced to admit that he'd misjudged his prisoner's vicious streak. A knife had sprung out of nowhere and slashed at his neck. Only his height and his instinct had saved him. The one, because in straining upwards, Lais had inflicted nothing worse than a flesh wound. The other, because in jumping backwards, he slipped on a loose lump of rock (hence the skid marks) and knocked himself out on the bole of the tree. Believing she'd succeeded in slitting his throat, Lais had left him for dead.

'It is too close to dawn,' Tarraco pointed out, when Orbilio suggested they row back to fetch reinforcements. 'Come daylight, they will be on their guard. I must act now, while I have the advantage.'

'Count me in, then,' he'd said, but the Spaniard refused to even help him to his feet.

'You've lost too much blood,' he sneered, propping him against the tree trunk instead. 'You will be liability to me, not asset.' Expertly, he ripped Orbilio's tunic into bandages and wound them round his neck and head, his fingers none too gentle on the lump. 'Stay here,' he ordered, handing over his broad, hunting dagger. 'Keep a lookout, and you,' he barked at Claudia. 'You stay with him.'

'While you go fighting one against thirty?' How bloody typical!

'I have quiver and bow.' Tarraco grinned. 'And I have plan. You wait here.'

But he should have known he was wasting his breath. As he padded towards the villa, a flash of yellow appeared at his shoulder. 'Just curious.' She shrugged. 'Wondering how you plan to take on the whole gang single-handed.'

'Easy.' He laughed. 'You watch this.' And hefting a

large jug of olive oil on to his shoulder from where he'd hidden it behind a potted palm, he scurried along the far wall of the villa, pausing to pour oil under each door as he passed and leaving a trickle which joined them all up. 'Is what we Spaniards call a diversion,' he said, arching one eyebrow in jest.

Claudia's heart was pounding. Any minute someone could walk out of the villa. Catch them at it . . .

'What about the rain?' she asked. Surely it would extinguish the flames?

Tarraco's response was a snort of disgust at so juvenile a question, but a second thought had occurred to her. Sure, the wooden doors would catch fire, the drapes inside, the tapestries, the rugs, the upholstery. But so too—

'Once this fire takes hold,' she said, 'the whole house will go up—' she paused to make sure he was listening '—with every antique and treasure.'

The olive oil faltered mid-pour. 'Yes,' he whispered, 'I know.' Then the flow continued at its old, steady rate, and despite the thunderclaps and the hammering of the rain, Claudia could hear her heart pounding louder.

'So.' He dribbled out the last few drops of oil and tossed his long mane back over his shoulders. 'Are you ready?'

Will I ever be? Claudia drew a deep breath. 'Naturally.'

'Then stand back,' Tarraco said. 'It begins.'

Looking back, so many things happened at once that Claudia had trouble piecing them together. The rain didn't help. Torrential, obscuring, drumming down on the paths and the roofs. Thunder, lightning, a dozen fires breaking out. From every door, screaming figures burst forth and, if they weren't in a state of advanced hysteria as they came out, then the hail of arrows Tarraco loosed from his bow quickly hastened it.

'The army,' someone shouted. 'They have us surrounded.'

'Run for the boats!'

'Too late, they've been holed!'

'The north shore,' someone else yelled. 'Head for the north shore and swim.'

Like a swarm of angry bees, the servants scuttled up the hill, while behind them, the western wing of the villa crackled like the dry tinder that it was. Windows popped, fireballs ran through the corridors, fanned by the swirl of the storm. Tiles fell in, smashing, crashing, as flames licked along wooden floors and gobbled up dry timber rafters. The smell of burning oil mingled with the stench of peeling paint and plaster, of wool and cotton and hemp. In the kitchens, pots cracked in the heat, glass exploded, shelves collapsed as they burned through, dashing jars and crocks to the floor. The stink of burning pepper, leather and vinegar turned the night into acid.

His quiver empty, Tarraco hurled it into the flames. 'Bastard!' he spat. 'Lais didn't fall for it.'

Claudia followed his gaze. Whilst the flames swirled high into the air along the domestic quarters and storerooms, the atrium and the courtyard had halted their progress. Even fire couldn't find a purchase on marble! And beyond the atrium, in the calm lee of the peristyle, the gangleaders toughed it out . . .

'I suppose that was the end of the oil?'

In reply, Tarraco flung his bow into the furnace and

kicked a flowerpot at his feet. 'I should have risked being seen in the courtyard!' he spat. 'I should have poured the oil through that hidden door first!'

He was wrong, of course. Despite the lateness of the hour, such was the state of emergency on the island that few were asleep. Tarraco would have been dead the first time he set foot in the garden. But as he stormed up and down, chewing on his knuckles and swearing at himself under his breath, Claudia knew that to point this out would not quell his anger.

'Here!' she called.

With his face black from temper and smoke, Tarraco turned towards her. Just in time to catch the spear which came flying towards him. 'What's this for?' he growled.

As the roof of the storehouse collapsed in on itself, Claudia jabbed a finger in the direction of Lais' chamber. 'I thought it was about time we hunted some bears,' she said.

There's at least one hide I want nailed to my wall!

XLI

They may not have fallen for the cheap diversion, nevertheless Lais and her cronies were far from relaxed. One peep behind the second tapestry revealed four people in varying degrees of agitation.

On the left, Cyrus, half-drunk, throwing his chubby hands in the air in a frantic effort to convince Kamar that the fire was the result of a lightning strike on the villa. Janus-fucking-Croesus, how could it be the army? He was the tribune, for gods' sake, didn't he have the garrison firmly under control? No buts, Kamar, that was hysteria spewing from the mouths of frightened slaves. They too, he snarled, hand on his scabbard, were overreacting.

At the far end of the room, Pul had his great curved blade drawn and was swishing it about in a series of practice decapitations, and Lais, old Stonypuss herself, was marching up and down the lamplit chamber, clenching and unclenching her fists, shouting to everyone to sit down. Just sit down and shut the fuck up.

'Now!' Claudia whispered. There'd never be a better time, they were rattled and edgy and, despite how they saw themselves, all four were offguard at the moment. 'I'll take Lais and Kamar,' she hissed, 'and leave the soft touches for you!'

Beside the Argonaut tapestry, Tarraco grinned and

hefted the spear in his hand. 'Are you sure?' he mouthed back. 'Is not too late to swap.'

Out in the courtyard, a spark from the west wing dodged the raindrops and was caught by the long line of clipped box. For a count of five, it was touch and go between wet leaves and oily resins, then whoosh! Half a bush was alight in an instant.

Claudia and Tarraco watched the flames zip along the line and exchanged glances. What he had failed to achieve, nature had amended. Another minute and the fire would spread to this wing . . .

Claudia's eyes flashed to the bed and the bulky tables and chests. There was only one way into that room. Therefore only one exit. She swallowed hard. An hour ago, in the underground tomb, she would cheerfully have barricaded Lais into her den and set light to the fire herself. But that was theory. This was practice. Could she hack it in cold blood?

Was there an option?

One boat, which the Spaniard had hidden. Four killers. Three survivors, one seriously wounded. If she ran fast enough, she would not hear their screams as they burned alive in that room . . .

Claudia's hands were shaking as she turned to face Tarraco, but one glimpse of his rigid jaw was enough. White knuckles gripped the cherrywood shaft of his lance and in his right hand, he weighted a short stabbing sword. For him this was now a crusade. A matter of honour, self-respect. All those years of pandering to petulant old women, long nights making love with the lights off, there was a debt to be settled, for which he was prepared to lay down his life.

Suddenly his dark eyes circled round to hers and there he was, looking past the reflection of the burning bushes to lay bare her emotions and scour her soul.

'You must go,' he rasped. 'Take the patrician back to Atlantis. This is my fight, not yours.'

Talons gripped Claudia's gut. Orbilio, white from loss of blood, lying underneath the willow. Cal, sprawled red and helpless on the shingle. She had sworn to avenge the one, and now the other's life depended on her rowing him to safety. Another box tree burst into flames. Due to the pressure of making that one vow of vengeance, Claudia sought refuge with the one man outside the unholy mess in Atlantis – only to find him in it up to his eyebrows. And willing to die for the cause. This is my fight, he had said. He was right. Showers of resinous sparks hit the door, the door jamb, and the drapes.

But it was also Claudia's battle.

Lais had left Orbilio for dead, had condemned Claudia to an agonizing death. That she was responsible for the death of a number of innocent victims was one thing. *Now it was personal.*

'For goodness sake, Tarraco,' Claudia winked as she swept aside the Golden Fleece, 'someone has to show you how this thing is done!'

As she flung open the secret door, she thought she heard a man tell her that he loved her, but then again, it was probably the crackle of the flames around the threshold and the growl of the sky overhead.

'Ladies!' she breezed. 'Am I interrupting your embroidery lessons?'

Eight eyes swivelled and suddenly each figure was frozen like marble. For one brief, delicious second, Claudia felt the same rush of power that Medusa must have felt when, with one look, her victims all turned to stone! But the moment was fleet, broken by the sudden rush for weaponry. Beside her, Tarraco began kicking over tables and chairs, to confuse and distract the enemy, then the sobering tribune and Pul lunged towards him.

Claudia advanced towards the self-styled Queen of the Lake and her lanky physician, brandishing the knife in her hand.

'By the gods, you meddlesome bitch,' Lais spat, 'you've no idea how I hate you!'

'You're not just saying that to make me feel better, are you?' Claudia shot back. From the corner of her eye, three men were slugging it out and it was clear, from Lais' lack of action, that she expected her own men to win. Her assumption was probably correct . . .

Kamar, however, had gone straight into panic, giving Claudia a chance to shorten the odds. Jabbing the knife at his face, she danced towards him, and with each step she advanced, he backed up, until finally his back was hard up against the wall and the blade was an inch from his nose.

'I surrender, I surrender,' he squealed, holding both hands up. In the glow of the lamplight, Claudia noticed a satisfying weal down his cheek. 'Let me go and I swear, on the life of my mother, I swear I'll tell you everything. Names, dates, the lot! P-please. Let me go.'

Last time, buster, I believed you were scared. Now you've wet yourself, I know you mean business!

'Scumbag!' Lais turned on Kamar. 'Sell me out, would you?' Her lip curled back. 'I don't think so!'

Something flew past Claudia's ear. Kamar screamed,

his eyes bulged. 'Lais?' he spluttered weakly and, disbelieving, goggled at the cleaver which protruded from the pit of his stomach. 'Lais!'

'How very kind,' Claudia told her. 'I didn't realize you were on the side of the good and the great.'

Across the room, Pul dropped to his knees, blood pouring from a deep cut on his chest, and Claudia heard the clash of raw metal as Tarraco engaged Cyrus in hand-to-hand combat. Around the door, flames had taken hold of both tapestries, blocking the only way out . . .

'You!' the older woman sneered at Claudia. 'Think you're a match for me?'

Nonchalantly, Claudia tossed her thin blade from hand to hand and back again. 'More than.'

And I don't want you dead, after all, Lais, my love. I want you alive. Screaming for mercy in front of the families of those you have either murdered or driven to ruin . . . Oh, yes. I want you alive!

The place was a bloodbath. Against the wall, Kamar had slumped to the floor in a puddle of urine, gibbering, clutching the handle of Lais' cleaver as thick scarlet fluid pumped through his fingers. Pul was back on his feet, the three men slithering and slipping in red, sticky pools as steel crashed against steel. The knees, Tarraco! Slash at the knees! But Claudia dare not call out, lest the tribune or Pul tried the tactic . . .

'Well?' she asked Lais. 'What are you waiting for?' Behind her, one of the rafters caught alight. 'Old bones too stiff to take a young woman on?'

'Bitch!' Lais spat. 'You'll pay for that insult!'

The more agitated Lais became, the more mistakes she would make, and in contrast, the calmer she portrayed herself, the more confident Claudia actually felt. She followed Lais' glance to where her henchmen were fighting the wrath of her husband. No doubt that his passion doubled his efforts, but the battle could still go either way—

'Then you'd better hurry,' Claudia said, 'I'm booked for a massage at eight.'

That did it. With a hiss of fury, Lais hurled a footstool through the air, and as Claudia ducked, she surged towards the table. Smoke had obliterated the three fighting men, but not the fruit knife Lais was after.

'Shame,' Claudia tutted. 'Just four inches, eh? No wonder you couldn't get enough of the Spaniard.'

Under the pancake of cosmetics, rage coloured her ravaged face and a claw lashed round the hilt of the fruit knife. Hard eyes glittered in the smoke-filled room, twin mirrors of the blaze round the door frame. Come on, come on, Claudia willed. Lunge at me, Lais. She twizzled her own thin-bladed knife in the air as a taunt. Lunge at me, you old bag.

A stranger to physical action, Lais made an ineffectual thrust through the air.

'Tut, tut.' Claudia tightened her grip on the object she'd seized and hidden behind her back. 'Is that the best you can do?'

Lais glanced round. She was alone in facing the enemy. She had no option but fight—

For a dance of twelve steps, they sized up and parried, oblivious to the flames and the smoke, until with a blood-curdling scream Lais lost her temper. She charged forward, stabbing hard. Claudia dived, sticking out a judicious foot as she fell. Lais tripped, and Claudia smiled to herself.

Gotcha! Dropping her knife, she grasped with both hands the piece of wood she'd concealed behind her back and cracked it down hard on Lais' head. The harpy's eyes rolled upwards and she sank face forward on to the mosaic floor.

'Nothing communicates quite like a piece of four by two,' Claudia told her unconscious majesty, picking a splinter out of her finger. 'And how are you feeling, Kamar?' The physician was incoherent with pain and fear and shock. 'Up to standing trial? I think we can patch you up enough for that.'

The fire had taken a hold, crackling the rafters and devouring Lais' prized treasure chests. Remus! The ceiling would crash any minute . . .

'Tarraco?' Suddenly she couldn't see for the smoke. '*Tarraco?*'

She was coughing now, couldn't speak. Tiles showered down, sending up clouds of plaster and clay and knocking Claudia off her feet, and when the dust settled and she hauled herself upright, she could feel rain on her face. The ceiling at the far end had gone.

Pinned under a rafter, Kamar's feet twitched in their death throes . . .

Above her, flames spat and crackled, the plaster began to bow. The doorway was a wall of orange fire. Holy shit, they were trapped. Whoever was left from the fight, they were trapped . . .

'Tarraco?' This time, Claudia's voice had a tremulous quality.

'Here,' a voice rasped. 'Over here.'

Stumbling across the overturned furniture, slipping in puddles of rain and blood, Claudia was aware of two men on their knees, their weapons long gone, slugging it out in a fist fight. Then one saw the knife which Claudia had dropped and he lunged – and through the black and red, the blood and the smoke, Claudia recognized Cyrus. She screamed as he reached it before her, his fist closing over the hilt. As Tarraco frantically clawed at the air, Cyrus raised himself high, brought up his fist, took aim, then . . . keeled backwards into the rubble!

'What the . . .?' The Spaniard turned. In the doorway, a man with high patrician boots was beckoning them towards him. He was barely able to stand.

'I thought you might want your dagger back.' Orbilio grinned.

'Then why did you give it to Cyrus?' Tarraco grinned back, hauling himself to his feet. One arm hung limp and useless at his side, there was a cut down his cheek, a slash near the collar bone and what looked like a stab wound in his thigh.

Claudia had an idea she'd be the one on the oars to Atlantis!

Miraculously, though it was charred and smoking and black, the door jamb was no longer alight. Drips of water trickled down and over the threshold.

'That was the purpose of your atrium pool, wasn't it?' Marcus asked. 'Emergency fire-fighting equipment? Now are you two going to stand there all day, or do I have to carry you both, one on each shoulder?'

Hauling Lais across the smoke-filled chamber by her dyed hair (and none too worried about any obstacles the old bat might encounter), Claudia paused, panting and coughing, in the doorway. 'Do me a favour, Orbilio,' she wheezed. 'Next time, come to the party earlier!'

'What?' he flashed back. 'And break up your cosy girl talk? No fear.'

She watched him stagger down the atrium, his prisoner now well secured, though still comatose. Perhaps it was just as well, in the long run, that Lais was alone in facing trial and public execution. Isolation and loneliness at the end of her life would be just as much punishment as being hated and reviled, laughed and spat on. The minions might have got away, but without their mastermind, they'd be simple thugs, easy to trace. At least Lais would get her comeuppance!

Oh, no! 'Where's Pul?' she shrieked. 'Where the hell's Pul?'

'Calm down,' a thick accent soothed, and Claudia followed the direction that his bloodied finger indicated.

Flat on his back, his walrus moustache pointing up to the open sky through the rafters, the massive Oriental stared up at the rains through one slanted, almond eye.

But only one eye.

A spear was sticking out of the other.

'Is speciality of mine.' Tarraco shrugged modestly.

When she laughed, the laughter felt good, but for some reason, her eyes had filled with salt water, and there was a low humming sound in her ears.

Outside, Orbilio had tied Lais to a post and was fetching the one boat which hadn't been holed.

'What will *you* do?' she asked. The roof of Lais' hidden chamber had long since collapsed, melting and contaminating the contents of her treasure chests. The storehouses had gone, kitchens, two whole wings, there was precious little left of the villa. Tuder wouldn't have recognized the place, she thought. But maybe the ancient Etruscans who buried their dead might . . .

'There is nothing left, that's for sure,' he said with a sigh. 'Nothing to salvage, nothing—' he broke off, blinked and looked away '— to stay for. I shall go back to Spain.' Suddenly his dark, dark eyes were boring into hers. 'I don't suppose . . .?'

No, Tarraco. Don't suppose. Please – never suppose. Something wet dribbled down Claudia's cheek. The rain, of course. What else. Louder and louder, the strange humming sound filled the air.

'W-what?' She cleared her throat and started again. 'What's that noise?'

On the foreshore, Orbilio was using every last ounce of effort to heave Lais into the boat.

'That?' Tarraco let out a snort of ironic laughter. 'That is Memnon. The colossus. Did I not tell you that, one day, you would listen with me as he calls to his mother, the dawn? The statue is hollow.' There was a sad, sad smile in his eyes. 'The warm air makes a resonance. Like a song.'

Claudia stared up at the sky and out across the lake to Atlantis. The torrential rains were easing to a drizzle, soft and gentle on the waters of Lake Plasimene. The thunder and lightning had burned themselves out, and now the sky was bright in the east. The fluke heatwave had finally been killed by a fluke storm.

Who says life does not mirror nature?

As she heaved on the oars, with Orbilio slumped white-faced and asleep in the bow and Lais out cold, Claudia listened to the mournful song of the fifty-foot colossus.

'Hey!' She cupped her hands round her mouth to

ensure her voice carried back to the island. 'I haven't thanked you,' she yelled, 'for saving my life in the tomb.'

'No,' a deep voice echoed back, 'but you will!'

As she reached for a kerchief to blow her nose, Claudia felt something hard under the seat. A woodcarving. Curious, she pulled it out. A peacock, with all its tailfeathers displayed! Laughing through her tears, Claudia squinted back to the island, to the man with dark eyes and a long mane which hung like drapes to veil his expression, but he'd been swallowed up by the island.

As though he had never existed.

Black Salamander
by Marilyn Todd

What better opportunity for a beautiful young widow than to join a prestigious trade delegation bound for Gaul? There was the fanfare as the procession left Rome, the breathtaking journey through lush Alpine meadows. And let's not forget the promise of riches for delivering a certain pouch, sealed with the sign of the black salamander.

Except things are never that simple when Claudia Seferius is involved. There's a rockfall, for a start, which leaves the party stranded as well as five men dead – and one death is not accidental.

All Claudia wants to do now is to get out of the valley they are trapped in and hand over the pouch. But there are those who will go to any lengths to stop her.

And suddenly Claudia finds herself plunged into a deadly game of high treason, in a land where warriors still hunt human heads and where wicker-man sacrifices are far from rare . . .

Claudia's latest mystery, *Black Salamander*, is now available in Macmillan hardback.

The opening scenes follow here.

I

Don't you just hate it when that happens? Claudia pulled her wrap tight to her shoulders, gritting her teeth as the trap bounced over yet another rut in the road. You're presented with a once-in-a-lifetime opportunity to join a prestigious trade delegation headed for Gaul (expenses paid of course!) at the time of year when Alpine meadows are at their lushest, yet here you are, twelve days into the trip, and you haven't seen a single Alp – not one – thanks to weather which has turned out more January than June. It's cold, it's wet, it's windy, but that isn't the half of it.

'Are we clear of the danger zone yet?' she asked the driver, poking her head through the gap in the canvas which shielded the car from the rain.

It was only last year, remember, that Augustus finally persuaded the Helvetii that resisting the might of the Roman Empire was not entirely to their advantage and even then his charm hadn't been universally appreciated. A burned village here, a town sold into slavery there, his tactics hadn't won all the tribes over and Libo, the tile-maker, had already paid the ultimate price. A taciturn, some might say secretive, individual, all he'd done was wander off the path to relieve himself in the bushes and he'd been found where he squatted, a stab wound straight to the heart.

'Dunno, miss.' The driver shrugged. 'Hope so.'

How very reassuring! Claudia glanced round. Protected by the pines, this mountainous terrain was perfect for a guerrilla attack; the delegation a sitting target as they skirted this deep-sided gorge. She shuddered. Wooded slopes fell two hundred feet to meet white waters swirling over jagged, black rocks while, high above, their granite-topped tips were obscured by the low heavy clouds. Would a hostile clan attack an escorted convoy in broad daylight? One could never tell with the Helvetii! For a hundred years, they'd been a thorn in Rome's side.

'Hello, gorgeous!' A shiny wet face poked its head under the awning. 'Hard to credit yesterday was the midsummer solstice.' He shook himself like a dog. 'Thought you might be feeling the jitters, what with the road barely wide enough for a wagon. Ha!' His eyes rolled upwards. 'Did I say road? Not like Rome, eh? Anyway, I've brought a skin of wine to take your mind off the lumps and the bumps and the bruises.'

Without waiting for encouragement (which was probably as well, because the wait would have been lengthy indeed), Nestor leaped into the moving rig, securing the canvas behind him. 'According to Clemens,' he said, referring to the stumpy little priest who seemed to know everything, 'this is the border between Helvetia and the land of the Sequani.'

Thank heavens! A Gaulish tribe, friends of the Empire! It was to their capital, Vesontio, the delegation was headed, which means they'd arrive in what? Three days from now?

'That river down there marks the boundary.' Nestor edged a fraction closer as he unstoppered the wineskin and Claudia reminded herself of the promise she'd made yesterday. Namely that if this stocky little architect touched her up just one more time, she'd rip out his gizzard and feed it to the wolves she'd heard howling in the night!

Not that Nestor was poor company, far from it. Relentlessly chirpy and a fount of tall tales garnered from travels which had taken him the length and breadth of the Empire, hours which would have otherwise dragged on this wet, miserable journey spun past, because when it came to spooky legends, Nestor had no match. He talked of Helvetian bear cults, of deep, sacred caves guarded by the skulls of seven bears arranged in a ring, or chilled the blood with tales of Druids, making human sacrifice by burning their victims alive in effigies made of whicker.

Nevertheless, it was quite astonishing the number of times he'd 'accidentally' brushed against her breasts, how often his hand had come to rest against her thigh, the regularity with which she'd felt his breath on the back of her neck. Take him to task, of course, and Nestor was quick to blame circumstances – the jolt of the wheels, a judicious pothole – but Claudia had given him clear warning yesterday. Keep your distance, or there'll be a wolf out there licking its chops!

'You've never been to Vesontio, have you?' He didn't wait for an answer. 'You'll love it! Prettiest city in the whole of Gaul in my humble estimation, and commanding as it does a broad loop of the river and with a mountain rising behind, it's not only beautiful, it's a natural citadel and is quite impregnable. And you know how impregnable translates to an architect, don't you?' He chuckled knowingly. 'Prosperous! That's why I love Vesontio so much!'

Funny how his hand needed to clasp her wrist whenever he made a point.

'That city's crying out for a delegation like ours,' Nestor continued. 'Oh yes.' As a self-made man, he'd never quite lost his barrow-boy accent. 'This'll make us all rich, mark my words.' He squinted out through the gap in the canvas, using the bump of the rig to annex Claudia's elbow.

'Nestor, which part of the word "no" are you having trouble with?' she asked, but so engrossed was Claudia in recalling the real objective behind making this journey that there was no sting in her rebuke.

Sure, the delegation would cover her expenses, raise her commercial wine-growing profile and provide her with numerous contacts for trade – unfortunately those were long-range proposals. When you've been blackballed and cash flow is tight, to hell with pretty views and a travelogue! The immediate objective is cash; cold, gold, glittery coins which Claudia could trickle through her fingers and replenish gasping coffers with. Her eyes darted to a satchel swinging from a hook above Drusilla's cage. She pictured the soft yellow deerskin pouch tucked inside. The one sealed with a golden blob of wax imprinted with the sign of the black salamander.

'Nestor!' Somehow he'd managed to combine the task of unstoppering the wineskin with a fingertip alighting on Claudia's nipple. 'I told you yesterday, no more funny business, but you didn't take a blind bit of notice!' She had to raise her voice to drown the rumbling sound from outside. 'The fact that you have no respect for a woman, that hurts. But you know what hurts most?'

'What?'

'This!' Claudia squeezed his testicles as hard as she could. 'Touch me again, you odious wart, and I'll geld you!'

'Landslide!' The powerful voice of a legionary boomed the length of the line. 'Move! Fast as you can – run for it. NOW!'

Claudia's stomach flipped somersaults. Sweet Jupiter! The danger after all came not from hostile Helvetii.

The danger came from a rockfall!

II

Imagine thunder. Imagine a stampede of wild Camargue stallions. Imagine earthquakes and a volcanic eruption. Now put them together! The very ground shook beneath the wheels as the driver cracked his whip. The mares bolted forward and, as her nails dug deep into the grain of her maplewood seat, Claudia thanked Jupiter for the skill of her driver.

With the stone trackway potholed and scarred and treacherously steep, coated with an ooze of wet mud which had turned it into an oilslick, only the driver's expertise kept this light trap on its course. Twice the wheels skidded. Drusilla's cage slid to the left, it slid to the right. The axle caught on a rut. Rocks crashed behind them, clattering, splintering, bouncing down the ravine. Horses screamed on the perilous bend and she clung to the rig as the wheels bounced high off the ground and crashed down again. We'll turn over, she thought, a wheel will spin off. How far now down the gorge? A hundred feet to the bottom?

Boulders the size of a stable block thundered past, ripping up sixty-foot pines, oak trees and beech. Fragments broke off, thumping, thudding, wrecking their way to the riverbed.

'Gee up! Gee up there!'

The mares needed no encouragement. Their eyes wild

with terror, foam flecking their cheeks, they galloped ever closer to the wagon in front. Claudia's clenched knuckles were white, she daren't breathe. One slip from a rig up ahead, the whole column would go down like gates in a gale. Plummeting into the void.

Sweet Juno, could they truly outrun it?

Nestor had gone. At the first yell of the soldier, he was off, faster than a rock from an Iberian sling, his eyes still watering, his face as red as a turkey cock's wattle. Idly she wondered whether things like this had happened to him before on his travels, whether rockfalls were a regular occurrence?

'Madam!' The canvas was jerked open, rain began driving into the cart. 'You have to get out!'

'About bloody time, I must say!' Claudia stared at the bleached face of her bodyguard, hurling himself into the jostling rig. 'Where the hell have you been?'

'Backtracking up the road like you told me,' Junius puffed, grabbing the handle of Claudia's trunk. 'Come on. Quick!'

'Brilliant. When that creep Nestor started pawing me, where were you? Sightseeing!' At her feet, Drusilla howled like a banshee. 'What's the point of having a bodyguard, if he's not around to protect your body?'

'Sightseeing!' he exclaimed, his left hand closing over the strap round the cat's cage. 'You gave me specific orders to – oh, madam, just jump, will you?'

Claudia stared at the young Gaul. 'Has your mind been possessed by a lunatic's?' With mares at full pelt, wagons racing behind and boulders bouncing down the hillside like inflated pigs' bladders, Junius tells her to jump? 'I'll be pulped like an olive for oil!'

'Madam,' he warned, his face pinched with worry. 'This whole mountain is going!'

Shit! Slinging her precious satchel over her shoulder, Claudia scrabbled onto the buckboard. Rain and dust slammed into her face.

'You what?' the driver said. 'Bleedin' 'ell, are you sure?' But Junius's face answered for him. 'Then forget jumping,' he said, clambering onto the buckboard, 'let's stop this column. Pull up!' he yelled, standing upright as he hauled on the reins. 'Stop your carts!' The authority in his voice caught their attention. 'Stop your carts!'

Junius wasn't the only one who'd seen what was about to take place. A horseman surged his way up the path, past quivering mules and women wailing in fright, ignoring the confused shouts of the drivers. 'Get out!' he yelled. 'Everybody out!' There was more than a tinge of panic to his voice. 'Huddle as close as you can to the rock!'

From deep inside the mountain came a low menacing growl. Claudia glanced up. Typical of the countryside, massive overhangs of granite jutted out, the softer limestone below having eroded away. The fissures above wobbled precariously, and it was this Junius and the others had spotted.

Suddenly, June or not, she was shivering.

'Croesus!' somebody cried. 'It's coming right at us!'

MARILYN TODD

I, Claudia

Pan Books   £5.99

Claudia Seferius has successfully inveigled her way into marriage with a wealthy Roman wine merchant. But when her secret gambling debts spiral, she hits on another resourceful way to make money – offering her 'personal services' to high-ranking citizens.

Unfortunately her clients are now turning up dead – the victims of a sadistic serial killer . . .

When Marcus Cornelius Orbilio, the handsome investigating officer, starts digging deep for clues, Claudia realizes she must track down the murderer herself – before her husband discovers what she's been up to.

And before another man meets his grisly end . . .

MARILYN TODD

Virgin Territory

Pan Books   £5.99

It just wasn't fair. When you marry a man for his money, you expect him to leave you a shining pile of gold pieces. *Not* a crummy old wine business. How was the new young widow Claudia going to pay off her gambling debts now?

So when Eugenius Collatinus asks Claudia to chaperone his granddaughter to Sicily she jumps at the chance to escape Rome. It should be easy – Sabina Collatinus, she is told, has recently completed thirty years' service as a Vestal Virgin.

Or has she . . .?

Claudia's suspects she is escorting an imposter. And then a woman's brutalized body is discovered . . .